Nightmare Along the River Nile

A Story of Twentieth Century Slavery

S. E. Nelson

Nightmare Along the River Nile
A Story of Twentieth Century Slavery

Copyright © 2010 S. E. Nelson

All rights reserved. No part of this book may be used or reproduced by any means, graphic, electronic, or mechanical, including photocopying, recording, taping or by any information storage retrieval system without the written permission of the publisher except in the case of brief quotations embodied in critical articles and reviews.

This is a work of fiction. All of the characters, names, incidents, organizations, and dialogue in this novel are either the products of the author's imagination or are used fictitiously.

Library of Congress Control Number: 2009910872

Printed in the United States of America

Dedication

This book is dedicated to all the men, women and children who are still held in bondage anywhere in the world.

Chapter 1

I was feeling relieved after my high school exams. I also felt confident about my performance, though I tried my best not to show it to my fellow students. Education hadn't been easy, especially for us students from northern Uganda. Endless wars that brought about untold misery and poverty had been going on for as long as I could remember. Fortunately the constant encouragement by my mother coupled with the fear of disappointing her transformed me into a good student.

I always remembered my mother saying, 'Edgar, your father worked hard but had no education, and look how he ended up.' She would pause and then continue, 'Mark my words, son. With education, people may not like you, but they will respect you.' She even insisted on fetching water herself from the borehole a mile away so that I would not take time away from my studies. Luckily for me, I had been given financial support by the Catholic church to fund my education.

All these thoughts went through my mind as I walked towards the nearest pub with my three best friends: Wilbur, Sam, and John. We had decided to celebrate the end of the final exams by having drinks.

'Eddie, you are too quiet. What's the matter? Aren't you happy we have finally completed the exams?' Wilbur asked me.

My friends called me Eddie most of the time. Wilbur, or Willy, as we called him, was very carefree. His family was well-off and lived in the capital city of Kampala, so I wasn't surprised by his easy attitude. At six feet, Wilbur was the tallest of the group. Sam, John, and I were about an inch shorter, but Sam and I were bigger in size.

I smiled and patted Willy on the back. 'Relax, Willy. I am coming to the pub with you to celebrate, aren't I? And here we are.'

All four of us were joking and laughing as we entered the pub. At my insistence, we chose the booth farthest from the door. I didn't want any of my teachers to see us in a pub. I still respected them even though I had finished high school.

Wilbur ordered some beers, and we started drinking and talking about everything else but school. This went on for a while as Wilbur, good on his promise, kept our bottles coming. We talked about our plans for the next several months while we waited for the exam results.

I slowly realized that out of all my friends, I was the only one who didn't have any plans for the immediate future. Wilbur Ochom had a job with his father waiting for him in the city. John Kimuli had already started working at his uncle's gas station in Jinja, and Sam Ssenyonjo would be driving his minibus taxi and pocketing the money. I kept my thoughts to myself, not wanting any pity from my friends.

Suddenly, an idea popped into my head and I raised my beer bottle for attention. There was instant silence as they all turned to me. I put the bottle back down.

'Guys, I have made a decision to be a volunteer worker for the Catholic church that sponsored my education. I want to teach children in the camps.'

Everybody looked at me in disbelief. John tried to say something but merely shook his head in resignation.

It was Wilbur who finally found words. 'Look, Eddie, you don't have to act like a saint.' He paused and took a sip of his beer. 'I know a few people who want to hire honest people like you. I could get you a job,' he finished.

'Hey, Eddie, you could work with me in the minibus until you get steady work,' Sam added with a big smile.

I was moved by the offers from my friends, so I looked down at my beer to get my composure back. 'Thanks a lot for your offers, guys. You're true friends, but I have made up my mind. This will give me a chance to be with my mother for some time. I really haven't spent much time with her since I started high school. I'm sure things will work out for the best,' I said.

All of them nodded slowly, even though I could tell they were not happy about it since the area was not safe. I checked the time and noticed it was getting late.

John eased out of his seat and headed for the phone booth. More drinks were brought before John came back with a big smile on his face. 'Gentlemen, you will be staying at our place for the night,' he said, looking around.

I sipped the beer in silence and then looked at my friends in wonder. We were about to embark on different paths. Some were going to be successful while others were not. *Life is always like that*, I thought with sadness. We finished our drinks and took a taxi to pick up our luggage from school before heading to John's residence.

We were welcomed by his sister and brother and shown where we would sleep. After a nice dinner, we sat in the living room, where we got involved in different discussions. Finally, one by one we retired to our respective bedrooms. I could not fall asleep for a long time, as I was thinking about my future and weighing the uncertain period ahead.

Sleep finally came in the form of a strange dream. The little I could recall the next day was that: *I was being chased by armed men through a dense overgrown tobacco plantation while trying to move away the leaves that were hitting my face. I kept running harder, urged on by my mother. Somehow she reached out and caught me with both hands, but some sort of force kept pulling me further and further from her until she was out of sight. She kept pleading for me not to abandon her.*

I woke up suddenly with tears in my eyes, unable to understand what was happening. I felt better when I realized I had been dreaming, but I still kept wondering why the dream had felt very real. I checked my watch and realized it was six-thirty a.m. I got up and went for a run to clear my head. I tried to figure out the meaning of the dream, but I couldn't make any sense of it. The more I thought about it, the more disturbed I became. I didn't care what people said about dreams not being real. In this dream, my mother had seemed too real to be ignored.

I arrived back a little after eight o'clock. I had been gone for a whole hour and a half. Everybody had already freshened up and gone to the dining room for breakfast. I greeted them and went straight to the bedroom for my shower kit. I felt a lot better after showering and changing into fresh clothes for the journey, but the dream was still in my head. I tried to ignore it. Who knows, maybe I had too much to drink last night, I thought to myself as I joined others at the breakfast table.

'Morning, Eddie, how was your night?' all of them intoned in unison.

'Pretty good, although I had a strange dream,' I answered with a smile.

Everybody around the table laughed heartily, including Maggie, John's sister, who teased me and wanted to know about my dream. I wasn't sure what to say, so I avoided her eyes and concentrated on eating breakfast.

We finally finished the breakfast and thanked our hostess. I snuck away to the bedroom and straightened the place out before picking up my suitcase and mattress and walking into the living room. Students always took their own mattresses to boarding schools.

'Gentlemen, we would not want to keep the bus waiting now, would we?' I said with humor.

John looked at his watch quickly. 'Well, we still have some time, but let me check on my uncle and see if he can give us a ride to the station. I'll be right back,' he said, walking towards the door. His uncle lived nearby.

I put my luggage down and joined the others in the living room. In a few minutes we heard the sound of a car engine, and then John hurried inside the house. 'Eddie, you are lucky. We just got a ride. Let's get you on that bus.'

I got up, shook hands with Maggie, and started to pick up my luggage.

'I will help you with your things,' Sam shouted, taking the suitcase from me. Wilbur picked up the mattress, and we all headed for the door.

'Thank you for the ride,' I said to John's uncle, Mr Bill Kimuli.

He brushed off my gratitude and opened the passenger doors. 'Anything for my nephew. Get in quickly,' he said jokingly as he started the car.

As the car pulled off, I waved to Maggie until the house was out of sight. She was an impressive girl, very humorous and obviously very intelligent.

'You know, the road to your area is dangerous these days,' John's uncle shouted above the noise of the car. 'You should disembark at Malaba and wait for the usual military convoy.'

I nodded in agreement but did not commit myself by saying anything since I did not have a lot of money.

We got to the Jinja bus station as they were announcing the bus to Gulu.

'There is your bus, son, hurry,' Mr Kimuli shouted as he parked the car on the shoulder of the road. We quickly got out and ran towards the bus. I inquired about the fare, and to my relief not much had changed in the four months since I last took the bus.

'Well, what are you going to do, Eddie? Will you wait for a convoy or head straight to Gulu?' Wilbur asked, looking me straight in the eye.

I shrugged. 'I don't know, Willy. But don't worry. It's not the first time I've gone home, you know.'

Sam and John looked at me with uncertainty. 'Eddie, I haven't kept up with the situation up north; but let me write down the license plate number of your bus anyway,' Sam said as he walked to the back of the bus with a pen and a piece of paper.

Sam came back with a concerned look on his face. 'Look, Eddie, I really think you should change vehicles at Malaba and wait for a military convoy.'

I nodded, and we sadly hugged one another before I climbed onto the bus.

'Don't forget to send us some kind of message when you arrive home,' Wilbur shouted above the noise of the bus engine.

I got a seat next to a window so that I could talk to my friends before the bus took off.

'Hey, guys come around here,' I shouted loudly through the window.

John arrived first, but the bus was starting to take off. 'Don't forget to write,' he shouted.

'You can call the number I gave you for the Catholic mission. I will definitely be there tomorrow,' I shouted back.

They were now chasing after the bus while waving to me.

'I will call you tomorrow morning!' John shouted.

The bus was moving very fast, and it was impossible to hear their words as we waved hard at each other. The bus joined the main road, and the station started fading until I lost sight of my friends. I sat back in my seat and relaxed. The boy next to me seemed too young to engage in a constructive conversation, so I reached into my jacket pocket for a Sidney Sheldon novel and started looking for the right page. It was going to be a long journey.

Along the way I must have dozed off because I suddenly woke up feeling uncomfortable.

The conductor was tapping my shoulder. 'Excuse me. Your fare, please,' he said.

I rubbed my eyes, sat up, and looked around. 'How much does it cost to Malaba?' I asked him.

The conductor looked at me in surprise. 'You mean they didn't tell you? This is a direct service bus.'

I shook my head. 'They said something about a military escort at Malaba because of rebel activity.'

The conductor smiled and shrugged. 'You know, young man, there are times when the rebels hit even when they see the military. It's all in God's hands.'

I reached in my pocket and paid the full fare to Gulu.

The conductor took the money and thanked me. He must have seen my concerned look because he said, 'I tell you what—we shall talk to people at the next rest area and get the full picture of what's ahead of us.' Then he walked off.

I reached down to the floor and picked up the little novel that I had dropped. *Maybe I am being paranoid. How else could these buses keep moving on these roads if there isn't any degree of safety?* Every time I went home, it was a nerve-racking experience.

I looked at the boy on my right. He was about fifteen years old. I decided to talk to him. I learnt that his name was Rob and that he went to school in Kampala. He said he was going to visit his grandparents for the holidays.

'Don't you think it's unsafe to venture so far from home?' I asked.

He shrugged his shoulders. 'Papa said it's safer than it's been for years, especially since they introduced military convoys.'

I learnt that he was in senior two at a reputable school and wished to continue with his education up to university, for engineering. I sincerely hoped the boy would achieve his dream.

The driver announced that the bus would stop at a rest area in a few minutes for some minor repairs. I checked my watch. It was getting late, and I was feeling hungry. I welcomed the idea of stopping and getting some food. Also, the conductor would hopefully find out more about the rebel situation in the area. The bus slowed down and made a turn into an area where numerous vehicles were parked.

'Welcome to Kali. We shall leave here at six-thirty. You have roughly an hour and a half. Please be back on time, otherwise we will leave without you,' the driver announced through the microphone.

I got up and followed the rest of the passengers off the bus.

'Hey, Eddie, it looks like it's going to be a long journey to Gulu,' Rob said to me with a big smile. I squeezed his shoulder and smiled back. He was about six inches shorter than me, but he was built like a wrestler. I thought he was pretty big for his age.

As we descended from the bus, Rob pulled on my hand and said, 'Come on, Eddie, I have been here before. I know a good restaurant where we can eat.'

I obliged and followed him through the maze of cars. I could use a good meal, not to mention the restroom. The restaurant was clean and newly painted, which meant it might be expensive. Oh, what the hell, I thought to myself.

'Hey, Rob, where is the restroom?' I asked.

He pointed to a white door in the corner. 'Don't forget to get the toilet paper at the counter if it's a long call,' he said, smiling.

I nodded and changed directions. I got the roll at the counter and then went straight towards the restroom. Afterwards I washed my hands and face and also combed my hair. I felt much better as I walked back into the dining room.

'Over here, Eddie,' Rob shouted when he saw me. 'I hope you don't mind, but I ordered for us and the food is on me.'

I was surprised and embarrassed. How can I let this boy buy a meal for me? I started to protest, but something in the boy's eyes made me relax. There wasn't any arrogance, just happiness.

'All right, Rob. I will accept this one time on the condition that I buy the drinks.'

'Okay, let's shake on it,' Rob said, giving me his hand.

I took it and squeezed it. He jumped up from his seat like a demon. I let go of his hand and burst out laughing.

'Damn! I'd be crazy to let you do that to me again,' he exclaimed as he shook his hand.

The waitress brought our meals of meat stew, mashed potatoes, and lettuce on the side.

'Excuse me, Miss. Can you please bring us a couple of soft drinks?' I asked. Rob asked for a Fanta, and I ordered a Sprite. 'Oh, and can you make two separate bills, one for food and the other for drinks?' I asked. She nodded and left to get the drinks.

I prayed before our meal, a habit I had picked up at home from my mother, and then we dug in. The meal was delicious and very timely. I ate all the food on my plate in silence and didn't look up until I was finished.

'Thanks, Rob, I really needed that,' I said, reaching for my drink. Rob raised his Fanta in a toast, and we both gulped them down. I looked at my watch and noticed we had spent about an hour in the restaurant. We still had about thirty minutes, so we chatted some more before we settled our bills and headed for the bus.

By the time we got there, everybody was back in their seats getting ready to go.

'Hurry up! We almost left without you,' shouted the conductor.

The bus started moving before we were fully seated. The conductor was checking tickets and at the same time issuing new ones for the newcomers. When he got to our chairs, I reached over Rob and touched the conductor's hand.

'Did you find out if the road is safe?' I asked.

'There hasn't been any rebel activity in a while, so we are heading straight to Gulu,' he said. He checked his watch. 'If all goes well, we shall arrive at around nine.'

That meant we still had a journey of two and half hours before we got home. I thanked him and sat back in the seat. I closed my eyes and started daydreaming about home and my new volunteer job.

Some people in my hometown lived in protected areas that were sustained by contributions from various churches and organizations. I was looking forward to teaching in these areas. I liked teaching; it gave me a sense of self-worth. I also wanted the children to have a better future. I hated seeing hopelessness in our people.

The bus slowed down. I opened my eyes and elbowed my young friend Rob. 'Hey, what's going on?' I asked.

He stood up to peep through the front windshield and then quickly sat down, his eyes wide with fear. 'Oh no, I knew I should not have come.'

I stood up and leaned over to take a look. We had stopped in a park, not too far from the road. There was some kind of roadblock, but something didn't seem right. A lot of thoughts started running through my head. Suddenly, something exploded very loudly, and I was thrown towards Rob. Another loud explosion followed, and then silence reigned all around. The bus headlights went off and everything became dark.

'What's going on, Eddie?' Rob asked.

I didn't know what to say. I just put my index finger on my lips. 'Shh ... I believe we are in deep trouble,' I whispered.

There was some commotion outside the bus, and then a powerful light emanated within the bus. The light moved silently from face to face, slowly going towards the back. I felt a surge of fear. *These couldn't be the rebels.* They were too relaxed. They didn't seem to be in any kind of hurry. Nobody dared say a word. I could feel my body shaking.

'Listen, everybody!' a male voice shouted in fluent English. 'I want you to walk towards the front and out of the bus, starting with the seat in the back. Now!' he finished harshly.

People started walking out of the bus, and Rob and I followed silently. The man with a flashlight was standing next to the driver's seat. Behind him was another man with a pointed gun. I noticed a leg protruding from under the driver's seat, and I recognized the clothing. It was our driver. My heart sank. *Oh, my God. The explosions! The bastards had murdered him. But why? He had slowed down the bus as they requested, but they had still killed him.*

Suddenly, the reality of our situation dawned on me. These were the rebels. I prodded Rob to hurry up. I didn't want to see any more death.

'You! Stay!' a voice barked.

I hoped it wasn't me they were calling and kept walking down the stairs.

'I mean you, going down the stairs, come back.'

I turned around to face him, scared stiff. He motioned with a flashlight for me to climb back up, which I did. He kept looking hard at other boys and kept motioning the strong-looking ones to stay behind until there were five of us. One woman tried complaining about her son, and they simply told her to go and wait for him outside. When she refused to go, they laughed and told her to take him. As the two were walking down the stairs, they were mowed down by bullets. The woman and her son fell outside the bus.

'Okay, everybody! That should be a lesson to you. We are not here to play around, understand?' the man with the flashlight said.

We all nodded, too dumfounded to say anything.

'I want everything cleared out of this bus and thrown through the windows on the right in ten minutes flat,' the man said to the five of us boys. 'Now move!'

We almost fell on top of each other as we hurried to unload the luggage. We worked fast, throwing things out the windows. Urged on by the rebels, we even broke a few windows. We finished quickly and were told to step out of the bus to join the others in the line. A lot of flashlights were outside, either pointing at us or at the bus.

'Now listen, you morons, I don't like to repeat myself! Everybody get your things quickly and form a line,' a man with a big flashlight shouted.

I was extremely frightened. I realized that the only hope we had was if by chance an army convoy passed by, but the odds of that happening were one in a million. In the meantime, all I had to do was try my best to cooperate with our captors.

They ordered us to start walking towards a hill deep inside the park.

'No talking. You hear!' the man with the big flashlight shouted again. I took him to be the leader because he was commanding everyone.

We kept climbing up for what seemed like eternity until we arrived at a flat area.

'Halt!' the leader screamed. 'I want everybody to sit down and turn around. Look this way!'

We all did as we were ordered. He stepped back from us. Suddenly there was a big explosion and our bus was on fire way down in the park. Our captors all laughed loudly as if it was funny. I felt sick to my stomach.

'Attention!' the leader shouted. 'As you have seen, we punish with death, so don't push us. If you behave, your time with us won't be bad,' he said and then walked away to join the other rebels.

I was trying to figure out what I had done to deserve this, but I kept drawing a blank.

'On your feet, we have a long journey ahead of us!' the leader shouted.

I didn't look back, I just picked up my things and followed the rest. *My nightmare had just begun.*

Chapter 2

John tried to eat his breakfast but couldn't. He just didn't have any appetite. He missed his friends, especially Edgar, and looked forward to talking with him this morning. John was very impressed with Edgar and felt lucky to have him as a friend. Edgar was selfless, good-natured, and very principled. John was sipping his juice, deep in thought, when he heard a voice.

'Aren't you going to work today, John?' his sister Maggie asked.

John was supposed to report for work at his uncle's gas station. 'I will go in later, sis. Right now I have to make some phone calls,' he said as he headed to his bedroom.

They didn't have a phone in the house, so he decided he would go to his uncle's place, which was nearby. He would call Wilbur and Edgar today and maybe Sam if he could reach him. He searched around for his address book but couldn't find it. After retracing his steps, he remembered where it was. He walked over to the corner of his room where he put his dirty clothing and retrieved the book from his blue jeans.

He checked himself in the mirror before he looked at his watch. It was ten-thirty in the morning. Before walking out of his room, he rummaged through his pockets to make sure he had his wallet, a habit he had picked up when one of his late father's housekeepers took off with his wallet.

The walk to his uncle's residence took less than three minutes. He greeted his auntie and cousins and then asked them if he could use the phone. His aunt nodded and told him to proceed. John smiled. He dialed Wilbur's number first and waited as the phone rang in Kampala.

'Hello, may I talk to Wilbur, please?' John asked.

Wilbur came on the line shortly. 'Hey, Willy, this is John.'

'Hey, John, how are you? Hold on a minute.' There was a pause and a sound of voices as Wilbur talked to somebody in the background. He came back to the phone.

'John, was it you or Sam who wrote the license number of the bus that Eddie took yesterday?' He sounded serious.

John fidgeted for his address book. 'It was Sam, but he gave me the number. Hold on.' John looked for the number and then read it to Wilbur.

'What is the matter, Willy? Why do you need the number? Please don't keep me in suspense,' John pleaded, suddenly worried.

Wilbur took a deep breath.

'Look, John, this may be nothing, but there were ambushes on some vehicles yesterday around the park just after Karuma Bridge. That's why I'm concerned. They said that the vehicles that were attacked were the ones that took the direct route without waiting for the army to escort them.' He paused and then added, 'But that would exclude Eddie since he was supposed to get off at Malaba and wait for the army escort.'

John felt a little relieved but wanted to know more. 'Willy, do you have today's paper? Is there any way you could find out exactly which vehicles were ambushed?'

'Let me turn on 'Radio Uganda' right now and find out exactly what is going on,' Wilbur said.

At the same time, John was thinking hard about another way to find out more about the situation. Suddenly, an idea popped into his mind.

'Willy, are you still there?'

'Yes, I am here.'

'I'm going to call the number in Gulu that Eddie gave me, and then I will go to the bus station. Surely they would know if one of their vehicles was ambushed. Willy, go and dig up as much as possible. I will do the same here. Let's talk again this afternoon at one o'clock,' he added as he glanced at his watch.

'Okay, John, talk to you later,' Wilbur said, hanging up.

John put the phone down. He was agitated, and the people in the room looked at him anxiously. He had to give them some kind of explanation. 'We are worried about our friend who went home to Gulu yesterday. Some vehicles were ambushed yesterday evening on the way there.' He turned around and dialed the Catholic offices in Gulu to find out if Edgar had arrived.

'Hello, Catholic Enunciate Gulu. May I help you?' a lady's voice answered.

'Hello, this is John Kimuli. I would like to inquire about one of the pupils you sponsor,' John said.

'Can you hold on, please?' she said and then called to somebody else.

'Yes, this is Father Benedict, may I help you?' a deep voice intoned. John repeated what he had just said to the lady and mentioned Edgar's name. He told the Father that Edgar was planning on volunteering with them. The Father asked him to hold the line while he asked around.

Father Benedict came back on the line in a few minutes. 'Son, I have asked around and nobody has seen Edgar.'

John told the Father why he was concerned.

'I will send somebody to his mother's house to find out if he is there. We should have an answer in half an hour,' the Father added.

John felt like he had been hit by a bolt of lightning. Tears welled up in his eyes.

'Father, I hope Eddie is okay. I am afraid to think the worst. I will go to the bus station and find out more. I will call later,' he said.

John put the phone down and stood up. He knew he had to say something to his relatives—they were watching him closely. 'Edgar didn't make it to work, but maybe he is at home with his mother. I will see you all later,' he said weakly as he walked out of the house.

The bus station was about four miles away, but he decided to walk. His thoughts were a mixture of apprehension, confusion, and hope for his friend's safety. He almost got run over by a car as he was crossing the road. The driver yelled a few choice words at him, but John didn't care. He was busy thinking about Eddie.

The more he thought about the rebels, the angrier he got. *What kind of ideology is it that leads to kidnapping unwilling people and making them serve in their army? Surely a student isn't of any use to them.*

He was so deep in thought that he didn't hear a car honking behind him. He turned around and saw his uncle's vehicle moving slowly next to him.

'Son, I heard about your friend. Come on—hop in. I will help you get some more information,' his uncle said, opening the door for him.

John hesitated because he wanted to be alone, but he didn't want to hurt his uncle's feelings so he entered the car. 'Hi, Uncle! Aren't you supposed to be working?' he asked as he entered the car.

His uncle looked at him with concern. 'Yes, I am, but when I went by the gas station and you weren't there, I decided to check on you.' He paused to light a cigarette. 'Son, how much do you know?' Mr Kimuli asked, looking at his nephew.

John looked down and cleared his throat. 'Well, a few vehicles were ambushed by the rebels yesterday evening, and Edgar didn't make it to work at the Catholic mission today.' His uncle patted his shoulder and engaged the gear. The car slowly eased off.

'Don't lose hope, son. Let's first go to the bus station,' he said seriously.

They drove in silence. There wasn't much to say, and speculation would only bring about more confusion and despair. They finally arrived at the bus station.

'You sure you want to go in, son?' his uncle asked with concern in his voice.

'Yes, Uncle. I want to know if Eddie's bus was involved,' he answered as he stepped out of the car.

Mr Kimuli could tell by the tone of his nephew's voice that the boy was worried. He shut the car doors, and together they walked towards the station office. The office was situated near where Edgar had boarded the bus the day before. Even now there was another bus being loaded with people heading north to Gulu.

The office was small, with only two chairs facing one another and a small table in between. John knew it would be better if his uncle asked the questions. He pulled his uncle to the side and gave him the license plate number of the bus.

Mr Kimuli approached the man seated in one of the chairs and greeted him cordially before sitting down opposite him. 'Sir, I have some questions concerning a passenger that took one of your buses to Gulu. Can you help me?'

The station operator looked at John's uncle for a moment before answering, 'I will help as much as I can.'

Mr Kimuli took the address book from John and then looked at the man and said, 'Our boy took the bus yesterday morning. Here is the license number of the bus he took.' He leaned over as he showed the man the number. 'The bus was supposed to drop him in Malaba, and then he was going to proceed to Gulu. Do you know the whereabouts of the bus?' Mr Kimuli asked.

The station operator got up, avoiding Mr Kimuli's eyes. He was clearly agitated. 'Look, you may ask at the main offices in Kampala. I don't know much about what happens to buses once they leave here. Can you please step outside now? I have work to do.'

The change in the man's attitude surprised both John and his uncle, and they retreated through the door.

'Uncle, why did the man behave like that?' John asked, confused.

Mr Kimuli scratched his beard, deep in thought. He had taken a good look at the man. The fellow looked poor. He was also hiding something. Maybe he could give him some money and get the information they needed. 'John, go and get in the car. I will be right back,' he said, handing John the car keys and stepping back into the office.

John was almost certain that something bad had happened. He noticed the daily paper nearby and perused through it. There wasn't anything in the paper. The ambush had happened after the papers had been published.

Mr Kimuli came out of the office and walked towards the car.

John noticed that his uncle was clearly distressed. He hurried towards his uncle and handed him the keys. 'Well?' John asked as he quickly got into the car.

'Son, you have to be strong,' Mr Kimuli said, looking straight ahead. 'That bus was supposed to go through Malaba to get an escort, but the driver decided against it to save time. They fell into a rebel ambush. The rebels shot four people; the driver, the conductor, a woman, and her son. The bus was burnt to the ground.'

Mr Kimuli lit a cigarette and puffed on it before starting the car. He drove in silence while smoking his cigarette until he pulled into his driveway. 'Take it easy, son, we will talk a little later,' he pleaded with John, who was already walking towards the house.

Everybody in the house seemed to sense what had happened. It seemed to John that they tried to look away. He walked straight to the phone and picked it up while glancing at his watch. It was already past one o'clock. He dialed Wilbur's telephone number.

'Hello, may I help you?' asked the voice.

'Yes, this is John. May I talk to Willy?'

Wilbur came on the phone. 'Hello, John, what did you find—' he started to ask, but John interrupted.

'Listen, Willy, I just came from the bus station. It is bad news.' He paused. 'Eddie's bus was ambushed. The bus was burnt to the ground and four people were killed. The others, including Edgar, were taken by the rebels,' he finished with pain.

'Oh no!' Wilbur said and then fell silent, absorbing the news. Even though the news had confirmed the ambush stories, he had hoped that Eddie had escaped the incident.

'Are you still there, Willy?' John asked, and then he continued to talk. 'Apparently the stupid driver decided to take a shortcut through the park to save time and bypassed Malaba,' he said.

Wilbur took a deep breath. 'John, the information I got said that three passenger vehicles were hijacked in the park and burnt down by rebels.'

John was listening and at the same time trying to figure out what to do. 'We have all been friends since childhood, Willy. If our roles were reversed, Eddie would do anything to help us. We have to look for him. We can't abandon him,' John said.

'Of course not. I agree with you 100 per cent!' Wilbur shouted into the phone.

'Very well,' John said. 'We should get together as soon as possible. We will need resources.' He paused. 'I have a piece of land in town that my father left me, which I can sell. Willy, can you tell Sam? I will be in touch with you this evening or tomorrow at the latest,' John said as he hung up. He proceeded to call Father Benedict. Edgar's mother would have to be told.

* * *

Wilbur dialed Sam's home phone number immediately. Mr Ssenyonjo, Sam's father answered the phone.

'Good afternoon, sir, this is Wilbur Ochom, Sam's friend. I wanted to speak with Sam.'

There was a pause on the other end. 'Yes, Wilbur. Sam has mentioned you. He is not here now. He is at work.'

'Sir, can you tell me which stage Sam works from? It's very important that I see him now.'

'Sam works on Ntinda stage. Is everything okay?'

Wilbur didn't see any reason not to tell Mr Ssenyonjo the truth since they needed all the support they could get. 'Mr Ssenyonjo, if you heard about me then you must have heard about Edgar, our other friend.'

'Oh yes,' the older man said.

'Sir, the news I have isn't very good. The bus Eddie took was hijacked by rebels, and he was kidnapped.'

Mr Ssenyonjo was quiet for a minute. Then he said, 'That is terrible news, son! Please let me know if there is anything I can do to help.'

Wilbur had learnt early on in life that one never turns down an offer in times of need. 'Yes, sir, as a matter of fact we will need all the help we can get.'

'Listen, son, let me know what I can do. Try to stay strong,' the older man said.

Wilbur thanked him and hung up the telephone. He turned away from the phone and walked to his bedroom. He decided to stop at his uncle's place later. His uncle, the Honorable Dickens Ochom, was a member of parliament. He could perhaps help to find Eddie. But first Wilbur had to track down Sam.

He picked up his wallet and notebook and headed for the garage. His father had given him a small car as a present for completing high school. Wilbur opened the garage wide and drove the car out. It was already two-thirty, and though he hadn't eaten, he wasn't hungry.

He drove towards the taxi station, thinking about what needed to be done. One thing was certain—they needed money and lots of it. They also needed to get information about the rebels and their sympathizers. He parked his car on a side street near the taxi station.

The downtown area of Kampala was always busy with vehicles and people moving erratically, not to mention hawkers stepping in the way. Wilbur pushed his way through the crowd and then sprinted across the street towards the taxi station.

Kampala had become unbelievably crowded in the past few years. There were lots of children standing around asking for money. Many young people from the north who were fleeing from the rebels and poverty had landed in Kampala but could not find jobs. Wilbur paid close attention to his wallet. Pick pocketing in this area was a norm. He also tried to avoid stepping into water patches or the garbage that seemed forever underfoot. He cursed himself for having taken this route and swore not to return that way.

Wilbur thanked God when he finally reached the taxi stand and started searching for Ntinda stage. He asked a few hawkers where it was, but they eyed him strangely, telling him to get lost and mind his own business. Finally, he found an old lady selling some clothes who directed him.

At Ntinda stage, he looked around trying to locate Sam, but it was to no avail. A teenage boy approached him and asked him if he could help. He hesitated, remembering the abuse he had just taken from the hawkers, but common sense prevailed.

'Do you know Sam Ssenyonjo? I have something for him,' Wilbur lied.

The young man smiled. 'I know Sam. Give it to me and I will guarantee he gets it.'

Wilbur could tell a con when he saw one, so he ignored the boy. His eyes kept looking up and down at cars coming by the stage; and by some divine luck, Sam got out of a little van and walked towards a group of other drivers. He hadn't seen Wilbur yet.

'Excuse me!' Wilbur said, pushing the astonished boy aside. He walked towards Sam. He was about three yards from Sam when he decided to call out to him instead. No sense going through all those introductions.

'Hey, Sam!' he yelled.

Sam turned and their eyes met. There was an instant smile on Sam's face. *Obviously Sam still doesn't know what has happened.*

Wilbur gathered that the best way to break the bad news was to say it as quickly as possible.

'Sam, how are you? Let's get a cold drink,' he said as they embraced.

Sam led him towards a soda stand. Wilbur paid for two, giving one to Sam. They both took a quick swig. It was very hot.

'Look, Sam, I have bad news.' He paused. 'It's about Eddie ... he was kidnapped by rebels last night.'

Sam staggered a little and almost dropped his drink. Wilbur reached over and grabbed Sam's arm.

'Jesus Christ!' was all Sam managed to utter.

Wilbur reached for an empty soda crate and pulled it over.

Sam sat down heavily, not yet steady on his feet. 'I can't believe what I'm hearing. How the hell did this happen? Didn't they say they would get a military escort to Gulu? Damn it!' he cursed.

Wilbur looked around to clear his mind. 'Well, the driver decided to take a shortcut to Gulu ...' He then related the story to Sam.

'Those damn bastards! Why the hell are they taking students?' Sam cursed.

Wilbur put his hand on his friend's shoulder to calm him down. There wasn't a lot else he could do.

'Have you talked to John, Willy?'

Wilbur nodded. 'It was John who broke the whole thing. He talked to Father Benedict in Gulu, and when he found out that Eddie hadn't reported to work, he went to the bus station in Jinja.'

Sam handed what was left of the drink to the attendant and shook his head silently.

'Can you believe that John's uncle had to bribe the bus officials in order to get information from them?' Wilbur added.

'Hey, Sam, come on! The van is full—we have to go now!' the conductor yelled.

Sam shook his head. 'No, Richard, I am not going anywhere. I might crash. Just unload them.'

The conductor looked unsure and confused. 'But ...' he started saying.

Wilbur stood up. 'Get up, Sam. I will drive,' he said as he pulled on Sam's arm. Sam got up reluctantly, and they both walked slowly towards the van.

Wilbur took the van keys, and to make room he asked one of the passengers to disembark, which the man did while cursing them. Wilbur started the engine, and then they slowly eased off. The station was a tough area to drive through, but fortunately Wilbur was an experienced driver. The only hassles were the constant stops and taking directions that the conductor gave him.

The passengers talked about all kinds of things, and frankly most of it was very interesting, so it was a good way to forget about his problems for a while. Wilbur drove the minibus through the city and suburbs until they got to their final stop. They loaded other passengers and headed back. They did this a couple more times. This isn't an easy job, Wilbur thought after a few trips.

Sam was stretched out in his seat next to Wilbur, just listening to the music on the van's stereo. He had been deep in thought since hearing the nightmare that had befallen Eddie.

They finally loaded their last batch of passengers heading back to the city. On the way, the conductor stepped out with Sam and finalized their daily business before he left for his residence. Wilbur pulled over where he had left his car.

'Everybody out! This is the last stop!' Sam shouted while opening the doors. In Kampala, people knew better than to argue with taxi operators, so they left the car one by one until the last one had disembarked.

Wilbur and Sam sat quietly for a few minutes.

'Listen, Sam, we will need money to help Eddie. John is going to sell a small piece of land, and I am going to hit my father for some,' Wilbur said. 'Your father also offered to help when I told him about our problem earlier,' he added.

Sam, who had been unusually quiet, suddenly turned and looked back at his friend. His eyes were full of fire and determination. 'I know two men who can give us information. They are former rebels in the Lord's Resistance Army—LRA.'

Wilbur tried to say something, but nothing came out of his mouth. Sam realized the confusion in his friend's expression and smiled a little.

'They were rebels but they didn't want to fight anymore, so they escaped and assimilated into civilian life. Sometimes they report to the rehabilitation offices for counseling. Otherwise, one would not know by looking at them that they used to be rebels,' he said.

Wilbur nodded his head slowly. 'I see what you are driving at, but will they help?'

Sam smiled. 'Look, there is nothing money can't buy. I will flash them some and ask them to provide us with useful information. Maybe they can tell us the names of rebel collaborators that can be bought.' He paused. 'I have even heard that people can be bought back from these rebels. I will arrange a meeting with them this evening and let you know the meeting place.'

Wilbur nodded and got out of the van. He got inside his car, started it, and rolled down the window.

'Talk to you tonight,' he shouted to Sam, who was sitting in the driver's seat of his minibus. They drove off in different directions.

Chapter 3

The journey was long and very tiring. As we walked, we kept seeing small towns at a distance on our right and left. At one point somebody behind whispered a name of a town, and I realized we were heading north.

We finally stopped and rested on top of a hill overlooking another town. A young man said the town was called Rom and also said that it was his hometown. Unfortunately, he hadn't realized a rebel was sitting next to him. The young man was grabbed by the collar and taken to the rebel leader. The leader calmly brought him in front of the whole group and ordered everybody to gather around. The rebels made a semicircle behind us.

'My name is Commander Okello,' the leader said. 'I am going to show you what we call a baptism. All of you must look. Anybody who doesn't look or closes his or her eyes will also be baptized.'

He motioned to two other rebels to bring the boy forward and make him kneel down in the middle, facing us.

'Look up at them!' one rebel screamed. Suddenly, the other rebel produced a small axe from the back of his pants and hit the boy on the back of his head. The boy fell forward—dead. I could not believe what I had just witnessed. *These rebels are animals.*

One woman put her hands over her face and almost got beaten, but the Commander held his soldiers back. 'You will pay for that later,' he told her.

They ordered us to form a single line again and walk silently. There was a soldier behind every third person. We kept walking through the bushes, up and down different hills. This excruciating cycle went on and on until I lost count of the number of times we did it.

I was feeling so hungry and tired and angry and sad. I felt every negative emotion that existed. I started wondering where God was or if he really existed. *If he really does exist, would he let a man treat a fellow man in this barbaric way?*

My thoughts were interrupted by Commander Okello. He was telling us that if we needed to relieve ourselves, this was the time. We left one by one until we were all finished. Meanwhile, some rebels who had been sent ahead came back and started talking to the Commander.

They were laughing as they talked to him, and their laughter kept getting louder. It was all very sick. *Here we are, tired and miserable, and these hooligans are laughing.*

The Commander ordered us to start walking again.

I estimated that eight hours had elapsed since we started walking, so I believed the time to be about three-thirty in the morning. I didn't dare look at my watch. Only God knew what the future held for us, but I could hear my mother's voice telling me to stay strong and not give up as long as I am alive.

I started to dig up some pleasant memories of school with my friends and of home with my mother. I thought of the work I would have done with Father Benedict. I had been looking forward to teaching the orphans, playing with them, and giving them hope and a sense of belonging. *How ironic that I am now probably in a worse situation than them.* I looked back at my past mistakes with regret, but I still maintained some hope of surviving this experience one way or another.

We passed by another small trading centre. This time, the Commander ordered the rebels to tape our mouths shut. They also tied a rope around our waists and joined the rope to each captive until we were all secured. The rebels walked in front of us and behind. Commander Okello sent a few soldiers ahead.

After a few miles, I realized that the reason we had been tied was that the Ugandan Army soldiers' barracks was nearby. In the barracks yard I noticed a big vehicle next to a small jeep. I wanted to shout out, 'Help!' but I was not ready to become a martyr—not yet, anyway.

After about an hour, the sun started to rise. I quickly glanced at my watch and saw it was about five-thirty. I estimated that we had passed the barracks an hour earlier. These barbarians still hadn't taken my watch, though I had no doubt they would soon.

They had already removed the duct tape from our mouths, thank God. I guess they wanted us alive. We are no good to them dead, I reasoned. While laughing at us, the rebels kept ordering us to watch where we stepped.

'Besides, it's you that will die, not us,' they bragged.

We walked and walked until we arrived on top of another hill, where we were told to stop.

Commander Okello walked around us, praising our good behavior. 'We didn't encounter the cowards of the Ugandan Army, and none of you rebelled except for the big-mouthed boy. That was unfortunate.' He paused. 'We will walk on for a little while, and then you'll be able to relax,' he said nicely, almost smiling.

We started walking again. The rebel leader had a good command of the English language and appeared to be educated. I couldn't figure him out. *How can this man talk in a civilized manner and at the same time be very cold and heartless?* I wondered. All of this was beyond my comprehension, so I just kept walking in the footsteps of the young man ahead of me.

Most of the captives were young girls and young men because most of us were students captured on our way home for the holidays. I thought about how Uganda was losing a generation. These rebels belonged to the LRA, which operated from southern Sudan against the Ugandan government. Nobody understood what they stood for. The rebel leader, Joseph Kony, was from the Acholi tribe of northern Uganda. The man was busy depopulating his people, especially the young, who were the future of the Acholi.

A lot of things were going through my mind. These wars with the rebels had been going on for years, and if there had been a serious effort to stop them, they would have been over. *Does anybody really care?* I was old enough to know that everything had a price. Maybe the Ugandan government could get rid of Kony by using paid mercenaries or assassins. This kind of thing had been done even before Jesus was born. *Hadn't it?* Surely it wasn't only in movies.

I was starting to get angry again, but I knew I had to curb my anger if I was to survive this ordeal. We finally arrived at the top of a hill, where we met other captives like us, guarded by other rebels. They put all of us together and told us to sit down. I estimated there were more than eighty captives in total.

Commander Okello reminded us that if we followed orders nothing would happen to us. He walked around, looking at us one at a time. 'You are now in Sudan, in our area of control,' he began, 'so don't get any ideas of escaping. If you do, you will suffer a very painful death. You will soon meet the Commanders that will be in charge of you.'

The Commander called to one of the soldiers. 'This is Sergeant Okumu. He is going to feed you, and if you need anything, just ask him. If you have any questions for me, this is the time to ask.' Nobody uttered a word. Commander Okello walked over to one of the captured girls and asked her name.

'Agatha,' she responded.

He turned to go, and then he stopped and looked back. 'Agatha, pick up your things and follow me. Sergeant, get a bag for everybody to deposit their valuables,' he said before he walked away with the scared girl half-running after him.

The sergeant laughed aloud, and I wondered what was funny. Then he spoke in Luo, the Acholi dialect. 'That girl is one of the lucky ones because she will be treated well, like any Affande's (Commander's) girl.'

He tossed a bag to the captive at the end of the line and shouted again in Luo and Swahili. 'Put everything in the bag. That includes money, watches, rings, and anything else you have on you. I don't have to say what will befall you if you don't do as I say,' he stated, and then he whistled very loudly.

'All of you stand up, and when you are done, sit down!' he ordered.

We all started emptying pockets, removing anything we had on us, and depositing items into the bag. After about half an hour, we were finished.

They divided us in two groups. Women and girls went on one side and men and boys on the other. We were ordered to leave our property where it was and moved to two, separate temporary enclosures, where we were told to strip and be searched.

Everything went all right until one man was found with something in his rectum. He was told to walk around naked and show everybody where he had hidden his little bundle of money. It was very embarrassing for the poor man, but I guess that was how the bastards meant him to feel. After this, they took him to a place where he was given a hoe and a shovel with which to dig his own grave.

I felt like I was in a dream. But this wasn't a dream; *it was a nightmare and it was real.* The man's hands were tied behind his back, and he was told to lie inside the grave. We were all brought near the grave at gunpoint to watch.

Commander Okello had come back to oversee the burial of his captive. He picked two boys, each about fifteen years of age, and told them to pile soil on the man.

One of the boys tried to refuse, and a soldier shoved two handfuls of soil into his mouth. The poor boy started choking and developed spasms, and he died shortly thereafter. He was also put in the grave.

The soldier laughed in delight, saying, 'Greet the devil on your way.'

Finally the whole sick episode ended and we were marched back to a place to sit down. We were then given porridge to drink. It was hard to swallow, although we were all hungry.

We were later introduced to Commanders Beba-Beba and Nyoka Kali. By this time we had been divided into two groups that included both men and women. I was told to gather my group's things, which we would carry to wherever we were going. The soldiers lined everybody up next to the bags. There were extra bags, so it was decided that some men would lift more bags.

Our group's new Commander was Nyoka Kali. He instructed us in Swahili on how to behave. Commander Okello came to wish us well before we started marching. I was put at the back near some of the rebels.

As we were leaving, I took a glance to my right and saw someone preparing a meal. It was Agatha, the girl Commander Okello had chosen. I could see she had already changed into some kind of decorative cloth that women wrap around themselves when they are doing chores. I felt sorry for her, but who knew, she was probably better off than us, who were heading into the unknown.

I overheard one of the rebels bragging that since he had money he would go further inland to buy army fatigues. I gathered the newly acquired money was ours.

The terrain was rough and very trying, and the weather was just too hot to bear. I kept hoping that maybe a miracle would happen and I would leave this place. The small hills were quickly becoming mountains. In geography classes, I had never learnt that there were mountains in Sudan. I was amazed.

We kept walking and only stopped once when our Commander, Nyoka Kali, was easing himself. The sun was going down and the weather was becoming unbearable, but we walked until we came up to a pond that was probably fifty yards long.

'You have ten minutes to rest. Water will be passed down for you to drink.' The Commander motioned a soldier to pass a jerry-can of water down the line. He even allowed us to wash our hands and feet. When the jerry-can finally got to me, I drank a little water. When we started walking again, the soldier told me to carry it. This gave me an opportunity to drink the rest of the water that was left inside. I was happy that I was able to fully quench my thirst.

The terrain got even rougher, and some women started stumbling. Commander Nyoka Kali slapped them and gave them a stern warning.

After a distance of about twenty miles, he told us to stop. He looked at his watch and then inquired who could speak English. The soldiers behind me shoved me forward. He motioned for me to come, and I hurried towards him.

'You know Swahili?' he asked.

'I know enough to interpret, sir,' I murmured.

'Okay, interpret!' he ordered.

'This area is perhaps one of the most dangerous places anywhere around,' he began. 'There are dangerous animals here. If you are left behind, you will wish you were dead. If any of you feel that you can't continue, tell me now and I will leave you. If you come along, you shall suffer but not as much as you will if you stay here.'

I quickly interpreted what he had said into English. No hands went up.

He ordered his men to bring the remains of some dead bodies. Within a few minutes, some rebels brought decomposed bodies near where we were waiting. The smell was unbearable, so they quickly took them back.

'Now you have seen for yourselves what happens to the people left behind. These dead people, you see, got tired a week ago. They said they couldn't continue, so I just left them.' He paused. 'So go ahead and tell me if you want to stay. I swear on my mother, not a single bullet will catch you,' he stated seriously. I interpreted.

Nobody said a word. We could hear hyenas howling nearby. The man was right.

'Let's go now,' he ordered.

We started walking again. The fear that he had instilled in everybody had worked miracles. We walked as if we had just started the journey, although the terrain was getting worse.

I heard the soldiers behind me complaining about the hilly Kinyeti area. They said that in the mountains, if falling and breaking your back didn't kill you, hyenas would have you for supper. They also said that out of the seven people they had left behind, three were unaccounted for and they didn't believe the captives had walked back to Uganda.

They were laughing as they talked about this. The fact that they got pleasure out of other people's misery baffled me. *What kind of people are they?*

We kept walking as Commander Nyoka Kali talked on his radio in some code. 'Ndiyo,' he shouted in Swahili, meaning, 'Yes.' I was glad that I understood all the three languages spoken here: Swahili, English, and Luo, my mother tongue.

'Now everybody hold on. We will be home soon,' Nyoka Kali stated as he lit a cigarette.

I interpreted. At this point all of us were exhausted beyond measure. We must have been walking for over twenty-four hours.

Our pace slowed down, and soon we met another party of rebels in a different type of uniform. The Commander greeted them, showed them his captives, and then shouted, 'Forward!'

We walked uphill at a slower pace. The new Officers in charge had consumed some alcohol, so they were slower. Most of them were smoking cigarettes and laughing as we walked. Suddenly, we noticed a large, flat area in the valley below us. Again we were cautioned to walk in a straight line. We came to a tall tree, where we rested for a while before walking a little further and finding ourselves in a large camp nested between trees. We were taken to a special area that had barbed wire around it and told to enter.

'Okay, we will see all of you tomorrow and cleanse you of evil spirits. Food will be brought to you shortly,' Nyoka Kali said in Swahili.

I quickly jumped up to interpret.

He smiled and motioned to me. He gave me a few cigarettes. I didn't smoke, but I thankfully took them, thinking they might come in handy. I later offered the cigarettes to one of the guards of the compound as a friendly gesture. I knew that in places like this, the more friends you had on your side the better.

Chapter 4

Wilbur pulled into his uncle's driveway at about seven-thirty in the evening and honked the horn of his car. The security guard waved to him and opened the gate. Government officials normally had security cameras at their residences, so Wilbur knew he was being observed from inside. He parked his car and got out. The door opened before he could knock, and his cousin Lillian rushed out to hug him. Wilbur had called ahead and told her the bad news without going into details. She pulled Wilbur towards the sofa.

'Oh, my God, that's really terrible about Sam,' she said as they sat down.

Wilbur shook his head. 'No, cousin, it is not Sam. It's Eddie!' he said quietly.

Her eyes started watering, and she quickly got up and walked away. 'I will call Dad, Willy,' she said weakly.

Wilbur had brought Edgar to his house during the previous holidays because they only had five weeks until the finals and they needed to prepare. They had visited his uncle's house, and Lillian had met Edgar. Wilbur suspected they had liked each other. He even recalled that Lillian visited his home much more frequently during that time.

Everything suddenly dawned on him. She had fallen for Eddie; poor girl. He was still deep in his thoughts when Lillian came back into the living room and offered him some juice.

'Willy, are you sure?' she asked as she sat next to him.

Wilbur gulped his drink and looked at her. She still had tears in her eyes.

'Lillian, he didn't arrive at his home in Gulu, and the bus he was riding in was burnt to the ground and four people were killed.' He paused and took another sip. 'That's conclusive enough for me,' he said quietly.

Lillian reached into her pocket, pulled out an envelope, and gave it to him. 'I know you are going to try and help him. Here is my contribution. It is only three hundred dollars, but I hope it can help,' she said, standing up. 'Here comes Dad. Please do the best you can for Edgar,' she said to both of them as she walked away.

Hon Ochom was coming down the staircase. He was a tall, heavy-set man with an air of authority. As he came into the living room, he looked at his daughter and then at Wilbur. A concerned look crossed his face.

'Are you all right, son? I see Lillian crying. Has something happened?' he inquired without pausing. Wilbur nodded as he got up and shook his uncle's hand respectfully.

'Uncle, one of my best friends has been kidnapped by the rebels of the LRA. His name is Eddie. He is the one I brought here during the holidays,' he stated and then sat down.

'Oh yes, I remember him. A very humble young man. Was he caught up in an ambush? Tell me everything,' Hon Ochom said as he sat down.

Wilbur proceeded to tell his uncle the whole story and mentioned that he and his friends were determined to help Edgar. His uncle listened intently and then got up and started pacing up and down the living room without uttering a single word.

Finally, he walked to the liquor cabinet, poured himself a drink, and then sat next to his nephew. 'This is going to be a very trying period for you and your friends,' he said. He paused and sipped his drink. 'It will take some planning. I have a friend who lives outside of Okaru, in southern Sudan. His son came to me for help a few weeks ago. He attends Makerere University. I believe he is still ...' He got up without finishing the sentence and walked to a cabinet.

He looked through some papers and finally found what he was looking for. Then he walked to the telephone, picked it up, and dialed.

'Hello! May I please talk to Hassan Lara? It's an emergency. He is in room B2-11,' he stated and waited.

A lot of thoughts were going through Wilbur's head. Could his uncle really get a captive released? He had no idea, but he was hoping for the best.

'Hello! Is this Hassan?' Hon Ochom asked. 'Good. This is Dickens Ochom. How is your class schedule, Hassan? Can you come to my house tomorrow morning?' He listened for a little while. 'Good. When do you have your holidays?' He listened again. 'Good. See you tomorrow at ten o'clock in the morning. Goodnight.' He put down the phone and exhaled.

'Wilbur!' he exclaimed as he took a seat. 'This isn't going to be easy, but it is worth a try. This young man has finished his exams for the term and is going home for the holidays, so the timing is good. I want to give him a message to take to his father, Al-Hajj Musa Lara, who can hopefully help us get your friend,' he said as he leaned back and took a sip from his drink. 'Tell me again—when did the rebels ambush your friend's bus?' Hon Ochom asked.

It occurred to Wilbur that he was with Eddie the day before yesterday morning. He looked up with sadness. 'I was with Eddie yesterday morning. He was captured in the evening,' he said, spreading his hands in despair.

Hon Ochom walked to the liquor cabinet for a refill. 'So they must have arrived at the LRA's camp tonight,' he stated. 'It takes at least a day of serious walking to get to the Kinyeti mountains, and then maybe another day to get to the flatlands where the rebel camp is located,' he said as he walked back to where Wilbur was seated.

Wilbur hadn't realized his uncle knew so much about the rebel movements. He decided to keep the burning questions of how his uncle knew this to himself. Right now all he wanted was to get his friend out of there as soon as possible.

'Uncle, you said the young man Hassan is going on vacation. I was thinking that he could go with us and maybe help us get Sudanese IDs in case we need to cross the border.'

'That's exactly what I had in mind, in case you boys wanted to go that far,' Hon Ochom said. He hadn't been prepared for his nephew's determination, and it took him by surprise. He felt a sense of pride. He would of course provide everything the boys needed to get the boy back.

'All right, son. Let's meet here with the young man at ten o'clock, tomorrow morning,' Hon Ochom said, getting up.

Wilbur got up too and they shook hands. Then he headed for the door with his uncle close behind.

'Drive carefully, son. I will see you tomorrow,' Hon Ochom said as he closed the door behind Wilbur.

'Goodnight, Uncle,' Wilbur called back as he walked to his car. He waved to the guard as he drove off. When he checked the time, he saw it was approaching to nine o'clock. He needed to be home in time for Sam's phone call, so he drove fast. Luckily there were few traffic cops that roamed about at night. Wilbur entered in his father's driveway and sprinted to the door.

His brother Tom opened the door. 'Hello, Willy, how are you?' Tom asked. Wilbur just shrugged. 'You received a phone call from Sam. He said to meet him at Cissy's Pub in Rubaga. He said you would know why.'

Wilbur turned around immediately and headed for the car. He stopped suddenly and turned around. 'Hey, Tom, what time did Sam call?' he shouted.

'About ten minutes ago,' his brother said.

Wilbur jumped into the car and backed out of the driveway very quickly. He drove through the city like a madman until he arrived in Rubaga. He found the street, then slowed down looking left and right for Cissy's Pub. He finally found it and parked on the street. He took a deep breath before stepping out of the car and walking across the street. He had a lot of questions to ask, not to mention three hundred dollars of beginner's cash from Lillian.

Sam was seated with two other gentlemen on the veranda outside the pub. The place looked all right, but that was beside the point. Wilbur needed to be alert for this meeting. He pulled up a chair and sat before greeting all the gentlemen around the table.

Sam asked the waitress to bring a beer for his friend.

'Sam, I'm sorry for the delay. I was at my uncle's place. I have some interesting news to tell you later,' Wilbur said.

'Gentlemen, this is my friend, Wilbur. Willy, meet Mr Jad and Mr Olwa.'

The former rebels shook hands with Wilbur.

Sam continued to talk. 'These gentlemen and I have been talking. They have told me some things that are very distressing, but there is still hope,' Sam said. 'I will let Mr Jad brief you.'

Wilbur looked at the man who used to be a rebel. He didn't look different from any other man on the street. He was average height and very slim, and he had penetrating eyes and a couple of scars on his face but nothing extraordinary.

When Mr Jad spoke, he spoke slowly with no trace of malice at all. 'Mr Wilbur,' he said, 'Mr Sam has already told me about your friend and I am really sorry. First, I will give you the names of two Commanders of the LRA who are powerful and can be approached for the release of your friend.' He paused to light his cigarette. 'Commander Okello and Commander Nyoka Kali can remove any captive from the camp before they are sold into slavery.'

Wilbur couldn't believe what he was hearing. *Sold into slavery?* His hands started shaking. He put his beer down to avoid dropping it. He had heard about this slavery thing, but he really hadn't taken it seriously.

'Hold on, Mr Jad, you mean the captives can be sold as slaves?' he asked in astonishment.

The former rebels nodded their heads in unison.

'Most young men and women are sold to the Arabs. They put chains around them and head north,' Jad said and paused to let the impact of what he had just said sink in.

Wilbur felt like jumping on the man there and then. He could not believe this man was sitting here telling him these things with a straight face. These men had been part of the barbaric group. *What kind of war are these barbarians fighting? Surely this is a devil's war—enslaving their fellow men?*

Sam seemed to sense the anger that was engulfing his friend's mind, and quickly stepped in to stop the inevitable fight. 'Willy, you must understand that most of the fighters that the LRA is using are also captives, who had no choice but to take arms,' he stated and ordered another round of drinks.

Jad looked a little concerned. He lit another cigarette before talking.

'A lot of people escaped from the LRA during the Ugandan army operations in the north. That is why he started selling people into slavery. He does this in order to buy ammunition and food for his soldiers. It's better to act quickly and soon if your friend is to be saved from the chains. There is a man named Oyu, an ex-rebel who lives in a little town outside of Madi Opel. He lives near a primary school. He used to be one of Kony's men in Uganda. I am not sure if he still is.' Jad paused and looked at Olwa, the other rebel.

Olwa decided to interject. 'There is also a woman called Joyce Akello, who lives in the same town. She owns a hair salon and a bar on the road that goes to Kitgum. The bar's name is Sukuma Chini. She also works for Kony. When I was a rebel, I saw her come to see him in Sudan.' He took a cigarette from Jad and puffed hard. 'I have heard that she is a clever businesswoman and will do anything for money. If she wants somebody released, Kony will release him or her. She is still a collaborator,' he added.

Wilbur digested everything and realized that even though most of what he had heard was unpleasant, they were making progress. He thanked the men and apologized for his anger.

He remembered that he had promised John he would be home, but since it was getting late he asked Sam if he could use his mobile telephone. He dialed John's uncle's number.

'Hello, may I talk to John, please?'

'Oh hi, John, I am using Sam's mobile unit, can you call me back?'

John called back and Sam answered. He talked to John for a few minutes and then handed the unit to Wilbur, who updated John on the latest developments and the impending meeting at his uncle's house. John said he had sold his two-acre plot for about five thousand dollars, which wasn't bad considering he had to sell it in a hurry. He added that he had talked to Father Benedict again, who told him that Eddie's mother had collapsed when she heard the news about her son. The Catholic mission was looking after her, and luckily she was in a stable condition.

After the phone call, Wilbur and Sam talked to the men for a little while longer before leaving them. Wilbur drove Sam to his home, which wasn't very far from Cissy's Pub.

'Sam, did you walk here from home?' Wilbur asked as they drove.

Sam nodded. 'I didn't feel like disrespecting the minibus by driving it without passengers,' Sam joked. They both burst out laughing. Sam was a jokester. That was one of the reasons they had clicked as friends in the first place.

They parked in Sam's father's driveway and started making plans for the next day. Wilbur recounted the meeting with his uncle.

'Sam, why don't you come with me to my uncle's house for the meeting with Hassan Lara tomorrow morning? We need to be there at ten o'clock in the morning—that's if you can get a driver.'

Sam nodded. 'I already got a driver to work for me until this situation is over. I will be there for the meeting if you can give me a ride.'

They were silent for a while, and then Wilbur started smiling. Sam looked at him curiously. 'What is going on, Willy? Are you going nuts on me now?'

Wilbur smiled a little longer, enjoying the suspense. Then he pulled the envelope out of his pocket and handed it to Sam. 'Go ahead, open it.'

Sam opened it. 'Where did you get this?'

Wilbur continued to smile. 'It's a contribution from my cousin, Lillian. Do you remember her?'

Sam nodded, 'Yes, but why would she …?'

Wilbur smiled again. 'It seems she really liked Eddie. The poor girl cried when she found out what happened.'

They sat quietly for sometime, each deep in thought. Then without warning they abruptly bid each other farewell.

They would need all the strength they could muster for the coming weeks.

Chapter 5

The cold weather was unbearable, and I had left my jacket in my bag, which the rebels had taken. The temperature must have been $5\,^{\circ}\text{C}$, equivalent to $37\,^{\circ}\text{F}$. We were huddled together in an area of no more than half an acre. Luckily the sun was rising and a little perseverance was all that was needed.

I had found a way to escape reality by reminiscing about my life back home. I recalled all the adventures I had with John, Sam, and Willy during school times and holidays. I even daydreamed about the job I would have been doing at the Catholic mission, taking care of orphans and widows. I especially remembered the peace I always felt when I was there. I dared not think about my mother.

I finally dozed off, and when I woke up the rebels were in the middle of organizing us according to age and gender. The ages were organized in three ways: over thirty, between fifteen and thirty, and below fifteen. They did this for both men and women. We were then taken to a stream nearby for baths and allowed to exchange our clothes for clean ones. Later we were marched in front of the Commanders to be inspected.

That is when I noticed the men with turbans. They wore white clothing and simple sandals. They were the ones doing most of the inspecting. These strange men told us to turn around carefully and then checked our ears, mouths, teeth, etc. They selected some people and told others to rejoin the captives. This went on for quite some time.

I was among the people who were selected.

We were marched to another big shed where the men with turbans re-inspected us. Then we were taken to a little room where we were told to strip. We were checked again, after which we were told to dress. Then we marched in front of other men with turbans and the Commanders of the rebels. That was the first time I laid eyes on Kony, the notorious leader of the LRA rebels. He had long, braided hair.

I had seen him numerous times in the newspapers back home in Uganda, but being in his presence made me feel a chill right to the bone. *What kind of person is he?*

Kony was talking to men with turbans. He was using an interpreter.

They called us forward, two at a time, and took us to another shed, where we were told to sit down. Some sort of negotiations began.

I saw an older man with a turban writing figures every time the negotiations were completed. I did not know what was happening. *Were we being sold?* I had heard about it but never believed it.

It finally dawned on me that we were indeed being sold to these Arab-looking men. *Oh my God. This is not happening to me.* Tears welled up in my eyes.

I was ordered to go to the kitchen, light a piece of firewood, and bring it back. On my way, I met the rebel to whom I had given cigarettes the night before. He told me to be humble and not cause any trouble. 'That way you will have a chance to survive,' he said. He told me that when we reached our destination I would know what the future held for me.

This did not make me feel any better. I looked at him for some kind of hope, but deep in my heart I knew it was too late. He just tapped me on the shoulder and told me to hurry. The only choice I had was to try and survive as long as I possibly could. I took the firewood and gave it to the man who had sent me.

We were advised not to complain otherwise punishment would be very harsh. They brought some older men to talk to us in our own language. We were also told that the consequence of any escape attempt would be instant death.

A fierce looking man in a turban came and put us in a circle, and then he demonstrated to us what he would do if we didn't follow his commands. He pulled out a shining sword, chose one of the captives, and told his men to hold the captive down.

With a swift movement, he cut both of the man's Achilles tendons.

The wounded man was screaming so loudly that they had to put a cloth around his mouth. After a few minutes he passed out. The swordsman motioned to another one of his men to use some herbs on the wound and bandage it.

The turbaned man asked all of us if we had seen what they would do to disobedience of any sort.

We all answered in unison, 'Yes.'

The evil man smiled and puffed on his pipe, and then he left with a little smile on his face.

I had seen mean people in my life, but this man was *the devil incarnate*. I felt very weak and defeated. I tried to stay optimistic and positive, but it was hard to do. I looked in the faces of my fellow captives. I could see some of them had tears in their eyes, but not a single one of them dared to cry out loud. I also saw a look on their faces that I hadn't seen before in all the days we had been together. It was a look of despair and an acceptance of the inevitable. I knew I had the same look on my face.

We were bound together in twos, with chains locked on our wrists. The process kept going for a long time, as if it was never going to end. I noticed that some of the young girls were going through the same thing except that they were chained by their waist.

Eventually we were given food, which we could only eat using our one free hand. Afterwards we were ordered to rest because in a few hours we had a long journey ahead of us. We were still chained.

Before I closed my eyes, I realized with regret that I hadn't seen or communicated with the jolly young man from the bus, Rob. I never laid my eyes on him again.

Chapter 6

Wilbur lay down on his bed and thought about everything that had happened and what they had learnt so far. There were lots of risks and uncertainties in trying to free their friend. He felt like he was being spun around in the eye of a storm.

Why did this happen to Eddie? he wondered. Wilbur had no answer to that question, so he focused his mind on how to rescue his friend. He thought of something he had heard somewhere. 'Every human being goes through trials; the difference that separates people is how they handle these trials and overcome them.' He couldn't remember the exact words or where he had heard them. Maybe it was something his father had told him.

He sat up in bed and turned on his bed lamp. He picked up a pen and started writing down some notes. He wrote down the names of the rebel collaborators: Mr Oyu, an ex-rebel, and Ms Joyce Akello, a businesswoman and close friend of Kony.

The first option was to approach both of these people with money and promise them more after they delivered Eddie. He didn't want to think about the other option. If, God forbid, Eddie had already been sold, then their best bet was to use Al-Hajj Musa Lara to try and buy Eddie back.

Everything depended on how fast things could be done. Wilbur reached for an aspirin lying on the table, swallowed it, and tried to sleep. He finally slept restlessly.

* * *

On the other side of town, Sam came to the same conclusion. If anything was to be done, it would have to be done with the help of the rebel collaborators or Willy's uncle's friend in Sudan. They had to find a way of entering Sudan safely without becoming victims of violence themselves. He drank some water and prayed for sleep although he was exhausted.

Sam didn't recall when he finally fell asleep, but he woke up the next day still feeling weak and tired.

* * *

The ringing phone woke Wilbur from a fitful sleep. He checked the time and saw it was nine o'clock in the morning. He reached over to the table and picked up the phone. 'Hello!' he said in a sleepy voice.

'Hey, Willy, it's Sam. Are you still sleeping? Have you forgotten about our appointment at ten?'

Wilbur sat up in his bed, trying to get his bearings. 'Thanks, Sam, I will be there in a few minutes.' He hung up, picked up his towel, and headed for the bathroom.

He realized he didn't have enough time to take a shower, so he washed his face and brushed his teeth very fast before running back to his bedroom. He quickly put on some jeans, a T-shirt, and some sneakers. He picked up his car keys and his wallet and headed for the main door, stopping only to say hello to his cousin, who was visiting for the holidays.

'Good morning, cousin. I have to run. No time for breakfast. I will call later.'

His cousin was wide-eyed, waiting for more explanation.

'I will be at Uncle's house. I have an appointment with him,' Wilbur said as he glanced at his watch and ran out the door.

The drive to Sam's place was full of the usual morning traffic—crazy drivers breaking all kinds of rules. He finally made it at nine-thirty.

Sam was waiting outside his house and quickly jumped into the car. They drove off towards Willy's uncle's place in Kololo, a high-end neighborhood.

'Hello, Willy, how was your night?' Sam asked, but he did not wait for the answer. 'You know, after thinking about the whole thing, I realized that we have two main obstacles. One is locating Eddie. The other is getting him out.'

Wilbur nodded in agreement. 'I know that too, Sam. What I don't know is if we can pull it off without professional help.'

Sam looked at his friend, puzzled. 'Willy, what the hell are you talking about?' he asked earnestly.

Wilbur was quiet for a moment, thinking of the best way to explain what he was trying to say. 'Sam, what I mean is, looking at this thing realistically, we are not equipped. We are just students, and things may become dangerous. To succeed, we may need professionals.'

Sam took some time to think about what Wilbur had just said. He recalled how he had fallen asleep still puzzled about how to handle this situation. He cleared his throat. 'I agree with you absolutely. We are not knowledgeable about these things. We will need reliable people who are familiar with these issues.'

He sat back in the car seat and stretched his legs. 'Willy, have you talked to John today?'

Wilbur shook his head.

Sam reached for his mobile and dialed John's uncle's number. 'Hello, my name is Sam. I'm John's friend. Is he there, by any chance?' He listened. 'Oh, okay, thank you. Please tell him I will call back at about eleven-thirty in the morning,' he said and hung up.

'He is not there, so I will just call after the meeting with your uncle,' he said to Wilbur. 'We should have a real plan by the time we call him.'

Wilbur nodded. They were coming to his uncle's driveway, so Wilbur slowed down. He checked his watch. It was five minutes to ten. 'Good, we made it in time,' he said as he turned into the driveway, pausing to wave to the security guard who was opening the gates.

He parked the vehicle, got out, and stretched. Sam did the same. The weather was great this morning, warm with a nice breeze.

Cousin Lillian opened the door. She hugged Wilbur and extended a hand to greet Sam. 'Welcome, please come in,' she said enthusiastically.

They both entered the house and took their seats. She turned to go and then stopped. 'Oh, Hassan, the Makerere University student, called a few minutes ago. He should be here any time,' she said and then walked towards the kitchen.

Soon after Lillian left, somebody knocked on the door. Wilbur went to open it. He turned the knob and to his surprise came face to face with John. He tried to say something, but John walked past him, grumbling.

'What the hell is going on, gentlemen? Are we in this together or have you decided to go it alone?' he asked seriously.

Both boys avoided his eyes as he sat down.

To their relief, Lillian brought a tray of tea, and biscuits and laid it on the table in front of them. She greeted John before setting cups in front of each of them. She went back to get another cup.

'Would you boys like something more to eat?' she asked as she came back. They all shook their heads. She smiled sweetly and headed back to the kitchen. Although they had a cook, Lillian liked to help out in the kitchen, the reason being that she loved cooking. Sam was the first to speak.

'John, we just called your uncle's house a few minutes ago and left a message. We thought we would call with something more concrete after the meeting.'

Wilbur interjected, 'Moreover, you live far away. We didn't want you to have to come all the way here.'

John smiled. 'That's okay, guys. I am just uptight right now because of this situation, and the days are rushing by so fast,' he said apologetically. He looked at Wilbur. 'I called here last night before you and Sam phoned me. Your uncle mentioned that you were coming this morning to meet someone, so I hoped on a minibus.'

There was a knock on the door, and everybody was suddenly alert. 'I will get it,' Sam said, getting up. Wilbur and John poured themselves some tea as Sam came back with a well-dressed young man in his mid-twenties. They all stood up and introduced themselves. The young man was Hassan Lara, a student at Makerere University.

Wilbur excused himself and walked to the kitchen area to talk to Lillian. She was resting her head on the table.

'Lilly, are you all right?' he asked.

'Yes, Willy, as well as can be expected under the circumstances,' she said with a sad smile.

'Lilly, the young man from the university is here. Can I have another cup?'

Lillian got up, walked towards a cupboard, and removed a cup. 'Here you go,' she said, handing him the cup. 'I will go and get Dad.'

Wilbur returned to the living room and poured some tea for Hassan. 'So, Hassan, how is school going?' he asked trying to make a conversation

'Not bad. The only problem is the waiting period before graduation.'

There was silence as everyone sipped their drinks. Finally, Hassan took charge of the conversation. 'It's very unfortunate about your friend. I shall do what I can to help.' He realized he had surprised them. 'I came here yesterday evening because Hon Ochom's call seemed urgent. He told me a little about what happened.'

Wilbur had already guessed that much. He put down his cup of tea and pulled his chair next to Hassan's. 'Look, this is a difficult time for all of us. We have been friends for a long time—Eddie is like our brother,' he said and scratched his temple as he looked for the right words. 'We will do everything we possibly can to bring him back,' he said with finality.

John and Sam nodded their heads simultaneously.

'Good morning, young men, how are you?' Hon Ochom greeted them as he came down the stairs. They all stood up at the same time. He shook their hands and patted his nephew on the back before he sat down. He turned to Lillian, who was standing by the door and asked her to bring another pot of tea. She left.

He looked at each one of them slowly. 'So have you all been introduced?' he asked.

They all nodded.

'Good. Let's get down to business. We don't want to waste any more time,' he said.

Hon Ochom turned to look at Wilbur. 'So, did you have your meeting with the former rebels last night?,' he asked as Lillian was pouring his tea.

Wilbur had forgotten that he had told his uncle about it.

'Yes, Sam, and I met with them,' he said. 'They told us a lot of things and also gave us some names of the LRA collaborators that we can contact.' He motioned to Sam to take over.

'Sir, the rebels claim that Kony only started getting involved in slave trading recently, after most of his fighters escaped. He still has collaborators in Uganda who help him monitor troop movements.' Sam went on to tell them about Mr Oyu and Ms Joyce Akello. 'The rebels said Ms Akello is in direct contact with Kony and can get anybody out.'

Hon Ochom still hadn't touched his drink. He was busy writing all the information down. Finally he cleared his throat and removed his glasses. 'Well, young men, this is good information. I hope you didn't have to pay too much for it.'

He perused his notes and finally closed the notebook. 'I have been doing my own personal investigation, but I haven't been able to come up with much.' He sipped his drink and examined his notes again. 'You will need to hire professionals along the way. Hassan is the son of my good friend who lives in Sudan. I will send a message to his father asking for help in that area.'

He poured some more tea from the teapot into his cup and looked at the young men. He could see anxiety in their eyes, a hunger to do something. He sipped his tea. 'Before we make any plans, do you want to add anything?' He looked around at all the young men, but everybody was silent.

'All right. Let's begin,' he said. 'Lillian, hold all the phones or take messages, and can you please pass me that book on the shelf?' Lillian did as told and then left.

Hon Ochom looked at his nephew. 'Can you please secure the door?' Wilbur nodded and stood up to shut the door. He knew his uncle very well. This was serious business.

Wilbur's uncle looked around at the young men. 'Okay, I will begin with you, Wilbur. Are you ready to do this?'

Wilbur nodded, 'Yes, sir.' Hon Ochom turned to Sam.

'Yes, sir,' Sam said.

John didn't wait for the question. 'Yes, sir,' he said.

'Good, that is settled,' Hon Ochom said. He sighed and looked at Sam. 'Since your ex-rebels are deserters, we have no reason to doubt them. We need to approach the collaborators. How do you suggest we do this?'

Sam scratched his head in thought. 'I would suggest that we approach an elder that has good community standing. We need someone that the rebels would not suspect as a spy.'

They all nodded their heads emphatically in agreement.

'Like a priest, a Bishop, or a Father—someone that the woman Akello would believe,' John interjected.

Hon Ochom looked at John and smiled. 'Very good. I know someone who can give us the name of such a man. Give me a few minutes.' He got up and walked towards the phone.

The boys started exchanging ideas quietly. 'Willy, maybe you should be the one to head north and approach this woman since you speak the same language,' Sam said.

John shook his head. 'We all go together.'

They all looked at each other with uncertainty.

John looked at his friends. 'Guys, we have already lost too much time, and we can't afford to lose any more. We should go together to Kitgum, and when we get there Willy can go and meet this woman.'

They all agreed. Hon Ochom came back and sat down. They told him what they had decided.

'Excellent. You will stay in my house in Kitgum,' he began. 'As for Wilbur being your choice to deliver the message, that also is wise,' he said.

Although Wilbur's grandfather was originally from the Teso district, he had settled in Kitgum when he got a job there and married his grandmother. His father and uncle had grown up in Kitgum and adopted the language, which they had passed on to their children.

Hon Ochom checked the notes he had written down and raised his eyes to meet the boys'. 'I have talked to Bishop Jonathan, who has given us the name of a person who will help us. He is Father Otim, and he lives a few miles from Madi Opel. I have instructed my secretary to type a letter and take it to the Bishop for a signature. The letter will be addressed to Father Otim.'

He paused and checked his watch. 'She should be here by four o'clock with the signed letter, so if there is anything you want to take care of today, you have a few hours to do it,' he said, getting up from his chair. 'Lillian, tell the driver to get the car from the garage—hurry!' He turned to Hassan.

'And, Hassan, you will come with me to my office.' Looking at the other boys, he stated, 'Okay, young men, go and get ready. Let's meet here at five o'clock and don't forget to bring the bags.' He went upstairs without looking back.

The three friends bid Lillian a good day and headed for their car, leaving Hassan behind. They all entered Wilbur's car quietly and backed out of the driveway. There was a moment of silence as everybody thought of what to do in these next few hours.

It was John who broke the silence after they entered the main flow of traffic. 'I will go straight to Jinja and get a few things together. You can pick me up on your way north.'

'Willy, drop me at the nearest taxi stand, please,' Sam said loudly.

Wilbur suppressed a smile.

Sam motioned to one of the taxis. 'Come on, John, I will drop you at the Jinja stage,' he said, jumping out of the car.

'Willy, see you at five,' Sam said as they jumped into a taxi.

'Okay, Sam. Later, John,' Wilbur shouted as he pulled off in his car.

Wilbur's problem wasn't simple. He only had about one thousand dollars in the bank and the three hundred his cousin had given him. He realized he needed more money. He decided that his best bet would be to approach his father, whom he had only briefed a little about the matter. He drove straight to Main Street, where his father co-owned an import and export company.

He checked the time as he pulled into a parking spot opposite the place. It was almost one-thirty. He didn't have too much time to work with. He had to use the little time he had productively. He half-walked, half-ran to his dad's office, opened the door, and entered.

'Good afternoon, Grace. May I see my father? It's an emergency!' he stated seriously.

'Just a minute, Willy,' the older lady said as she stood up and headed to Mr Isaac Ochom's office.

'Please send him in,' Wilbur heard the reply from his dad.

Wilbur was halfway to the door by the time the lady turned around to inform him. She shrugged and continued to her desk. *Young people these days are always in a hurry*, she thought.

Wilbur knocked on the door and turned the handle. 'Dad, I'm sorry to burst in like—' he began, but his dad motioned him to the chair.

Wilbur sat down and said, 'Dad, I know I didn't tell you a lot about what is going on. It's because we get home at different hours and I also—'

His father again stopped him in mid sentence. 'Son, I know what is going on. I just talked to my brother. Now, tell me what you need,' he stated.

Wilbur hesitated. He didn't want to impose a big burden on his dad, who had not only made his life comfortable but had also always been there for him.

Mr Ochom noticed his son's hesitation. 'I have eight thousand dollars here in the safe that I know you will need for transactions with the lunatics,' he said, reaching into his desk safe. 'Here is a letter for you to take with you. It is addressed to Al-Hajj Abdul Asuman, a very good friend of mine in Nimule, Sudan. He will help in any way he can when you get to Sudan.'

Wilbur began to open his mouth to say something, but his father continued talking.

'You see, son, Uganda doesn't have any diplomatic relations with Sudan. Entering Sudan with Ugandan identification papers would be utter suicide. Al-Hajj Abdul will help you to get Sudanese identification papers.'

'Thank you, Dad,' Wilbur said with deep gratitude.

'One more thing, Wilbur. Take my instant camera—you will need pictures for your IDs.' Mr Ochom came around the desk and hugged his son. Tears came into his eyes, and he turned around.

'The films are right on the end table ... Good luck, son. Be careful out there,' Wilbur's dad said, walking to the window and wiping tears from his eyes.

Wilbur felt tears wet his eyes too, but he simply closed the door and walked out of the office. He crossed the street and got back into his car. He turned to look up at his dad's office.

It took time for him to compose himself. He looked at his watch. He had to get to the bank before it closed, so he started the car and quickly joined the flow of the traffic. Within a few minutes he was at the bank. He closed his account and walked out.

The day had been productive so far. Hopefully God will continue to be on our side, he thought as he entered the car and put the money together with what his father had given him.

    Wilbur had nine-thousand-three-hundred dollars altogether and he was sure his uncle would also contribute. Not bad, he thought as he started the car and slowly eased into traffic; his mind was calculating all the issues that needed to be taken care of.

    He would go home and pack his bag and also pick up his dad's camera. He would pack only the necessities. To Wilbur, the first phase of the mission was moving along smoothly.

Chapter 7

'Driver, please hurry up. We don't have all day to listen to your music. We have things to do,' Sam said, rather agitated.

John merely smiled and shook his head. Sam had always been impatient. One would think he would be a bit more sensitive considering he drives a taxi too, John thought, but he didn't say anything.

Sam then turned to John and said, 'Listen, John, we may be going to a different country, so you will need to exchange some of your money for dollars.'

John merely smiled. 'I already thought about that. That's the first thing I will do when I get to Jinja. There is a bank that closes late, so I will exchange the money there.' Sam looked at his friend with admiration.

The taxi came to a stop.

'Here you are, John. See you soon,' Sam said.

John got out of the cab and waved to Sam as he walked to his taxi stand.

Sam turned to the driver. 'To Standard Bank at the corner, quick,' he said as he reached into his pocket for some money.

A few minutes later, the cab driver pulled over in front of the bank; he was used to uptight customers. Sam paid and jumped out. He was glad he had remembered to bring his bank book this morning. Since banks closed at four, he wouldn't have been able to make it if he had to go home first. He walked straight to the teller and asked to withdraw money.

'Are you sure you want it in one batch, Mr Ssenyonjo?' the teller asked.

It took him all the self-control he had to stop from cursing the lady. *Why do they always ask such questions when one is withdrawing one's money? They never ask anything when one is depositing it.*

'Yes, please,' he said firmly.

The lady hesitated for a second and then reached for the money and started the counting process. She finally finished counting and slid it over to him. He reached over for the bundle and stuffed it into the little bag he had brought with him. He thanked her politely and then asked her if their foreign exchange bureau was open.

'Oh yes, it is right over there,' she said, pointing to an office in the corner. Sam thanked her again and walked hurriedly to the foreign exchange office. He entered and was greeted by a friendly lady who offered him a chair.

She started explaining the exchange process, but he stopped her in mid-sentence and asked for a calculator. The exchange rate was around two thousand shillings to one dollar. He removed the money from the bag and handed it to her, but kept six hundred thousand shillings. She took her time counting the money. Some of these bank people were always nervous handling large amounts of money. Sam had worked for a long time driving and managing money for his father and uncles, and experience had taught him that whenever someone was nervous around money they were not to be trusted.

She finally finished counting it, and then she reached under her table and pulled out a bundle of dollars. She again took her time counting the dollars. Then she put everything in the money-counting machine. She finally finished and gave Sam the money.

Sam, who was very streetwise, first checked the validity of the notes to make sure they were not fakes before he quickly counted it. As expected, they added up to five thousand dollars.

'Could I have a couple of those rubber bands, please?' he asked the lady.

'With pleasure, sir,' she said sweetly as she gave them to him.

He ignored the beautiful, inviting smile and tied both bundles of money—shillings in one pile and dollars in another. Then he put both of them in the inside pockets of his jacket.

He said goodbye to the lady, who wasn't smiling widely anymore, and walked out of the bank to get a taxi. These women really don't care anymore, he thought as he entered the taxi. *People are dying daily of AIDS*, and she really believes I'm going to buy my own death sentence? He shook his head.

'Sir? Where to, sir?' the driver inquired.

'I am sorry. Please take me to Rubaga—I will show you the way,' he said and sat back.

During the ride, Sam thought about a lot of things. The night before, he had resigned from his job and recommended a good friend he had known for a few years to take over driving his minibus. The operations of the minibuses rested with his father, but his mother would receive all the daily income from the minibus that Sam had acquired.

The taxi pulled over in front of his father's house; he paid the driver as he stepped out. The taxi drove off. He stood still, surveying the area for a few seconds. According to tradition, this place held a lot of secrets, but to Sam it was simply a beautiful place to live. He especially enjoyed the vast gardens around his home. He smiled as he walked up to the front door, holding the house keys.

The instant he stepped inside, he knew he wasn't alone.

'Hello, son, I have been waiting for you since noon,' his father said as he extended his hand to him.

Sam took his father's hand as he closed the door behind him. 'But, Father, aren't you supposed to be working?' he asked, still puzzled.

His father ignored the question as he guided Sam to the living room. 'Son, I know why you resigned and I admire you for it.' Sam tried to say something, but his father stopped him with a gesture. 'I haven't finished. I want to offer you something, and I don't want you to turn me down.'

Mr Ssenyonjo reached into his pocket and pulled out an envelope, which he gave to his son. Sam took it and put it in the inside pocket of his jacket without uttering a word.

James, the housekeeper, called from the kitchen. 'Master Sam, I have done what you told me to do.'

Sam smiled. He had called ahead and asked James to pack his bag. He could always rely on James; the boy was efficient. 'Thank you very much, James. Please bring the bag down here.' He looked at his watch; he was running out of time. He used his mobile unit to call Wilbur Ochom's house. He was told that Wilbur wasn't at home.

He asked to talk to Mr Ochom and was given his office number. He then called Wilbur's dad, who was very pleasant and gave Sam his brother's number.

Sam dialed it and got Lillian on the phone.

'Hi, Lillian, this is Sam. I know everybody is waiting for me. Can you please tell them I am on my way?' he asked.

The familiar voice of Hon Dick Ochom came on the phone, 'Hello, Sam, how are you?' he asked.

'I am fine, sir. I am almost done here at home, I should—'

Hon Ochom didn't let him finish what he was saying. 'Don't worry, Sam. It's okay as long as you get here before dark.'

Sam was relieved. 'Thanks a lot, sir. I was getting worried.'

'See you later,' was the reply.

Sam put his phone back into his pocket and looked up with surprise. His father was coming from the kitchen with a tray holding two glasses and two soda bottles. He set the tray on the table between them and popped open the bottles. He poured some into both glasses and offered one to Sam.

'I wish you good luck, son,' Mr Ssenyonjo said as he raised his glass.

Sam was not in a drinking mood, but he didn't want to hurt his father's feelings, so he raised his glass too. He also realized that he had not told his father about all of the risks involved. He made up his mind not to discuss them with his father, the reason being that it would include a lot of explaining and he didn't have enough time.

Mr Ssenyonjo took his time refilling the glasses. 'You see, son, your mother doesn't want to say goodbye to you. She said she would rather see you when you get back.'

That was understandable. Sam knew his mother was a very emotional person, and frankly he would rather not deal with her at the moment. That's why he had chosen not to say anything to her in the first place. He noticed that James had brought his bag. He checked the time; it was approaching six o'clock.

There wasn't any point hanging around any longer, so he stood up and embraced his father. 'Father, please tell Mom I will see you both very soon. I will keep in touch,' Sam said.

His father turned and called to the housekeeper, 'James, help Sam with the bag.' Then he added with emotion, 'Sam, your mother and I will pray for your safe return.'

Sam opened the front door for James and looked back at his father one more time; his dad's eyes were teary. He had never been close to his father even though he loved him, but this time he felt a closeness he hadn't felt before. He waved to his dad and closed the door behind him.

Sam and James walked to the taxi, which was waiting outside.

'James, you take care of my parents,' Sam said, putting his hand on the boy's shoulder.

The boy was a little sad. Master Sam had always been good to him. 'Master Sam, when are you coming back?' he asked in anguish.

'I don't know, James, but I hope to be back soon,' he said as he got into the taxi with his bag. They waved to one another as the cab moved off.

'Where to, sir?' inquired the taxi driver.

'Kololo, near the airstrip—I will show you,' Sam answered. He felt hollow inside. He hadn't seen his mother, but maybe it was just as well. It wouldn't have been a good idea knowing how emotional she was.

'Hey, driver, turn off the damn music. It's giving me a headache,' he stated as the taxi proceeded to his destination. He wanted to think and the music was interfering with his thoughts. *Life isn't fair. How could Eddie be caught up in this mess? He is an incredibly good guy, and a great friend.* Sam recalled what a good listener Eddie was and how he was always the first one to jump in and stop the fights. Eddie didn't like violence; he always said violence was never a solution.

Sam shook his head in frustration as the cab entered Kololo area. He then started giving directions to the driver. This area of the city was for the rich. The houses were large and spacious; some of them could be called mansions. A smile crept onto his face when he thought about the source of some of these riches. Money that came from numerous foreign agencies intended for development projects was instead diverted straight into the pockets of corrupt officials.

'Hey, driver, slow down and turn right at the next entrance,' he shouted.

The security guard opened the gates without interrogation. The cab entered and stopped next to the rest of the cars in the compound. Sam got out with his bag and paid the driver before walking to the main door.

To his surprise, the door was opened by Wilbur's uncle. 'Come in, Sam,' he said cheerfully.

Sam smiled as he picked up his bag and entered the house. Hon Ochom closed the door and followed him into the living room.

Everybody was already seated; Wilbur and Hassan were deep in a conversation. He deposited his bag in a corner and shook hands with everybody before he took a seat.

'Sam, what will you have to drink?' inquired Lillian, who had appeared out of nowhere.

'Oh, hello, Lillian. I will have some tea please, thank you,' he said politely.

Hon Ochom cleared his throat. 'I am glad everybody is finally here. We all have to be very attentive,' he said as he took a sip from his glass. 'You young men are entering a world of very treacherous people, so remember—don't trust anybody. With the exception of the people in this room and John. The only other people you can talk to are the ones whose letters you are carrying,' he said.

Hon Ochom stood up and paced the room in silence.

'Don't show your emotions in front of anybody else, and don't let anybody know you are carrying money. Otherwise, you will invite trouble or even instant death.' He picked up his glass and went to refill it.

Everybody was silent. Sam took the opportunity to drink a good portion of his tea. Lillian was sitting on a little stool by the kitchen door, looking through a newspaper.

Hon Ochom came back. 'Young men, you might be gone for weeks or months, so always be resilient. In moments of weakness, rely only on each other. Remember, you are students visiting a teacher,' he said seriously. 'Does anybody have anymore to add?'

'Yes, I certainly do. It's not that I don't have faith in the letters we are carrying, but I would like to know exactly what I have on me,' Wilbur said, pulling the letter his father had given him for a friend in Nimule, Sudan from his pocket.

He proceeded to open it. Everybody was quiet, including Hon Ochom. Wilbur read it quietly, and when he was finished he smiled and passed it to Sam. The letter went through everybody's hands.

Hon Ochom smiled. 'So would you like to read my letter too?' he asked.

Wilbur fumbled. 'No, sir, this is not about trust. Of course I trust Dad. Since you have been fully involved in this from the beginning, you know the risks. My father, on the other hand, is on the sidelines. He might make a mistake and write something without intending to,' he finished, sweating a little. He reached for his soda and took a swig.

'I agree, son. You have to be very careful,' Hon Ochom said. 'I want you young men to remember that not everyone you deal with will wish you success. There will be many wolves in sheep's clothing, so the less they know about your intentions, the better,' he said thoughtfully.

'We leave tomorrow morning. I will go with you up to Malaba, and I will arrange a security convoy to accompany you up to Kitgum,' Hon Ochom said, settling into his seat. 'Wilbur, when you go to see Ms Akello, do not act desperate. Make it look as if you know what you are doing.' He paused and took another sip of his drink. 'Father Otim will introduce you to Ms Akello as a student, and you might have to produce your student ID card. It is very important that you don't volunteer any information unless she asks. Remember, she will be suspicious.' Wilbur nodded.

'Any questions?' Hon Ochom asked, looking at each of the young men.

'Yes, Uncle, what if she wants to know how the Father knows me?' Wilbur asked.

'That is a good question,' his uncle said, reaching into his coat pocket and pulling out an unsealed envelope. From the envelope Hon Ochom pulled a two-page, type-written letter addressed to Father Otim from Bishop Jonathan.

'Ms Akello will be told that a businessman named in this letter is the one who referred you to him. The letter instructs Father Otim on what to do and states that you will handle the financial negotiations with the lady. Feel free to read it now before I seal it.'

Wilbur read the letter. It was very precise. Mr Ochom sealed the letter and gave it back to Wilbur, who put it in his jacket.

It was getting dark, and lights had been on for a while. Lillian called them to dinner. Hon Ochom got up first and led the way to the dinner table, followed by Hassan and the two friends. They first washed their hands, and then Lillian led them in prayer before dinner. She prayed for Edgar and everybody who was going on the trip.

The food was delicious; mashed potatoes, mixed vegetables, and roasted chicken.

All through dinner, they talked about football and other topics not related to their upcoming mission. Afterwards, they went back into the living room to discuss some final points of their upcoming trip.

'Young men, I hope you all had a nice meal,' joked Hon Ochom.

Sam belched and excused himself, rather embarrassed.

They all laughed.

'Good, I'll take that as a yes. In the morning all four of us will use the same car. My driver will follow closely behind us,' he said. 'We shall pick your friend John in Jinja and go up to Malaba together,' he added. 'Wilbur, please call John and tell him to be ready by seven-thirty. We will leave here by seven, so make sure you are up and fed by then.'

Hon Ochom patted his rather large stomach. 'Okay, young men, I will see you in the morning. We old fellows have to go to bed early to avoid getting heart attacks, so I am bidding you all goodnight. Lillian will show you to your respective rooms,' he said, walking towards the stairs.

After Hon Ochom left, Sam called Lillian and asked her for a fresh envelope and a pen. He reached in front of Wilbur, pulled the torn envelope towards him, and looked at it carefully. Everyone watched him, wondering what he was doing.

Lillian came back with a pen and an envelope and handed them to Sam.

'Thanks, honey,' Sam said with a smile, making Lillian blush. He took both envelopes and positioned them evenly. Using the black pen, he scribed Al-Hajj Abdul's address so perfectly that no one could tell the difference. 'Here you are,' he said, passing the good envelope to Wilbur.

They all looked at the envelope and then at Sam, still amazed by the forgery.

'Lillian, may I have some more tea, please?' Sam asked.

'Me too,' Hassan added.

Wilbur laughed, 'While you are at it, cousin, make it three.'

Lillian walked towards the kitchen.

All of a sudden, Wilbur remembered what he had to do. 'I have to call John and tell him to be ready by seven-thirty,' he said as he stood up.

He came back shortly. 'John will be ready. I had called him earlier and told him to get a duplicate picture of Edgar from the school. Thankfully he got it, which reminds me—bear with me a second,' he said and walked to his bag. He opened the bag and removed a camera and some film. He walked back to where they were sitting.

'We need to take pictures for our IDs. Hassan, you have a Sudanese passport, I assume?' Wilbur asked. Hassan nodded.

'I don't mind being a cameraman,' Hassan said.

'Lillian, do you have a few more bulbs in the shop?' Wilbur asked.

'Yes, but the security light in the back of the house is powerful enough. It might be better to use that,' she answered.

'Okay. Let's go and do this,' Wilbur said and led the way. Lillian opened the back door, and sure enough the light was very strong.

Sam asked Lillian for a stool. He stood on the stool and turned the light so it faced the wall above their heads. 'Wilbur, stand over there by the wall,' he said. 'Okay, cameraman, go ahead and snap.' Sam requested with a smile.

Hassan took the first set of photos of Sam and Wilbur. They all waited anxiously for them to develop. They repeated the process a couple more times until they were satisfied that their pictures didn't look like mug shots. They kept some film for John's picture.

Sam climbed on the stool again and reset the light.

'Well, that wasn't too hard, was it?' Wilbur inquired. Everybody laughed as they went back into the house.

They got a pair of scissors and cut the passport photos to the size they wanted. They let Lillian keep the rest.

'Well, boys, finish your drinks and I will show you to your rooms,' Lillian said. They drained their cups, picked up their bags, and followed her to their rooms. Each of them had their own room and a bathroom with a shower.

They paused to say goodnight to each other.

'Remember, you have to wake up early. Breakfast will be ready by six. Goodnight,' Lillian said as she left.

Chapter 8

We had been walking for days, and the situation kept getting worse. People were hungry and many others were getting sick. The men who got sick and couldn't walk anymore were instantly killed. The sick women were treated better, and some were given donkeys to ride on. I had lost all sense of time since we were taken from the LRA's camp some days back.

Sometimes we walked during the day, but mostly we walked at night. Usually, it was just emptiness around us—there was nothing in sight. It was very hot during the day and extremely cold at night, so we huddled together for warmth. At some point we went through a swampy area where two middle-aged men drowned, the reason being that we were tied in twos and if one went down so would the other.

I could not fathom the meaning of what was happening to us. I had reached a point where I didn't dare think about the people I had left in Uganda; it was too painful. I just prayed to God Almighty to forgive me for all my sins and to please spare me any pain.

The vegetation had been getting sandy and drier, and so had our diet. It had changed to two handfuls of millet and water per day. I started thinking that I would not make it; death was inevitable. The only thing that kept me going was thinking of my dear mother in Uganda whom I missed very much. As much as I tried to suppress all memories of the past, I couldn't get her out of my mind.

After some days, we saw a town at a distance but did not go near it. Instead we were taken to a dark basement in a warehouse located on the outskirts of the town. The women had been separated from us and taken somewhere else. I am not sure how long we stayed in this dungeon. I couldn't tell the difference between day and night. I lost all sense of time.

The only time we saw any light was when some men brought a big lantern to feed us or check if the drums used for defecation and urination were full. If they were full, one of us would have to dump them. Occasionally they came and took one or two captives upstairs. That would be the last time we saw those captives. Since we didn't have guards and could tell when they were coming, we were able to converse in quiet tones.

I started talking to a young man sitting next to me. He introduced himself as Jimmy Abiriga, and I told him my name. He was a bit older than me and at least two inches taller, and he was bigger as well. He told me that he had just finished training as an accountant in Kampala but didn't get a chance to use his trade.

Jimmy knew a lot more about the situation we were in than I did. He told me that this kind of slave trade existed even during Amin's regime. He had heard of people being taken up north, thinking they were joining the army, only to be made into slaves for wealthy Arab farmers here in Sudan. Jimmy concluded by telling me that the only way for someone to get out once he was a slave was to buy his freedom.

This information really depressed me. I was quiet for a long time. I didn't have a penny to my name. How would I be able to pay for my freedom? Jimmy saw my distress and told me to be patient and to always do everything I was told.

The most sickening thing he told me was that once you were a slave, the slave master could do anything to you, including beating you. I merely shook my head in disbelief; I couldn't believe what I was hearing. Jimmy and I conversed in English most of the time. I could not speak his native language and he could not speak mine.

I told him about my family and about how my father had abandoned us at an early age and it was only through faith in God and my mother's hard work that we survived. Jimmy also shared his experiences of atrocities committed on his tribe—the Nubians—since the liberation of Uganda and subsequent regimes.

'But, like the old saying goes, we are in the same boat without any radar,' he said with a small smile.

The man at the end, who was tied to me, developed diarrhea and eventually died. I was made to dig a large pit in which to bury him in the extreme corner of the dungeon. I prayed to God that he hadn't infected me with this deadly disease.

There wasn't any medicine around, and although most deaths in our group had occurred during the journey, people were still dying in the dungeon. I wanted to live and hopefully find a way to escape when I got the opportunity, but the more I talked to Jimmy, the more I knew that my life depended on divine intervention.

Finally the leader of the group who had bought us came into our dungeon to count us. He was accompanied by some of his men. For one reason or another, some people had passed away since we left the LRA's camp. The slavers looked at us carefully, untying the ones that were sick and weak looking.

They put the sick men in the corner and gave them certain herbs rolled like cigarettes. They were then ordered to smoke the rolled herbs and pass them around to the other sick men. Finally the slavers put a rope around their waists so that they were all joined together and then took them upstairs. We never saw them again.

I had started to feel sick but didn't show it, having recalled my conversation with Jimmy earlier. He had warned me that to survive one had to show strength and obedience. According to Jimmy, the worst thing one could do was to play sick, because that meant one was worthless to them. These men were ruthless and murderous. They really didn't give a hoot about us; to them we were merely property.

After the sick men were taken, everybody was quiet for a long time. The mood was too depressing. Fortunately my wrist was tied to Jimmy's.

He nudged me and I turned to look at him. I could see his eyes although it was dark.

'I think we will be moving out of this hole soon,' he whispered.

I looked at him, not comprehending what he meant.

'You see, I figure they removed the sick to be sold off before we continue.'

'How do you know, Jimmy?' I whispered.

He leaned over and whispered in my ear, 'You see, when I was young I used to listen to Arabs talk to my uncle, who was a trader, and I picked up most of the words.' He paused. 'I heard one say that they had to move us soon because if they didn't, all of us would perish. The other one answered that we shall move after selling the weak.'

I looked around the dungeon, but because of the darkness I could not count how many of us remained. 'Jimmy, do you realize that there are not many of us left?' I whispered back into his ear.

He nodded and used his fingers to squeeze mine. 'Be strong, Eddie—that's the only way we shall be able to leave here,' he whispered.

We leaned back against the wall and waited for our fate. I preoccupied my mind by thinking about the work I would have been doing at the mission. I thought about Father Benedict, the humble man who had sacrificed his good life in Europe to come to Africa and contribute to humanity. I couldn't fathom that kind of sacrifice.

The Father had told me about his childhood in Italy and how his own father owned a farm with a lot of sheep and his mother worked in a cloth factory. I once asked him why he had decided to come to Africa, especially to Gulu, which was a war-torn area. He said that helping people was his calling. He also said that if we didn't have God with us, all we had was for nothing.

Now more than ever I realized his point. Here we were, slaves or properties that were disposable, and yet we were students, professionals, and businessmen. We were all in the same boat, the rich and the poor, so Father Benedict was right all along. I assumed he and my mother knew of my misfortune by now. I had to be strong and live to see them and all my friends.

Jimmy nudged me. 'Don't think too much; it's not good for you. If you do, you have to think positively.'

I nodded. 'I wasn't thinking about this misfortune,' I whispered. 'What I just concluded was that one has to eat what is on one's plate and not wish for what one doesn't have.'

Jimmy turned and smiled at me. 'Yes, Eddie, but be positive. The fact that some of us are being sold now is good,' he whispered. 'It means that selling has begun, and although we shall be re-sold, we shall be alive and out of this hellhole,' he added with a sigh.

I was now more curious about the events that happened in these places, so I decided to ask him as many questions as I could. 'Tell me, Jimmy, what will happen to us, and please tell me everything. I need to know.'

He eased himself closer to me, nudging the fellow next to him a little. The man grunted. I guess he had been sleeping.

'You see, Eddie, I was trying to spare you the truth, but since you insist I will tell you. I have to warn you—some of it is not pleasant,' he stated in a whisper.

I hesitated. *Do I really want to hear anything that will depress me? Or should I just wait and see what happens?*

I made up my mind; it was better to fight the enemy I knew than be taken by surprise. 'Yes, Jimmy, do not spare me the inevitable. It is better to know what the future holds,' I whispered back.

He hesitated for a while, and then he leaned over and put his mouth next to my ear. 'Soon we shall be re-sold to other buyers. Some slaves will work the fields, others will be used as studs to reproduce more slaves.'

Jimmy must have sensed my anguish because he added, 'You know, Eddie, all these things are mental. You have to stay strong.' His breathing became quick. 'Eddie, I am sorry to say this but I have to tell you—all of us, without exception, will have our Achilles tendons cut,' he whispered into my ear.

My heart sank like a ton of bricks. I had heard enough. I was so distressed by what Jimmy had just told me that I felt nothing but hatred in my heart. I hated the rebels, the slave traders, and the slave owners. This had to be the number-one sin in God's book.

The door to the dungeon opened, and two men brought down some pails. It was time to eat. They had put a little thing that looked like cowhide in front of everyone the day we arrived. The men put the pails at the end of the line and stood a little distance away, puffing their pipes.

The rules were simple; we took a handful of millet from the pail, put it on a plastic plate, and passed the pail down until it arrived at the end. If there was some millet left, we reversed the process. We had to eat the millet first, and then the water was passed down the same way. We all swallowed water from the same pail. No one was allowed to spill water under any circumstances.

I was at the end of the line and I worried about being infected by the sick, but I had no choice. I drank the water and passed the bucket back to Jimmy and the process continued. I noticed that the two men who had brought the pails were arguing loudly about something. They assumed nobody knew their language. Jimmy was eating slowly, but I could see he was paying attention to what the men were saying. I was glad that at least I would know of our demise.

I leaned back against the wall and relaxed, thinking about my mother. I prayed for my mother to be strong. I thought about my friends at school—Wilbur, John, and Sam. One of them must have called the Catholic mission in Gulu and realized what had happened.

Although I knew that my friends would try their best to do something, it was farfetched to imagine them ever having any success in getting me out of here. I was lost in my thoughts when Jimmy nudged me. I was instantly alert. The guards had left with the two pails.

'Eddie, are you awake?' Jimmy asked.

'Yup, I was just daydreaming. What's up?'

Jimmy Abiriga just stared at a point on the opposite wall and said, 'You know, Eddie, I listened to the two men when they were having their argument,' he whispered in a low tone. He turned and faced me. 'In case we are bought by different people, take care of yourself and don't forget what I said.'

'I won't. Thank you, Jimmy. It's been nice having you with me for the last few days,' I squeezed his hand.

From his look and tone, I knew that my time had come. There was nothing else to say or do.

Soon after, the upper door of the dungeon opened and a group of men walked down the stairs. There was a door in the extreme corner that I thought never opened, but one of the men opened it. I could see a small room and inside were some type of stairs going up.

Another man entered the dungeon with a lantern. Jimmy nudged me, so I turned and looked at him. He merely moved his head up and down, which meant that the time had come for me to go.

A bunch of guards approached me with lanterns. They released the hand that was tied to Jimmy and then handcuffed both my hands. Our eyes met and we had an understanding.

I had accepted the inevitable, so I was calm and relaxed. I was told to get up, and I went with them obediently. I didn't want any additional problems.

We entered the small room; only a few men could fit inside. I knew what was going to happen to me. I was told to kneel down. I instantly did what I was told.

'Keep your eyes looking straight ahead,' shouted one man in Swahili. Then, just like lightning, I felt a sharp sting in my Achilles tendons. Then came an unbearable pain. It hurt so much that I instantly felt weak and passed out completely.

When I woke up, I was in a different room that was very large and had windows with ventilators. I could feel fresh air coming inside, which I hadn't felt in a long time. There was a little light coming through the ventilators, and from the smell of the air I knew it was dawn. I felt a sting in my Achilles tendons and slowly remembered the events of the night before.

My mind was at peace, even though I had been maimed. My only goal was to live. I rested against the wall and dozed off. By the time I woke up, there was enough light in the room to see the faces of other captives. Each one had some kind of bandage on their Achilles tendons, but surprisingly the handcuffs were gone.

Somehow my mind was eased, probably because of a combination of things; the air, the light, seeing other people in the same condition as me, and not to mention having my hands free for the first time in a long time. Whatever the reason, I felt better.

I started crawling slowly around the room, looking for Jimmy. I almost missed him because he was in a strange position; his head was bent to his chest. I nudged him and he looked up. He slowly eased himself towards the wall.

He suddenly recognized me and smiled. 'Hello, Mr Brave Goliath, you really made yourself some friends,' he said quietly.

I was taken back by his statement, and he noticed my confusion.

'I mean you never screamed when they worked on you, man, and I heard them say that you were brave.'

I looked away and shook my head. 'You know damn well screaming wasn't going to help me,' I whispered, 'If anything it would have given those evil bastards a kick, and I wasn't going to give them the satisfaction. I clenched my teeth till they hurt.'

Jimmy patted me on the shoulder in understanding. 'You really are something, Eddie. I'm glad we have become friends.'

'Jimmy you are talking too loudly,' I whispered.

He shook his head negatively. 'They can't hear us. There are toilets flushing above us.'

I relaxed and sat near him. 'Tell me frankly, Jimmy, have you ever heard of anybody who has succeeded in leaving this hell?'

He again shook his head negatively.

My shoulders slumped in resignation, but Jimmy tapped on my shoulder. 'Wait a minute—I have heard of people buying their freedom after working for years, and I have also heard of some being bought back by friends or Christian organizations.'

I nodded my head in understanding. I was trying to figure out what my friends would do in such a situation. 'Jimmy, I have very good friends back home.' I paused, collecting my thoughts. 'I believe they would approach any organization that has some connections in Sudan and try to get me back.'

Jimmy was very quiet for moment, deep in thought. 'Let's assume they try. How would they know that Kony didn't retain you at his camp?' he asked.

I took my time to think about his question. Although Sam and John had money, they didn't have any connections in the north. Wilbur was a different story; his uncle was a member of parliament with a lot of power in the government, and he was from the Acholi area in the north.

'I have a good friend with an uncle in the government. His uncle could probably find informers who could go to Sudan to talk to Kony, so with luck they would find out our demise.'

Jimmy merely shook his head, 'You know, Eddie, it is good to have hope, but the best thing we can do is face reality and try to survive this. Daydreaming will not help you,' he said quietly.

Jimmy had a point. The chances of ever being rescued were less than zero, so why even bother one's head about it? We were quiet for some time, enjoying the fresh air that was coming in through the ventilators. I slid down against the wall, and before I knew it I was fast asleep, not knowing why I was suddenly overtaken by exhaustion.

I was awakened by the noise of the doors being opened. Sunshine burst inside with so much intensity I had to look away and close my eyes again.

A young black man without a Turban came around and gave everyone a plate and a cup. He then moved around serving millet bread and some kind of soup. We were hungry, and within a few minutes everybody was finished.

The meal wasn't as bad as what we'd been having in the dungeon, and the soup definitely contained of some sort of animal.

While the utensils were being removed by the black youth, the slavers came in and ordered anybody who wanted to use a toilet to do so, as we wouldn't get that opportunity soon. One by one we started crawling towards the loo. Jimmy and I were the last ones to go. Afterwards we talked about what kind of work the slaves did up north. He said that if we ended up working for farmers, we would probably be working in the fields.

'Can you believe that this kind of thing happens in this century and the whole world knows but decides to keep quiet?' Jimmy said with a small smile. 'You know, Eddie, if either of us ever gets out of here alive, we should make it our life's commitment to expose this injustice to the whole world,' Jimmy stated seriously. 'Agreed?' he asked.

I nodded.

'Let's shake on it, then,' he added. We shook hands.

'If I ever get out, I will make sure the whole world knows about it,' I said. Jimmy told me that he suspected our next move would be towards the north-western side of Sudan.

As the sun was going down about an hour later, the same young man opened the door. He told us in broken Swahili that it was time for our journey, so everybody tried to get up. Standing up sent lightning bolts of pain down our legs, so some people crawled while others walked using the wall for support. It was like learning how to walk again. *The bastards have made us into babies.*

A truck was waiting outside. We entered it slowly. The enclosed cabin we sat in was surrounded with wire mesh and had a black canvas on top which hid us.

Slowly the truck started pulling off.

Chapter 9

They all sat around the table for breakfast. It was six-thirty in the morning. Lillian said a prayer for breakfast and for the journey. They all ate in silence. Apart from the radio broadcasting the news in the background, the only other thing that could be heard were the forks digging into the eggs. They finished the breakfast in record time.

'Okay, Lilly dear, get the driver to bring the car around and help us with the bags. If anybody can think of anything else that we have missed, now is the time to speak up,' Hon Ochom said as he pushed his chair back. 'Let's go, young men. We have a long journey ahead of us.'

The driver helped with some of the bags as they all headed for the door. Lillian walked behind them towards the car and said goodbye, tears freely flowing down her cheeks. Hon Ochom talked to the driver as they put the bags in the trunk of the four-wheel-drive vehicle. He then talked to his nephew privately before they came back to the rest of the group.

'Come on, young men, we shall use the Range Rover,' he said. Wilbur sat in the driver's seat with his uncle next to him. Hassan and Sam sat in the back.

'Drive carefully, son,' warned Hon Ochom. Wilbur just smiled. The driver and two armed guards were in Wilbur's small Toyota Corolla.

The Rover went in front, and the small car followed them. They could see Lillian waving to them until they hit the main street. They drove fairly fast since the traffic was light and the road towards Jinja had recently been renovated.

Hon Ochom didn't take long to break the silence.

'Young men, look at this as an operation,' he said. 'Wilbur, remember not to show your hand to that Akello woman, and try to take the lead on financial negotiations.' He paused. 'Start by offering her five hundred dollars as a down payment. If that doesn't work, go up but do not exceed one thousand. You can promise her two thousand or more after she brings Eddie. Understand?' Wilbur nodded. 'Just be firm and decisive. You have your student ID, right?' Wilbur nodded again. They were quiet for a while, listening to oldies by Billie Holiday.

'Don't sleep in that town after meeting her,' Hon Ochom warned Wilbur. 'Just drive straight back to Kitgum. Tell her that Father Otim has your complete trust and will know how to reach you.' He paused. 'Once you arrive in Madi Opel, just go straight to the Father's house and give him your letter of introduction from the Bishop. He will make an appointment for you to meet Ms Akello. Assure her you will be around, and then disappear the same night and go back to Kitgum,' he said firmly.

'Remember, Wilbur, and the rest of you too,' he said, looking around, 'people like this Akello woman are treacherous. If she fails to get Edgar, she will still try to set you up and take everything.' He turned up the volume of the radio and leaned back in his seat.

The rest of the journey was uneventful. The beautiful countryside passed at terrific speed. The silence was broken when the signs reading, 'Welcome to the Source of the Nile,' started appearing everywhere. This meant they were near the town of Jinja.

'Wilbur, slow down so that the driver in the small car can keep up with you,' Hon Ochom said.

They passed the petrol station where John worked and made a right turn on the street to John's house. The town had a few vehicles moving about, and most of the roads needed repair.

'Uncle, I think it's best to first check at the residence of Mr Kimuli, John's uncle,' Wilbur said as he quickly headed for the house.

When they stopped, Sam jumped out of the car and went towards John's uncle's house. He was greeted warmly and told that John was at his home and so was his uncle.

As Sam was leaving the house, John's relatives asked him why they had armed men with them. 'Oh, the guards are accompanying

Hon Ochom. He is with us.' He turned and walked back towards the car, ignoring the goodbye speeches that usually went with every trip one made. This was typical of his culture. It never failed. He opened the back door and jumped in.

'Let's go to John's house. Everybody is gathered there, including Mr Kimuli,' he said.

John's residence was a few minutes away. The moment they pulled into the driveway, John came out of the house to meet them. He invited them inside, and Hon Ochom checked his watch and mentioned that they couldn't stay long. The guards took their positions outside the house.

The rest followed John inside, and greetings were exchanged. They were offered something to eat, but they declined, having just had breakfast an hour before.

Mr Kimuli got into a conversation with Hon Ochom, and Wilbur and John stepped outside as Hassan took pictures of John. John's sister produced a pair of scissors to cut the photo to passport size. All of the small pictures were given to Hassan, including Eddie's, since he would be the one going to Nimule in Sudan to get the ID cards.

Soon after, Hon Ochom stood up and insisted on leaving immediately. The four young men and Hon Ochom walked towards the car. John hugged his sister, brother, and uncle before entering the vehicle.

'Always think before you act, son, and don't assume anything,' Mr Kimuli advised John. Wilbur started the vehicle.

'I love you,' shouted John's sister amid tears.

Sam was glad when they hit the main road. *Why do women always cry when they bid someone farewell?* Sam wondered. One should cry at something really bad, like death or the forced capture of Eddie.

Sam's thoughts were interrupted by Hon Ochom's voice. 'Young men, I guess you know roughly how everything will proceed,' he said and chuckled. 'I will go over the whole plan again so that there is no misunderstanding.' He paused. 'You will join a military convoy in Malaba, which will escort you all the way to my residence in Kitgum. You should be safe there.' He paused again to let everybody absorb what he was saying.

'Wilbur will go to see Father Otim and meet with Ms Akello in Madi Opel. He will return to Kitgum immediately after meeting the lady,' he said and looked around at the young men. They all nodded.

'Good. Hassan won't stay with you in Kitgum. He will proceed to Nimule in Sudan to meet with Al-Hajj Abdul, and then he will proceed further north to his home.'

'When Wilbur comes back from Madi Opel, the three of you must head for Arua and stay at Arua Inn. You should leave Kitgum within three days, four at the most. I believe it will take Al-Hajj Abdul Asuman at least two days to arrange the papers and bring them to you in Arua,' he finished, glancing at everybody.

'Sir, the town where Wilbur is going is a dangerous place. What if, God forbid, he falls into a rebel ambush?' Sam interjected.

Hon Ochom nodded. 'I have already thought about that. We shall try to minimize the chances of that happening,' he said.

That was good enough for Sam. The way he saw it, this deal was the best they could get under the circumstances. If all went well, Father Otim would read the Bishop's letter and immediately make plans for a meeting with Ms Akello. It would be up to Willy to convince her of his sincerity. She would probably get suspicious, but then greed would take over.

The journey wasn't as long as Wilbur had thought. They arrived at the border post of Malaba in less than two hours. Hon Ochom went to talk to some officials, and he was told that they would have to go to a post near Tororo for assistance, so they continued northwest.

Hon Ochom didn't seem too concerned about the in-convenience caused by the delay.

'Uncle, is there anything you want us to do after we get to Sudan?' Wilbur asked.

Hon Ochom shrugged. 'Well, besides being very careful so that you don't blow your cover, I can't think of anything else. Your father's friend Al-Hajj Abdul Asuman should be able to take it from there.'

Wilbur continued, 'If Ms Akello is successful in getting Eddie, how will we conclude the final payment?'

His uncle smiled, 'Good question. The letter you will give Father Otim has instructions on how to get in touch. Tell him to inform the Bishop about any new developments. Please emphasize to him that Ms Akello will only be paid when Edgar has been brought back from Sudan and not before.'

'Oh, and Hassan, if possible you should arrange to travel to Nimule tonight or tomorrow. The sooner you get the IDs the sooner these young men will be able to travel into Sudan.'

They listened to music quietly as both cars cruised towards Tororo. The road wasn't bad, and the weather was mild with a little drizzle as they approached the town. In Tororo, they were directed to the place where they would find a military convoy.

After traveling for about thirty minutes towards Karuma Falls, they saw a sign warning of a roadblock and military presence. They slowed down and followed the instructions of the soldiers in charge of the roadblock, and then they stopped at what looked like an office building.

Hon Ochom's bodyguards waited outside the office, forbidding anybody from entering while Wilbur's uncle was inside. He emerged from the building and sent one of the guards to get the young men. Wilbur, John, Sam, and Hassan followed the guard to the office.

'Come over here, young men. Meet Captain Patrick Aine. He will be going with you to Kitgum,' Hon Ochom said.

Captain Patrick Aine, was tall and lean and looked like he was a few years older than the boys. He greeted them one by one and expressed pleasure to be of service. They also met a Major Thomas Owino, the head of the military detachment.

'Now, young fellows, can you leave us for a few minutes? The Captain and I have things to discuss,' Hon Ochom said, looking at his watch.

The boys had been around long enough to know what that meant; money was going to change hands, and the fewer people who knew the better. They fled out of the office very fast and headed for the Range Rover.

It was obvious this place was highly militarized. There were heavily armored vehicles and all kinds of military equipment everywhere. The soldiers looked battle hardened and very serious; they only talked to one another and avoided eye contact with civilians.

There were about fifty civilian vehicles waiting to be escorted. The civilians were sitting by their vehicles or buses, waiting patiently for the military escort. The route they were about to take was notorious for rebel ambushes.

Hon Ochom finally came out of the office accompanied by the Captain, and they walked towards the Range Rover. He smiled broadly and said, 'Young men, the convoy is leaving in a few minutes, so we barely made it on time. I will leave you with Captain Aine.'

The driver had moved all their bags into Wilbur's little Toyota. The only thing left was to say goodbye.

Hon Ochom called them to the side, and they stood in a small circle next to their vehicle.

'Remember, young men, rely only on one another. Do not trust anybody else! Wilbur, somebody will get in touch with Father Otim about the rest of the payment in a couple of days, so don't use any more money than you need to,' he said as he motioned to his driver to come over.

'Take Wilbur's vehicle around the back and fill her up. Hurry!' he said to the driver and gave him some money. The driver took the Toyota for a refill and was back in a few minutes.

Hon Ochom bade the young men farewell and gave each of them some pocket money as he shook hands with them, and he passed his nephew a large envelope. He reminded Wilbur to give him daily reports if possible, and then he walked to his Range Rover followed by his driver and bodyguards. Within a few minutes, they were heading back towards Kampala.

'Young men, are you ready to go?' the Captain asked. They all nodded in unison.

'You have already been cleared, so you will follow directly behind my Land Rover,' he said firmly. He turned and walked towards his vehicle followed by his bodyguards.

'Okay, gents, let's do what the Captain just said,' Wilbur said as he opened his car door. Everyone quickly entered the car.

Wilbur started the car and eased closer to the Captain's Land Rover. The vehicle leading the way was very large, with big tires and numerous guns pointing in all directions. The Captain's Land Rover was second, followed closely by Wilbur's Toyota. The journey towards the north had begun.

When Sam glanced back, he noticed that for every ten vehicles or so, another large armored car and jeep followed. The armored vehicles had different types of guns. It was quite a sight. Sam felt like he was already in the battlefield. He nudged John, who was sitting next to him in the back seat.

'Do you see what I see?' he asked.

'I sure do. I feel like I am on the front line. The only thing missing is a gun in my hand,' John responded.

'This is why we begged Eddie to get an escort. I wish the stupid driver had listened,' Wilbur said with disgust. They were quiet for some time, looking at the scenery.

As they headed north they could see the Nile River in the distance. The beauty was breathtaking. Vegetation was varied, with all types of trees and animal species. The convoy moved at a reasonable speed, not too slow and not too fast.

The soldiers in every vehicle were one hundred per cent alert, facing different directions and ready to act at a moment's notice. A few miles ahead, the soldiers hurriedly removed what looked like another roadblock, and the convoy moved on.

'Tell me, Hassan, do you always use this route when going home?' John asked.

Hassan shook his head. 'Not usually. I have used it twice since I started school, but back then it wasn't too bad. These days I bypass this area and take a plane to Arua.'

The convoy picked up some speed.

They entered Acholi district shortly before five as they passed through Murchison Falls National Park. They couldn't help but notice the beauty of the place. Unfortunately, the rebels used this park for hiding. There had been no incidents thus far, and they hoped that their luck would hold. Suddenly, the convoy stopped about fifty miles inside Acholi district. One of the armored trucks and a jeep with multiple guns passed them and took positions in front. Everybody in the little Toyota realized that they had started celebrating a little too early and became fearful. None of them had ever been in a situation like this before.

There was a quick succession of gunfire coming from machine guns and other handheld weapons. The rat-ta-ta-ta sound from the guns kept going without pause in between heavy thuds from the bigger guns. Jeeps full of soldiers with raised guns kept passing by.

The drama lasted about thirty minutes, and then there was total silence, which made everybody uncomfortable. The Captain walked by their vehicle and waved to them before entering his vehicle. The slow-moving process of the convoy began again.

They had traveled for just about a hundred yards before they saw what looked like two people lying on the side of the road. The convoy stopped, and some soldiers walked to the bodies and removed their weapons before searching their pockets. There seemed to be other bodies nearby, but the boys didn't want to look. They had seen enough.

After a few minutes the convoy started to move again, and John nudged Sam to look at a trail of blood leading into the bushes. 'Sam, why don't the soldiers go after these rebels? Isn't that their duty?'

Sam looked at John with a surprised look on his face. 'John, would you go after them if it were you?'

John was expecting an answer from Sam and not a question, so he just looked away. 'I don't know what I would do. I am not a soldier,' he said.

Sam looked at John and smiled. He decided to let the issue rest.

The convoy continued to move slowly, passing through Gulu to drop some people off before proceeding to Kitgum. The intellectual talk in the car had since stopped, as reality had set in about what they were facing. They finally arrived in Kitgum at a quarter to seven in the evening. The convoy broke up, and the boys were told to follow the Captain's Land Rover to Hon Ochom's residence.

This time they drove quickly, and Wilbur followed with ease since he knew the area. He hadn't said a word since the encounter with the rebels. They arrived at the residence in a few minutes. They pulled in behind the Land Rover and parked in the far corner.

The Captain motioned to Wilbur, who quickly jumped out of the car and headed for the Land Rover. Wilbur chatted with the Captain while the others got out of the car and removed their bags.

The housekeeper helped them carry their things inside. The house was well cared for, with modern furniture in the living room and dining room.

Wilbur joined them soon after and said, 'I think I will get a ride to Madi Opel tonight with the military boys,' he said, looking at each of them. 'It is safer and much more reliable, so here are the car keys,' he said, reaching for his bag.

Sam held out his hand. 'Wait a minute, Willy. Don't you think it would be better to take a couple of pants and shirts just in case you stay there for a few days before you get in touch with Ms Akello?' he asked.

Wilbur hesitated and then nodded.

'I have an extra bag,' John added, reaching for a small bag and removing the things in it.

Wilbur opened his bag hurriedly and removed a few belongings. He then deposited some of the envelopes he was carrying in the bag that was staying behind.

'I won't need all these. What I need is the introduction letter and a little over a thousand dollars,' he said.

John was already stuffing his things inside the bigger bag.

'Hey, Willy, you might need this,' Sam said, handing him a wad of Ugandan currency.

Wilbur started to say no but realized that it wouldn't help, so he accepted the money and stuffed it into his pants pocket. He locked his suitcase and handed the key to Sam.

Picking up the small bag, Wilbur headed for the door. 'Guys, I won't say 'bye. I won't be gone for long.'

Hassan went after him. 'Hey, Willy, be careful. I will see you in Nimule,' he shouted.

Willy turned as he entered the jeep. 'Take care, Hassan,' he shouted back as the driver started the vehicle.

Chapter 10

As soon as the boys arrived at Wilbur's uncle's house in Kitgum, Hassan asked the housekeeper to find out if it was possible to get transportation to Gulu.

About twenty minutes later, the man came up to Hassan as he chatted with the boys and said, 'Excuse me, sir, there is a bus that is going to Gulu with an escort. It's leaving at nine o'clock.'

Hassan looked at his watch; he had about thirty-five minutes. This was an opportunity he didn't want to miss. 'Gentlemen, I can get transportation with an army escort. I can't lose this opportunity,' he said, reaching for his bag. He opened it, removed a camera, and gave it to John.

'What is this for?' John asked, confused.

'Well, I used it to take your photos, but it belongs to Wilbur. Can you give it to him when he gets back?' he asked.

Sam was thinking the camera might come handy later. 'No, keep it. We might need it in Sudan. Willy can get it from you when we see you. I'll drive you to the bus station,' he said, getting up.

Hassan put the camera back inside the bag, and they both headed for the car. 'See you soon, John,' Hassan shouted as they walked to the car. The housekeeper came along to show them the way to the station.

Sam started the car and backed it out of the compound expertly.

'Now, Hassan, tell me your plan,' Sam said as they headed towards the city centre.

'It's simple. I will go to Gulu and find an escorted convoy to Pakwach, and then I will head north to Arua. I should arrive there in the morning and then get the first bus to the border. I have done it a few times before.'

'You mean you will be in Nimule tomorrow?'

'Yes. If all goes well, I will be in Nimule tomorrow evening. I will get a hotel for the night and see Al-Hajj Abdul Asuman the day after.'

Sam smiled as he pulled into the parking lot next to the bus station. To his relief, he saw some military presence. 'That's a good plan, Hassan. I am glad you are on our side,' Sam said as they got out of the car.

The bus driver had already started the engine, but they still had a few minutes before departure. Sam talked to some Military Officers, who insisted he give them some soda, another way of asking for a bribe, which he did. He had already prepared for this. Soldiers were not well paid and sometimes depended on bribes to supplement their income.

Sam came back to the car. 'Hassan, you will have military escort up to Pakwach,' he said. Hassan was very pleased to hear this.

The conductor announced that it was time to depart, so they shook hands as Hassan boarded the bus.

It is really sad what the war has done to this area, Sam thought to himself. All businesses were closed. Most of the people went home early to sleep or to hide from rebels, who normally attacked under the cover of darkness. The bus joined the military convoy, and slowly the vehicles started leaving.

'Come on. Let's get out of here before it's too late,' Sam told the housekeeper. He visualized the state of their whole plan as he backed out of the parking lot. Everything had been going well so far, maybe a little too well; something had to go wrong somewhere.

'Tell me, my friend, do you get rebel attacks around here?' he asked the housekeeper. 'And before you answer, my name is Sam. What is yours?'

The man smiled and said, 'I am Tim Opong. No, we don't get rebel attacks in the city anymore, but there are plenty in the countryside.'

Sam drove steadily towards the house. 'Tell me something, Tim, have you ever had any rebel problems at the residence?'

Tim took a long time answering the question, possibly weighing its impact. Whatever the case, Sam had his answer so he patted Tim on the shoulder. 'Don't worry about it, my friend. I didn't mean to sound like an interrogator.'

Sam's attitude must have relaxed the man, because Tim bent his head and spoke slowly. 'A few years ago, rebels raided Hon Ochom's residence and killed his wife and oldest son. I got shot in the arm,' he narrated sadly.

Sam was shocked, but this answered a lot of questions that had been nagging him. He had been surprised that Hon Ochom lived in the house without anybody else but sweet Lillian.

'Tim, please excuse me, I'm sorry I asked. You don't have to tell me anymore. I'm glad the good Lord saved your life.'

They were coming to Hon Ochom's residence, so he slowed down and turned into the driveway. There were a few armed soldiers, and Sam wondered what they wanted.

'Tim, who are these army men and what do they want?'

Tim smiled a little, 'Sir, the Captain who came with you told us some soldiers would be coming to the house for guard duty,' he answered.

This also made sense. Hon Ochom had talked to the Captain in private when they were in Tororo. Apparently he had arranged for their security while in Kitgum. Sam was not surprised by what Wilbur's uncle had done. The man was impressive.

They got out of the car, said hello to the soldiers, and entered the house.

John was sipping some tea and relaxing in a large chair. 'You guys took your time getting back,' he remarked.

Sam came and took a seat next to him. He reached for the teapot and poured himself a cup. He took a sip before he spoke.

'We waited for the convoy to leave before we headed back,' he stated. He took another sip. 'What's up with all the soldiers? I saw at least six.'

'Oh, them. There are actually eight, and they've been assigned to guard this residence for the next few days,' John answered.

They both drank their tea in silence. Sam was wondering how Willy was doing. He had left about an hour ago. He must be halfway to Madi Opel by now. From Sam's understanding, the place was at least two hundred miles from Kitgum. If the roads were good, it should take three hours, but if the road was rough the journey could take anything from six to eight hours. He silently wished Willy a lot of luck; the guy had some tough work ahead of him.

Sam and John chatted for a little while before they started yawning. 'Have they shown you where we will sleep?' Sam asked.

John nodded. 'Yes. We have a large room with two beds. There is a shower nearby. Come! I am kind of beat.' He stood up and started moving. Sam followed him.

* * *

Wilbur and the army convoy had been traveling for three hours. The roads were certainly bad, and Wilbur was glad he hadn't brought his small car. He was sitting with the Captain in the Land Rover. He was surprised that the Captain had chosen to continue past Kitgum, so he decided to pry.

'Captain, to what do I owe the pleasure of getting an army escort?' he asked with good humor.

Captain Aine looked at him for a long time before he decided to answer. 'You can call me Patrick. You see, I already had orders to go to Madi Opel and do some reconnaissance there, hoping to find the rebels' main supply route. Lucky for you, your uncle asked us to take you along.'

'I am very grateful, Patrick. Thank you,' Wilbur said.

There were four vehicles; the big one in front, which the soldiers called the mamba, the Land Rover they were in, and two open jeeps following behind. The road was generally quiet and uninhabited, and there wasn't any sign of life. Wilbur was thinking about how the area had been destroyed by the rebels. He had heard that people in the area had been moved to large camps for their safety.

'You are too quiet, my friend. Are you having second thoughts about your trip?' Captain Aine asked jokingly.

Wilbur shook his head. 'I was just wondering where people in these parts are. I haven't seen a soul in hours,' he answered.

Captain Aine smiled a little before his face became serious. 'You see, Wilbur, these rebels started hiding inside the civilian population and thereby caused unnecessary civilian casualties.' He paused and lit a cigarette. 'So it was decided by the government to put civilians in protected camps that are guarded by the army.'

Wilbur decided to take a chance. 'Isn't that like being in a large prison?'

Again the Captain smiled. 'No. You see, these camps are voluntary and people are allowed to leave them during the day and go to their farms to cultivate or go to the shops to get food.' He paused and looked at Wilbur closely. 'You may think of them as prisons, but the fact is that people don't get abducted from these camps,' he said in conclusion.

His radio signaled an incoming call and he turned it up. He talked for some time, gave some kind of instructions with military emphasis, and then hung up.

The Captain turned to Wilbur; he was a little out of breath. 'This is what I was afraid would happen. A group of about fifty rebels has been sighted north of Madi Opel,' he said as he lit another cigarette.

'Sir,' one of his escorts shouted, 'we are arriving in Madi Opel!'

Captain Aine merely nodded and kept quiet. The town came into view a few minutes later. 'Tell them to observe radio silence, Sergeant,' Captain Aine ordered. He turned to Wilbur and said, 'I have somebody who will take you in a civilian car. Your uncle insisted on that for some reason. I personally believe one is safer with the army,' the Captain said. 'We shall go back to Kitgum the day after tomorrow. If you are ready, we will take you.'

'Captain, what time will that be?' Wilbur asked.

'We will leave early in the morning. Six o'clock sharp.' The Captain turned to the soldiers with them. 'Sergeant, tell the others we will find them at the detachment. Driver, take the first left,' Captain Aine ordered his men.

'Yes, sir,' both answered, and the sergeant relayed the instructions using the radio. The Land Rover took the left turn, drove down the street for a while, and then pulled over.

They all got out and walked to a little cottage off the street. Captain Aine knocked on the door, and somebody opened it. They talked for a little as Wilbur watched from a distance. The Captain called to Wilbur and told him to bring his bag. When Wilbur approached, Captain Aine introduced him to the man standing at the door of the cottage.

'This here is Michael Mutu. He will take you to Father Otim,' he said and then added, 'If you are ready to go back to Kitgum the day after tomorrow, this is where I will find you.'

Wilbur nodded, hoping he would be ready by then.

Captain Aine bid him farewell and left. Mr Mutu extended his hand. 'Please, call me Michael,' the man said.

'All right, Michael, call me Wilbur or Willy, whichever suits you,' Willy said as they shook hands and went inside.

Chapter 11

Hassan Lara had been traveling all night. He was now in a van moving between Arua and Nimule town which was located on the border of Uganda and Sudan. There was no traffic and the weather was good, and apart from the poor road conditions, the journey has gone smoothly.

He had slept for most of the journey to Arua, except for when the occasional noise from the people in the bus woke him up and prompted him to check his belongings to make sure he hadn't been robbed. Robbery was a common occurrence on these types of trips. It paid to be alert. He had come with a few novels to occupy him in between periodic naps. He was looking forward to checking into a hotel and getting some uninterrupted sleep.

Hassan knew the journey ahead into Sudan had many challenges, and he wanted to be ready when the time came. He had taken these trips before and knew what to expect.

Unlike other Eastern African countries, Sudan was extreme in most things, full of unpredictable weather and people. The extreme weather, poor vegetation, and constant conflicts had led to death and starvation. The superstitious people believed that these catastrophes had something to do with a punishment from God or the devil. Hassan did not believe in this analogy.

They arrived in the border town of Nimule, where he would spend the rest of the afternoon before crossing into Sudan to meet Al-Hajj Abdul. Hassan checked into a little hotel named 'Border-Pride Lodge' and was quickly shown his room.

Hassan lay on the bed, and his mind recalled all the recent events. It had all started when Hon Ochom had called him to the house. He woke up and looked at his watch; it was late in the afternoon. He took a shower and slowly dressed, thinking of his next move.

He had grown up in Sudan and was familiar with the way things worked; there was a different kind of order from the neighboring countries. He safely hid the letter and the photographs in his jacket pocket as he headed for the door and locked it behind him.

The border town of Nimule was a busy trading area, full of people from the three countries of Uganda, Sudan, and Congo. It was fairly easy to cross over the border and do business. The few SPLA guerillas who were stationed on the border didn't bother anybody. Moreover, people from the border town in both Uganda and Sudan were from the same Nubian tribe and spoke the same language.

Hassan had already decided to make his way into Sudan without talking to too many people, so he crossed the border and kept moving until he arrived at some shops. He decided to approach a man who was leaning against a wall.

'Hello, would you by any chance know the residence of Al-Hajj Abdul Asuman?' he asked in the native Nubian language.

The man looked at him for a little while. 'Maybe, but why should I reveal the man's residence to you?' he asked.

Hassan was taken by surprise, but he also realized that indeed he had phrased the question badly and decided to apologize and rephrase.

'I am sorry for my rudeness. My name is Hassan Lara, and the reason I would like to see Al-Hajj Abdul Asuman is because I have a message for him,' he said apologetically.

The man came closer to him. 'Do you have any paper to identify you, sir?' he asked.

Hassan produced his travel papers and gave them to the man. He could tell the man couldn't read, but that didn't mean he was stupid. The man gave him the papers back and told him to wait there.

People in this part of the world were usually very suspicious of strangers, the reason being that the only life they had known involved persecution from their government, so any stranger could be presumed to be a possible spy. If you wanted things done you had to be humble and tread very carefully.

Hassan entered one of the shops and bought a cold drink. He sat down and drank it slowly. The man came back after a little while and motioned him outside. Hassan quickly downed what was left of the drink and went outside the shop to talk to the man.

'I have been told to take you to see Al-Hajj Abdul, so follow me,' he said as he turned to go. Hassan knew better than to ask any questions, so he just followed him quietly.

They walked through a maze of corridors and alleyways until his guide stopped, knocked on a door, and shouted, 'Hamid!' - which was probably his name.

Somebody opened the door a crack, peeped out, and then closed it. The door was then opened fully, and a young girl invited both of them in. Hassan followed the man into the house, where they were offered seats.

A few minutes passed before an elderly man came into the room. The man was tall and distinguished looking. He was about sixty years of age, and he had penetrating eyes. He regarded Hassan carefully before greeting him.

'I am Al-Hajj Abdul Asuman. And who are you, young man?'

'My name is Hassan Lara. I have a letter for you, sir,' he said, handing the older man an envelope.

The man took the envelope in silence and walked to a seat in the corner. He carefully opened it and perused it. 'How is my friend Isaac Ochom doing?' Al-Hajj Abdul asked, still looking at the letter.

Hassan was so mesmerized by the man's stature that he almost missed what Al-Hajj Abdul said. 'He is doing fine, sir. I was just with his son in Kitgum yesterday evening,' Hassan answered.

Al-Hajj turned and thanked Hamid for bringing the visitor and bid him farewell. Hamid left. Al-Hajj Abdul stood up, went to another room and asked someone to bring some tea. He then brought a chair and sat opposite Hassan. 'Now, tell me everything and don't leave anything out,' he said in a cordial manner.

The man's attitude relaxed Hassan, and he recounted the whole saga. He started with how the boys had been friends since the early days of secondary school. He then detailed the unfortunate accident that had befallen one of them on the way home to do volunteer work for the church, and he concluded with how Mr Isaac Ochom's brother, Hon Ochom, had asked for Hassan's help on the account that he was friends with Hassan's father and Hassan was Sudanese.

Al-Hajj Abdul did not interrupt Hassan; he just kept nodding his head up and down in understanding.

'I see this isn't going to be easy,' he said after standing up. 'As you know, our country is vast and very complicated. We have a lot of factions, fiefdoms, warlords, and militias.'

Hassan was about to say something, but Al-Hajj Abdul interrupted. 'I didn't say it's impossible, but it's going to take some work and resources,' he finished.

'We have the money, sir,' Hassan said.

The man ignored him. 'Now, you said your name is Hassan Lara?' he asked and Hassan nodded. 'You mean you are the son of Al-Hajj Musa Lara?'

'Yes, sir, I am attending Makerere University in Uganda.'

'That is good. How is your father?'

'He was well the last time I talked to him, sir. I am going to see him after leaving here,' Hassan said. 'Sir, we also have a favor to ask. The four boys will need to get some identification cards while they are in Sudan. I have their photographs.'

He reached into his coat pocket and pulled out the photos of John, Wilbur, Sam, and the school photo of Edgar.

'So they intend to come here to Sudan?' Al-Hajj asked.

Hassan nodded; he figured it was obvious but decided to answer anyway. 'Yes, sir, they are trying all angles.'

'Do you have luggage with you, son?'

The question took Hassan by surprise. 'Oh, yes, sir, but not here. Sir, I was also instructed to give you this.' He handed over another envelope. He paused, trying to remember what else he had been told to tell Al-Hajj Abdul.

'Is there any other thing you were told to give me or tell me?' the older man asked.

Hassan couldn't think of anything, so he shook him head.

The tea was served with hot pancakes stuffed with meat.

'Eat, eat, I will see that you get a safe passage to get your luggage. I assume you are coming back here?' the older man asked, walking away.

'No, sir, I booked a hotel, not knowing if I would be able to find your residence.'

'No problem! I will see that a room is prepared for you, and somebody will go with you to collect your things,' Al-Hajj Abdul stated and disappeared behind the inner door.

Hassan just kept quiet. He knew the culture and also knew he didn't have a choice in the matter. To refuse would be considered rude. The familiar tea was mixed with ginger root that was a bit spicy. Hassan realized he had missed it.

Al-Hajj Abdul came back with another young man about the same age as Hassan and introduced him as Ghani, his son. Ghani was instructed to escort Hassan to his hotel and help him get his bags.

As they were about to leave for the hotel, Hassan remembered another message.

'Sir, I forgot to tell you that the boys will stay in the Arua Inn, until they see you,' he said.

Al-Hajj nodded and dismissed them with a wave of his hand. 'Hurry up, young men. It's getting late. Ghani, if there is a problem talk to the Chief Customs Officer,' he added as they walked out of the door.

The way back to the hotel was very quick. It was late in the evening, and only experienced local people could walk through these alleyways without getting lost. Most of the SPLA border guard had already gone to their drinking joints; the few present at the crossing didn't even look at them.

When Hassan arrived to take his luggage, the hotel manager was surprised but co-operative. The young men gathered the luggage, left the hotel, and talked about school and football as they walked. They got back to the house in less than thirty minutes. Hassan was shown where he was going to sleep. Soon after, dinner was served, and then they turned in for the night.

Chapter 12

Michael, true to his word, got transport for Wilbur in an old, dilapidated truck. They traveled in it for a while until the truck broke down fifteen minutes from their destination. It was becoming dark, but they managed to negotiate with local villagers and hired some bicycle taxis to take them to Father Otim's house.

Wilbur was glad Sam had advised him to bring a few things. They hired four bicycles. Wilbur and Michael sat on the one's with padded seats. The other bicycles carried the two men who were their lookouts; one in the front, and another in the back. The journey continued in silence but then the bicycle in front suddenly stopped.

Using signals, all four bicycles and the passengers left the road and hid a few yards away behind the bushes. They didn't have long to wait before a group of soldiers passed by on the road.

'Michael, why are you hiding from Ugandan soldiers?' Wilbur asked.

'You see, my friend, some of these soldiers can be almost as bad as the rebels, especially at night. Many of them are corrupt and can easily take your money and leave you stranded,' he said quietly.

They pushed the bicycles back onto the road. Michael directed the riders to the Catholic apostolate, and they rode on quietly. Finally the front rider turned off the road and stopped by a dimly lit house. Wilbur and his rider followed suit.

'That will be fifteen thousand shillings, gentlemen,' one of the riders said.

Wilbur removed a flashlight from his bag and counted the money for them. The boys left in silence. Michael knocked on the house door. People in war zones don't like to open houses at night unless the caller explains the circumstances. The door opened a small crack.

'Father, you have a visitor from Kampala,' Michael shouted.

'Don't you realize how late it is?' a voice inquired.

'We realize that, Father, but our truck broke down. That's why we've arrived late,' Michael answered.

The door opened wider, and a small man motioned for them to enter the house. They were ushered into a well-decorated living room.

'Excuse my rudeness, but it is not usual to receive visitors this late,' the man said. 'I am Father Otim,' he added, offering his hand.

'I am Michael Mutu from Madi Opel, and this young man is Wilbur Ochom. He has come to see you from Kampala.'

They shook hands and sat down. Wilbur reached into his bag and gave Father Otim the letter from the Bishop. The father walked to a table, picked up his reading glasses, and silently read the letter. He took his time folding it and putting it away. 'I will see if the spare rooms are in order,' he said and walked out to the corridor. The Father came back shortly and showed them to their rooms before bidding them goodnight.

The nights were unusually quite in this area, not even a bird could be heard. This was deceptive since they were in one of the most dangerous places in northern Uganda. Wilbur remembered his uncle warning him not to trust anybody and to be alert.

He lay on the bed thinking. He was hoping the lady, Ms Akello, would be receptive and want to do business with him, and the sooner the better. This would give him ample time to get away. From what Wilbur knew, the lady could be dangerous if she became suspicious. He finally fell asleep and had a good rest.

Wilbur was awakened by the sound of metal rubbing against metal. At first he was confused, but then he got himself together. Maybe somebody was cleaning saucepans. He checked his bag and removed necessities before heading to the bathroom. Luckily there was water in the bathroom, so he was able to brush his teeth and clean up.

By the time he had changed into fresh clothes and headed out of his room, the noise had stopped. The house smelled fresh, and a lot of air was coming in from outside.

'Morning, sir, I have a note for you from Father Otim,' the cleaning lady said as he approached the sitting room. She handed him a piece of paper.

Wilbur took the note and read it. All it said was that the Father had gone to arrange a meeting with Ms Akello and would be back as soon as it was done. Wilbur picked up a nearby book and tried to busy himself with it.

The lady brought some breakfast and handed Wilbur another note. 'I am sorry, sir. Here is a note from your friend who brought you. It had slipped my mind,' she said apologetically.

It was from Michael. He wished Wilbur luck and hoped to see him on his return. So my escort decided to take off, Wilbur thought to himself, but he didn't take it in a bad light. After their arrival at Father Otim's residence, Michael's presence wasn't necessary.

Chapter 13

A sharp pain in my feet woke me up, and I realized we were still in the truck. The pain was unbearable but I tried to ignore it, knowing everybody else was feeling the same way. I couldn't tell how long we had been traveling, but the journey was long and uncomfortable.

Somebody was humming a song. It made me feel strange and kind of empty.

'Jimmy!' I called out quietly.

'Eddie?' somebody called out next to me. The voice was weak and faraway. I couldn't tell if it was Jimmy calling or somebody else.

'Jimmy, is it you?'

'Yes,' he answered quietly. Though he was the nearest person to me, we had somehow moved farther from one another.

'What is going on?' I asked, easing myself towards the voice.

He cleared his throat. 'The truck has refueled twice, so wherever we are going, it is far from where we started. I hope it won't be much further.'

Jimmy was quiet for some time. 'Eddie,' he began again, 'I was thinking about home. You know, I had a girlfriend in Pakwach. We had started living together and selling secondhand clothes. And when I was leaving for Kampala the last time she told me to take more money and enjoy myself. It was almost as if she knew something bad was going to happen, being in love and all. I agreed and had a good time in Kampala. I'm glad that I did.'

I paused, not knowing what to say, but I also didn't want our conversation to end. 'Don't worry, Jimmy, however you look at it, we shall be free. This is the twentieth century,' I said slowly.

He burst out laughing as if he had suddenly lost his mind.

'Shh... they will hear you,' I said quietly.

Jimmy continued laughing for some time and only stopped when he had to say something. 'You see, Eddie, this practice is accepted by some people in this country as normal. This country has a lot of primitive warlords that still regard a human being as property. How else could one explain the maiming we have just undergone? Before there are any changes, the people have to first know they are doing something wrong.'

'Yes it's frightening that this is happening in this day and age. Worse still that a so-called freedom fighter is the one selling his own people,' I said in disgust. I was still trying to think of a way out of this hell. 'Tell me, Jimmy. Is Rokon near the Republic of Central Africa? I heard the men talking about it,' I asked.

'Not really, but you are right. We seem to be heading north-west, which would probably mean we are heading towards Rokon.' He turned to me and said, 'I know what you are thinking. Just forget it,' Jimmy said with a warning that was more than his normal quiet tone. 'You are not the first guy to be sold into slavery, or the first one to think of escaping. If you want to stay alive, stop thinking.'

We were silent again. The truck finally stopped and the doors were opened. It was very late in the evening, and it was getting cold. A strong breeze was blowing as well.

'Everybody get out. This is the last stop,' a small, stout man announced.

The whole group started to get up. Most of us were grunting in pain as we moved out of the truck. Pieces of steel were put to the opening and pinned to the ground to help us slide down. It was done so fast and perfectly that I realized this kind of human transportation was probably very common. We moved towards what looked like a large tent.

There were camels and donkeys nearby, and people were sitting around talking to one another in low tones. The place had a strange feeling, as if it was a marketplace. Later I found out that I was right. We were in another kind of marketplace, and we were about to be auctioned again. They were preparing the area.

I nudged Jimmy. 'Hey, Jim, it looks like we are about to be re-sold to other slavers. Am I right?' I asked.

He just nodded in despair. 'Yes, my friend, but these things are to be expected and more.'

I wasn't sure what he meant, but I let it go.

The slavers lit some kind of lanterns and arranged them in a large square in front of them. I looked around at my fellow captives and realized that one person was missing. I thought that maybe he had been sold earlier to somebody, but deep inside I felt that most probably they got rid of him.

Jimmy seemed to know what I was about to ask before I did. He must have seen me mentally counting the captives. 'You were asleep when they threw him out of the truck in the afternoon,' Jimmy said quietly. I started thinking about the man's family and how they would never know what had happened to him. It was all so depressing.

'You know, Eddie, to these people you are useful only if you are alive. Don't torture yourself by counting. It will only depress you.'

He was right, of course. I looked at the men who were whispering to one another while looking at us. I felt bitter, but I also knew that all these slavers were illiterates. They were landowners who lived in another age; their only care was their own survival.

'If I wasn't a captive I would almost feel sorry for these people, Jim. I really don't think they know any better. They look like the ancient creatures that one reads about in the Bible,' I said and looked at him.

He chuckled quietly. 'I am glad you finally see it the way it is. These folks live in Biblical times, or rather, Koranic times in this case,' he said slowly.

The slave traders came and started taking people in pairs and parading them in front of the Mullahs. Then the bargaining started.

Before they got to us, Jimmy leaned towards me and whispered, 'Eddie, this might be the last time we see each together. Please don't forget our deal; this practice has to be exposed.'

The thought of separating from Jimmy made me frightened. The auction picked up, and the slaves were undressed and inspected roughly. Finally, I was taken to the lit square and inspected all over. I was bought by a Mullah named Sadiq Bin Fahad and put in a separate group. The group had about six other men, and I prayed that the same Mullah would buy Jimmy. They sprayed us with some kind of paint on our backs; mine was red. My friend Jimmy Abiriga got a different color. I got very concerned.

'Does the difference in colors mean we will be separated, Jim?' I asked, feeling totally defeated and lost.

'Come on now, Eddie, you knew it was bound to happen sooner or later,' Jimmy said. He had a point, as depressing as it was.

Jimmy put his finger to his lips, and I realized that he was listening attentively to our new masters. He kept listening to the slavers, and then he turned to tell me what they said.

'Eddie, we will be working in different farms but living in the same houses.'

The news was like a fresh injection of life in me. I thanked God for it. I was not as strong as Jimmy, and I really needed a friend. I didn't know how I would live through this nightmare without him. It was amazing how things worked out. I had met Jimmy out of misfortune, but I already considered him a close friend.

They finally ended the auction. There were fourteen slaves in our group.

'Do you know what they were saying?' Jimmy asked.

I shook my head.

'Don't look at them, but the skinny one said their boss would use some of us to breed,' he said in a flat voice. 'Apparently they have some young girls that they bought, and they want to breed them.'

I looked at Jimmy, but he was staring into space. The Mullah was laughing at the young Arab men with him.

Jimmy listened and related it to me, saying, 'I believe the reason they were laughing is because the younger men wondered why their older brother didn't let them breed the girls. Apparently the slave masters don't believe that men of mixed race make good workers. It's archaic thinking, but then again so are they.'

All I could do was shake my head in disbelief.

Jimmy patted me on the shoulder. 'We have finished the first hurdle, my friend.'

Chapter 14

Wilbur decided to take a walk around the little town. He was finished by eleven o'clock and decided to go back to Father Otim's house. He was also thinking about his meeting with Ms Akello and hoping that Father Otim would be back by the time he got back there.

Wilbur entered the house using the side door and met the maid in the corridor, who informed him that Father Otim was waiting for him in the living room. He quickly went there

'Good morning, Wilbur! Have you had breakfast?'

Wilbur nodded. 'Yes, Father, thank you.' He sat opposite Father Otim.

'I met with Ms Akello and Mr Oyu this morning and made arrangements for you to meet Ms Akello at her bar at lunchtime. Apparently she wants to meet you alone,' he added.

Wilbur was taken by surprise. He had done his planning with Father Otim in mind. 'Why doesn't she want to meet me in your presence, Father?'

Father Otim spread his hands in ignorance. 'You see, son, some people operate strangely. Nothing will happen to you, trust me,' he said firmly.

Wilbur stood up and walked to the window. His mind was weighing up the whole situation. He looked at his watch; it was already eleven-thirty.

'At what time am I supposed to meet her, Father?' Wilbur asked with apprehension.

'There is no particular time. All you have to do is show up at her bar around lunchtime and order something. She'll contact you. I did not make an appointment with Mr Oyu.'

That was good enough for Wilbur because the person he really wanted to see was Ms Akello. 'That's okay, Father. I don't need to see Mr Oyu just yet.'

Wilbur sat down again opposite Father Otim and raised his eyes to meet the Father's. 'The most I intend to offer Ms Akello today is one thousand dollars, no matter what amount we agree on as final payment.' He paused. 'We will arrange to give you the rest of money when the deal is done, but not before we see Eddie,' he said. He stood up abruptly and then quickly sat down again. 'Father, on second thought, let's pray before I head out.'

Father Otim smiled at the young man. The boy had both brains and guts—a rare combination. He reached for a Bible and opened it. 'And the Lord shall give you the wishes of your heart,' he read, and then he prayed for the Lord's hand to be on Edgar and to keep him safe.

Wilbur got up, suddenly feeling very strong and purposeful.

'Okay, Father, I will go down the street and get a taxi to Sukuma Chini. I believe that's the name of her bar,' he said as he walked towards the door.

'Yes, that's the name. God be with you, son. I will see you later,' Father Otim said.

Wilbur walked to the street and looked left and right for a bicycle taxi. There were none around, so he sat in the shade of a tree and waited. He started to rehearse his plan. He'd go to the bar and buy himself a drink. He'd take it easy and relax, and if possible he'd order something to eat and wait to be contacted by Ms Akello. One thing he wouldn't do was try to contact her.

The bicycle finally arrived, and Wilbur sat on the padded carrier.

'Can you please take me to Sukuma Chini?' he asked in the local language.

The young man nodded and rode. The town wasn't too bad weather wise, and if all the fighting would stop, the area was fertile enough to sustain growth in the agricultural sector. There were a few older people in this town. Most young men and women had moved to the big towns, joined the rebels, or been captured and sold into slavery.

The third option made him shiver. *How can the world sit back and watch people get sold as slaves in this day and age?* He shook his head when it dawned on him that the world was very different from what he had thought a few days ago. His mind was working overtime. *Do people know that slavery is still happening?* The truth was that before now he was among the few who didn't know. How could he not have known that this was happening—to his people, for that matter? He felt ashamed.

The bicycle pulled over in front of the bar, and he paid the driver. He looked around the place carefully and was surprised by the silence. He knew one thing for sure; he had to take care of this little deal with Ms Akello and then get the hell out of this town—fast. He entered the bar.

It was dark, and only after his eyes grew accustomed to the darkness did he get his bearings and take a seat near the window. He motioned the bartender to come over. The man rushed over as if he had been expecting to be called. 'Why don't you open some windows to get some light in here?' he asked.

The bartender shrugged as if Wilbur's request was strange, but he proceeded to open a few windows. The place was well decorated for a village bar, and there was enough room in the middle of the floor for dancing.

Although he was tempted to order a beer because of all the heat and this being a bar, Wilbur ordered a soft drink. He had to be alert for this meeting. The bartender brought the drink.

'Tell me, do you have any kind of food to eat here?' Wilbur asked.

The bartender, who had lost interest in him, probably for only ordering a soft drink, suddenly came closer to the table. 'Sir, I can send someone to buy a hen and then roast it for you. Would that interest you?' he asked.

Wilbur thought about it for a second and agreed readily. 'Please do, thank you,' he said. The idea of ordering chicken was good. The lady he was going to meet would get the impression that he was going to be around for a while.

'A large roasted one would be about five thousand shillings,' the bartender commented to make sure Wilbur had the money.

Wilbur nodded and took a swig of his drink. 'Please, can you hurry up? It's getting late and I haven't had any lunch.' He gave the bartender a ten-thousand-shilling note.

The bartender called to a boy who was somewhere in the back and then left with the boy, giving him instructions.

Wilbur finished his drink and was starting to wonder if Ms Akello was going to be a no-show when suddenly a strikingly pretty older woman entered the bar and nodded to him before heading straight for the bar area.

The bartender also saw her. He rushed behind the bar and poured some kind of drink into a glass and passed it to her.

Wilbur averted his eyes when she looked at him. Then he banged his bottle on the table slightly to get the attention of the bartender.

The lady picked up her drink, walked straight towards him, and almost knocked the table over. Wilbur could not ignore her anymore. He looked up at her.

'Madam, would you mind joining me, please?' he said as he stood up and pulled out a chair for her.

'Thank you,' she said in perfect English. 'I was hoping you'd ask.'

There was only one thing to do to confirm she was the one.

'I am Wilbur,' he said, giving her his hand.

'And I am Joyce,' she said.

Wilbur turned his head towards the bar. 'Please bring me another drink and bring one for the lady. Thank you,' he called out to the bartender.

The lady started sizing him up. 'Excuse my asking, but aren't you a student?'

'Yes, I'm a student, but I am currently on a long vacation. I assume you're a businesswoman?'

She nodded and smiled. 'I do a little business, but in this town it only gets busy on market days. Otherwise it is very slow.'

The bartender brought their drinks and left them quickly. Apparently he knew when to be scarce. The lady was still busy studying Wilbur. She suddenly changed.

'Young man, I like to talk frankly because I believe it saves us all a lot of misunderstandings. So let's talk,' she said and then sipped her drink.

She sure doesn't waste any time, Wilbur thought to himself. Although Wilbur knew that she was putting on a front, he was still taken aback by her straightforwardness. He nodded, not knowing what to say.

'I'll begin, Wilbur, by saying that the only way we can work together is if we agree with one another that this little transaction will stay between the three of us; you, me, and the Father,' she said with conviction.

'Absolutely, that's the only way I would have it. This is basically a financial deal we are talking about,' Wilbur said casually. She smiled.

'All right then, give me the details of the fellow you want and tell me all you know about what happened,' she stated as she removed a pen and a paper from her pocket.

'Before we begin, I would like us to get the price out of the way,' Wilbur said.

She shook her head emphatically. 'There is no way we can do that without you briefing me.'

Wilbur shrugged when he realized that she was very serious. He proceeded to tell her the whole story about their last day with Edgar and what he had intended to do during his vacation. He also told her the day Edgar's bus was ambushed. After he was done, he was so exhausted that he was glad when the bartender brought his roasted chicken.

'Excuse me, can you bring an extra plate and please cut the fowl up into small pieces?' he asked, avoiding the woman's eyes. Wilbur could tell that she was controlling and manipulative. He had not forgotten that this was the same person who managed to turn other people's misfortune to her advantage. The bartender brought the extra plate and water to wash their hands.

'Can you get some tomatoes, pepper, and salt, please?' he asked the bartender, delaying the answers the lady was looking for. He downed his drink before he looked at the lady again. She was observing him and waiting patiently.

'Do you mind if we eat first and then talk after?' Wilbur asked.

'Suit yourself, young man,' she answered casually.

The bartender brought the sliced tomatoes and salt and pepper. 'Is that all you would like, sir?' he asked.

'Freshen our drinks, and that will be all, thank you,' Wilbur said.

The bartender left.

The lady just ate a few pieces of chicken, even though there was more than enough food for both of them. Wilbur ate until he felt satisfied. They left the rest of the chicken for the staff. The boy came back with water to wash their hands.

'All right, there is no point beating around the bush, so name your price, Ms Akello,' he said firmly.

'Such a turnaround after some food—you must have been starving. In these kinds of circumstances, we negotiate,' she said easily.

Wilbur was again outsmarted by the woman. The woman probably wanted to take all of his money, but she failed to realize that Wilbur was city-born and not easily manipulated.

'All right, Madam, I will give you one million shillings (five hundred dollars)—half now and half later,' he said easily.

She absorbed this without showing any emotion. 'I would think that if I am to try to get in touch with people in Sudan I would need international currency.'

Then Wilbur made his first mistake. 'I will pay you in dollars if you want,' he said and immediately regretted having opened his mouth. The lady would think he had a lot of money.

'Okay. Let's assume that I negotiate for your friend's release. I would have to go through numerous people, each of whom would expect payment.'

Wilbur decided to go ahead and make his original bid in dollars, wanting to conclude this deal as soon as possible. 'I will give you an initial five hundred dollars, and then you will get the rest when Edgar is released,' he said firmly.

She looked at him as he sipped his drink. 'Is that the best you can do?'

The question shook Wilbur. He thought he had prepared himself for this meeting. The woman was a real devil. She was trying to make him put a price tag on his friend. He decided to go ahead and negotiate, ignoring the implications involved.

'Tell me, Ms Akello, how much do you think everything would cost? I want a figure that includes everything,' Wilbur said firmly.

She smiled. 'I would say that to be able to go through the various middlemen to find your friend and bring him here, you would spend three thousand dollars,' she said and took a sip of her drink. She had expected a shocked young fellow but was surprised by the young man's reaction.

Wilbur looked straight into her eyes. 'Okay, Madam. I am willing to pay a deposit for your expenses, and Father Otim will give you the rest when Eddie is freed.'

'How much will you pay now?'

'Well—' Wilbur began, but he was cut short by Ms Akello.

'Can you make it fifteen hundred?' she asked.

Wilbur reached into his pocket, pulled out some money, and dropped it in front of her. 'This is your deposit,' he said.

She took the money and counted it. 'I see only one thousand dollar here. When do I get the rest?'

'The rest will be given to you by Father Otim when he gets Edgar.'

'Okay,' she said, 'make sure two thousand is in his hands soon. But, remember, there are no guarantees and no obligations,' she said.

Wilbur nodded in understanding. She would not return the money even if she doesn't get Edgar.

She raised her glass. 'To our success.'

Wilbur also raised his glass, although he was feeling uneasy.

He looked at his watch, and then he stood up, pulled twenty thousand shillings from his wallet and put it on the table. The bartender quickly took it and thanked him.

Wilbur walked towards the door, followed by Ms Akello.

'I assure you, Wilbur, I will get your friend if he is still alive.'

He shook her hand. 'Ms Akello, please don't let us down.'

Chapter 15

Wilbur walked to where a small motorcycle was parked. 'Are you doing any taxi work?' he asked a young man standing by the bike. The young man nodded.

'Where to, sir?' he asked as he started the little motorcycle.

'Let's go to Father Otim's residence at Catholic Nuncio.'

The little motorcycle cruised down the street, but the driver took the opposite direction from the one that Wilbur had taken earlier. After a little while, the man turned to speak to his passenger.

'Sir, a man named Oyu would like to see you. He has already paid me.'

Wilbur was angry at first, but then he realized that Mr Oyu might give him some useful information.

'All right, man, but next time you decide to surprise someone, you had better bring along a note,' Wilbur said.

The motorcycle finally pulled inside a well-kept yard and eased closer to a modest-sized, one-story house. A lean medium height well-dressed man opened the door and came to meet Wilbur.

'Hello, sir, I am Oyu. I would like to apologize for the surprise,' he said, offering his hand.

Wilbur took the man's hand and shook it. He shrugged. 'It is okay, Mr Oyu. I am not complaining, though I was surprised,' he said, walking with the other man towards the house.

The house was well furnished, but anybody could tell that it had seen better days. They sat down. A middle-aged lady came to greet Wilbur, and then a young boy brought some beer. Wilbur hesitated and then thought, why not, one beer won't hurt me.

'The reason I brought you here, sir, is to brief you about Joyce Akello,' Oyu began as he poured his beer into a glass. He also opened a bottle for Wilbur and poured him some.

'Have you talked to her?' Wilbur asked.

'I got in touch with her after Father Otim came to me. Unfortunately, the group which took your friend has already crossed into Sudan.'

Wilbur decided to tell Oyu about the arrangement he had made with the lady. He had nothing to lose by talking about it.

'Mr Oyu, as you know, I met Ms Akello. I gave her a deposit. I will give her the rest when we get our friend,' Wilbur confided.

There wasn't anybody in the vicinity except for them, but Oyu still eased his chair closer to Wilbur. 'That woman is a wolf. She will do anything for money, but since she wants the balance, she will deliver your friend,' Oyu confided quietly.

Wilbur reached into his pocket, pulled out some money, and gave it to Oyu. 'Thank you for warning me about Ms Akello. Please take this as a token of my appreciation.'

Oyu hesitated and then reluctantly took the money. 'I want you to know that this isn't necessary, but I will do my best to gather information on your friend,' he said before putting the money his pocket.

'That's fine. I have a feeling that this isn't going to end quickly,' Wilbur said, standing up.

Oyu walked him to the motorcycle outside. The boy was still waiting for him patiently.

'So are you going to be at Father Otim's place?' Oyu asked.

Wilbur had been expecting the question and had already decided how to answer it.

'Yes, I want to see what I can do from this end. If I go anywhere it will be because I have run short on funds.'

They shook hands as Wilbur sat on the motorcycle.

Something was bothering Wilbur. This man, Oyu, had supposedly been a rebel and quit. What bothered Wilbur was the place where the man had decided to settle down; it was right on the route the rebels used when they came to Uganda.

The motorcycle headed for Father Otim's place in a hurry. Wilbur was happy by what he had achieved already. There wasn't anything else to be done here; all he had to do was to wait. The bike finally arrived at the house. Wilbur tried to pay but the boy refused, saying he would be paid by Mr Oyu. Wilbur insisted on paying a tip, which the boy accepted and then rapidly left.

Wilbur entered the house and was met by Father Otim.

'Welcome back, Wilbur. How did it go with Ms Akello?' he asked.

Wilbur smiled slightly as they entered the living room. 'I found out why she is able to play both fronts and come out unscathed. She is smart and extremely cunning. I had to stay on my toes the whole time.'

'She sure is. I believe only God can help people like her. By the way, the Captain sent a message for you, wanting to know if you still want to go to Kitgum with him,' the Father said.

'Yes, Father. My friends are waiting for me. I would like to go back as soon as possible. Otherwise they will worry,' Wilbur said, pulling over a chair.

Father Otim called the young man who was in one of the rooms, quickly gave him instructions, and sent him off. 'I had guessed your response, so I took the liberty of arranging your transportation in advance. One of my parishioners is going to Madi Opel. I have asked him to take you.'

The maid brought them some tea and yams. Wilbur could not help smiling as he remembered the way his mother used to serve yams. Father Otim read a few verses in the Bible and prayed for Wilbur's safe journey back to Kitgum.

The car arrived at six-thirty in the evening, and after bidding everyone farewell, Wilbur started towards the vehicle followed by Father Otim.

'By the way, Father, Ms Akello will get in touch with you for the second half of the payment, if she is successful in delivering Eddie. My uncle will be in touch.'

The Father nodded and wished Wilbur more blessings and a safe journey.

The trip back to Madi Opel was quiet. The man who gave Wilbur a ride was a serious Catholic man. He did not utter a single word. Wilbur thought that maybe the man had detected some liquor on his breath and decided to deliver him to the next town—fast. That suited Wilbur just fine, because to be honest he was tired of being nice to everyone. They finally arrived in Madi Opel at around eight at night.

'I want to thank you very much, sir,' Wilbur said, reaching inside his pocket for some money. The older man refused, and this time Wilbur did not insist. The guy was odd.

Wilbur got his bag out of the backseat and walked to the taxi station. He got a taxi to take him to Michael's residence. On arrival, he paid the taxi driver and then walked to the door of the small cottage and knocked.

Michael opened the door and stepped back in surprise.

'What! I had already given up on you. Come in, Wilbur,' he shouted with pleasure.

'How are you, Michael? So, you left without letting me know?' Wilbur teased Michael as he placed his bag down in the corner.

'It was the right thing to do. I wanted to give you some room to operate without distractions,' Michael answered motionlessly. 'Let us go to the club around the corner so that you can fill me in on your adventure,' he added.

'Good idea. It will give me the opportunity to thank you properly,' Wilbur said without hesitation. He was feeling safer away from the small town where Ms Akello and Mr Oyu lived.

'I will buy the drinks,' Wilbur said as he walked to the door, 'Your turn will come another time,' he added before Michael had a chance to refuse.

They walked to the club making jokes, and on arrival they decided to sit outside and enjoy the fresh air. The bartender came to them and took their order.

'All right, Wilbur, you can now tell me all about your mission,' Michael said.

Wilbur thought about how much he should tell Michael.

'Well, after you left, we contacted someone to arrange a meeting, and we succeeded in meeting this person. Now we have to wait for results.'

'You mean you will be coming back here?'

Wilbur nodded. 'I might come back if it's necessary,' Wilbur answered.

A young girl brought the drinks, smiling shyly. After she left, Wilbur asked Michael why they let an underage girl work in a nightclub. The comment made Michael laugh hard, and he motioned for the girl to come.

When she came, Michael leaned across the table and asked, 'How old are you, young lady? I just had a small disagreement with my friend here about your age,' Michael said.

The girl looked down. 'I am eighteen years old,' she answered softly.

'I won't believe it unless you show me your card,' Wilbur said. Michael kept laughing hard. 'Girl, please show him your card.' The girl smiled and walked away.

'Michael, have you found out what time the convoy is leaving?

'They should be leaving very early in the morning, about six o'clock. We should drink a little bit more and head home to rest.'

They talked for a little while longer and then decided to call it a day. On their way out, the little girl thanked them for the tip. They bid her farewell and left for home.

Wilbur patted Michael's shoulder as he said, 'You better be glad you are not a betting man, my friend, because you just lost.' Michael laughed even harder.

Wilbur could tell that the girl was underage but he let it go.

Michael was a jolly fellow, and he was still laughing when they finally entered the house and prepared to go to bed.

Chapter 16

Joyce Akello had been apprehensive after talking to Oyu and Father Otim, but after meeting the young fellow Wilbur, she was convinced beyond doubt that an opportunity had arrived for her to get paid. She got in touch with a few rebel Commanders that she knew were in the area and bid her time.

She also found out that Wilbur Ochom had gone to Madi Opel, so she took the opportunity to test the waters. She went to Father Otim's residence at about six in the evening and knocked. The door was opened by the Father.

'Oh, come in, sister,' Father Otim said as Joyce entered.

'Father, I have some leads on what the young man was looking for. I just need your assurance that you will pay if I go ahead and investigate it.'

'Oh, dear sister, I give you my word and that of the Bishop that you will be paid after the boy arrives. I believe you made an agreement with young Wilbur?' Father Otim asked, and she nodded.

Joyce refused to stay and have a drink, saying she had to start on the mission right away if she was to be successful. She also mentioned something about how the young man had touched her heart.

Father Otim walked her to the motorcycle taxi and bid her farewell, wishing her a successful mission.

Joyce Akello had been told that Commander Nyati Okello was in the area, and she had sent a message to him. She went to her club to get a bottle of Johnnie Walker, which was Nyati's favorite, and planned her next step.

'Did Steven leave something for me?' She asked the bartender when she arrived.

'Madam, he left this for you and said he would get in touch with you about the other matter later,' the bartender said as he handed her an envelope.

Ms Akello took the envelope without a word. It was her policy not to chitchat with her employees. She took the letter and her drink and then walked to a table next to the window, sat down, and opened the envelope.

The letter was from Nyati Okello, extending greetings and making an appointment to meet in the usual place. She sipped her drink and thought about how she was going to approach this little problem. She checked the time. It was close to seven o'clock in the evening. She stood up and walked to the bar area.

'Hand me a bottle of Johnnie Walker and let me sign for it,' she ordered.

There were only a few people in the club but it didn't matter, since she had plans to expand it to include full time music, which would make it the ultimate club in town.

'If someone comes looking for me, tell them to leave a note,' she said as she signed for the Johnnie Walker. She put it in a paper bag and walked out of the club, straight towards the motorcycle taxis. She was heading to her other business, where she would link up with Steven, and from there she would head to her final destination to see Mr Nyati.

She smiled to herself as the motorcycle burst to life and headed out into the night. She always got what she wanted, and there was no reason to begin losing now. She had to play her cards closer to her chest this time. Men were the same to her—the only difference between them was their degree of resistance, but all of them had a breaking point.

The motorcycle taxi stopped in front of her other shop and she got off, stopping only to pay the driver. When she entered the shop, the workers greeted her, and as usual she just nodded to them and continued walking to the back office door. She knocked and announced herself.

A surprised Steven unlocked the door. 'Well, I wasn't expecting you for another hour, but since you are here we can proceed. They are only here for tonight.'

She nodded and smiled; Steven was the only employee she trusted to run sensitive errands. They had been together for a long time.

As usual, they used the back door to sneak out. The door opened into a hallway that somehow ended up in a row of tall bushes behind the building. They walked quickly through, in silence, until they arrived at the house where Commander Nyati Okello was waiting. Two rebels appeared from nowhere with their guns cocked. They established Joyce and Steven's identities before melting back into the bushes.

Steven knocked on the house which was opened without hesitation, a sign that the people inside had heard them coming long before.

'Joyce, I hope you remembered to remain silent when coming here,' Nyati said. She nodded. 'How have you been, my love?' Nyati asked, embracing her.

She embraced him back, and together they walked hand in hand into the next room, leaving Steven in the living room. She offered Nyati the package, and he smiled contentedly as he pulled the Johnnie Walker bottle out of the bag and admired it before unscrewing the cap.

Joyce brought two glasses, and he poured some for both of them. He snuggled next to her and started kissing her in between drinking his favorite whisky. As usual, she put everything to a stop and looked at him.

'How is my favorite man?' she asked sweetly.

'Oh, come on, baby, you know I miss you,' he said, trying to pull her towards him.

She resisted. She faced him and became more serious. 'Baby, you know everything has got its time and place. Right now I am trying to find a boy that you have. I believe you can help me get him back, and then who knows … I might thank you properly,' she said as she refilled his drink.

'Okay, what's the boy's name? Give me the details,' Nyati said impatiently as he downed his whisky.

She reached inside her bag, retrieved a piece of paper and a picture, and passed them to the Commander.

Nyati took the piece of paper and walked to the door. He opened the door and called his assistant, who had a very good memory for these things. There was a moment's wait, and then a young man came and Nyati told him to enter. They whispered to each other while looking at the paper.

Nyati nodded and dismissed the man before closing the door. He walked to where Joyce was and sat down.

'Well, what did he say?' she asked.

Nyati knew this woman too well to get on her wrong side, so he decided to tell her the truth. 'We took him with other students after the operation in Karuma Falls, but my assistant believes he was among the workers that were taken. Sorry, baby,' he said weakly, reaching for the bottle. He sipped a little as he lit a cigarette.

'You mean he was taken by the Arabs? I thought all that had come to an end,' she said, suddenly standing up. She was very disappointed by this revelation.

'We still remember the people who took him. They'll be back the day after tomorrow. He could be bought back,' he said apologetically.

She sat next to him again, suddenly realizing that the slender chance of getting the boy back lay with this man and maybe two others.

'Baby, I promise I will get this boy back for you,' he said and kissed her.

'I know you will, honey, but I would like to come along too. This young man is a special case. My future business plans depend on getting him back,' she said and kissed him back.

Nyati fumbled with his pants and jungle boots. His heart was beating very fast. He knew he should control himself, but since becoming a rebel he had spent most of his time moving, and when he returned to the camp, he was too tired to have sex, or the girls had been sold by the time he woke up.

He finally managed to remove everything and was surprised to find Joyce relaxing naked beside him. He quickly turned, and the match began. They enjoyed themselves for a few minutes, and as usual he spent himself too quickly. She held him in her arms.

'Honey, I have to get this young man if I am to retain my business, you understand?' she said.

He sat up. 'We will get him back all right, and if you want you can come with us and talk to the Arabs,' he said easily, lighting another cigarette.

Joyce liked this man. He was powerful and straightforward. If Nyati said he would do something, it usually got done. The soldiers in a few towns had found out that the fellow always did what he said he would. Unfortunately for them, some of the people found out too late.

'Thanks, baby. I know I can always count on you,' she said, getting up. She had to get back and plan a trip. 'Honey, I wish I could stay, but as you know, if I delay people will start wondering. Send somebody to meet me across the border,' she said as she put on her clothes.

She quickly straightened herself in the mirror that hung on the wall and turned to say goodbye to Nyati, who was already standing behind her. He started trying to kiss her, but she smiled and firmly headed for the door.

'Joyce, baby, thank you very much, and I look forward to seeing you soon,' he said.

She just gave him a little peck and walked to the outer room.

'Steven, hurry up. Let's go and check on the business,' she said.

As she walked out of the house, she waved to the rebels who had reappeared from the bushes. She and Steven went the same way they had come and entered through the back of the shop. Nobody in her shop had noticed that they had left. She removed a set of keys from her bag, went straight to a cupboard, and opened the lock. She retrieved papers revealing information about Ugandan Army troop movements and supply routes.

She intended to use this information when she reached the rebel camp in Sudan.

Chapter 17

A strong, pungent smell woke me. I looked around and realized that it was the stuff the slavers were smoking. We had been moved to smaller tents, and every thirty minutes a young Arab man counted us. We were given some kind of bread. I couldn't tell what it was made of, but I knew for sure it wasn't wheat.

Jimmy had dozed off; he looked peaceful and relaxed. I wished I could get some sleep. It was the only time I could temporarily forget about my predicament unless I had nightmares about it. I was fascinated by Jimmy. I had never met a man who used reason to deal with the unthinkable. Jimmy's ability to free his mind was a gift from God, and I hoped to learn a lot from him.

I thanked God that he had brought Jimmy into my life, especially at this trying time. I strongly believed that God had sent Jimmy to help me deal with this horrendous situation. Jimmy was closer to the door of the tent. He must have moved in his sleep.

Alas, he now seemed to be awake. His eyes looked at me once, and he winked. Son of a gun! The guy hadn't been sleeping at all. He was listening to the slavers' conversations the whole time. I was impressed.

I started thinking about my predicament. I didn't fancy being made into a breeder. I had stopped talking to girls in my mid-teens after hearing and seeing numerous examples of what AIDS did to people. AIDS had killed a lot of young people, leaving mostly the elderly and the children. As far as I was concerned, it was the deadliest disease on the planet, and I didn't want to die from it.

I felt tears well up. How can God let my life end like this? I had been a responsible person and I went to church, got good grades in school, and avoided bad groups. I was even sure I had passed the exams to attend Makerere University. I couldn't believe that I had done all this only to end up as a slave in some godforsaken foreign country.

I was overcome with sadness. I closed my eyes and prayed that God wouldn't let them turn me into a stud to breed more slaves for the Mullahs.

Finally, Jimmy straightened slowly, trying to avoid anything that would raise suspicion. He looked at me closely.

'What's up, Eddie? Have you been crying, man?'

I shook my head. 'I can't help it, Jimmy. I just saw my life pass by. I can't believe I may end up being used as a stud, Jim. In this day and age when AIDS is rampant, I really don't want to …' I broke down, and Jimmy patted me on the back.

'Look at it this way—the worst is to be raped by the slave masters and be turned into their sex slave,' he said.

The thought of being raped made me very frightened. Fortunately Jimmy changed the topic.

'Eddie, I was listening to them. They said some slaves bring with them a disease that infects their necks, and then they die immediately. I know that it isn't AIDS. From what they are saying it sounds like meningitis,' he said slowly. 'They also said some young slaves are needed as workers because most of the others have become old and have been sold to a town merchant. Better than getting killed, I suppose,' he added.

I thought that maybe I could find a way to talk the Mullah into having me do some other work. Surely a man like that had different kinds of paperwork that needed an educated person?

All of a sudden it hit me that these were ancient people and probably did not know what education was. Once again I felt defeated.

It had been dark for a while. I gathered it was about ten at night. The few men still at the marketplace were preparing for something. Finally, they told us to get up.

'Oh, I forgot to tell you, we are leaving soon. The journey will be on foot, so stay strong,' Jimmy said.

They tied a rope loosely around everyone's waist and then tied it to a camel. This was done with two rows of slaves.

The Mullah who had bought us started to speak Arabic but soon realized that nobody knew Arabic and was frustrated.

Jimmy raised his hand and said that he knew a little bit. The Mullah was pleased and ordered Jimmy to be untied and to interpret his words. He told us that he had his gun, which he showed us, and a good horse, which he patted, and warned that if anyone attempted to escape he would be chased, caught, and then shot in the middle of the desert. His body would then be left there to be eaten by vultures.

He stressed that the best way for us to survive would be to do what we were told, and he wouldn't tolerate any complaining. All of us would be given different jobs that would change from time to time. He reminded us that we were his property and he was not to blame for our situation since he did not go into the jungle to capture us; he had merely bought us just like he bought a camel or a donkey.

I was thinking that if there were no people like him willing to buy other people, then the situation would not exist. I could not understand how a man in his right mind could think that he owned a fellow man. I had momentarily forgotten that I was dealing with a primitive being.

The Mullah walked to where the tents were being folded and supervised the work. He looked like a serious man, even with fellow Arabs. He went and talked to other slavers and then came back to where we were. He talked to Jimmy in Arabic for some time, and then Jimmy interpreted.

'Is there anybody that doesn't feel ready to walk now?'

Nobody raised his hand.

The Mullah again talked to Jimmy, pointing at the donkeys that were standing in the shade. He told us he didn't like losing his property, so we shouldn't worry—no punishment would be given to anyone for being tired.

Suddenly three hands went up. The Mullah went to look at them and then ordered Jimmy to loosen the rope around their waist. They were taken to where the donkeys were, lifted, and put on them.

There was a sudden wail from the Mullah, and then we started walking slowly. The animals, especially the camels and donkeys, weren't forced to move fast since most were loaded. We started walking and kept going for what seemed like hours.

One of the men started softly singing old Bible hymns and waited to see if the slavers would complain, but when they didn't everybody, including me, joined in and the journey became more bearable. I was reminded of a black American movie I had seen at Wilbur's house, but this wasn't a movie. We were slaves, and the century was coming to an end.

I didn't want to but couldn't help it—I started feeling sorry for myself. Nobody really cared about what happened to us! Nobody in the developed world even noticed that there was slavery going on right here. I sincerely believed that if somebody told President Bill Clinton about this, he would do something.

As we walked, I noticed that since leaving the rebels' camp we had used either small mountain trails or side roads that had no military presence. That meant we were bypassing SPLA territory. The SPLA would have rescued us for sure.

I also noticed that the Mullahs who had bought us looked different from the men who brought us from the LRA's camp. These ones had a light brownish complexion with bigger noses. They also looked scarier.

My thoughts were interrupted by someone tapping my shoulder, so I turned.

'How is my friend?' Jimmy asked. He was sitting on a horse, the reason being that he had to run back and forth to interpret the Mullah's commands. I had to look up to make sure it was really him.

'Well, I don't feel really bad, but I could be better. Isn't it dangerous to talk to me?' I was thinking that they might hear us and take his benefits away.

'I don't think so, my friend.' He paused and then added, 'I am the only man here who can speak both Arabic and Swahili. These languages are finally coming in handy for us, so just hold on,' he said, handing me a bottle of water. I hesitated at first.

'Come on, now, you know you are thirsty,' he said.

I took the bottle but kept walking. I gulped most of it before handing it back. 'Thanks, Jim,' I said as he rode away. Now that is a resourceful man, I thought to myself. In a few hours, Jimmy had managed to turn the situation to his advantage. I could see him riding up front with the slavers and talking to them, but I knew better. Jimmy hadn't joined them, not by a long shot—he was using them. He hated the bastards just like the rest of us.

Truth be told, the ancient or primitive weren't too intelligent. Jimmy had already fooled the bastards by pretending to be an obedient servant. I was sure that if he could find a way, he would kill them. I silently asked God to forgive me for these bad thoughts.

We had walked for a long time. At first I wondered how they knew the way, but soon I figured it out. One of the slavers went ahead of us and would make the route signs by planting a lantern in the direction we were supposed to take. That was why when we passed by a lantern, someone retrieved it. I could see Jimmy holding a few. That was smart. They had a few brains after all. Enough at least to get home, I thought sarcastically.

Jimmy came riding by. I motioned him over, and he came.

'Hey, Jim,' I whispered, 'can you find out how much we are worth to them? Who knows, we might be able to buy our way out in the future.'

He looked at me, hesitated, and then nodded, 'I know, Eddie. That's my ultimate purpose, but not yet. Don't start getting any funny ideas before we have a plan.'

Jimmy passed something to me. It was desert bread made like a pancake. It was bland, but right now everything tasted like baked chicken. I munched it unceasingly, and then he passed me some water to wash it down.

I swallowed some of the water and passed the bottle back to Jimmy. I felt a pang of guilt about the special treatment, but I also wanted to survive. I was glad it was night and hoped nobody saw us.

'I don't know how to thank you,' I started saying.

'Don't,' Jimmy said, riding to the back of the line. I was truly thankful to have him on my side. I knew he was going to gather as much information as possible, and we would discuss it whenever we got a chance or when we were allowed to sleep.

Suddenly I saw a lantern reflecting in something that looked like a lake. We were in a semi-desert, so it was probably an oasis. It was not more than a mile away. Our pace slowed down considerably, and I could tell we were going to make a stop.

We finally arrived at the oasis and were told to rest and bathe. A crude-looking soap was given to us to share as we moved to the part of oasis where slaves washed up. Our bathing area was created by having us remove sand with our hands until we had made a pit deep enough to hold about three full drums of water. We dug a trench to carry the water from the oasis to this pit. After the pit was full, we put sand back on the trench to block it.

We all washed up slowly without being rushed. Some of the slaves had infections on their Achilles tendons, and these were treated by Jimmy, who had been given medicine and penicillin injections. He finally came to give me an injection.

'But …,' I started to protest.

'But what?' he asked as he opened a new needle quickly. He seemed to read my mind. 'Don't worry, I got different needles for us. Hurry up.' He injected me. He opened another needle, and I quickly injected him.

The chances of getting AIDS and other diseases through cross infection were increased by using same needles, but apparently these people either didn't care or didn't even know; most probably the latter.

'I supposed these ancient people don't know that using the same needles is dangerous to their workforce,' I commented.

Jimmy nodded. 'That's why I only injected the few with infections, but I don't want to push my luck with the Mullah. Unfortunately, a few people will have to be sacrificed,' he said, handing me some antibiotic ointment to smear around my wound.

I thought about what he said. We were just property of these people, and of course a few of us had to be sacrificed.

We didn't stay at the oasis very long; perhaps forty-five minutes. They tied us up again and the journey resumed. This time I was put in the extreme back and tied loosely by Jimmy.

'You know, being in the back is better. You don't get stepped on often,' he said with a smile. 'This will give your Achilles tendons time to heal, though without proper surgery we are bound to have the pain in our veins for as long as we live,' he said quietly. I thanked him for being thoughtful.

I had been wondering about something, so I gathered this was as good a time as any to ask him. 'Tell me, Jim, why do they maim only the men?' I asked.

Jim laughed hard as the caravan kept moving.

I thought the slavers might be angered by seeing one of us laugh. 'Jim, don't you think it's utterly stupid to laugh out loud like that? The slavers will hear you.'

'Nope. On the contrary, my friend, they believe I am laughing at you, and I will keep them believing that.' Jimmy paused. 'To answer your question, these people believe that girls lose their value when they are maimed. They believe that women are weak and die quickly from depression or something.'

'I'm glad they don't maim the girls, but it's silly to think women are weak. You and I know how strong our women are,' I said sarcastically.

Jim agreed. 'Well, these people come from a different time.'

He paused. 'By the way, I heard that we will be arriving at about six-thirty in the morning, so hang in there. We only have a couple of hours left,' he added before riding to the front.

He must have told the Mullahs a lie, because shortly after he joined them up front they laughed loudly, as he had predicted. I shook my head. What a man! He has already studied these primitive people and knows how to manipulate them. I admired him.

Chapter 18

Wilbur felt something shake him and opened his eyes. At first things were not clear, but slowly his eyes adjusted to the surroundings. He was cooped up in a small bed in a room no bigger than a large cupboard.

'What …?' he started to ask.

'Wake up, Wilbur, the convoy is here. It's time to go,' Michael said. Wilbur slowly sat up and recollected his bearings.

'Okay, Michael, just show me where I can go and wash up. Last night's buzz is still in my head,' he said, getting up slowly.

Michael directed him to the bathroom. 'Hurry up, Willy, you know soldiers work on time,' Michael urged him.

There was no time to wash his whole body, so Wilbur soaked his head in water and quickly washed his face and hair. Finally he felt awake enough to begin the journey. He walked to where his bag was, opened it, and removed a towel.

The door opened and in entered Captain Aine.

'There you are, my dear fellow!' he exclaimed coming to Wilbur.

Wilbur was still feeling the effects of the night before. 'How are you, Captain?' Wilbur managed to ask while drying his head.

'I didn't do too badly this time. I only lost two men and five are injured. The enemy lost more,' Patrick stated without emotion.

Wilbur could not understand why the man seemed unaffected by his loss, but he kept those thoughts to himself. 'I will be ready after I brush my teeth and straighten the bed,' he said, walking towards the little bathroom

Wilbur was thinking as he brushed his teeth. These wars were becoming a daily reality in Uganda. Death was either by a bullet or

AIDS. He came back and picked up his bag. 'Okay, Captain. I am ready to go,' he said.

Patrick patted him on the shoulders and opened the door to the outside. 'All right, let's rock'n'roll,' he joked using an American accent, then he stepped outside.

Wilbur came out behind him and stopped for a while, giving his eyes time to adjust to the morning light. There were four vehicles; the big mamba, two jeeps, and the Land Rover. After adjusting to the light, Wilbur followed the Captain to the jeep in the middle. Michael was standing by one of the vehicles, talking to an Officer. He saw them, came towards the jeep, and handed Wilbur a soda, which Wilbur was very thankful for and swallowed immediately.

'Thank you, Michael, I really needed this,' he said.

'I know … Now, Willy, when do we see you in these parts again?' he asked.

'I may come back soon to check on developments, but if I don't, I will keep in touch,' he answered as he discreetly slipped some money in Michael's hand. Money was the most appreciated way to thank people during hard times.

Wilbur could see that Michael was surprised, but he just smiled then entered the jeep.

The convoy finally started moving, and they waved to Michael as they left. Wilbur was hoping that the trip from Madi Opel back to Kitgum would be as smooth as the trip in. They drove slowly, as was usually the case with military convoys.

'Tell me about your mission, Wilbur. Was it a success?' Captain Aine probed.

Wilbur was suddenly alert; he didn't want to jeopardize his contacts with the rebel's informants by revealing any information to the government.

He turned and looked at the military man. 'Yes, sir, but why don't you tell me about your mission?' he asked, smiling.

Patrick studied him for some time before he burst out laughing. 'Okay, Willy. I will tell you something, and this is a secret.' He glanced at Wilbur. 'We know all the rebel collaborators in these areas and even the rebels themselves, but we have decided to leave them alone and just monitor them,' he said with finality.

Wilbur was taken aback, not knowing what to do. He finally decided to say something. 'Thanks a lot, Patrick. I'm reluctant because my friend's life depends on it,' he said quietly.

'Well, I really hope you succeed in securing his release. Believe me—we know how cruel and unfeeling it is to use civilians as shields during a conflict.' Captain Aine shook his head before continuing, 'I strongly believe that without informants this man Kony and his rebels would have been history by now.'

They rode in silence for some time until they were stopped by some civilians. Captain Aine motioned for a soldier to talk to them, and while they waited for the soldier to finish, he turned to Wilbur.

'Did you like that place?' the Captain asked.

'The area was too quiet. One wouldn't have known that the place was on the front line unless told by somebody!' Wilbur answered truthfully.

The Captain was about to say something, but the soldier came back from his little talk with the natives. 'Sir,' he said, 'they are reporting a rebel raid about one mile and a half from here. They claim the rebels were headed for another town further up.' The soldier pointed in the direction the convoy was heading.

Captain Aine pulled out a map and carefully perused it. He told the soldier to put the civilians in the Land Rover and move ahead but stop before the little town and wait for them to catch up. 'I have to make sure we don't run into an ambush,' he said, then he left and ran towards the mamba.

The soldier told the civilians to board the Land Rover. They sat between the rows of soldiers, and the vehicle took off. The big mamba took off uphill through the bush. The other vehicles seemed to be following each other very slowly. Wilbur's jeep was the last vehicle to leave.

Suddenly, the peaceful atmosphere was broken by fire from the machine-guns, and the heavy thuds from the mamba. The convoy came to an abrupt stop. The Land Rover dropped off the civilians and moved forward. The driver of Wilbur's jeep jumped out of the vehicle and talked to the soldiers in the other jeep. Then he quickly turned to Wilbur.

'Excuse me, sir, have you ever shot a gun?' he asked very sternly.

Wilbur, who was in shock, just shook his head.

'Well, this is the time to learn. It's your life or theirs,' he said as he retrieved the gun.

Wilbur had no time to think; he was just reacting. The soldier quickly showed him how to load an AK-47 and fire. He also showed Wilbur the safety and the rapid fire switch.

'Did you get that?' the soldier asked. Wilbur nodded, not knowing what else to do.

'Okay. Do it!' the soldier ordered, pointing towards the wild terrain surrounding them.

Wilbur knew it was not the time to argue. He wasn't ready to die, so he aimed at the bush and pulled the trigger. The first shot shocked him so much that he almost fell over, but after a few more tries he felt comfortable.

'Good, try a few more times,' the soldier said, and Wilbur did as he was told.

The fire from the mamba seized momentarily. Everybody's rifle or machine gun was pointing towards the bushes. Wilbur could see lights from the little town about a mile away.

Suddenly, like lightning, some figures appeared over an embankment, and the soldiers started jumping out of the vehicles and shooting at the same time.

'Jump out!' the driver shouted to Wilbur, who was already halfway out. 'When we stand and move ahead, you come along so that you won't be shot by mistake,' the driver shouted amid the gunfire. Wilbur listened carefully, but his eyes were glued on the embankment.

The figures that had been coming forward had stopped. The soldiers started moving ahead, and Wilbur didn't have a choice but to follow suit. He noticed that the soldiers slanted their bodies and that their movements weren't coordinated, which he later learnt reduced the surface area for a bullet to hit. He did the same; he felt like a robot.

They came under fire. 'Chini!' someone shouted.

Wilbur knew it was a Swahili word for 'down', so he dove to the ground. One of the soldiers got up, took a couple of steps, threw something, and went down again. There was a tremendous explosion. The driver had already jumped on top of Wilbur seconds before the bang.

'Never look into the explosion, okay, sir!' he said as Wilbur realized that an explosive had just been thrown and there was a large cloud of smoke twenty yards from where they were. There was another command, and the soldiers got up and moved ahead while shooting. Wilbur saw figures running away and shot in their direction, not necessarily aiming at anyone.

'Halt!' a radio command came through.

The gunfire stopped. Wilbur looked at the driver, 'Why have we stopped?' he asked.

The driver looked at him and smiled. 'The aim is to finish the resistance without getting hit. If we had followed them, chances are we would have come under friendly fire. You did well.'

Everyone started heading back to their vehicles. One injured soldier had been taken ahead for medical care. Wilbur sat with the soldiers who were not involved in evaluating the battle damage. He noticed that they were not acting wary of him anymore, and their attitude towards him was markedly different—friendlier.

The shock of what had just happened to him still hadn't sunk in.

Finally the soldiers who had gone to evaluate the damage came back with a lot of guns and papers they had removed from the bodies.

'Eight rebels are dead, but I believe there are more because there was blood trailing away,' the Officer in charge stated.

The radio transmitter crackled, and he picked up the headset and listened.

'Okay. We will move towards the town at a steady pace, over and out.' He hung up.

They all entered their vehicles and continued slowly along the main road towards the little town. There was some gunfire still coming from automatic rifles. Wilbur thought it came from the Land Rover that had left the main group earlier, but the two jeeps kept moved steadily towards the little town.

They finally sighted the Land Rover and halted the vehicles. All the soldiers jumped off, leaving only the drivers. Wilbur went with them to the top of the embankment to have a better view.

What Wilbur saw he would never forget; he quickly looked away, feeling nauseous. There were dead bodies everywhere. *What is the use of being a rebel if you are going to end up like this?* Wilbur asked himself.

It was easy to figure out what had happened. The rebels had retreated back towards the little town but had been met by fire from the bulletproof mamba that had gone ahead.

There was complete silence as the soldiers watched.

'Do you see the massacre down there?' the driver asked.

Wilbur nodded; he couldn't trust himself to talk. His feelings about war had changed in the last forty-five minutes. Before today, Wilbur had thought that the rebels kept up the struggle because they believed in winning eventually, but now he wasn't sure.

'May I ask you a question, sir?' Wilbur asked him.

The driver, who seemed to have relaxed, merely smiled and said, 'Go ahead, my friend.'

Wilbur paused, trying to put everything into perspective.

'Tell me, is it normally like this?'

The driver shook his head. 'Nope, it has not been like this since I joined the army,' he said as he lit a cigarette. 'I have never seen this much loss of life. We took them fully unaware.' He paused to puff on his cigarette. 'It all comes down to the people,' he continued, 'Once the people get fed up of the bull, then they cooperate,' he added.

'You mean the people we encountered were responsible for the rebels' loss today?' Wilbur asked in disbelief.

The soldier nodded. 'They were responsible for the whole thing. God knows how they fooled them, knowing our convoy was coming,' he added with confidence.

Wilbur could see the mamba coming from the direction of the town.

The soldiers disembarked started piling all the dead rebels in one place; the civilians were helping them. Every time the civilians found a dead rebel, they shouted in delight.

The whole thing made Wilbur feel like throwing up, so he walked behind one vehicle and did exactly that. Afterwards he felt thirsty, not to mention there was a bad taste in his mouth, but there was nothing to drink nearby so he approached a middle-aged man who was standing nearby.

Wilbur still had his gun with him so the civilian looked at him suspiciously, and Wilbur could see that the man was frightened.

'Don't be alarmed; I'm also a civilian like you, believe me. Can you go to the shop for me, please?'

The man smiled and took a deep breath, 'Sure, for a moment I thought you were going to accuse me of being a rebel. Where is the money?'

Wilbur produced some money. 'Hurry, take this bike, get a crate of soda, mixed bottles, one bottled water, and some chewing gum,' he said, taking a bike from a stranger and handing it to the man.

Just before the man left, Wilbur called to him, 'Hold it, my friend! Leave your tax documents and identification.' The man was puzzled at first but finally complied and left, pedaling fast.

'He will be back,' Wilbur said to nobody in particular, then he told the owner of the bicycle to wait. The baffled man who saw Wilbur's gun just moved aside and stood there.

Captain Aine tapped Wilbur on the shoulder. 'How are you doing? It wasn't too bad, was it?' he inquired, looking at the gun in Wilbur's hand.

Wilbur just stared at the pile of dead people and shook his head.

'It was easy this time. They got themselves betrayed,' the Captain said as he lit a cigarette. This was the second person to tell Wilbur this, and neither of them had anything to gain by it. Wilbur looked up at the Captain. Many commanding soldiers would have kept that information under wraps and taken full credit for the smooth operation. Whatever Patrick Aine was, he was too good to be a soldier. This man should have been a teacher, a doctor, or even a priest, Wilbur thought.

Wilbur asked the Captain for a cigarette; he had heard that it helped with nausea. The Captain complied, sensing the young man's distress. Wilbur started coughing after taking a puff, and everyone laughed at him.

Fortunately, the messenger came back with the drinks and handed Wilbur his change. Wilbur gave some money to the messenger together with his documents.

He approached the bike owner. 'Thank you very much for the use of your bicycle. If you wait around you can take the bottles back and get the deposit that was left at the shop.'

'Thank you, sir.' The man smiled and moved back to where he was originally standing.

Wilbur rinsed his mouth with some water, chewed a piece of gum, and then drank the rest of the water. The soldiers helped themselves to the drinks.

'You know, Willy, the first time it happened to me I was near Lukaya in Masaka district,' the Captain said, unscrewing the bottle cap and taking a swig.

'What do you mean?' Wilbur asked, opening up another piece of gum.

'Throwing up, Willy. I threw up the first time I saw people dying in battle. As a matter of fact, I almost quit,' Patrick said, taking another drink. 'That nausea feeling happens to everybody,' he said.

'Everybody, that's for sure, sir,' the Lieutenant standing nearby added.

Someone was counting the victims and the prisoners. The prisoners were lying on the ground with their arms tied behind them. They were a few yards from where Wilbur stood. He walked over slowly and looked at the rebels.

'Why, some of these boys are not even fifteen!' Wilbur exclaimed.

'That's true. The boys only died accidentally. Usually they raise their hands and give up. Besides, all these young people were kidnapped by the rebels and were forced to join. Most who are caught have no choice,' the Captain said.

The dead bodies were put in a makeshift grave and left behind for later burial. If they were lucky, a priest would come by later and say a few words. Wilbur silently hoped that would be the case.

The soldiers boarded their vehicles and headed for Kitgum, driving through the town centre as the people screamed with joy. Wilbur was feeling uneasy about all of it.

The rest of the journey to Kitgum was uneventful, and the soldiers were quiet except for an occasional groan from the injured soldier. They entered Kitgum late in the afternoon.

Chapter 19

Sam and John were busy talking about what to do in case Wilbur was delayed coming back from his trip. They hadn't arrived at any clear solution. Sam preferred sending somebody to Madi Opel while John preferred going there to investigate.

'You have to be kidding,' Sam said in a joking but serious manner. 'There is a war out there, and we don't even speak the language. If something happened to both of us, it would look stupid even to God himself,' he added sarcastically and then walked towards the window to investigate the sound of a diesel vehicle outside.

'Hey, John, look!' he screamed as he ran towards the door and outside. He kept running full speed until he got to the jeep.

'What's the matter, Sam? It's only been two days!' Wilbur exclaimed in surprise.

'I know, man, but we had started thinking of what we would do in case you didn't show up today,' Sam answered, a little embarrassed.

'And what did you boys come up with?' Captain Aine asked with a smile.

'I preferred sending someone to investigate, and John wanted us to go there,' Sam said as John joined them.

'What!' the Captain exclaimed looking at John. 'Are you serious? That would be suicide. Why don't you ask your friend here what we went through today?'

The two boys turned to Wilbur, who just said, 'I will tell you later.'

Wilbur went to say goodbye to everyone in the convoy. The other boys shook hands with the Captain and started towards the house.

'Hold on, guys. I have to find out when they are going to Pakwach,' Wilbur shouted, turning back towards the jeep. The Captain, who had heard Wilbur, picked up the transmission unit and talked for a while. He glanced at his watch and turned to Wilbur.

'It is four-thirty now. We leave at six-thirty. You've got less than two hours to finalize what you are doing here.' He turned and nodded to the driver and they took off.

'Well, I'm glad I'm back,' Wilbur said, walking towards the house behind Sam. John had become quiet after having been abashed by Captain Aine.

Sam noticed it. 'Come on, John, it was just a suggestion. We hadn't done any of it anyway, so just forget it,' he said casually.

Wilbur quickly took a shower before going into the kitchen to get something to eat.

'Good afternoon, sir,' the housekeeper greeted him. He was standing in the doorway that led to the backyard. 'Can I get you something to eat? The food is ready,' he said.

'That's good. Do you have some bottled water in the house?' Wilbur asked.

'No, sir. There is a shop nearby. I can run and get it.'

Wilbur gave him some money. 'Ask everyone what they want before you leave, and get yourself a drink,' Wilbur said.

The boy disappeared into the living room. John had come into the kitchen and was warming some food on the stove.

'How did the trip go, Willy?' he asked.

'It only got bad coming back today. We were caught in a gunfight with the rebels,' he answered, looking at the food on the stove.

John stopped suddenly, 'Oh, my God. Did some people die, Willy?' he asked.

Wilbur nodded, 'Yes unfortunately. One of the soldiers in the army was injured, but a lot of rebels died. The rest were taken prisoner. We brought them with us.'

John looked away, shaking his head. 'I am sorry you went through that. You know, man, I really never felt like we were in a war until this trip. I mean—'

Wilbur cut him short. 'I know exactly what you mean. You can't really feel it until you get into a gunfight and you see people falling down like in a damn movie,' he stated as he reached for a plate and started putting some food on it.

'Let me help you, Willy,' John took the plate from Wilbur and proceeded to put some food on it.

'Take your time,' Wilbur said as he left to join Sam in the living room.

The housekeeper came back with cold soft drinks and Sam and Wilbur started chugging them down.

Finally, John brought a tray of food and Wilbur, who was famished, started eating immediately. The Irish potatoes were fried, and the sauce was delicious and had chunks of meat in it. There was also a salad of tomatoes and green peppers. John had also put avocados and mangoes on the side, which the boys had brought with them from Kampala.

Wilbur ate until he felt stuffed. He turned to his friends with a wide smile. 'You have been doing fine, I see,' he said jokingly, 'Thanks for the meal, John. It was delicious.'

Sam stood up. 'Guys, it's a quarter to six. We should go and prepare our bags.' He disappeared into the bedroom.

'I will come after a little while. I don't have much to pack, anyway,' John said.

Wilbur told John some more about his trip.

John looked at his watch and realized that he had only ten minutes. 'I will go and bring my bag, Willy. I am glad you are back safe,' he said as he walked towards the bedroom.

Sam and John both came back after a few minutes with their bags.

'So how did both of you enjoy this town?' Wilbur questioned.

Sam and John looked at one another, wondering what to say, and then they both shouted simultaneously, as if they had planned it all along, 'Boring!'

Chapter 20

When we left the oasis, we started walking a little faster. It was getting colder and colder. This place is cursed, I thought to myself. It was too cold at night, too hot during the day, and very dry. I gathered that by now we were in a semi-desert. There was hardly any vegetation.

The people in my country didn't realize how good they had it. The equator ran through the country, so most of the land was fertile and the weather was usually mild. And then there were the various lakes and River Nile running through the country. I felt a sudden longing for my country. I was still deep in thought when I saw what looked like a big enclosure with many small, flat houses and one big one.

Jimmy rode back to where I was. 'Eddie, we have made it through hurdle number two. The third hurdle is being able to leave this godforsaken place and go home to our people, so stay strong and keep up the hope,' he said.

The big gates to the enclosure were finally opened and we entered into a large compound that was half the size of a football field. We walked to the centre and Jimmy was told to count us. We sat and waited as Jimmy counted us, and then led the sick to a house in the corner. I was tempted to join them, but Jimmy firmly refused, saying that if things got too bad he would figure out a way to get me there.

The Mullah summoned Jimmy and talked to him for a moment before entering a large house. Jimmy walked to another house that didn't have a door. After about ten minutes, he came out and called to me loudly.

I was angry but mostly scared. Why in hell did he have to shout? I wondered as I walked to where he was. 'Jim—' I started saying, but he raised his hand.

'Eddie, trust me on this. It's better that these slavers know who you are and start to like you. They will think you have accepted their conditions and will be less likely to punish you. And one more thing—do not smile at them. Otherwise they'll think you want them, and I don't have to tell you the rest.' He led me inside the dirty house, which as I had guessed from the fumes, was a kitchen.

There were about four young black girls in the kitchen preparing breakfast. I figured they were also slaves. Jimmy talked to the man in charge. The man was of mixed heritage (half Arab, half black) and must have grown up on this ancient farm. I came to the latter conclusion after I looked closely at his Achilles tendons and realized that they were normal.

The man gave me bowls and a jug full of a porridge-like substance. This was to be our breakfast. I walked with this container and the bowls to where my fellow slaves were sitting and started distributing the porridge. Jimmy stayed in the kitchen even though I kept some porridge for him; I believe he was eating with the half-Arab caretaker.

He finally came to where we were sitting and told everybody to follow him except me. I had to take the utensils back to the kitchen area. The half-Arab caretaker told me in broken Swahili to wash the utensils, which I happily did.

I noticed that the girls were looking at me pleasantly. I decided to take a chance and talk to them. Not knowing how to ask for soap in Arabic, I asked in my language and instantly one of them answered and gave me the soap. I wasn't surprised because most of the kidnapped people from Uganda were from the same area and spoke the same language. I thanked her and asked her how many other slaves they had at the farm.

The girl said it was only them because some militias had raided the Mullah and his brother and robbed the previous slaves during a fight. I asked her about the caretaker, who was now half asleep in the corner. She answered that he had been born at the Mullah Sadiq's brother's farm, who had passed away. After his death, all of his property and his wives reverted to Mullah Sadiq as per tradition.

I asked her when she had arrived here. She replied that she arrived to this sheikdom when she was kidnapped in senior one (eighth grade). She had spent two years in this place as a slave.

'All we do is cook and clean, but that will soon change,' she said sadly.

'What do you mean?' I asked.

'Some of you were bought so that you can mate with us in order to produce more slaves for the Mullah,' she answered sadly. I had suspected as much.

I decided to change the subject. 'Were all of you in the same school?'

She shook her head. 'No, we were in different schools, but we were all captured in Kitgum and Madi Opel. We are all about the same age,' she answered without emotion. 'They brought us around the time the boys were taken from the Mullah, but he refused to breed us, saying that we were too young,' she added.

I was still puzzled. I pointed at the caretaker. 'Please forgive my question, but wouldn't it have been cheaper to use him?'

She paused for about a minute. 'The Mullah claims that slaves of mixed-race make bad workers,' she said. I remembered that Jimmy had told me something like that before. She pointing at the man, 'And as for him, he prefers men. He only started smiling today. His heart was broken when the thugs kidnapped the men.' She gave a small smile.

I shook my head, suddenly feeling frightened. I remembered what Jimmy had told me about some men being used as sex slaves. I would rather mate with a girl.

She looked at me closely, and so did the others. 'What is your name?' she asked. I told her.

'Well, Eddie, my name is Mary.' She proceeded to introduce the other girls. 'Since we know you, I hope they choose you to mate with us,' she said. I prayed that wouldn't happen.

I noticed something strange about these girls. They didn't have any emotions even though they were all very young.

'Seriously, haven't they fooled around with you girls?' I asked.

They all shook their heads in unison. 'The Mullah would hang anybody that attempted to touch us. He is the one who decides everyone's fate,' Mary intimated.

'Since you've all been around for a couple years, maybe you can answer one question. What are the chances of a person getting his freedom?' Deep inside I knew what the answer was going to be. They all smiled and shook their heads.

'No chance,' they answered at the same time. 'And don't even think of running, because you will be caught, tortured, and then hanged. I guess you saw the tree outside, didn't you?' one of them said.

I felt defeated and weak. I had already noticed a big tree with a ladder on the side of the compound. I also noticed the girls looking at my tendons. I knew what they were thinking. *How can you think of running when you have already been maimed?* I had to think of another plan. Losing the ability to run didn't make me useless. I had gone to school to learn how to use my brains, not my physique.

Jimmy came into the kitchen. 'I see you have some new friends. I guess it would be more bearable if you know one another in case you are chosen to breed them,' he said.

I felt a surge of anger. 'I guess you're right, but you didn't have to be so blunt about it,' I snapped.

Jimmy looked at me with a smile. 'Eddie, the sooner you face facts the better. Moreover, it will help you to cope. You should be occupying your mind with questions like, "Where are we? What's the name of this place?" he said, still smiling.

Jimmy had a point. The most important thing was to find out where we were and then calculate the distance from here to wherever. 'You are right, Jim. Please accept my apologies.'

Jimmy brushed off my apologies, walked to where the man was fast asleep, and got two cups. He poured some dark tea in each cup and brought it over, handing me one.

'Salute!' he said.

I raised my cup, all the while wondering how Jimmy could salute at a time like this.

The liquid was bad, but it was better than the porridge.

Jimmy walked to the corner and came back with a few pieces of bread. We ate until I felt satisfied. 'Thanks, Jim. That helped a lot,' I said.

He simply looked away.

The girls were looking at us. They seemed to have adapted better to their circumstances. *Was it because of their immaturity, or are women generally more accepting?* I wondered. I was still wondering about this when I heard Jimmy's voice.

'We are going to look at the Mullah's farms tomorrow, Eddie,' he said. 'He keeps telling me these things. I think he wants me to be an overseer, in which case you will be my assistant,' he added quietly.

The girls were now doing some kind of knitting in the corner. I still had a lot of questions to ask. This was my opportunity, and I didn't care what Jimmy thought.

'How many wives does the Mullah have?' I asked the girls.

They laughed. 'Oh, he only has five,' one of them answered scornfully.

I looked at Jimmy as if I wanted to confirm, and he nodded. 'Eddie, for a Mullah that is very few, believe me.'

I had another nagging question that was inappropriate, but I figured what the hell. 'How do they hope to get any of the girls to have babies if they send them to different studs?'

Jimmy laughed. 'Oh, they know the fertile ones. When they're mating, the Mullah's wives are nearby to monitor the progress. They use the same man, and after a few months they know if the man is fertile or not,' he said, still laughing silently.

'What if the lady can't have babies?' I asked, hoping that they wouldn't meet the same fate as escapees.

Jimmy looked at me and shook his head. 'I know what you are thinking, but no, nothing like that happens. She will continue doing housework or they let her do some light work on the farm,' he answered easily.

Suddenly I became suspicious. How did Jimmy know so much about slavery, more than any regular guy would? I hesitated to ask, but I liked him so I had to come straight with him.

'Hey, Jim, there is something that's been bothering me for some time, and I have to ask you. How come you know a lot about what happens in these slave camps when it's your first time as a slave?'

He looked at me with a smile. 'Well, Eddie, I understand your suspicion, but first I want to remind you that my Achilles tendons were also cut.' He paused and collected his thoughts before he proceeded. He turned to me and sighed.

'Years ago, before the movement government came to power in Uganda, I had an uncle who dealt in ivory and exotic animal skins like leopard, cheetah, and python. I was only in my mid-teens.' He stopped there and asked me if I wanted a refill of the black tea. I agreed, and he left with both cups, filled them, and then came back and handed one to me.

'My uncle took me on some of his trips. We used to go to Zaire, which is now "The Democratic Republic of Congo," and meet business-people that sold all kinds of things, such as diamonds, gold, ivory, and animal skins. The minerals were too expensive for my uncle to trade, so he mostly dealt in ivory and skins.' He paused. I didn't dare interrupt him, so I sipped my tea casually.

'He would buy things and take them through northern Uganda and then to Sudan. If it was ivory, we would go with three more men to carry it, but ivory trade was illegal, so we couldn't take the main roads. That's when I learnt to ride a horse because we used the bush trails and besides walking, there was no other mode of transportation.'

He sipped more tea. 'One day we came across a slave market by accident. My uncle paid some money to guarantee the safety of ourselves and our goods. Before letting us go, they put us in an enclosure near the captives and I had a chance to talk to them. I saw people being sold like cattle, and being young I remember I almost fainted. The relief I felt after we were let go is hard to explain. That was my last trip to Sudan until now,' he finished and sipped the little tea that was left in his cup.

I felt embarrassed to have made him say all that. 'Sorry, Jim, I shouldn't have pried,' I said, looking down on the floor.

Jimmy stood and patted me on the shoulder. 'Eddie, it doesn't matter. I have been trying to get that burden off my chest for a long time. Although I promised my uncle fifteen years ago never to mention it, the incident has never left my thoughts,' Jimmy said, walking towards the entrance.

I followed him out, after bidding the girls goodbye. We walked in silence and entered the big dormitory, where the rest of our fellow slaves were resting. The blankets had already been distributed. Jimmy told me that we would collect our own elephant grass to sleep on later on. We had to make the best of everything in order to survive, even if it meant sleeping on elephant grass instead of mattresses.

Chapter 21

Hassan woke up very early and bid farewell to the family of Al-Hajj Abdul Asuman. Ghani, the son of Al-Hajj Abdul, accompanied him to the taxi stand. They sat on the benches and waited. It was windy and cold, but by six-thirty the weather started warming up.

Ghani managed to find a ride for Hassan. It was a pickup that was going to Magwe through the towns of Pageri and Moli. Hassan reminded Ghani that the boys would be at the Arua Inn the next day and someone should get in touch with them there as soon as possible. They bid each other farewell, and the vehicle finally left the station.

The pickup moved slowly because as usual the roads hadn't been repaired since the 1950s. Occasionally they were stopped by the Sudan People's Liberation Army, which was in charge in the southern part of Sudan, but the soldiers let them go.

They finally got to Pageri and stopped to load some dried fish and other merchandise. Hassan got out and had something to eat. The pickup left an hour later and continued on its mainly quiet journey, northward.

A few years had passed without any big battles, but rumor had it that a while back, there had been a bombardment of bacteria bombs in the neighboring towns by the Sudanese Army, using Russian-made planes.

The vehicle experienced mechanical problems, so Hassan and the other passengers, who were all continuing to Moli, decided to approach a trader who owned a small minibus. After much bargaining, he agreed to take them.

Hassan knew that it might be impossible to get to his father's house that day, so he decided to sleep in either Moli or Magwe, depending on how their journey proceeded.

The journey was treacherous due to the heavy rain that started to pour just before they headed out. The passengers had to disembark a few times to give the vehicle a push. Luckily all the passengers were co-operative and the journey proceeded agreeably.

When they finally arrived in Moli, the town was surprisingly dry. The driver was determined to proceed up to Magwe despite the reluctance of some of the passengers. The passengers relented after realizing that the next vehicle wouldn't be available for a few more days. Some passengers disembarked at Moli but others took their places, so the vehicle was still full.

The driver bought some petrol from a bootleg dealer and refilled the minibus. The next stage of the journey wasn't as difficult as the previous one, and they finally arrived in Magwe without any incidents.

Hassan was very thankful for the safe arrival. He gathered his bags and looked for a motel, which he fortunately managed to find near the taxi station. The hostess was very kind and managed to get Hassan some warm water for a shower. She also gave him a late dinner of fried rice and roasted meat, which was delicious.

After eating, he listened to the radio for a bit. The first channel was religious, but he wanted to hear the news so he continued searching. Most people in the southern towns were Christians, but just like in Uganda, Christians and Muslims got along well. Hassan didn't feel out of place, even though he was a Muslim. He decided to call it a day, having failed to find a good channel, and had a very restful sleep.

Hassan woke up at about eight o'clock in the morning and started weighing his options for the journey home. In this part of Sudan, any movement from one town to another involved tremendous risks, and one had to be extra careful. He brushed his teeth, washed up, got dressed, and then went to the reception area.

After talking to the hotel hostess, he came to the conclusion that both of his options included risks, though one was much longer than the other. The longer journey had a better road, but Hassan would have to change vehicles twice before arriving in his hometown. This journey would take at least a day, and he would have to go through Okaru and pass through many roadblocks with soldier searches, which almost always resulted in robbery if one was lucky; the unlucky ones disappeared.

Hassan decided to take the shorter route through the hills and bypass the town of Okaru. He decided to rent a motorcycle that would be able to traverse the rough terrain up to his uncle's house. The rest of the journey home would have to be made on horseback. His uncle, Mr Adam Wani, would provide the horse. Hassan had been to his uncle's village before with his father Al-Hajj Musa Lara, but he had never taken this route.

Serious discussion between him and a motorcycle rider were concluded and a price was reached. Hassan knew that the price was too high, but he agreed because the alternative was unpredictable.

They began the journey at a steady speed on small roads that were more like paths. These paths were mostly used by traders on foot and on bicycles. This area was also notorious for being a slave route, and at times dead people or escaped slaves were found in the bushes.

The motorcycle driver, whose name was Yasin, knew the way, and he liked to talk so he chatted the whole time. They stopped a few times to stretch their legs. They finally arrived on the outskirts of the town in the early afternoon, having gone through all kinds of difficult terrain.

Usually Hassan took a small airplane to Torit and then got transportation to his hometown. All this traversing had been caused by the packages he had been given by Hon Ochom to take to his father. It was almost certain that if one went with too much money through roadblocks, one would be robbed and most probably killed, and most people knew which roadblocks to avoid.

They entered the town and headed for his uncle's residence, which Hassan had no problem locating. He was so relieved to have arrived safely at his uncle's place that he gave Yasin a big tip on top of his ridiculous fee.

Mr Adam Wani was happy to see his nephew, but he was surprised to see him get off a motorcycle until Hassan explained to him that he had special letters for his dad from Hon Ochom in

Kampala. Hassan explained what had happened to Edgar and the mission the boys had decided to embark on to rescue him.

His uncle mentioned that he had heard of some slave dealers who had been going to the Kinyeti Hills to buy slaves. He took the details of the situation and promised to look into it. He tried to convince his nephew to spend the night, but Hassan was determined to go home.

Mr Wani, who was a very powerful chief in the area, gave Hassan a horse and sent some nomad warriors to accompany him. They were known as fierce fighters. He also escorted his nephew for a few miles before turning back. He begged Hassan to think about marriage as soon as possible, promising a small herd of goats the moment he decided to settle down.

'Please don't forget to tell your father that I will come to visit in a week. Hopefully I will have information about the boy,' he said as he took off with his other fighters.

When Hassan got home in the early evening, he was exhausted but happy. Al-Hajj Musa Lara and Hajat Zibeda, Hassan's mother, were very excited to see their son, but Hassan refused to divulge too much about his trip because many people had come out to greet him and welcome him home.

After taking a shower, Hassan was given some food. The fighters that had accompanied him were also fed and given a decent place to sleep, and their horses were rubbed down and fed.

Hassan was finally able to talk to his father privately and hand him the envelopes from his friend Hon Ochom before he retired to his bedroom. He slept longer than usual, possibly because he felt relieved that a burden had been lifted from him. In the morning, he brushed his teeth, washed up, and changed into clean clothing before he went to look for his father.

Al-Hajj Musa was sitting in his favorite place in front of the house, under a tree shade. He saw his son and motioned to him. 'Hello, son, come join me and have a cup of tea.'

Hassan picked up a small stool nearby and walked with it to where his father was seated. 'Good morning, father,' he said, bending a little to shake his father's hand, as was the custom.

'Good morning, son. Did you have a restful night? You must have had a rough journey.'

Hassan smiled as he reached for a cup and poured himself some tea. 'Yes, sir, I didn't sleep much since I had important documents for you and also because I had to go through Nimule for the boys' identifications.'

Father and son exchanged some small talk about Hassan's school, and his father inquired about his friend, Hon Ochom. Finally Al-Hajj Musa cut to the chase.

'I understood most of what Hon Ochom wrote in his letter. Is there anything you would like to add?' Al-Hajj Musa asked.

Hassan started to shake his head but then remembered something. 'Sir, Hon Ochom's nephew, Wilbur, went to a border town near Madi Opel to meet with a rebel collaborator who is apparently very influential with the rebels. Wilbur went to offer her some money in exchange for returning Edgar, so we shall hopefully know what came of that meeting in a few days,' he finished.

Al-Hajj Musa had been nodding his head while Hassan was talking. 'This collaborator is a woman?' he asked with a surprised look on his face.

'Yes, sir. Apparently, she can return a captive if they are still in rebel hands,' Hassan said.

'Interesting ... I have already sent the boys that brought you with a specific request to my brother to send a group of men to the Kinyeti Hills with instructions to buy back a few captives. During this process we shall know what happened to the boy and hopefully find out which group of Arabs took him.'

He paused and sipped his tea. 'What did Al-Hajj Abdul say about all this?' his father asked seriously.

'Sir, he promised to send some traders in the general direction of Rokon to see if some slaves had been taken around there lately. He also said that if the boy had been sold into slavery, he was long gone and the best way would be to buy him back,' he answered.

Al-Hajj Musa scratched his beard, deep in thought. 'The problem might arise only if the Mullah refuses to sell him back to us. That's why we need a few more facts from my brother's men in order to handle them,' he said as he poured some more tea into his cup.

Hassan felt very defeated. For some reason, he had assumed that the moment they found the Mullah who had bought Edgar, everything would fall into place, and the boys would then buy him back to freedom, but now there seemed to be all kinds of obstacles. Although he didn't know Edgar personally, Hassan had bonded with his friends and felt a connection to him.

'I assumed that it could be solved with money. I didn't realize that some of these Mullahs would be difficult to deal with,' he said.

Al-Hajj Musa nodded his head, 'You see, son, our country is divided into two parts—the one in the north and us in the south. The Arabs in the north, where these Mullahs are from, behave as if they are above the law. They regard us, black people, as half human. To be able to deal with these people we need to hire warlords to attack them and kidnap the slaves when they are working in the fields, but there is a catch,' he said, sipping his tea slowly. 'The warlords must be fellow Arabs to be able to get close to them. These are the most treacherous people ever created,' Al-Hajj Musa added.

Hassan was confused and it showed. 'But, sir, we are Muslims and we were taught to regard all people equally,' he said, looking at his father.

'Son, I will say this. Not every Muslim is a good Muslim, just as not every Christian is a good Christian. The same goes for all other religions. Not every black person is a good person either. Different people behave differently and interpret their faith differently,' Al-Hajj Musa concluded and stood up. 'See you later, son,' he said as he walked away.

Chapter 22

They heard the sound of a car horn, and all three boys stood up instantly. A minute later there was a knock on the door. Sam opened it, and Captain Patrick Aine entered smiling. 'Are you boys ready to hit the road?' he asked.

'Sure, Patrick,' Wilbur answered, 'Unless you want a drink before we head off.'

Patrick said they were pressed for time and should leave. The boys had decided to leave their car behind. They grabbed their bags and headed towards the door, bidding the young housekeeper goodbye before they got into the Jeep. The vehicles were the same ones that Wilbur remembered. Captain Aine insisted that Wilbur sit in the front seat and handed him a gun.

Sam and John looked at one another, a little bit confused. Wilbur, realizing their confusion, decided to offer an explanation.

'I guess I didn't really explain everything about our encounter with the rebels. I was taught how to use a rifle to defend myself,' he said flatly.

'You mean you fired a gun, Willy?' Sam asked, intrigued. Wilbur nodded.

'Well, I guess I would do the same thing if our roles were reversed,' Sam said. 'As a matter of fact, I wish I knew how to use it,' he added.

Wilbur gave him a quick look but kept silent. John was too shocked to say anything. He couldn't imagine himself ever firing a gun. The rest of the journey from Kitgum to Gulu was uneventful. The countryside was pitiful, devoid of construction or farming, but the soldiers remained very alert.

'You know, this rebel activity has brought a lull in agriculture and other activities,' Captain Aine remarked.

Everyone in the jeep was quiet for some time, digesting the information. They had not seen a single person for miles until they entered Gulu district, about twenty miles from the town. One thing was noticeable. People in this area seemed to either dislike or fear the Ugandan military. There had to be a reason for this kind of fear.

'Tell me something, Wilbur. Why do these people seem to be afraid of the military?' John asked.

Wilbur glanced at him. 'John, I think Patrick might be able to answer that question much better than me,' he said and looked at the Captain.

Captain Aine chuckled and glanced at John. 'I guess you should know yourself since you are a civilian. Generally in war zones or places of constant conflict people tend to be suspicious of people with guns,' the Captain answered.

John nodded his head in pure agreement.

Wilbur remembered that it hadn't been the case in the little town where he had fought with the rebels. I guess every place is different, he thought to himself. They kept moving slowly until they entered Gulu town.

The town centre had some activity, though one could tell that it wasn't anywhere close to the towns in the southern part of Uganda. They finally got to the place where the convoy was waiting to escort cars and took off with them.

Wilbur was getting tired of holding the gun. Do these soldiers believe that because I fired a gun once to protect my life, I am now like them? he wondered. But he decided to stay quiet. Why scratch a wound before it healed?

As the convoy was leaving Gulu, Sam and John were quietly discussing different things, ranging from tourism to other income-generating activities. What a shame that nothing could be done because of the insecurity.

The road from Gulu town to Pakwach wasn't bad. The nearer they got to Pakwach, the more people they saw cultivating their gardens, walking about, or riding bicycles from one small shopping centre to the other.

Soon the situation completely changed, and people could be seen talking or bargaining about some business.

'Excuse me, Captain. Aren't there any rebels in this area?' Sam asked Captain Aine, who was puffing on a cigarette.

'There used to be a few rebels around here sometime back, but people started realizing that they were the ones losing out, so they began reporting the suspected rebels and their informers. In no time the government brought security back into the area.'

Sam didn't ask anymore. He hoped that the Captain was right since Wilbur and Edgar were from this unstable area and had little tolerance for the rebels and their cause.

They were glad when the convoy finally arrived in Pakwach. The time was about ten-thirty at night.

'All right, boys, here we are. I wish you luck on your journey to Arua tomorrow,' Captain Aine said, smiling.

Wilbur pulled the Captain aside, and together they walked a little distance away from the convoy. He had already put aside an envelope for the soldier. He knew that these soldiers worked very hard and sacrificed their lives but were not well paid.

'I don't know how to thank you, Patrick. I hope we shall meet again,' Wilbur said, hugging the Captain and slipping the envelope into his pocket.

Captain Aine winked in understanding, and together they walked back to the convoy, which took off towards the taxi station.

The three friends picked up their bags, headed up the street, and checked into the only decent hotel in Pakwach. It was cheap, so they got separate rooms. Although they were hungry, they decided to take quick showers before having a meal. They took their time getting ready before finally meeting in the dining room for dinner. They ate in silence as they devoured their meal and quenched their thirst with soft drinks.

Wilbur was the first to talk. 'Gentlemen, we'd better start making suggestions about what we shall do when we arrive in Arua,' he said.

John and Sam both nodded to his suggestion.

'Okay, let's get a booth in the corner and continue our discussion,' Sam suggested, rising up from his seat.

The waiter came to them, and Sam quickly settled the bill and led the way to the booth. After they settled down, they ordered some beer. Wilbur told them about his stay with Father Otim and Michael in Madi Opel and his talks with Ms Akello and Mr Oyu. He also mentioned how nervous he was while negotiating with the lady but did not let her see it.

'Ms Akello and I finally agreed on a deposit of one thousand dollars, and that she would receive two thousand dollars when Father Otim got Eddie. She let me know that this kind of business was a gamble, so there are no guarantees but she would try her best. In other words, cross your fingers.' Wilbur stopped talking and looked at his friends. He noticed that John was shaking his head.

'Willy, are you saying that this woman can keep the thousand dollars and not deliver Eddie, just like that?' John asked and snapped two fingers quickly in remonstration.

Sam smiled and patted John on the back. 'Yup, when you decide to do something illegal like we are doing, you gamble with your money and sometimes with your life,' he stated.

Wilbur nodded his head in agreement; he was glad Sam was street-smart. 'Sam is right. We have to be prepared to lose money to achieve our goal, and anything could happen to any of us, just like the battle I was involved in with the rebels.'

John was quiet for a second, and Wilbur knew a question was coming. 'Wilbur, did you shoot anyone?' he asked.

Wilbur hesitated a little before replying, 'When the rebels were coming toward us, I fired at them, but I don't think I killed anyone. John, I don't know how you feel about it, but I couldn't lie down and wait to get slaughtered like a lamb. Remember, these rebels are deadly and this isn't a John Wayne thriller. I really felt the bullets buzzing by. I was afraid for my life.' He poured some more beer into his glass.

John could see the anguish that his friend had gone through and was embarrassed for having asked the question. He decided to ease the situation. 'You know, Willy, even though I have never been in such a situation, I have been in a lot of street fights, and I have never turned the other cheek,' John said jokingly.

They were silent for some time until Wilbur took the lead again. 'We shall be able to communicate with my uncle when we arrive in Arua. Hopefully by then he will have an answer from our Ms Akello.'

Sam and John nodded their heads in agreement.

'Moving onto the next topic, I believe that by the time we get to Arua tomorrow, Al-Hajj Abdul Asuman will have brought our travel documents,' Wilbur said.

'I suggest that we get Sudanese money just as a precaution,' Sam added.

John and Wilbur agreed.

'We have to be ready for everything. By the way, Hassan still has the camera,' John added, looking at Wilbur.

They sipped their drinks slowly, each thinking about the mission ahead and trying to figure out how they could simplify it.

'We should have contingency plans in case, God forbid, these barbaric rebels have already sold Eddie,' Sam said.

They were silent for a while, and then John raised a question.

'Do you guys think Hassan told Al-Hajj Abdul everything?'

Wilbur felt a lot better knowing that his friends were thinking along the same lines as he was. 'I sure hope so,' he said. 'If, God forbid, Eddie has been sold, then we will have to rely on help from Al-Hajj Abdul and Hassan's father. Both of these men have lived in Sudan all their lives and have numerous contacts.'

Sam sipped some more of his drink; his mind was working fast even though he was a little tired. 'John, the way I see it, Hassan must have told Al-Hajj everything. How else would he explain getting us counterfeit identification cards? Moreover, Willy's dad knows Al-Hajj very well, so he must trust the man,' Sam concluded as he reached for his drink.

They all raised their glasses together. 'To our success,' they said in unison and then downed their drinks.

'Well, gentlemen, I think we have covered most of the immediate big problems and should call it a night,' Wilbur said, getting up from his seat.

John motioned for him to sit down. 'If, God forbid, Eddie has been sold, he would have been taken up north. It would take a lot of time to find out where he is. We will need divine intervention,' John said.

Suddenly all the other fellows got gloomy and looked at him intently.

It was Wilbur who spoke first. 'John, I hope you are wrong, but if you are right then we need all the prayers we can get,' he said slowly.

'You are right about that. I mean about the prayers, because the way I see it to get Eddie back would take a miracle,' John said, getting up. He walked out of the bar, followed by Wilbur and Sam.

They didn't even wait for their change.

Chapter 23

Sam woke up and saw that the sun was already up. Looking at his watch, he noticed it was eleven o'clock. He quickly washed his face and brushed his teeth before he put on a clean pair of pants and a clean shirt. John woke up with a tremendous headache, so after a quick shower he rushed to the shop to get some aspirin.

Wilbur, who also woke up late and weak, decided that a cold shower might help, so he jumped into it. He had a hangover and wanted to get rid of it, but he didn't believe in the old saying that one had to take another drink in order to neutralize the hangover. After showering he carefully dressed in some clean clothes and decided to walk to the restaurant for a cup of black coffee.

On the way to the hotel restaurant, he met John. 'Morning, John,' he said jokingly.

'Morning, Willy, I had a headache so I went to get some aspirin. Want one?' John asked.

'Sure, care to join me for a cup of black coffee?' Wilbur asked. John gave him an aspirin and they both entered the restaurant. The place didn't have too many people, which suited them fine. They chose the table in the corner, as they had the night before, and sat down. The waiter came, took their orders, and left as Wilbur nudged John to look towards the door.

Walking towards them was Sam with a big grin on his face. 'Sorry I am late,' he said.

'Hi, Sam, you look surprisingly fresh,' John said.

Sam smiled and sat down. He didn't look like he had been drinking the night before. On the contrary, he looked well rested.

'I heard you guys talking as you passed by my room. I also ordered the newspaper,' he said as he paid the boy who had just brought it. He passed some pages to John. 'Willy, you'll have to do with the middle part for now.' He gave the middle pages to Wilbur.

They took their breakfast in silence, exchanging papers and talking about the gossip that was in the paper.

'Did you notice that this is yesterday's paper?' John asked.

The other two fellows nodded.

'It takes some time for news to get to these parts, and in some areas it takes two days,' Wilbur said, standing up.

Sam stood up too. 'We better get going since we are using public transportation,' he said, moving towards the door. 'I will call a taxi.'

The other two paid for breakfast before heading to their respective rooms.

'You know, John, I really thought about what you said last night, and the more I thought about it the more I realized that the next part of our mission is going to be very tricky. I am glad we are all together,' Wilbur said, patting John on the shoulder before heading for his room.

They packed their belongings in a hurry and left their rooms as the taxi started honking outside.

Surprisingly, Sam was already outside with his bag. 'I will take your keys back to the front desk,' he said, extending his hand to them. Sam rushed off to the desk while the others loaded their bags into the trunk of the taxi.

The taxi driver drove them towards the station.

'Do you think we can get immediate transport to Arua, sir?' John asked the driver.

'Oh yes, transportation to Arua is easy depending on how much you want to spend,' he answered as they pulled into the station. They paid the driver and removed their bags from the trunk.

The taxi station in Pakwach was very busy in contrast with the stations in Gulu and Kitgum. It took them a few minutes to get a minibus taxi to Arua. The only inconvenience was that they had to wait for more passengers to fill up the minibus before embarking on the trip. The three friends were content with reading the newspapers as they waited.

At approximately one o'clock, the taxi left the station, and soon they were on the highway to Arua. They didn't talk to one another during the ride to Arua; they either looked at the scenery or read their papers. The other passengers were talking in a language that none of the boys understood. The roads were good, so the driver made it in less than two hours.

At the station in Arua, they disembarked and started looking for a taxi. The place was bustling with business. Hawkers were selling anything from dried fish to watches and radios. Looking at the people here and remembering Gulu and Kitgum, one came to appreciate the importance of peace and security.

The boys called a taxi to take them to the Arua Inn.

'Did you notice the difference between this town and Gulu or Kitgum?' Sam asked.

Both John and Wilbur nodded sadly.

'I agree. The contrast between this town and Kitgum is incredible. It's unbelievable,' John added sadly, remembering the abandoned buildings they saw in Gulu and Kitgum.

'I really don't understand why Kony started this cowardly war. It's sad to think of the suffering he has brought to his people. Damn it! This makes me so angry!' Wilbur said, looking out the cab window.

The taxicab pulled over in front of a hotel. It looked just as good as any of the hotels in Kampala. They paid the cab fare and removed their bags. The weather was sunny, and there was a little breeze blowing.

'Welcome to Arua Inn. Not bad at all,' Wilbur announced, picking up his bag. They walked over to the receptionist and inquired about rooms.

'How many days do you want to stay here, gentlemen?' inquired the beautiful young lady at the desk.

They looked at each other, undecided.

'Two days,' Sam said, taking charge. The lady gave them their room keys and directed them.

'Excuse me, madam, if we get any messages can you let us know immediately?' Wilbur requested before they walked towards their rooms. 'Thank you,' he added. Luckily their rooms were close to one another.

On entering his room, Wilbur noticed that it was spacious and had a double bed and a phone. 'Not bad indeed,' he said aloud, dropping his bag in the corner and jumping on one of the beds. He picked up the phone, but there was no dial tone. Oh well, it was too good to be true, he thought to himself.

Somebody knocked on the door. Wilbur went and unlocked it. 'Come in,' he said.

The lady at the reception opened the door but hesitated in the doorway. 'Sir, I am sorry I forgot to tell you. An older gentleman came here last night and left a message for you. He said he would be back this evening,' she said. 'Also, somebody left an envelope for you,' she added, handing Wilbur the envelope.

'Thank you,' he said, reaching into his pocket for a tip.

She shook her head. 'Sir, I don't like to take money that I haven't worked for,' she said seriously.

Wilbur was taken by surprise. 'What? This isn't a bribe. It's a tip. I want to thank you for giving me my messages,' he said slowly.

'But, sir—' she began, but Wilbur didn't let her finish.

'Please accept this with no strings attached. It would be an honor. Can you tell me your name, please?' he asked after mustering enough courage.

'My name is Caroline. I will accept it since you insist, and thank you,' she said, turning and walking away.

'Mine is Wilbur, but my friends call me Willy,' he called after her before closing the door. *Phew, now that's what I call a woman.* He opened the letter as soon as he sat down. It was from his uncle.

Hon Ochom said that he was pleased at the way Wilbur had handled Ms Akello and that she was making preparations to leave for the rebel camp immediately. The Bishop had relayed this message to Wilbur's uncle after receiving it from Father Otim. The letter also forbade Wilbur and his friends from leaving the Arua Inn until they had received further instructions from him.

Wilbur wondered how his uncle could have already received a message from Father Otim before they got to Arua. He stood up and walked out of the room, locking the door behind him. He went to Sam's room and knocked but there was no reply. The same happened with John's room. He decided to check the hotel lounge and headed there. He saw his two friends and walked towards them.

They were drinking some fruit juice. Sam motioned for the waiter to bring another glass when he saw Wilbur

'Guys, don't you think we are living a little extravagantly?' Sam asked when Wilbur sat down.

'No, no, don't even start,' Wilbur said, and they all burst out laughing. Sam was known for being frugal with his money.

'By the way, Willy, we saw you talking to that pretty belle, the receptionist. You do have the right idea. I should have thought about that one myself,' Sam said teasingly.

'Well, I don't see anything wrong with a little relaxation.' He grinned. The other two riveted their eyes on him with big grins on their faces.

Wilbur suddenly changed the subject. 'She brought a note from my uncle. He received a message through Bishop Jonathan from Father Otim. Don't ask me how. The message said that Ms Joyce Akello was preparing to go to Sudan to try to retrieve Edgar.' He looked at both of his friends. 'The three of us can't leave this place until we hear from him about Ms Akello's mission.' Wilbur then chugged down his drink until the glass was empty.

'She also gave me a message from Al-Hajj Abdul Asuman,' Wilbur added.

'What did he say?' Sam asked anxiously.

Wilbur spread his hands and answered, 'There was nothing to it. She only said that an elderly Muslim man came yesterday but missed us and said he will be back today.'

Sam started to order beer, but John stopped him. 'Guys, I think it's bad to drink when we are about to meet a Muslim clergyman.'

'Thanks, John, that was a timely suggestion,' Sam said and Wilbur nodded. It was approaching five in the evening. They entered the restaurant and ordered food, which they ate in a hurry. Their last meal had been the night before.

Wilbur called the waiter over. 'Excuse me. Do you have any English newspapers here?'

'You want today's paper?' the waiter asked.

'You mean you have today's paper?' Wilbur asked, with a surprised look on his face.

'Yes, sir, we get them daily at about noon. They come by air.'

'That's very good. Can you get us both dailies from Kampala?' Wilbur asked as he gave the waiter two bills. The fellow left quickly with the dishes.

Sam was shaking his head, 'Now that is what I call security.'

'Yup, it sure is, and good for us too because we shall be able to keep up with what's happening in Kampala,' Wilbur added.

John had been quietly thinking for some time. He looked at his friends. 'Guys, I was just remembering the time I called Father Benedict at the Gulu Catholic Mission. The lines weren't clear, but we could hear each other. Since Arua is more secure, most likely they have phones that work. We can tell Hon Ochom of our arrival and ask him to inform our families that we are okay,' he said.

Both Wilbur and Sam nodded. 'That's a good idea. Right now, Willy's uncle doesn't know our whereabouts. We should inform him where we are at all times in case, God forbid, anything happens,' Sam said.

The somber mood was interrupted by the waiter, who arrived with both papers.

'Thank you. By the way, is there any place in this town we can make a phone call to Kampala?' Wilbur asked anxiously.

The man nodded, 'Yes, sir, you can make a phone call to most places at the reception.'

Wilbur didn't wait for him to finish the sentence before he stood up. 'I will let him know that we are all fine. Is there any other message you would like me to give him?'

'Please ask him to pass on the same message to our families,' John said, looking at Sam. Sam nodded. They scribbled down the respective phone numbers.

Wilbur walked to the reception and found Caroline busy talking to a customer, so he took a seat in a nearby chair, picked up a magazine, and started reading.

Wilbur was startled when he heard his name. 'Yes,' he answered abruptly, but he quickly calmed down after realizing that it was Caroline calling him.

He walked to the desk smiling. 'Excuse me, Miss Caroline, I was wondering if it would be possible to make a call to Kampala.'

'Sure, but you don't have to call me Miss.' She smiled at him and he felt nervous all of a sudden. 'Do you have the number?' she asked.

Wilbur fumbled for a pen and scribbled the number on a piece of paper and handed her the paper. She reached under the desk for a phone, dialed a number, and asked an operator for a connection to Kampala. Soon after, Caroline read the number on the paper to someone and waited for a few seconds before handing the receiver to Wilbur.

'Hello, Lillian. It's Willy. How are you?' He listened as his cousin nearly screamed into the phone with happiness and proceeded to ask a lot of questions without pause.

He couldn't help but laugh. 'Yes, we are all fine … We are in Arua now … May I talk to Uncle, please?'

Lillian said goodbye to Wilbur and called her father to the phone. Wilbur and his uncle talked for about ten minutes before he hung up.

'I don't know how to thank you, Caroline. How much do I owe you?'

She looked at her watch, calculated, and gave him the total bill. He smiled, paid her, and thanked her again before walking back into the restaurant to join his friends.

Chapter 24

As soon as Wilbur entered the restaurant, he saw an older man sitting with his friends. It was the same man he had seen at the reception desk talking to Caroline. He immediately knew it was Al-Hajj Abdul Asuman, his father's friend from Nimule, Sudan. He calmly walked towards the group.

Al-Hajj Abdul stood up to greet Wilbur, and Wilbur bent over, greeting him as tradition dictated when one was meeting an elder.

'How you are, son? And how is your father?' he asked warmly.

Wilbur extended greetings from his dad and studied the man for a few seconds. The older man was very distinguished looking but also had an air about him that made Wilbur relax. Wilbur liked him immediately.

Al-Hajj Abdul said he had met with Hassan and then asked Wilbur about his trip to Madi Opel.

By now Wilbur had figured that Al-Hajj Abdul knew everything about their mission. There was no point in holding anything back. Moreover, he was a good friend of his dad.

'My trip was very eventful, to say the least. I met with unsavory characters and learnt how to use a gun. All in all it was a learning experience,' he answered truthfully. 'Oh, I just talked to my uncle on the phone and he sends his greetings to you, sir.'

The older man told Wilbur to extend his greetings to his uncle and father the next time he talked to them.

'How was Hassan when you last saw him, sir? Where is he? We are anxious to know!' Wilbur asked.

Al-Hajj Abdul smiled. 'First of all, I admire what you are doing for your friend, and I want to thank Allah for giving me the opportunity to meet you. As for Hassan, he should have arrived in his hometown by now. I had him accompanied without his knowledge. It's always better that way,' he said philosophically.

The boys looked at this older gentleman in wonder. They had the same thought. This old man must be very powerful to be able to do that.

'Sir, you must be hungry. Let us order something for you,' Sam said calmly as he ordered a coffee pot for them.

'My son, I will drink tea. If I drink coffee at my age, my heart beats very fast and causes all kinds of changes in my body,' he said teasingly.

The three boys burst out laughing, realizing that the old fellow had a sense of humor.

Al-Hajj Abdul reached under the table and pulled out a bag. He carefully opened it, removed the identity papers, and handed them to Wilbur. Wilbur took his ID paper and handed the rest over to his friends. They each looked at their papers.

'Sir, we want to know as much as possible about the situation we are in. It is important for us to know everything,' Wilbur said.

Al-Hajj Abdul nodded in understanding. 'Okay, young men, I will begin by telling you what I have learnt about the slavery business so far. It's true that some Arabs have been going to the rebel camps to buy slaves in exchange for guns and ammunition, and sometimes they use cash.' He paused to drink some tea. 'These slave dealers don't usually keep any slaves themselves. They just sell them off to the Mullahs, who use them to work on their farms.'

The three boys had their eyes fixed on him with questions on their minds.

Sam realized that without enough information about these dealers and their routes, they didn't have much of a chance to rescue Edgar. 'Sir, is it possible to find out which dealers go to the camps to buy people?'

Al-Hajj Abdul turned to look at Sam. 'That's a good question, son. I also asked the same thing. Over the past three years, due to some pressure from Khartoum caused by the European countries and America, the practice has gone underground. Only one group we know of goes to Kinyeti Hills, and it's sponsored by a warlord north of Makorro area. This group moves their slaves to a marketplace deep in the semi-desert. They usually move at night to avoid detection by the SPLA. I wrote down the names of these places.'

'Sir, you said Mullahs buy slaves to use in their farms. Do they sell them later, or do they keep them?' John asked.

Al-Hajj Abdul was enjoying his tea and kept smiling, clearly impressed with the young men. 'The Mullahs usually keep their slaves. Unfortunately, most of them don't live long if they work on these farms,' he answered, bending his head and staring into his tea. 'Your friend is a young man. If he has been sold into slavery, he will be around for a while, assuming he does as he is told. If he is as smart as you young men, I don't see why he shouldn't stay around long enough for us to find him,' he said, trying to reassure the young men in front of him.

Al-Hajj asked the boys if they wanted him to continue, and they nodded in unison. 'There are not many Mullahs who still do this business. There is a well-known one called Mullah Sadiq Bin Fahad. This Mullah isn't as harsh with slaves as the others, but he is very hard to negotiate with for rescuing somebody. The news I have is that three months ago he was ambushed by militias. His brother was killed, and every single slave was taken from him. That experience has left him a bitter man and very hard to deal with,' he said, looking at John.

'Another one is Mullah Isa Faquil. He is a small-scale buyer who has just started growing hashish near the Oasis of Vanil. He doesn't have any strong ties in the area and can easily be bought. Altogether this fellow doesn't have any more than five horses and donkeys combined. Another Mullah is Sheik Farid Maloof. He is known to be very cruel to his slaves but also greedy, so he is approachable.'

Al-Hajj Abdul cleared his throat and took another sip from his tea. 'Now we come to the most dangerous and treacherous warlord in that area. This man has about thirty fighters with weapons, and he used to grow hashish using slaves. The good news is that he eventually stopped growing it and prefers to let others grow it and buy from them. His name is Sheik Nadim Haddad. The news from my contacts is that he had taken a consignment of hashish up north and only got back last week. If your friend has been sold into slavery, we should thank Allah that he did not end up with this guy,' Al-Hajj Abdul summarized.

All three young men were quiet for some time. It was Wilbur who finally broke the silence. 'Sir, we don't know how to thank you for what you are doing for us. Is there any way to find out which Mullahs have bought slaves in the past week or month?' Wilbur asked intently.

Al-Hajj nodded his head. 'I took the liberty of putting some people on that mission. I figure if we know that, we can narrow our search base. That information should be coming to me very soon, and of course you shall know....Young men, do you have any more questions to ask me? I have to leave for Nimule tonight.'

All the young men shook their heads.

'Please tell your father when you talk to him next that I will do everything in my power to find the boy and bring him back safely,' he said, looking at Wilbur before he stood up.

The boys also stood up simultaneously and bowed to shake Al-Hajj Abdul's hand.

'Sir, do you mind if I walk you to your car?' Wilbur asked.

Al-Hajj shook his head. 'It is better if you are not seen with me for now.' He reached into his pocket and gave Wilbur a piece of paper. 'If you want to contact me for anything, use that address. It belongs to my son who lives nearby. May Allah be with you,' he said, and he walked straight to the door without looking back.

Everybody was silent for a while before Sam broke the silence. 'Now there is a prince among men. I am glad he is on our side,' he said as he motioned to the waiter. 'Can you bring us some beers please?'

The boys looked at him strangely.

'But Sam, we drank quite a bit yesterday. Don't you think it is better to take it easy?' John asked, looking at him.

'Yes, John, that would be a very good suggestion under normal circumstances, but I personally think we have a reason to be optimistic. I like what I heard from Al-Hajj Abdul. At last I have some hope that we shall get Eddie back. I couldn't have said that last night,' he said, perusing the notes he had written while Al-Hajj Abdul was talking. 'Yes, my brothers, I have some hope indeed,' he added as the waiter brought the beer.

They each opened the bottles and raised them in a toast.

'To Eddie's freedom!' they all said.

John eyes were moist with emotion. 'I tend to agree with you, Sam. This time I see a tiny light at the end of the tunnel. The way I see it, after we get some news from Kampala about Ms Akello's trip, we shall know how to proceed,' he said, taking a sip of his beer.

Wilbur was wondering what Al-Hajj Musa Lara, Hassan's father, had found out. He started thinking about their possible trip to Sudan and the challenges they would face. From what he had heard, things there worked differently from Uganda, especially when it came to trading in rural areas.

'You know, guys,' Wilbur said, 'I have been thinking hard about our possible trip to Sudan. I heard my father say once that the illiterate traders prefer commodities to money. We have to think of things to barter with them in exchange for information.' He paused. 'We could take some commodities like leopard skin or a snakeskin. Don't get me wrong. I am not encouraging this trade or forcing anybody to agree with me, but I don't think it would harm our mission if we took things that are loved by Arabs.' Wilbur finished talking, and then poured some more beer in his glass.

The other boys looked at him. They were advocates of animal rights, especially John.

Sam was the first to talk. 'It's very unfortunate to see that people kill these creatures for money, but if they are already dead and can help save Eddie's life, then it would be well worth it,' he said and looked at both John and Wilbur.

John was shaking his head profusely. He was totally against animal violations and was known to demonstrate for this cause.

'Look at it this way, John, we gave blood to the Red Cross a few times when we were at school to help someone's life, so if the skin of some dead animal could save someone, then I sincerely believe it's worth it as long as we are not involved in killing any creature,' Sam said and reached for his drink.

John was still shaking his head. 'No. I won't be part of this. Is that clear?' His eyes were serious.

Wilbur decided to change the subject. He clapped his hands together. 'Hey, guys, how about a little music and relaxation with members of opposite sex? And don't forget, we came here to visit our teacher.' The others nodded.

Wilbur walked towards the reception area. The little talk with Al-Hajj Abdul had given him tremendous confidence. He approached the reception desk and asked Caroline how work was going. She replied that work was fine though a little boring. She was being friendly, so Wilbur decided to take a chance and state his question before he lost his nerve.

'Caroline, my friends and I are not familiar with this town Do you know any good place for a night out?'

She smiled. 'There is a nice club not far from here with a nice atmosphere for dancing and relaxing,' she answered.

Here we go, thought Wilbur, feeling a bit nervous. 'Caroline, is it possible for you and some of your friends to join us this evening? We will be on our best behavior, I promise,' he said, not knowing how she would respond, but hoping she would agree.

She hesitated and looked at Wilbur. 'I can't promise, but if it's possible I will leave a message with my replacement at the reception in ten minutes. Oh, here she comes. I will see you later,' she said, smiling.

Wilbur smiled too and walked back towards the restaurant where his friends were.

'How did it go, Willy?' they both asked at the same time before he could even sit down.

Wilbur pretended to be angry and reached for his bottle.

'Didn't I tell you, Sam, that this would come to nothing?' John said, pouring himself a drink.

Wilbur suddenly smiled. 'Now, don't go jumping to conclusions. We will have our answer soon, so cross your fingers. Let me remind you that there is no place that is safe from you-know-what, so be careful.'

Sam looked at Willy and shook his head. 'You don't have to lecture us about AIDS, my friend. Everybody knows it's all over the place. Thanks for being concerned, but when it comes to women, it's every man for himself.'

They talked some more about the Arua girls, wondering if they were different from Kampala girls. Wilbur looked at his watch; ten minutes had past. He stood up. 'Give me a minute,' he said, walking away towards the door.

'That guy is something. Isn't he, John?' Sam asked.

John merely smiled and sipped his drink.

Wilbur came back quickly; he hadn't been gone for even a minute.

'He must have been turned down by the country belles. So much for a night out,' John said.

'Guys, leave those drinks. We are going for a night out with some beautiful women, and remember, women don't like to be kept waiting,' Wilbur said, turning around.

They all walked towards their rooms.

'Make it quick. We have only thirty minutes,' Wilbur added as he put his key inside the lock of his door and opened it.

Each of them was eager to unwind, so they got ready in a record fifteen minutes. They got a taxi and hurried to pick up the ladies.

Chapter 25

Joyce Akello listened to the report from Kitgum about the young man she had met a day ago, Wilbur Ochom. She planned to leave for Sudan in a few hours. She looked at the old man in front of her.

'Did you say his father was a permanent secretary, or was it his uncle?'

'Madam, the young man's father owns a big trading company and a mansion in Kololo, but the uncle, who is very close to the young man, works in the government. He is an Honorable Member of the Parliament.'

Joyce digested all this information in silence. 'Okay, keep talking,' she said.

'The young man had two other friends waiting for him at Hon Ochom's house in Kitgum. Their names are Sam and John. Both young men are from the central province.' He paused. 'I managed to talk to the housekeeper after they left, and he said something interesting. He said that he had heard the guards say that Hon Ochom himself had come up to Tororo to arrange for them to be escorted by a convoy all the way to Kitgum and Madi Opei to see Father Otim,' Mzee Francis Opi reported. ('Mzee' is a respectful way of addressing elderly men).

'Mzee, did you find out the last names of the two boys staying at Hon Ochom's house?' she asked.

The old man shook his head. 'No, but I heard that they were going to Arua and that the convoy would take them to Pakwach.' He paused again. 'When I was talking to the housekeeper, I found out that Hon Ochom has other houses in Gulu and even owns a soybean industry in Jinja,' the old man added.

'How much money did you spend altogether, excluding your fee, Mzee?' she asked.

'I only spent nine thousand shillings. I stayed at my daughter's house for the night,' the old man said quietly.

'You did well, Mzee Opio,' Joyce said as she reached into her bag and pulled out two ten–thousand-shilling notes and gave them to him.

'Thank you, Madam, thank you ...' he said, trying to kneel down.

'Don't do that, Mzee. Just go. When I need you, I will call you. Just remember our silence code,' she said, and then Mzee left through the back door.

Joyce reached for her gin and tonic. She was busy separating the useful information from the trash. By now the young man, Wilbur, had arrived in Arua. That was all fine with her as long as she didn't lose too much time.

Nyati Okello had sent a message to the LRA's camp asking the black Arabs to wait for some days for new business. They would arrive at the camp sometime tomorrow morning. She had to act quickly. Unfortunately, she had been informed that Nyati's group had been caught in an ambush with the Ugandan Army, and was wiped out, so she wasn't sure how to contact the rebel camp. She was still deep in thought when Steven arrived.

'What is it, Steven?' she asked without looking at him.

'Madam, the Assistant Commander managed to escape and is at the H-B safe house.'

Joyce turned fully and looked at Steven.

'He contacted me and I went there. From what he told me, Nyati had sent him to town for crude waragi and cigarettes. He bought the cigarettes but had a hard time finding the alcohol. After finding the waragi, he tied it on the bicycle and decided to ride in the direction his fellow rebels were heading, but all hell broke loose before he reached them. Apparently the rebels ran into an army convoy, which opened fire on them. The Assistant Commander decided to ride on high ground and pushed the bicycle through the bush until he got far enough to escape and get here,' Steven finished and took a deep breath.

'Steven, do you believe some might have survived? I am worried that they may be tortured enough to reveal that we are collaborators.'

'I don't know, but the Assistant Commander said that some were taken as prisoners. In any case, the only ones who know our names are Nyati and his assistant. Nyati is dead, so I wouldn't worry too much.'

'Remember, Steven, we are in this together. Don't think that just because you deliver messages you will get off free. This is a real war. Only the sharp ones will survive,' she said, drinking some more of the tonic. 'I already know about Nyati. I heard about the ambush,' she said, looking down.

Steven couldn't tell if his boss was remorseful or not. The lady was hard to read.

She looked up. 'I am glad that Nyati's assistant is alive. It will make things easier.' She paused. 'Now, Steven, listen to me carefully. Do you recall what we did last time we headed up north?' she asked.

He nodded. 'Yes, I remember everything, Madam.'

'I am leaving for Sudan in a few minutes. Do you still remember Fred's place?' she asked, and again he nodded. 'You will use the same way you took last time, and we shall meet there this evening. Bring the Assistant Commander,' she said as she looked at her watch. 'It's about four-thirty. If you move now, you should be able to arrive by seven. Use the bicycle—it's better. All the other things should be at the shop, so hurry,' she said, standing up. Steven left her.

She walked to her bedroom and changed into loose jeans and some sneakers. She also packed a few pairs of pants and T-shirts. She didn't expect to spend more than four days in Sudan. The fact that her friend Nyati was dead demanded that she go to the rebel camp in person, otherwise she wouldn't achieve anything. A plan was developing in her head slowly, but she would have to reach Lopodi before putting it into practice.

She walked outside her house, leaving her travel bags behind. She looked around before locking the door, a habit she picked up after the Ugandan Army ambushed her a while back in front of her door. She then walked to the motorcycle taxi station and called a fellow she knew who was also a rebel informer. She got on his motorcycle and headed for her bar. She told the man to wait for her as she made her way to her office in the back.

It took about fifteen minutes for her to finish all the things she had to do and to give the bartender instructions. He was used to handling the bar without her, so she wasn't worried about him. She then made her way to her shop and did the same. The young girl who relieved Steven sometimes was there. Joyce opened the drawer where the money was stored, put it in her bag and left. She didn't tell the girl much, only that she had given Steven an errand so she should close early.

They rode back to her house on the motorcycle. She picked up her bags and left, closing the door securely. The ride north was good, and they only saw a few people along the way. They stopped only once to push the motorcycle across a makeshift border that didn't have any sign.

Joyce was thinking about her mission. If the boy had already been sold, she would give the Arabs a lot of money to buy him back. They would accept it since they only paid ten to twenty dollars for each slave, which was pitiful.

She shook her head in disbelief. She did not approve of this slavery business. She believed in trading commodities, not people. She felt a quick pang of guilt for being a rebel collaborator. But what choice did she have? She had a business to run, and she didn't want any problems. Either way, she would hide Edgar while she renegotiated a higher price with Father Otim.

'Hey, Winston, move slower. I want to take a drink. I think better with something in my head,' she said, making the driver burst out laughing.

They were now in Sudan and less than ten miles from Lopodi. They moved slowly while Joyce thought about her plans for getting more money out of the Ochoms. She was very quiet, and Winston knew that normally when she got like this it was better to leave her alone. They finally arrived on the outskirts of Lopodi.

'Ms Joyce, should I take you to the same place where I took you last time?' Winston asked.

She glanced at him. 'So you remember, ah?' she joked.

'Yes, Madam, I don't forget anywhere I go during the day.'

'Okay, please take me to the place so you can go back before it's too late.'

After a few minutes they pulled into a long driveway and slowly proceeded to the house. She thanked Winston and gave him money before he left.

The lady of the house came out to greet Joyce and they embraced.

'How are you, Mama? It's been a long time. How is Mzee Thomas doing?' Joyce asked as they entered the house.

'He is all right, but he is always complaining of pain in his back. Otherwise he still goes to church daily,' the older woman said with a smile.

'Mama Rebecca, bring a glass. I brought some wine. I think you might even like it,' Joyce teased.

'Make yourself comfortable, my dear. I will be right back,' the older woman said, heading to the kitchen.

This wasn't the place that Joyce wanted to hide the boy, Edgar, but this was where she stayed whenever she came to the area. They were relatives. The older lady brought the glasses and poured the wine. Joyce drank very little. She had business to do. Besides, she knew her limits with alcohol. She just used it to keep the edge off.

'Mama, I want to meet people today for business before it gets late. I will leave my bags,' Joyce said, getting up and putting a bottle in her handbag.

'Come, my dear, I will get you a bicycle to town,' the older lady said, leading the way out of the house. They walked a little distance from the house before she called a boy and gave him instructions to escort her guest.

'Joyce, remember we will have dinner together,' the older lady shouted as she rushed back to the house.

Joyce walked with the boy until they arrived on the main street, where the boy hailed a bicycle for her. She thanked the boy as she got on the bicycle and headed towards the town.

She already knew how she would organize her trip to the rebel camp the next day. It had to be early so as to arrive there before midday. They finally arrived at the bar, and Joyce paid the rider. The fellow rode off very happy.

The bar owner, Fred Okot, saw Joyce and rushed towards her and embraced her. 'What do we have here? How are you, Joyce? You suddenly decided to grace us with a visit?'

'You look good for somebody who drinks daily,' she teased Fred with a smile.

'Oh, listen to you. What happened? You suddenly received the Holy Ghost?' he responded to her comment with a smile.

They entered the bar, which was surprisingly empty at six o'clock in the evening. 'Fred, where is everybody? Don't people drink here anymore?' she asked.

'They do, but most of them get here at seven or eight o'clock. Generally people here drink more on weekends. So, how is home and the rich folks there?'

It was funny how people in this part of Sudan regarded people in Uganda as rich folks.

'I brought you something,' she said, producing a bottle of Uganda Waragi from her bag.

Fred's eyes popped out of his head as he rushed to the bar and brought out two clean glasses. He again admired the liquor before he popped the top and poured some into both glasses. They drank and gossiped until Joyce realized that it was coming close to seven.

'Listen, Fred, I have a favor to ask you—actually, two favors,' she said.

'Go ahead,' Fred said.

'The first one is to give my two friends a place to stay tonight. I believe you remember Steven. He will be here with another friend. The next favor is about what brought me here today. I would like you to arrange a place nearby where a friend can stay for at least a month,' she said.

Fred was listening to his favorite girl as he sipped his favorite drink. He moved around to sit next to her.

'Of course you already know the answer to that, baby. Is there anything else, pretty girl?' he teased.

She had known Fred as long as she could remember. He had always been very nice to her and she liked him, but because of their childhood friendship she saw him more like a brother and could never have a romance with him.

'When are you getting married again, Fred? I heard that you have finally decided to take a companion since the untimely death of your wife, God bless her soul,' she said, looking at him intently.

'I don't think it will work out. She wants to go for further education,' Fred answered seriously. 'I wouldn't want to be accused of having interfered with her future goals, so I'm going to let her go,' he added, sipping his drink.

Fred tried to refill Joyce's glass, but she turned it down. 'No, Fred, that was for you. I have had enough today,' she added.

Joyce heard the sound of a metallic screech, and a minute later Steven entered followed by Nyati's assistant, whom she had never seen before, the reason being that it was always nighttime when she visited Nyati.

'Hello, strangers. We had started wondering where you were,' she said teasing with a big smile.

Steven interjected, 'Well, we took the longer way. Let me be the first to introduce Mr Masuma Lini, and, sir, this is my boss, Ms Joyce Akello, and her friend, Mr Fred Okot,' he said and stepped back. They all shook hands.

'Well, gentlemen, Joyce had mentioned your coming here, and you are very welcome. I will call somebody to make arrangements, but first, would any of you boys like some beer or waragi?' Fred asked as he moved behind the bar.

They both opted for beer, and he handed them bottles of Nile beer.

'Welcome to Lopodi, my brothers. Now, I will go and arrange your sleeping quarters,' he said as he walked to the back.

As soon as Fred was out of earshot, Joyce suggested they move to a table and turned to the Assistant Commander. 'I would like to know everything that happened. From the little I heard, it might have been a setup.'

Mr Lini nodded. 'The way I look at it, the reconnaissance didn't do its job because nobody informed us that the convoy was going to Kitgum. We blindly attacked the little centre, thinking that by the time the convoy came through we would be long gone,' he said and downed his beer.

Fred entered and announced that the rooms for the two gentlemen were ready. 'Now tell me, boys, how was your trip here?' Fred asked, trying to make conversation. He was completely oblivious of what they had been talking about.

'It was the usual,' Steven answered.

Joyce realized then that the conversation might get out of hand and decided to tactfully interrupt it. 'Say, Fred, don't you have some roasted chicken or meat here? These men are starving after the journey, and please, I insist on paying this time,' she added.

Fred was taken aback by the sudden change of topic. 'Well, we could roast a chicken for you. It will be ready in about fifteen minutes or—'

Joyce quickly interrupted him again. 'That's good, Fred. Can you get two more beers for the gentlemen and bottled water for me?' she asked, passing him some money. 'Oh, and Fred, you have some customers in the back,' she added as Fred returned and put drinks on their table.

'Duty is calling,' he said, hurrying away towards the customers.

Joyce turned to the soldier. 'Look, that ambush was strange. I will find out the leak as soon as I get back home. I am very saddened by the death of my dear friend,' she said, looking down. She took a sip of her water and turned to Steven.

'Steven, you will ride with me to where I am staying? As for you, Mr Lini, the sooner you go to bed the better. We have a long journey tomorrow. You can get your dinner sent to your rooms,' she said.

The soldier nodded. 'That sounds fine. I will retire to my room as soon as he shows it to me, and I will come with Steven to pick you up for our journey tomorrow morning.'

Fred came back smiling. 'It's a good night. The customers are multiplying.'

'Fred, how much do I owe you, including their sleeping quarters?' Joyce asked.

'Joyce, the money you gave me will cover everything including breakfast,' he answered, as he walked away.

'Now, Steven, drink up—we have to go. I need my sleep,' she said, looking at her watch.

She waved to Fred, who asked why she was leaving so early. She explained that she was tired and had to wake up early, and she promised to come back soon. She bid farewell to the soldier and then she walked to where Steven had parked his bicycle. During the ride to her auntie's house, Steven briefed her about their journey. She reminded him to bring Assistant Commander Lini very early the next day for their journey to the rebel camp.

Joyce didn't know where the new camp was due to constant relocations.

She apologized to Mama Rebecca for being late and explained how the people she went to meet had been delayed due to transportation problems. She greeted Mzee Thomas, and they ate while exchanging some stories before the old man retired to his bedroom for the night.

Mama Rebecca fed Joyce, and they gossiped about family and the news. It surprised Joyce that an old woman like Mama Rebecca knew about current events. She confided to Joyce that the rebels had restarted the old habit of capturing people from Uganda and selling them to Arabs who took them north to work on their farms. Mama Rebecca also told Joyce that she had heard from people that Joyce's name was mentioned among people who collaborated with the rebels.

'I beg you please, my daughter, be very careful. These boys cannot win if they are selling their own brothers and sisters,' she said tearfully.

Joyce embraced the old woman and tried to put her heart at rest. 'Mama, I only come here to see if I can do business with some merchants from Congo.'

Mama Rebecca showed Joyce to her bedroom and also showed her where they had put some warm water for her to wash up.

'But, Mama, don't you have anybody to help you? I see that you have too much work,' Joyce said, very concerned.

'I had a girl, but she ran away with a young man. Since then I haven't been able to get a replacement,' the older woman said.

'We shall see what we can do before I leave. Let me go and wash up,' Joyce said, picking up her towel.

'Sleep well, child,' Mama Rebecca said, closing her door.

Joyce washed up quickly and went straight to bed. But her mind couldn't rest. There was something that wasn't right about the events preceding Nyati's death. And how come somebody had mentioned her name to Mama Rebecca? *Could it be that somebody had seen her going to meet Nyati?* No, that was unlikely. She had been careful. She was sure that the leak wasn't in her town or the town of Madi Opel. *Then where is the leak?* Joyce's mind was working overtime.

Chapter 26

Joyce Akello lay in bed thinking about what Mama Rebecca had said. Being near the old woman had also brought up a lot of memories from her past. She started thinking about her youth.

Growing up, people always commented that Joyce should have been given more education by her late father. Unfortunately, he was only interested in getting some form of bride price by marrying her off to some peasant. As luck would have it, her auntie told her about her father's plans, and Joyce was able to escape.

That auntie was none other than Mama Rebecca. She had given Joyce five thousand Ugandan shillings, which at the time had some value, and told her to go to Kampala and try to get involved in business with her uncle.

Joyce had escaped to Kampala and rented a little room next to her uncle's residence. She started a business selling lunch and breakfast to construction workers. Using three thousand shillings, which was a lot of money at the time, she was able to buy plates, cups, and saucepans. She operated in the shade of papyrus reeds and an old tent that she had purchased for only four hundred shillings. She acquired the benches and tables from an old lady who had decided to sell her business.

After some time, her business prospered. She moved into a real building and even hired some help. She finally decided to introduce herself to the uncle who lived only a few blocks away. At first her uncle was angry because Joyce had stayed nearby for many months without telling him, but he was also amazed at how far she had come in business. She simply told him that she didn't introduce herself to him because she didn't want to be kidnapped and married off to an old man for two mere cows.

Her uncle had laughed very hard, and the two of them had walked to inspect her business. They became very close associates. All these thoughts passed through Joyce's mind as she lay in bed. She laughed heartily, as she remembered her history; tears came to her eyes.

The experience had taught her a big lesson, so she saved her money at a bank nearby and business kept getting better. A short while later, she moved into a permanent structure with cement floors that had pretty colors to make people feel at home. She even hung up big posters in town advertising her business. She managed to retain her customers by offering them credit. Her uncle was in the food transportation business, which suited Joyce very well because she became one of his customers.

When her uncle died two years later, Joyce quickly took over his transportation business and also kept the restaurant. She was very discreet and never told her employees anything other than what they needed to know for their job. Joyce was deadly serious when it came to business. When people tried to rip her off, she had them either arrested or beaten up until they paid her money in full.

During her uncle's funeral, her father tried to patch things up with her, but she never forgave him for trying to sell her off as a commodity. That was one of the reasons she was against what Kony was doing, but she kept those thoughts to herself. After all, she had a business to run in a tough area. She later gave her auntie Mama Rebecca all her money back and even offered her a partnership in Kampala, but her auntie turned her down.

The laughing brought Mama Rebecca to her room.

'Joyce, my child, what's the matter? I heard you laughing all the way from my room. Are you all right, baby?' she asked, coming closer to Joyce's bed.

Joyce sat up, still laughing. 'Auntie, I'm sorry if I woke you up. I was remembering when my father almost married me off to that old man and you gave me money to run away to Kampala,' she said, hardly containing her laughter. Mama Rebecca was already falling over the bed laughing before Joyce finished the sentence.

'I even went to Uncle's house but didn't enter because I was worried that he would kidnap me and send me back,' Joyce said, still laughing. 'I think I told you this,' she said.

By now, Joyce and her auntie were laughing so hard tears were streaming down their cheeks.

'Auntie, I want to tell you something,' she said after collecting herself. She was thinking of a way to say what she had to say properly.

'What is it, my child?' the old lady inquired

'Auntie, when I moved back home from Kampala, I really thought that the rebels and their intentions were noble. I agreed to collaborate with them not because I believed in them totally but because I also wanted to survive without trouble. They were strong then. Now I have come to the conclusion that they are misguided and can never win, so I will find a way out.' She paused and looked at her auntie.

'I was also thinking that I am not getting any younger, and I need family around me. Have you and Uncle thought about moving back?' she asked, looking at her aunt intently.

Mama Rebecca was taken by surprise but was also glad because she and her husband had indeed decided to move back to Uganda.

'Yes, my child. In fact, we have already decided to go back home, so we are in the process of selling this small place,' she answered.

They both embraced, tears running down their cheeks freely.

'I assure you my daughter, we shall be together. Now go to sleep,' Mama Rebecca said as she covered her niece. She stayed there until she was sure Joyce was asleep, and then she went to her bedroom.

Joyce woke up early to go to the bathroom. She looked at her watch and saw it was six-thirty in the morning. She realized that her fellow travelers would be coming anytime. She quickly washed her face up and brushed her teeth before going back to her room to put on fresh clothes. She was glad she had taken a bath the night before. She put some money in an envelope and put it on the bed.

She didn't feel quite as strong this morning. She hoped Steven had packed some water and snacks for her as she had requested. She slowly picked up her two bags and walked towards the door.

Before she could open it, someone pulled it from the other side and she came face to face with Mama Rebecca.

'Mama, I wasn't going to leave without telling you. I just got ready early because I have to wind up this business I started. I will also see if we can solve that housekeeper problem when I get back,' she whispered to her auntie.

'Just be careful, baby. Remember not to say too much,' her auntie said, embracing her. 'Come, let's go—there are two people on bicycles waiting for you,' she added as they closed the door and walked to the main doorway leading out of the house.

'Mama, please say bye to Uncle for me, and go look on my bed. I left a letter for you.' Joyce said and they embraced again.

Joyce sat on the soldier's bicycle carrier and rode away, waving to her auntie. Steven followed them. They exchanged greetings as they rode side by side.

'So, how was your night, gentlemen?' Joyce asked.

'Very well rested, aren't we, Steven?' asked the soldier.

'Yup, I feel very well except for a little hangover from last night.'

'Steven, I want you sober until I get back. We have work to do but right now I have a little business to do with the black Arabs at the camp, so I will be gone for about two days,' she said as they were coming to the intersection where they would part ways. Steven gave her a plastic bag of drinks and snacks.

'Please keep watch over the business and keep your mouth shut,' Joyce Akello advised Steven as they said goodbye to one another.

During the journey, Assistant Commander Lini revealed a lot of things to Joyce Akello that she didn't know. She found out that all the Commanders she knew were still at the camp, including Commanders Beba-Beba and Nyoka Kali.

Lini also told her that the provision of weapons had not been forthcoming, and that was one of the reasons why Kony had resorted to doing anything that would give him money to buy weapons. He told her about plans to capture as many schoolgirls as possible to be used in harems owned by powerful warlords up north.

The failed mission of Nyati and Masuma Lini had been designed to destabilize the Ugandan Army and take them on a wild goose chase while the other Commanders got ready to go to numerous schools in Kitgum and Gulu to abduct young girls.

This information made Joyce sick to her stomach because it reminded her of what almost happened to her as a young, innocent girl. She also knew that these rebels would amuse themselves with the young girls before selling them off to the Arabs as prostitutes.

They rode for about three hours before they finally reached the outskirts of the town of Logo Forok. The Assistant Commander didn't want to go through the town because the area chief had started to work with the SPLA and trouble could start at the sight of strangers, so they took a different route through the mountains.

The journey was hard, especially the part that included climbing hills and negotiating rocky trails. They couldn't use the bike going uphill, so they stopped many times so Joyce Akello could rest. She had spent years without doing exercise, and this was backbreaking.

'Tell me, Masuma, do you usually go through this pain every time you go back and forth to your camps?' she asked.

He nodded. 'We sometimes travel even farther into Sudan to pick up weapons and ammunition,' he said as he sipped some alcoholic drink.

'You shouldn't drink so much. It plays with your judgment, and since you carry a gun it's not a good idea. I could give you some water,' she said, reaching for her bag.

'No, Ms Joyce, but I promise not to drink again until we arrive at the camp,' he said, standing up. 'We only have a couple more miles, and then the rest of the journey will be downhill,' he said as he gave her a hand.

She stood up and they started walking again. She was happy she was wearing sneakers instead of her usual high heels. The higher they went, the colder it became, so Joyce put on a sweater. They finally started riding downhill, moving deeper and deeper into the dense forest.

They had just started walking again when suddenly soldiers in camouflage uniforms stopped them at gunpoint. After a brief period, their leader saluted Masuma Lini and the conversation became friendly as they escorted them to the rebel camp. The little encounter with rebels lying in ambush convinced Joyce to finish this little deal as soon as possible and head as far away as she could to rejoin civilian life.

They continued their journey and arrived at the LRA's camp around three p.m. The soldier leading them pointed to a little white tent on the outskirts of the rebel camp. Lini mentioned that it belonged to the black Arab, Mr Hamis Ali, who was camped with his horses, waiting for a chance to negotiate with Kony.

Lini left her in a tent and went to meet Kony and explain the tragic episode that had occurred near Kitgum. This made Kony very upset until he received news that Joyce Akello had come to the camp and could give him firsthand information about the matter. He told Masuma to let her in immediately.

Kony greeted her warmly and immediately asked her what happened.

'My lord, I would like to say that what happened to Nyati Okello confused me and has indeed disturbed me completely.' She paused to see if she had the man's attention. 'When he arrived, I paid him a visit and he was in good spirits. It's best to assume that somebody gave him wrong information,' she said.

Kony nodded his head in agreement. 'I already know who told him to attack, and I will deal with them,' he said. 'Now let us go. I have some business to do with Hamis. By the way, what's the name of the boy you want bought back?' he asked casually.

Joyce reached for the bag and pulled out a piece of paper. 'My lord, the name is Edgar Lapyem,' she answered.

Kony regarded the woman for a minute. 'Are you sure that by retrieving this one person you won't be opening a can of worms?' he asked thoughtfully.

'Yes, my lord, I am sure it will be safe. Otherwise I wouldn't have agreed to try,' she answered.

'All right, let's go to the courtyard where we will do business,' he said.

The people were already seated in the courtyard and waiting for Kony. Joyce had never been in such a courtyard gathering. Normally when she dealt with any of the Commanders they talked one on one. The strangest thing was that Kony had an interpreter for the exchange with the Arabs. They negotiated prices on young men and women, and finally they bargained on guns.

Joyce bid her time, and finally Kony asked about a slave named Edgar Lapyem. Joyce told them when she thought the young man had been taken. There was a discussion among the black Arabs, and finally they agreed that they could buy the slave back. Joyce had already put five hundred dollars aside, so she gave it to Kony, who in turn gave it to the Arabs with a warning not to play any games and to deliver the boy unharmed.

The meeting came to an abrupt end, and Kony took his guns and ammunition. The Arabs took the slaves to their tent and prepared to depart.

'Akello, I shall send a message to you about the boy. If he is still alive, you will get him. Now go to Mama's quarters and rest,' Kony said as he left with his Commanders to plan another operation. Mama was Kony's witchdoctor and only someone he respected could sleep in her quarters.

The next morning, Kony instructed some of his men to walk Joyce up to the outskirts of Lopodi. The journey home wasn't hard, but Joyce promised herself never to go on such an adventure ever again.

Chapter 27

Al-Hajj Abdul sat on a homemade wooden chair in his enclosed compound and digested all the information he had attained about the slave market. A few days ago he had sent two small-time traders to investigate the movement of slaves in the past month on the pretext of buying them again for the purpose of cultivating his farm.

He had given them some money and promised them more when he achieved results. Their other mission was to try to approach the Mullahs with the pretext of selling them goods. He had also given them Edgar's picture and asked them to be on the lookout for him. Al-Hajj knew that at some point they may have to negotiate with the Mullahs, who could even double-cross them.

These things could only be solved by a few people with much more influence and power than him. He felt drained with the puzzles in his head. He tried to think of how he could make a good attempt without causing too much damage or even totally failing in his mission, which was something he could not afford under the circumstances.

Isaac Ochom, the father of the young man, Wilbur, had helped Al-Hajj Abdul and his family escape from Sudan to Uganda during the war a few years back. They were able to live in Arua and Pakwach for some time before they returned to Nimule.

At the time, Isaac Ochom worked for the Uganda Transport Service as a Chief Officer in northern Uganda. He had personally authorized two trucks to cross to Nimule and retrieve Al-Hajj Abdul's family and his property when the war was going on and machine guns were blasting away.

This kind man had later provided a house to him free of charge for a period of two years. The way Al-Hajj Abdul looked at it, this was his opportunity to return a favor. He would risk his own life to help Isaac Ochom. Al-Hajj Abdul shook his head and then turned around.

'Amina! Please call Ghani. I want to ask him something,' he ordered a young girl who was cleaning nearby.

The girl quickly disappeared in search of Ghani. Ghani arrived after some time, bringing with him a pot of tea.

'So, son, you bring me tea before briefing me about your trip?'

Ghani didn't know what to say. He knew his father's temperament very well, and right now Al-Hajj Abdul was very serious.

'Sir, I wanted to leave you alone until you called me yourself, having heard that you'd just come back from a journey,' he answered quietly.

'Son, get yourself a cup and bring something to sit on!' he ordered.

Ghani ran inside the house and then brought out a mat and a cup. He put the mat in front of Al-Hajj Abdul and sat down.

'Pour yourself some tea, son.' Ghani poured himself a little tea and refilled his father's cup. 'Ghani, I need to know everything that happened. You followed Hassan Lara until Magwe?' Al-Hajj asked.

'Yes, sir, I was in a different taxi, so he never knew I was following him. I stopped after he hired a motorcycle. I asked people where Yasin (the motorcycle owner) had gone, pretending to be a friend, and I found out they were heading towards Hassan's town using a shortcut.'

Al-Hajj Abdul nodded and sipped his tea. 'That is a clever young man. I am impressed. The other route is very dangerous if one is carrying money,' he said. Then he looked seriously at his son. 'So how much did you find out in Magwe about slavery in Kinyeti?'

Ghani sipped some tea before he answered. 'Sir, I didn't find much in Magwe, so I proceeded to Ngarama, where I found out that another group had just gone by. I carefully asked about the slave trade market, pretending to be buying some for my boss.' He paused. 'I found out that they have made only one trip in the past month, but this time they only brought girls and boys. All the slaves were bought by a black Arab called Hamis Ali, who sometimes supplies guns to the rebels.'

Al-Hajj Abdul nodded his head in understanding and looked at his son. 'So they go by the Ngarama area to avoid running into the SPLA soldiers?'

'Yes, sir. There is a tale of an incident that happened to Hamis Ali which almost finished off his men when they crossed into the area belonging to the Liberation Army of Machair,' he answered.

'Now tell me, how do they move from Ngarama to the north? That is a very long distance?' Al-Hajj Abdul asked.

Ghani sipped his tea, hesitating to answer. 'Sir, I thought you might ask this question, so I got the information for you. There is a businessman there who has a big truck. He modified the truck so that it is rigged with wire mesh and covered all round with a tent. He rents it to Hamis, who loads it with slaves and drives them to a slave marketplace in the north.'

'You mean this man Hamis Ali doesn't have any problem with the government soldiers?' Al-Hajj Abdul asked.

Ghani shook his head. 'There is a rumor that Hamis sometimes takes packages of ammunition and guns to some other rebels supported by the government of Sudan, so he is given special treatment and can trade in anything he wants.'

Al-Hajj Abdul kept nodding his head as he listened to his son.

Ghani looked at his father. 'According to my source, Hamis started out as a go-between for the government and the rebels, but later on he started getting involved in slavery after realizing the tremendous profit in human trading.'

'Tell me, son, what did you find out about the powerful warlord Abasi El Mafi ? Does he have a hand in all this?'

Ghani shook his head, 'No, sir. Apparently Abasi El Mafi only deals in minerals and skins. I hear he has powerful fighters so the SPLA and the government leave him alone with his illegal business,' Ghani said.

Al-Hajj Abdul nodded.

'It is said that Abasi would sell his own mother for money,' Ghani added.

Al-Hajj Abdul smiled and stood up slowly. 'You did well, my son. I'm going to rest, Ghani. I will need you later,' he said, walking to the house.

'Okay, sir,' Ghani said, relieved that his father had approved of his work.

Chapter 28

Over the past two days, the three friends had had a small disagreement about the goods to take to Sudan, but they had finally agreed to do what Edgar would have done. He wouldn't have touched an animal skin for anything. During his final years at school, he had joined a lot of international groups supporting the preservation of wildlife.

All of them were feeling impatient and restless. They had been staying at the Arua Inn for three days and had done nothing besides taking in a few sights. They were eager for some kind of adventure, so they were looking forward to the trip to Aru, a small town which was located on the border of Uganda and Congo. They were going with Juma, another son of Al-Hajj Abdul who lived nearby.

They arrived at Juma's shop at eight-thirty. They had decided to stay booked at the hotel for three extra days, during which they hoped to have returned from this little trip.

'Morning, boys, how are you today? Are you ready to go?' Juma asked.

'Yes. How about you?' Wilbur asked.

'Almost. Let me get a few things, and then we will head out.' Juma was about to leave when Wilbur stopped him.

'Oh, by the way, Juma, we decided that we will only buy minerals.'

Juma stopped and turned around. 'Are you sure? You know, if the skins are well preserved, there are hardly any risks and the profits are tremendous.'

'Yes, we are positive. No animal skins,' Sam said in a serious tone.

Juma shrugged. 'Okay. I will be right back,' he said as he disappeared into the back room of his shop. Sam gathered that Juma, being a businessman, was disappointed because the profits on minerals wouldn't be as good as that on leather.

The boys had brought their passports in case they ran into a roadblock. Wilbur had reminded them of the war that Uganda was waging in Congo and had told them that being caught without any documents would be tantamount to being a rebel.

Juma Bin Asuman joined them after saying goodbye to his wife, and together they walked towards the taxi station.

'Gentlemen, this business we are going to do is not like buying cigarettes. If a person isn't double-crossed by the dealers, he is betrayed by his own mouth, so please talk about the weather or cars and nothing about why we are going to Aru,' Juma said as they neared the taxi station.

Sam, John, and Wilbur exchanged looks and smiled. The four boys, including Edgar, had always done things together and never uttered their business in public. Juma didn't know that they lived by a code of silence, even more so with this mission.

'Of course,' Wilbur agreed quietly.

'Good. We will board the taxi to Aru. It's more than a hundred miles south-west of here,' he finished quickly when they reached the taxi station.

The four of them got in the backseat of the minibus, and in about ten minutes the minibus was full. Most of the people in the taxi were women who went to Congo regularly to buy cheap textiles and sell them at a higher price in Kampala. Others were men with different business goods to sell in Congo, like radios, televisions, and watches, which were very much in demand.

The little, fully loaded minibus went slowly, so it was good that they had bought newspapers to read on the way. Wilbur had also borrowed a Time magazine from his new friend Caroline, with whom he had been spending time.

The scenery from Arua all the way to Aru was beautiful, with rolling hills which were cultivated with different kinds of food crops. This area was fertile because of the tributaries from the River Nile. The three boys were busy either admiring the scenery or reading.

Two hours into their trip, they came across a roadblock that was manned by military police. As agreed earlier, they said they were visiting a teacher in Arua but had decided to do some sightseeing as well. After the police did some light checking of the luggage, the minibus was let through and arrived at the Aru taxi station a little while later. They disembarked.

'Gentlemen, let's get a hotel in case we don't reach our objective today,' Juma said. The boys obediently followed Juma to the hotel which looked new and clean. It was cheap, so Sam quickly paid for four rooms and gave each one of them a key.

'Why don't we put the bags in one room so that we can proceed without wasting any time?' he suggested.

'Good idea,' Juma agreed.

John and Sam took both bags to John's room and hurried back.

All four quickly got motorcycle taxis and followed the leading cycle, which carried Juma. Aru was a small town built on both sides of the border, but business was more on the Ugandan side. When they arrived at the Boringo Club, Juma stopped the cycles and paid them.

'Gentlemen, we shall enter through the back. The owner of the bar is called Zambe, and he deals in gold. I brought concentrated nitric acid so we can test the gold before we buy. All right, let's go in,' he said, entering the bar. It was dimly lit and had a small dancing floor in the back.

The four of them got a table in the corner, and Sam asked Juma if he wanted a cold beer. Juma gratefully declined but clarified his position.

'I'm not as religious as my father. Once in a while I drink, but I don't usually drink before business.'

Sam ordered soft drinks for each of them and also asked if they could talk to Mr Zambe. The waiter said that Mr Zambe would be around in a few minutes and could they kindly wait for him.

Sam turned to Juma when the waiter left. 'Hey, Juma, is everybody really polite around here, or is it my imagination?'

Juma glanced around and said, 'Well, first of all his boss would be very pissed off if he didn't please his clients, and another possibility is that he is polite so that you will choose to stay and spend money.' All of them laughed at Juma's simple explanation.

Juma cleared his throat. 'Okay, gentlemen, let's get serious. For every game there are rules. When dealing with precious metals around here, you never reveal in advance how much you want to buy or how much money you have. What you do is negotiate for an ounce and then proceed from there, one step at a time,' Juma finished.

The boys were listening to him intently.

'Does he negotiate right here or somewhere else?' Sam asked.

Juma shrugged. 'Well, you only go to the private room after having an understanding per ounce. It's better to pretend that you want ten or fifteen ounces at a time rather than buying a kilogram or so,' Juma answered. He observed the questions on the young men's faces, especially on John's.

'It sounds like a risky business to me. We could keep our money and forget it,' John quipped.

Juma shook his head. 'I've dealt with this guy before on numerous occasions. He is okay. What I wanted to get across to you is how the game is played in case you do business while I'm not here,' he added, smiling. 'Gold is addictive just like cigarettes or alcohol. Sooner or later you will be back, mark my words,' he finished and sipped his drink.

They listened to music for a little while.

Although Wilbur knew vaguely how gold was tested to make sure it was pure, he still asked how it was done, so Juma explained it to him. Wilbur was happy that Juma's explanation coincided with his knowledge.

'How much does this fellow sell an ounce for, Juma? The last I heard gold had lost value on the world market,' Wilbur asked.

'I have bought an ounce for anywhere between $100 and $140. Before this hopeless war, I went even further into Congo, where I acquired it for as little as $50 or $60 an ounce and took it to Nimule, where I sold it for $200, no questions asked,' he answered.

In Wilbur's mind a lot of things made sense now. Juma had a little shop that sold cigarettes and soft drinks, but the man was knowledgeable, smart, and clearly had money. Wilbur was now sure that the little shop was a mere front.

'Juma, have you ever gone to Mahagi? Are the prices different?' he asked.

Juma hesitated and looked around. 'Yes, I have gone there, but I haven't been there since this damn war. The town is too militarized now. It isn't too far, though,' he answered. Sam looked at his watch. It was almost one-thirty, which meant that if Mr Zambe didn't come in soon they would have to spend the night, which was something they had hoped to avoid.

'So, tell me. How did you boys like the women in Arua? I saw you at the club. It was disappointing that the girls all left—not even one stayed!' Juma said, shaking his head. Everyone started laughing except Sam.

'Wait a minute, Juma, how did you know it was us?' Sam asked.

Juma sipped his drink rubbing tears out of his eyes. 'I guessed you were the ones my father had told me about. You fellows must be very important to him. The man has spent at least three years without coming to Arua, but he came to see you. He told me that some young men would be calling on me. That's all he said, but I wanted to know more so I had a young lady go to the Arua Inn and inquire about three young men staying there. The rest, as they say, is history.'

Wilbur shook his head in disbelief.

Sam just smiled. 'Do you and your father have a special school of investigation? I may consider joining it in the future,' Sam said jokingly.

Juma's eyes suddenly became serious; he was looking in the direction of the bar. 'Well, gents, there is our man. He will be coming over here anytime.'

All eyes turned towards the man talking to the bartender. He was dressed in a suit cut in the Congolese style. The man was almost six feet tall, light skinned and of medium weight. He appeared confident and unhurried. The man turned around and walked over to their table.

'Gentlemen, I apologize for the delay,' he said.

All four stood up to greet him. 'No need to apologize, we didn't have an appointment with you. Besides, these are hard days, so we are glad you are here,' Juma said, and then he introduced everyone to Mr Zambe.

'I am Zambe, but my friends call me Z,' he joked as he flicked his fingers to the waiter. The waiter brought them some drinks and quickly left.

'I wouldn't want to waste your time or ours, Zambe,' Juma began. 'We came here to see if you have some gold,' he added.

Mr Zambe took his drink slowly as if he hadn't heard, and then he smiled. 'Juma, you don't have to talk to me like that. You and I know what we deal in. It would be better to talk about quantity and money,' he said slowly, still holding his glass.

'Zambe, gold has been sliding and has not stabilized, so that means that unless one is smart there is a big chance of falling into a loss,' Juma said as he sipped his drink and handed Zambe the newspaper with the gold price quote.

Mr Zambe merely glanced at the paper and gave it back. 'I understand, trust me. I have also conveyed this to the people I buy from, so let's get to the business at hand. How does $120 an ounce sound?'

Wilbur shook his head. 'I think eighty bucks would be more realistic since most people are waiting to see how far it will slide,' he said.

Mr Zambe looked at Wilbur. 'I can't do it at that price, young man. The least I would sell it for now would be $100. I am willing to wait for the prices to stabilize.'

Sam and Wilbur looked at each other, and Juma shrugged his thick shoulders. John had decided that he wouldn't get involved in the matter.

'Mr Zambe, can we view the substance?' Wilbur asked, looking at his watch.

'Sure, let's go in my office.'

They all left the table and walked towards the back. The office was directly behind the bar. One had to move slowly to avoid hitting the crates of bottles lined up in the hallway.

'Gentlemen, you are welcome,' Zambe said as he offered them seats. He moved behind his desk and then tried out the combination of the safe that was located under the table. He pulled out a little box, opened it, removed a little batch of yellow stones, and put the stones on a tray.

'You boys want to test it to be sure?' he asked. Wilbur nodded.

Juma opened his bag and removed a little bottle containing acid, and then he took a small paper from his back pocket and gave it all to Wilbur who walked towards the table and put the paper on the tray next to the stones. He opened the bottle and poured the content onto the paper. The paper suddenly caught fire.

'Mr Zambe, can I test all of it?' he asked.

'It's up to you, young man,' Zambe answered with a smile.

Wilbur carefully used a steel spoon to gather the small stones together and then poured the acid on them. There wasn't any change. If anything, they were a little brighter.

'Mr Zambe, this is pure gold. Don't get me wrong, but you are the one who reached into the box. I would feel much better if I tested all the contents in the box,' Wilbur said with a little smile.

'Certainly, young man,' Zambe said, pushing the box towards Wilbur.

Wilbur opened it and used the spoon to test a little from each corner and did the same with middle. The results were the same.

'Thank you, Mr Zambe. I'm convinced. Can we measure everything?' he asked as he motioned Juma to pass him the small weighing machine that they had brought with them.

Afterwards, Wilbur handed fifteen hundred dollars to Mr Zambe, who was still smiling. Zambe counted the money and handed the gold to Wilbur.

'Thank you very much, gentlemen. It's been an immense pleasure doing business with you,' he said, offering his hand for a handshake.

'The same for us, Mr Zambe,' Wilbur said. With Sam's help, he carefully put the gold in another small bottle.

They put everything in their small travel case and left soon after. They retrieved their bags from the hotel saying urgent business had come up, and proceeded directly to the taxi stand.

Chapter 29

The journey back to Arua was uneventful, though the minibus was loaded with passengers so much so that it could barely move. Again it was Juma who kept them busy talking about the news. Luckily the roadblock had been dismantled so they were not checked.

'So, you boys never answered me. Do you intend to see the girls again or not?' he asked.

The boys looked at one another, undecided about what to say.

Finally Sam answered. 'Well, Juma, why not? They are beautiful. But, with the loud music in the club I barely got their names,' he said, drawing laughter from his friends.

The rest of the journey was full of jokes combined with the uncertainties of dating nowadays.

'These days you have to do an investigation on anyone you date; find out who she has dated and if her ex-boyfriend is alive or sick or dead. The whole thing is complicated,' Wilbur said, shaking his head and looking outside the window.

'Say, what you are thinking about, Willy?' Juma said.

Wilbur hesitated a little but gave in. 'I was wondering why people capable of making rockets and spaceships are unable to find medicine for this killer disease,' he said angrily.

All of them shrugged.

'Willy, are you sure it's not just your frustration coming out?' John asked, looking at his friend closely.

'Maybe you are right, John, but this thing is making the best years of my life very dull, that's for sure,' he answered.

'I have a suggestion to make!' Juma intervened seriously.

The boys looked at him in anticipation. 'Finish what you are doing as soon as possible and get married,' he stated. The few passengers near them agreed by muttering and nodding their heads.

'Well, I guess that's what we will have to live with for the rest of our lifetime,' Wilbur said.

The taxi finally got to Arua, and the four got out. Juma tried to shake their hands, but the boys refused to take his hand and insisted he come into the hotel to unwind with them. He agreed. John took the travel bag up to his room.

Wilbur stepped over to the reception and talked to Caroline a bit as the others continued to the restaurant.

'Mr Ochom … ah, Wilbur, sorry, you received a message. Would you like to have it now?' she asked.

'Oh sure, thanks,' he answered as he reached for the note from her.

'Caroline, thank you for the outing with your friends. I will see you a little later. Please excuse me,' he smiled and then walked towards the restaurant.

The boys were seated at their usual place in the corner.

Wilbur pulled up a chair and motioned to the waiter for a drink. John joined them a few moments later, after making sure that the contents of the travel bag were securely locked in his big suitcase.

The waiter served them and left.

'Gentlemen, I have a message from Kampala. We are receiving a visitor today,' Wilbur said, sipping on his beer.

'That's great news, Willy. This waiting was beginning to get me down,' John said cheerfully.

'Yup, I agree. That's fantastic news,' Sam added.

Wilbur had been thinking of a way to thank Juma without offending him. Clearly Juma didn't need the money.

'Juma, there must be a way for us to express our appreciation,' Wilbur said in a quiet voice.

Juma cleared his throat and smiled. 'Wilbur, I will come straight with you. I did this for my father, so I'm sorry, but in this case, gratitude is not necessary,' he said candidly as he sipped his drink.

'Thank you for taking us to Aru,' John said as the others nodded in agreement.

'You are welcome,' Juma said. 'Well, gentlemen, I have to get home now. I will keep in touch. Please don't leave without saying goodbye,' Juma said, pushing back his chair. They all stood up and shook his hand.

'See you soon, Juma,' Sam shouted as Juma left.

'A very principled man he is. Just like his father,' John stated quietly. The rest nodded.

'So who exactly is coming here to see us today?' Sam asked as he looked at his watch.

'The note didn't say, though I believe it's someone we know. The person is coming by air, so he should be here soon,' Wilbur said.

Shortly after Juma left, the waiter came to their table with a note and handed it to Wilbur, who read it and smiled before he got to his feet.

'Gentlemen, I have a surprise for you!' he announced and headed out. At first he didn't see her as he approached the reception, but he turned and there she was, his cousin, sitting on a sofa and reading a magazine.

'Lillian?' he asked, not very sure of himself.

'Willy!' she shouted as she jumped up and hugged him.

They looked at each other and hugged again.

'Lilly, I am really happy to see you, but why did Uncle send you all this way? Couldn't he find somebody else?' Wilbur said with concern.

'I insisted on coming,' she said with tears in her eyes. Wilbur pulled out his handkerchief and handed it to her.

'Lilly! Why in hell are you crying?' Wilbur asked. She hesitated a little.

'Please, tell me,' he pleaded.

'Well, the ambush you fell into was shown on the television and it was all over the newspapers,' she said quietly.

'You mean they mentioned my name?'

She shook her head. 'Dad called Captain Aine, and he told Dad everything.'

'I must admit it was rough, but I am okay, as you can see, Lilly. Now, where is your bag?' he asked.

'Oh, I already checked in. I got a room next to your three rooms,' she said.

Wilbur looked at his cousin seriously. 'I want you to know that I am fine and luckily I did not kill anybody.'

She looked up at him and nodded.

'Good, get your purse and let's go and join the others. You look different—I nearly didn't recognize you,' he said.

'What do you mean? I don't look good?' she asked as they entered the restaurant.

'Not that. You look more mature.'

'I see you guys are pretty comfortable,' Lillian said teasingly.

John and Sam's eyes suddenly opened wide when they saw who their visitor was. They stood up to greet Lillian joyously.

'Lillian, I will be honest, you really look smashing. Let me see. Did you do something with your hair?' Sam asked as he sat down.

Lillian looked down in embarrassment. 'Guys, stop looking at me like that. I only removed the braids. That's all.'

'Okay, Lillian. Can I have the pleasure of ordering you a drink?' John asked.

'Well, I will take some white wine since Dad isn't here,' she answered with a smile.

John ordered their drinks, and the waiter disappeared to get them.

'Father gave me a letter to bring to you,' Lillian said as she reached into her purse. 'And he made me promise that you won't read it in my presence, so please don't read it now,' she added as she put an envelope on the table in front of them.

John reached for it and put it into his pocket. The waiter arrived with their drinks, and they asked Lillian what was happening in the city.

'Not much has really changed except that you guys are not there,' she said with a smile. Everybody burst out laughing.

'That's the city, all right! It never waits for anybody,' Sam said jokingly.

'How is Uncle?' Wilbur asked.

'Stronger than all of us, I'm afraid. He has been working on something important. I don't know what it is, but he asked for a holiday. He told me to tell you that he informed all your families that you are well.' She turned to her cousin. 'I spoke to Uncle before

I came. He sends you his greetings and cautions you to be careful,' she added. Wilbur smiled.

'Lillian, you must be hungry. We haven't eaten anything since breakfast, before we went to Aru. Would you do us the honor of dining with us?' Sam asked.

'It would be my pleasure … Aru? But … oh, please forgive me. I don't have the right to ask. I don't mind having dinner with you guys, but you probably want to discuss some things,' she said quietly.

'Oh, come on, Lilly, this is us. Don't behave like a stranger with me—I won't accept it,' Wilbur said forcefully. 'We went to the little town of Aru this morning to meet a man who might help us in what we are doing,' he added.

She smiled. 'Thanks for telling me. Unfortunately, I have to leave immediately after dinner and go to sleep. I am taking an early flight back,' she said with a smile.

The waiter came and they ordered some food. Sam gave Lillian a phone number and a message to give to his parents. John did the same for his uncle and sister.

Their dinner was delicious as usual—rice, beef stew, and some salad.

After the meal, Lillian stood up. 'Well, I have to go and sleep. I will have to wake up very early to make the flight. Please take care of yourselves and I hope you find Eddie,' she said, giving each one a hug before she walked away.

'Just a minute, cousin, I will walk you to your room,' Wilbur said, running up behind her. 'Look, Lillian, we are going to read Uncle's letter and answer it. I will slip his letter under your door,' Wilbur said as they reached her room. Wilbur gave his cousin a big hug, promising to see her soon. He turned back and hurried towards the restaurant.

'Okay, guys, let's read the letter and then answer it so that Lillian can take our reply with her,' he said as he sat down and drank his beer.

John carefully opened the letter and started reading it. The letter stated that Wilbur's uncle had made an investigation. Through a person who had worked with Ms Akello for a long time, he had found out that she tried to get Edgar back but was too late. Edgar had already been sold into slavery. The Honorable advised them to let Al-Hajj Abdul Asuman and Al-Hajj Musa Lara do the dealing. He further reminded them that there was still time to change their minds if this course was too much for them.

Tears were running down John's cheeks when he finished reading.

'The bastards!' shouted Sam as he shook his head.

Wilbur was also sad, but he mostly felt a lot of anger towards Joyce Akello. She had not even contacted Father Otim to tell him this. *What kind of game was she playing?*

They ordered more beers and tried to calm their nerves by chugging them down. Neither of them was a big drinker, but this depressing news called for it.

John left and came back shortly with a piece of paper and an envelope. Wilbur took a pen and the paper, but before writing he looked around at his friends and waited.

'Our efforts to rescue Edgar by approaching the rebel collaborators haven't worked,' Wilbur said with sadness. 'The way I see it, we have two choices. One is to go all the way to Sudan and keep looking and the other is to bail out now.'

He took a sip of his drink and paused a little. 'Who thinks we have done enough and should bail out?' He looked at his friends. Neither of them moved. 'We shall continue, then,' he stated and they all nodded.

'Was that really necessary, Willy?' John asked.

Wilbur nodded. 'Unfortunately it was very necessary, however cruel it sounded. I needed to make sure that we were still of the same mind.'

They drafted the letter, explaining how they had met Al-Hajj Abdul when he came to visit them at the Arua Inn and that Al-Hajj Abdul had already sent people to the slave camps up north to get more information about the whereabouts of Edgar. They then thanked Hon Ochom for all his help and told him that they had decided to proceed to Sudan the next day. They also mentioned that they had acquired a little gold, in case currency became hard to negotiate with in Sudan.

They finally signed the letter—all three of them—and put it in the envelope, then they drank their beer in silence, each in deep thought. The news about Eddie had depressed them. It was Wilbur who broke the silence. 'Sudan is a mammoth country, and searching may take a while. We may have to stay in Nimule for a long time while we wait for news. Nimule is controlled by the SPLA, so we should be fine. Either way, if we are asked we just say we are visiting students,' he said in conclusion.

'I agree,' Sam said. John just nodded and motioned the waiter over to settle the bill before the three of them walked to their rooms in silence.

'Goodnight, guys,' John said, opening his room. Wilbur slipped the letter under Lillian's door. Sam and Wilbur bid each other goodnight and went into their rooms. *Tomorrow is the beginning of the second phase of our mission,* Wilbur thought as he lay down on his bed. He fell asleep instantly.

Chapter 30

We had just come from a backbreaking job that had been contracted by our slave master Mullah Sadiq to a man named Isa Faquil. The warlords in these areas had a lot of power. They grew hashish and sold it to drug cartels. Isa Faquil was one of these warlords. The job we did for him involved weeding very large farms, and the ground was very hard.

I grew weaker from the constant hard labor. Every evening I went to bed with aches and pains all over my body, knowing that the next day would be the same. I prayed to God for strength. Sometimes I wished I was dead, but that thought didn't last long because I wanted to live to see my mother again.

We lived in tents and ate the usual bread and porridge. Isa Faquil had about six slaves of his own. They told us that sometimes they spent weeks without seeing each other. From what they said, I gathered we were treated a bit better but we were all still slaves. To these Mullahs, we were property. As Mullah Sadiq had once told us, he had bought us in a market just like he would buy a camel or a donkey.

The human degradation I had seen in the past several weeks deeply disturbed me. The worst was what had been done to two slaves who had tried to escape. Sheik Farid had made a public demonstration for all of us to see. The slaves were tied to poles, tortured, and hung upside down. Even Jimmy, who always tried to stay in control, had cried silently.

That day Jimmy and I renewed our pact to reveal these injustices if we succeeded in escaping this godforsaken place. We wanted the whole world to know about what was happening. I had decided to learn as much as possible about the area. Jimmy told me as much as he knew, and I kept observing my surroundings.

One day while we were working for Isa Faquil, I saw a black man showing him animal skins. They were busy haggling about the price. I called to Jimmy, who was still our overseer. When he arrived, I pointed to the two men doing the transaction, and he just shrugged.

'But, Jimmy, he is a black man; how come he is walking free in this area?'

'Eddie, my friend, I can see you still don't understand much about the politics of this country. All right, I will explain.' He paused.

'When the Arab Sudanese couldn't defeat the militant blacks from the southern part, they resorted to using the method of divide and rule. Although blacks are detested by the northern Arabs, some of them are used as spies and given permission to trade. They are given documents which allow them to travel anywhere in Sudan. Sometimes they even sell guns to different facets of SPLA in the south so they can fight each other. That man you see there most probably has permission to trade,' he concluded. We watched the well-dressed black man take off on his fine horse after concluding the transaction.

A few days back, the Mullah's wives had prepared two of the girls to breed. I was selected to be one of the breeders. Thankfully, good old Jimmy came to my rescue by telling the Mullah that I was too drunk to perform, having felt hungry and mistakenly chewed the hashish leaves.

The Mullah and his friends, who were all smoking something in long pipes, had laughed hard and told Jimmy to find another slave. The Mullah preferred to see how strong the men looked before using them for breeding. That would give me some time before I was selected again. I was very relieved.

That afternoon when we came from Mr Isa Faquil's farm, our Mullah had a surprise for us. Among the slaves was a religious fanatic who kept preaching about God and our salvation. The Mullah decided to teach him a lesson. The man was stripped naked and later put on top of a naked girl. He tried to resist, but after a beating he eventually gave in. After that, the poor man never said a word again.

Again the Mullah reminded us that we belonged to him, and he said he could do anything he wanted with us. Though I had previously agreed with Jimmy about the hopelessness of escaping, my resolve to leave this place was renewed after what I had seen done to the men at Sheik Farid's farm and then again to the religious man. Jimmy believed that one of us would be successful in escaping.

As an overseer he had the power to order fellow slaves, so he made them sleep in the extreme corner. I asked him why he did that, and his only answer was that a fellow slave could get one killed much quicker than a rattlesnake in the desert, especially where he was concerned since he was treated better than the other slaves. He said desperate situations could lead to deadly results.

Later on, Jimmy made me his assistant on the pretext that I could count very well and that it had been my job when we were captured. That had been confirmed by other slaves, so I had been made the assistant overseer and slept next to Jimmy. We talked at night before we went to sleep.

'Eddie, do you remember what we saw on the way to Isa Faquil's farm?' Jimmy asked. 'That wasn't a tunnel—it was a military trench. I heard the Arabs talking to each other and saying that they wouldn't need a trench to fight the black army in the south because God had cursed us with stupidity.' Jimmy just shook his head. 'Eddie, I can't tell you the anger I felt by being called stupid. I could have exploded my eyes out, but I cooled myself down. I keep thinking about the men they hung upside down at Sheik Farid's farm and ... Anyway, I have decided to do a quiet study of all these places. One of us will leave this place,' he said sternly.

'Jimmy, I couldn't leave you behind after we have been together for all this time!' I protested.

He kept quiet for some time, and then he began to whisper slowly. 'Eddie, do you want to be a martyr like that stupid man who had to be beaten and kicked in order to lay with that naked girl?' he asked. 'No, don't answer. Just remember that by freeing yourself you will be freeing me as well, because I have a feeling that's the only chance I have to expose the truth. My hope is in your success,' he concluded.

We were quiet for a little while.

'Tell me, Jim, what made you come up with this today? Was it because we saw a free black merchant at Isa Faquil's farm, or was it the whipping that was given to the man?'

'Nope, Eddie, you know me by now. Before I talk about something this crucial, I would have had to seriously think about it.'

I nodded in acknowledgement. Jimmy never said anything without merit.

'Right now there are practically no wars in Sudan, but from June to October there will be fighting and some of us will be forced to help,' he said.

I sat up, wondering what the man was talking about. 'You mean they will make us into shields?' I asked, totally lacking comprehension of what he was talking about.

'Nope.' He shook his head and swallowed a little tea. Bringing tea to the tent was one of the privileges of being an overseer. 'We will be taken to dig holes for heavy guns and trenches for soldiers,' Jimmy said. 'From what I heard the guards saying, the Military Commander of the Sudanese Army has visited Mullah Sadiq and requested our services. Our first job would be to unload heavy equipment somewhere outside Juba. The little I heard was that the army wanted us to start digging military trenches before June,' Jimmy continued and then smiled. 'Apparently the Mullah agreed to this, almost kneeling on the floor … that coward. So, brother, we have two months to plan the perfect escape,' he said, quietly leaning back on his elephant grass bed.

'Do you really think we can pull it off, Jim? I would hate to end up hanging upside down like those men,' I started saying, but then I remembered the way Jimmy Abiriga operated and shut my mouth.

'You see, Eddie, all one needs is a simple diversion. It's a little something I have to work on, but it will still be risky. There is nothing in this whole situation that doesn't include risk. The escape will have to be done during war. I heard that sometimes slaves are made to stay there to help the government in things like retrieving the bodies and carrying heavy equipment.'

He sipped his tea. 'Just remember one thing. The first few miles you will have to crawl with your whole body on the ground in order to dodge the bullets,' he added.

I was angry that he was just referring to me and not both of us. 'I have one question for you, Mr Abiriga. Where do you come in? Say I manage to get away. Would I have to raise an army to buy you back? Maybe I could just ride back and rescue you?' I asked angrily.

He looked at me and just smiled. 'No, sir, you do neither. If we are to succeed, the man to contact would be Isa Faquil. I have heard that he is greedy and would help a slave escape if there was a lot of money involved,' he concluded.

Jimmy Abiriga had already thought this through and had made up his mind about me escaping. But why just me?

'Remember, Eddie, this is the only time we will talk about this. Don't even think about it for now. Just bide your time, and I will let you know when the time comes. Now go to sleep. We have work to do in the morning,' Jimmy said, covering his head with a blanket. I slept soundly that night; I felt better than I had felt since being captured.

Somebody was shaking my body hard. I tried to resist but they persisted.

'What?' I asked in a sleepy voice.

'Rise, Eddie, it's time to go to the kitchen for some porridge. I will be right back,' Jimmy said.

When we got to the kitchen, I saw Mary. I greeted her, but she merely looked at me and waved. A lot of thoughts passed through my head, but I kept silent. I greeted the other girls and sat down to wait for the porridge.

One of the girls finally walked over to me and tapped me on the shoulder. 'It's a sad day. Mary has been bought by a black Arab to help him with his house chores. She is leaving today for a place near Wali. That's why she is sad,' she stated quietly.

I looked at Mary. She was barely in her prime, but here she was being taken away to be used and abused. I was angry.

'What are you waiting for, Eddie? We have to get ready for our next job,' Jimmy said, walking into the kitchen. He stopped when he realized the mood in the place was somber. I picked up the jug of porridge and walked towards him.

'You know that girl named Mary? She has been bought by a black Arab to be his chore girl, but of course you know what that means,' I said.

'Let me help you with the jug of porridge. Get the cups. We have to go to the water ditch to wash up,' he said as he took the jug from my hands and walked towards our sleeping quarters.

I went to the corner where we kept our mugs and picked them up. I was angry with Jimmy. How could he be so insensitive about Mary's situation? I distributed the mugs to all the slaves and poured them their porridge. Then I gave them some pieces of crude, roasted bread.

Jimmy took his place in the corner and silently sipped his tea and ate some roasted bread. He invited me to join him, but I turned him down. For some reason I felt like I didn't know him. He didn't rush us to eat like he normally did before a job. He just sat there drinking his tea in silence. Finally he stood up and told one of the boys to wash the cups quickly because we had to go to the water ditch. He left us and walked to the Mullah's house, and in a few minutes he came back with a bundle, which he tied to a horse.

'All right, everybody, pick up some pails and basins—we have to go now,' he shouted, leading the way to the gate. He got off his horse, untied one of the camels, and then stood aside as the slaves, including me, were counted; two slaves were left behind to mate with the girls.

The place where we got the water was two miles away. This was the water we used for drinking and bathing. When we got there, Jimmy distributed the soap and told everybody to take a bath and scrub one another's back. He also took a bath like everybody else, and then he gave us some clothes after we finished bathing.

'Listen carefully, everybody! We are going to start working for some important people. If you know what is good for you, just do any work they give you and don't complain. Is that clear?' he asked in a serious voice.

Everybody said yes or 'Ndiyo' in Swahili.

It finally occurred to me that Jimmy had started acting indifferent after I told him about Mary. It was his way of coping with the situation and being strong for all of us. Otherwise something stupid would erupt, and the consequences were obvious. We finished dressing. We wore a sheet on the lower part of our bodies, and those who had another cloth used it for the upper part. We loaded the containers with water and slowly headed back to the Mullah's compound.

To our surprise, we found two men seated with the Mullah and talking with him. They were dressed in white trousers and white shirts that had a lot of pockets. Jimmy showed us where to unload the water containers and to wait for further instructions.

The Mullah called Jimmy, using the name he had given him—Jamal. Jamal went and had a long discussion with the Mullah and the men in white. I found out later that they were soldiers. I could see that the Mullah looked very unhappy. Finally Jimmy came to where we were and told us to pick up our blankets because we had to take a small trip.

I finally decided to abandon my anger and approach Jimmy. 'Jimmy, I know I keep apologizing to you, but I am really sorry. I realize that I need to learn to cope with this miserable situation. Please accept my sincere apologies,' I said, looking him in the eye.

Jimmy ignored my look. 'Eddie, for your sake and mine, I hope you stop getting emotional. You've seen quite a bit since you've been here not to let emotions take over you,' he said bitterly. His feelings had been hurt by my actions.

'Anyway, we are going to Juba on the Nile to unload equipment from a ship. The work will definitely be backbreaking and might take a long time. The Mullah complained that the last time they took his slaves they didn't return them for a long time, but as you can see he didn't have any choice in the matter,' Jimmy said without any emotion. He motioned me to follow him to the dormitory where we kept our few belongings.

We packed our stuff tightly in a sack and headed for the door. The air around the place didn't feel right. It felt like we were saying goodbye. The girls left the kitchen and stood in the doorway, looking at us in our white clothing as we lined up a few feet from Mullah Sadiq.

As the assistant overseer, I counted everybody. We had one more slave because the Mullah Sadiq had seized an extra slave from Isa Faquil until he was paid in full for all the work we had done. The two studs, or breeders, were also among us. The Mullah wrote down our count and gave Jimmy further instructions.

We were told to form a line. Jimmy was at the front and I was at the back. The two soldiers picked up the guns and horses they had left at the gate, as was customary before entering somebody's compound. I turned around to look at the girls, wanting to say goodbye but not knowing how. I just nodded to them. We started moving. The two soldiers rode their horses behind me.

Chapter 31

We stopped from time to time to rest and drink some water whenever we came across a water patch. Jimmy kept counting us to make sure all were present. After a few hours I changed positions with Jimmy because I couldn't speak Arabic. I moved to the front and Jimmy moved to the back so he could talk to the soldiers.

The route we were taking wasn't the same as the one we used to go to Isa Faquil's farm or even to the Oasis of Vanil, though we seemed to be walking parallel to both places. The temperature had been steadily rising during the past few weeks, and it was almost impossible to continue walking. Finally one of the Arab soldiers we were with pointed at something and rode towards the place at full gallop.

After a few minutes he waved, and the whole group set off in his direction. We arrived at a mini camp and were given a place to sit in a tent that already held about fifty other slaves dressed in white like us. The soldiers got off their horses and went to a separate tent that overlooked the one we were in.

Jimmy was summoned by one of the soldiers, and after talking to him he came and showed me a large container of water to carry to the rest of the slaves.

'Listen, Eddie, I have to be like this for now,' he said, handing me a mug to go along with the container. It took me a long time to understand what he meant. He was trying to say that he needed to act serious with all of us and for me not to take it personally.

I started giving water to our group, and we were later given some food. We felt a lot better after eating, but I was praying that we wouldn't have to walk again. I knew that if they told us to walk further, I would collapse and be shot dead by the soldiers.

Jimmy came back and counted us one more time. He told everyone in the tent to keep a close watch on each other, because if one of us escaped the others would suffer terrible consequences.

It was about six p.m. when the last batch of slaves was brought inside the camp area. I noticed that most of the ones from other camps had scars all over their bodies. I gathered that their conditions were more pitiful than ours.

Jimmy counted us once again and repeated the same speech as before to the newcomers. This time he asked me to help him count. Some of us were chosen to roast bread, and others made porridge in large drums, which we had as our dinner before we went to sleep.

Jimmy managed to get us a place in the corner of the tent, which gave us a little room to talk. 'So, what do you think?'

I didn't answer him quickly because I hadn't figured out the whole thing yet. 'Well, Jim, I don't really know what is happening yet, but I hope this little adventure will make us more knowledgeable about our surroundings.'

He absorbed my response in silence before asking how I felt physically.

'Well, besides the terrible pain in my ankle veins, I am all right.' I paused. 'How about you, Jim? How are you feeling?' I asked quietly.

'I am better than you. You know, Eddie, we are going to be doing backbreaking work, unloading pipes and other tools from the ship. You have to learn how to pace your body and not overstrain yourself—that's the secret.'

'Did you find out where we are going?'

'Same as I heard before—somewhere near Juba, along the River Nile. I believe the equipment is loaded into trucks then taken somewhere for oil extraction,' he answered.

There was a whistle blow and then another, and then they continued blowing before stopping abruptly.

'What was that, Jim?' I asked quietly.

'It's just a signal. Those soldiers you saw have the responsibility of guarding us. It's their way of alerting each other, I guess,' he responded. 'Now go to sleep. We have a hard day ahead of us tomorrow.'

I slept badly, seeing myself falling deeper and deeper into a bottomless pit. The dream was very disturbing and real. I woke up in the morning feeling sad and depressed. I didn't feel good, after that terrifying dream.

I was chosen to make the breakfast porridge. Others made roasted bread out of maize flour. I kept wondering why we hadn't been tied like we usually were. Then it suddenly hit me. These soldiers were from the real army that represented Sudan, and it mustn't be known that they supported slavery.

We ate fairly quickly before the soldiers counted us again and loaded us onto the trucks which were manned by a few soldiers, and the journey began. Jimmy and I sat way in the back. The trucks were the strong kind that were normally used to ferry heavy goods through rough terrain. The progress was slow, with frequent stops for the soldiers to talk with one another and re-map their route. There were no roads for many hours.

After a while, I started noticing that we were going through some shortcuts of prairie-like grass, which only meant that we were leaving the semi-desert behind us. I tried to keep a watchful eye on our surroundings. I noticed that the trucks avoided passing through town centres. This reminded me of the walk we took with the LRA rebels after our capture. *Why do people do things they are clearly ashamed of?* I wondered.

I managed to see one town clearly because it was in the valley. I felt like hitting myself for having failed to study the geography of Sudan. Unlike other African countries, little was known about Sudan apart from the fact that it was massive and the British had left in the 1950s. From what I remembered in geography classes, Sudan's size was compared to three combined U.S. states: Texas, New Mexico, and Alaska.

We kept moving at a slow pace, and finally after about four hours we passed by another town. Though the trucks sped through, I managed to read the name, 'Jebel', but the rest was in Arabic. I glanced at Jimmy and he nodded.

The people I saw in these towns were a mixture of black and Arabs, though for some reason they were walking and talking with each other. This didn't make sense to me until I remembered that some Arabs had dark skin.

We stopped a little way beyond this town, and all the trucks were fueled with diesel and the oil was changed. This was done by a black-looking Arab, but the man who went around writing figures in a book was clearly a light-skinned Arab. I assumed he was the owner of the gas station.

After a little ride, the trucks started heading south, moving parallel to a swampy-looking area. I kept wondering what exactly was happening, but as usual caution took over. Not a single slave had uttered a word since we had begun this morning's journey. The pace was now much steadier than before.

We finally stopped at an armed roadblock just before a bridge. There was a large river below the bridge, so I assumed the bridge crossed the River Nile. I knew that the LRA's camp was further south, on the other side of the Nile. We must have crossed the Nile before; most likely when we were in a truck after we left the dungeon.

The soldiers manning the roadblock were dressed much differently from the ones that had brought us. They had desert brown combat uniforms with brown caps, and each had a weapon and magazines of bullets hanging around their shoulders and waists.

I also noticed that the soldiers who brought us had lost their vigor. They either feared or respected these new ones. We were told to get out of the trucks and were searched one by one. The lines moved slowly; these new soldiers didn't seem to be in a hurry.

Once again we were searched in a very degrading manner. We would enter a little room and take off our clothes. Then we were told to bend over and spread our legs so that the soldier could make sure we were not concealing anything in our behind. We did as we were told because the consequences of refusing to do what they said were obvious.

I wondered what would happen to all these proud Arab men if perchance the Nile stopped flowing through their country or suddenly dried up. I remembered someone saying that the Ugandan dictator Idi Amin had once threatened to cut off the Nile's flow to the north.

After being examined, we were told to walk across the bridge, which we did at a slow pace. The other soldiers were searching the trucks at this point. We were led to a paved piece of land and told to stay put. The slaves I had seen in the morning had greatly fooled me by their numbers. I gathered that we were now in the hundreds. Maybe some other trucks had joined us.

The checking was over in about two hours, but the trucks didn't arrive for us until late in the afternoon. Jimmy and I found a small place in this large parking lot and sat down.

'Jimmy, did you see the towns that we passed through?'

He smiled a little and glanced left and right before he spoke. 'Yes, I memorized them all the way from the Mullah's enclosure. You see, Eddie, just like you, I concentrated on mathematics and sciences in school, because I thought I would be an accountant.' He paused. 'I know more about the politics of Sudan than the geography. I also know we are now east of Sudan and the river we have just crossed is the Nile. Didn't you notice the change in vegetation and climate?' he asked and I nodded.

'I noticed that we went through some short grass, and it kept getting longer the further south we went,' I responded.

Whatever this place was, it felt a lot better than the semi-desert where we had spent the past few months. I didn't know how long we had spent in slavery, but a lot of time had passed. 'Tell me, Jimmy, how long have we been down? I mean, how long have we been slaves, starting from when we got captured in Karuma Falls by those rebels?' I asked.

The question took Jimmy by surprise. 'What? Why do you ask that?' He looked at me with concern. 'Let's see, we were captured in February, and we are now in May. I would say it's been more than two months since our capture,' he answered.

'Thank you, Jim,' I said.

Somebody was calling for Jamal, and I realized it was one of the soldiers. A truck had just arrived. 'See you later, Eddie. Just relax and everything will work out,' Jimmy said, heading for the truck.

He received instructions from the soldiers, and when he returned, he told some slaves to board the truck and unload the food containers. Again we made two rows, and one by one we received our potion of the meal. Altogether they had at least eight drums of food. I realized with joy that the food was rice with some kind of stew mixed in. It had been a long time since I had had rice and stew.

There was half a drum of food left, and my group was the last to get served. It took Jimmy and his aid almost an hour and a half to serve all of us. Finally Jimmy gave his aide a good helping and motioned for me to grab a bowl, which he filled up before he poured the rest in his bowl.

'One thing about this work, Eddie, is you have to eat as much as you can,' he said when we sat down to eat.

Jimmy had managed to grab a bowl of water, so we washed our hands before we dug in. The meal was delicious and everyone was savoring it. We finished eating in record time. I hadn't had such a good meal in a long time, so I made sure I ate all that was in the bowl.

The utensils and the drums were washed by Jimmy's helpers and put back in the truck. Some other trucks arrived, and the soldiers called Jimmy to make an announcement for everybody to hurry up. We lined up in two lines as before and boarded the trucks.

We left the bridge area as the sun was going down. The trucks headed away from the bridge, made a right, and continued going parallel to the river for a few miles before they stopped. The soldiers told us to disembark and go through a big gate.

We ended up in an enclosed place with a very high fence—about twelve feet. Jimmy was again called by the soldiers and told to divide us in groups of fifty. He asked for my help in doing this. We were hundreds of slaves in this enclosure, which was about the size of a football field—much bigger than Mullah Sadiq's compound.

Jimmy distributed tents to each group. What surprised me most was that some of the slaves were mistreating one another instead of being compassionate.

I didn't feel good about the behavior that I was witnessing, but I remembered how Jimmy had told me that a desperate slave could be more dangerous than a desert rattlesnake. Our tent held people who had come with us from Mullah Sadiq's fiefdom.

'Jimmy, do you have any idea where we are now?' I whispered.

He shook his head. 'I will know tomorrow, but what I have confirmed is that we will be unloading things which are coming from Khartoum to be used in the oil fields.'

My mind was working fast as I looked around. With so many people like this, an outbreak of a disease like cholera or meningitis would be devastating. I finally fell asleep and dreamt of my mother talking to Father Benedict. She was telling him that she had faith that I would be fine because she had a vision of me telling her not to worry.

We were woken up at six o'clock in the morning and told to get ready. Jimmy told me to help re-count everybody. I finished in a record thirty minutes. We were again told to go through the small gate and were then led along a fairly large road to an area that was built right on the river.

There was a steel structure built in the deep waters that extended all the way to the river bank. I gathered that this was a docking area used to load or unload merchandise from ships. We were told to wait a little further away until we got more instructions. Trailers began to arrive at sunrise.

'Jimmy, did you notice how that dock was built?' I asked him as we sat under one of the deserted houses near the dock.

He nodded. 'Yup, that's the first thing I noticed. It is a state-of-the-art dock. It couldn't have been built by people in this country. They don't have any engineers that build anything close to that,' he answered philosophically.

I had been watching the preparations the soldiers were making. Something was happening today. 'Say, Jimmy, the trucks keep coming and the soldiers are busy on the dock. Do you think the ship is coming in today?' I asked, trying to make some sort of conversation.

'Yes, Eddie, I believe they received a message that there was a cargo coming in. Otherwise we wouldn't be here so early.'

Almost immediately there was a loud booming horn, and though I had never heard it before, I guessed it was a ship.

'There is your answer, Eddie. The ship is arriving,' he stated.

It took a few more minutes before a huge black ship slid slowly towards the docking yard. Jimmy's name was called, and the soldiers on the dock gave him instructions.

He told us we would be unloading pipes and put us in three different groups; some were told to go on top of the trucks, and others went with Jimmy inside the ship as he interpreted the instructions. I was with the batch that waited on the dock.

We improvised a method where we formed three lines that went from the dock all the way to the truck. In a few minutes some people came from the ship carrying pipes. We started passing pipes to the people next to us, who passed them on all the way to the ones who were in the trucks. By using this method, three pipes were loaded at the same time.

After the first set of pipes had been unloaded from the ship and some trucks had been filled and driven away, I began to appreciate the power of that water vessel. I managed to peep inside where Jimmy and some soldiers were talking; the ship was still full of pipes, as if nothing had been unloaded. It was then that I realized that whatever we did, this ship wasn't leaving the dock anytime soon.

Remember, learn how to pace yourself. Jim's warning sounded in my ears as we kept loading one truck after another. The pipes were very heavy and we were tired, but what really exhausted people were the constant commands from the soldiers.

Numerous accidents occurred; some were serious and others minor. Most were caused by the fact that it took time for people to learn how to work together. We got our lunch break sometime in the afternoon, mainly because there were no more trucks to load. Some slaves had been put in charge of cooking food, which comprised of brown rice and some kind of vegetable soup. We ate and rested a little while we waited for more trailers to arrive. I sat with Jimmy, who seemed to be in a very jovial mood.

'How do you feel—be honest?' he asked, looking at me and smiling.

I looked at the dock, and my eyes swept across the whole place. 'It's hard to tell, Jimmy. I took your advice and paced myself, but I am still a bit tired.'

Jimmy laughed. 'How is the food? Isn't it better than the porridge we ate at Mullah Sadiq's farm?' he asked.

I was a little disturbed by the way he seemed to be enjoying himself when he knew full well that we were still slaves. Jimmy noticed my apprehension.

Jim noticed. 'Hey, Eddie, I see you are still not able to control your emotions. You have to learn. It will help you to keep both your physical and mental strength intact, and try not to think too much,' he said, getting up. He was right, of course, as always. How does he do it?

Some other trucks arrived, and Jimmy walked to where the soldiers were and talked to them for a little while before shouting the orders. We had rested enough, so everybody took their plates to the cooks and walked to their respective places.

Work went more smoothly this time around. Pipes were being lowered into the trucks differently, thus avoiding the accidents that had occurred before. We were being creative and had acquired ropes. Using the ropes, they were able to lower the pipes slowly into the trucks, after which they were yanked loose. The process made the work a little easier, though the soldiers kept up the pressure.

We worked hard until there was barely any light left for us to see what we were doing. We were led in two lines back to the enclosure. Once again I helped Jimmy to count all the slaves, and then we walked back to our tents.

Chapter 32

The three friends had been staying in Nimule at Al-Hajj Abdul's residence for more than two months. They had gone there soon after returning from Aru. Getting information about Edgar's whereabouts had turned into a waiting game. Al-Hajj Abdul had insisted, and rightly so, that if they were going to succeed they would have to stay for some time in Sudan, learn the culture and the methods by which people communicated.

There was a rumor that very soon there would be a guerilla offensive against the Sudanese government. Another rumor was that a lot of equipment had been given to the SPLA by certain African countries acquainted with some of the guerilla leaders. During the movement of these guns, all civilian transport was halted so as to avoid Sudanese government spies from getting to know much about the type of weaponry that the SPLA had.

Decades back, the British abandoned their colony to a group of religious zealots called the Mahdi. The new rulers installed religious Sharia laws that encouraged the maiming and persecution of many non-Muslims and black people. The latter started to rebel, and the SPLA was born to fight for freedom of worship and association.

Later, the SPLA guerillas disintegrated due to differences of opinion, but once in a while they co-operated to fight the Sudanese Army. Al-Hajj Abdul told the boys about a conference which had recently taken place where the various guerilla chiefs had agreed to work together with a common goal of dislodging the Khartoum government.

The four boys, including Al-Hajj's son Ghani, had visited their friend Hassan and talked to his father, Al-Hajj Musa Lara, who introduced them to his brother Mr Adam Wani, a very powerful chief. They had been able to reconstruct piece by piece the routes the slaves had taken during the time Edgar was abducted. However, they said that it was difficult to get concrete evidence on the movement of one particular slave.

'Wilbur, you remember how Mr Wani talked about the warlords, who bought some slaves? Do you think we should pay them off and get Eddie back?' Sam asked.

Wilbur kept moving. They were walking on a small, paved road that led from Al-Hajj Abdul's residence to the main road heading to Pageri. Since arriving in Sudan, these walks had become a frequent way to get some exercise. To these young friends, this was a country that was completely stagnant. Everything in Sudan took a lot of time and patience.

In this part of the country, the people had their own simple government that only collected taxes to buy basic essentials and once in a while guns.

Finally, Wilbur looked at Sam and put his hand on his friend's shoulder. 'Sam, I am sure you have noticed how long things here take. As you know, Al-Hajj sent some people to investigate slave camps and get information. We don't know where Eddie is, so we have to be patient for now,' he said seriously.

They kept walking on this little path, each of them quietly digesting the information they had been given over the past months.

'It is probably just as well. From what I heard, these people can double-cross us and not deliver,' Sam said, answering his own question. He bent to pick up a few stones and started kicking each one to Wilbur, who tried to control them and kick them back.

'You are right, Sam. I don't think people like that can be trustworthy.'

Suddenly a thought occurred to Wilbur and he turned to face Sam. 'Say, Sam, since we don't have much to do, how about buying a football and sneakers to keep busy?' Wilbur knew Sam's weakness. Sam had been the Captain of the school football (soccer) team.

Sam's eyes lit up. 'That's a good idea, Willy. I bet John will go for it too. Come on, let's go into town. We might see some sneakers and shorts we could use.'

The two of them walked back towards the town. They had given most of their money to Al-Hajj Abdul to keep, but each had kept some for their personal use.

A few days later, Wilbur, John, Ghani, and Sam gathered some other boys and formed a football team, and they started practicing every day. They decided that they would start by competing with other local teams before playing teams like the Arua Boys. During the games Sam shouted himself hoarse.

'Look, think of this game as a country with eleven districts. Each district begins somewhere and ends somewhere, okay?' he shouted. They all nodded.

'You always stay in your district. Once in a while you visit your neighboring district, but quickly come back to your district. Are we together?' he asked loudly.

They all shouted back, 'Yes.'

He pointed at the centre forwards and wingers. 'You boys are like the police, and the ball is the criminal. The net is the jail. Your job is to lock up the criminal as many times as possible. Okay, boys, let's try that, and remember, pass the ball before leaving your district. And don't dribble unless you notice a gap in the enemy lines,' he finished.

The name of their team was Super Warriors, and John was their goalkeeper. On this particular day, they started out badly. The second half was about to begin, and the score was 1–0 in the other team's favor.

The Nimule crowd started gathering to see the teams play. Sam's team wasn't wearing shirts, but they all had similar shorts. The other team had full uniforms, but they were disorganized.

'Okay, boys, move around your district and don't forget to pass the ball,' Sam shouted.

Sam found an opening and bypassed a defender before placing the ball in the corner of the net for a score. The game was now even, but there wasn't enough time to make a new strategy, so Sam told his defenders to just clear the ball from their side of the field, and that did a lot to help. Sam then made a good corner kick to Ghani, who controlled the ball and sent a devastating shot into the opponent's goalpost, leaving the goalkeeper with no chance whatsoever. Now they were leading 2-1.

On Sam's instructions the team defended their goal by diverting every ball that came close to their side of the field. The final whistle brought about a lot of jubilation from Ghani and all the boys.

The local people had enjoyed the game. That was exactly what the community needed; some activity to cheer them up and take their minds away from their present circumstances. They suddenly became friendly towards the boys.

'You know, guys, I don't know how much it will cost us, but we must get some uniforms for the team,' Sam said. 'We shall have a few fundraising matches before we call in the team from Arua, but to tell you the truth we still have a long way to go, so we need more practice.'

Sam turned to the rest of the players. 'Guys, let's meet again for practice tomorrow at four p.m. If you don't show up you are out,' he shouted in Swahili as some of the players did not speak English.

It was getting late and the sun had gone down. The football field was almost a mile from Al–Hajj Abdul's residence. As they were heading home, people waved to them, and they felt accepted for the first time since they'd arrived.

'Guys, this feels good. Welcome to our new home,' Sam said.

All four of them burst out laughing and continued making jokes until they arrived at Al–Hajj Abdul's residence and prepared to shower.

'Hey, Willy, thank you for bringing up the idea of football, man,' Sam said as he picked up his towel and headed for the shower.

'I second that. The exercise really helped me relax, and it got me to start liking this town,' John added and Wilbur agreed. They now had something to look forward to.

Chapter 33

Al-Hajj Abdul Asuman welcomed back one of the men he had sent to investigate the slave camps. The two met in a little restaurant at the edge of Nimule town, located in southern Sudan, near the northern border of Uganda.

Al-Hajj Abdul was a tall, distinguished man with a full head of gray hair and a very dark complexion. He was from the Nubian tribe and looked about sixty-five years of age but no one knew for sure.

Rashid Omar, a small-time trader, was about twenty years younger. He occasionally conducted some business for Al-Hajj Abdul. The two men had known each other for many years.

'So how are you, Al-Hajj?' Rashid asked as they hugged one another.

'Oh, Rashid, you don't know how long I have been waiting to hear from you. How long has it been?'

'Almost three months, but I assure you, my friend, the journey was worth it. I learned some information about what you wanted and also managed to acquire some camel skins,' Rashid said with a big grin on his face.

'That's good news, Rashid. Come, let's find a quiet place where we can talk in privacy,' the older man said as he led his friend to a table in the corner of the restaurant.

Al-Hajj Abdul ordered some tea with special herbs and then examined his friend closely. 'You look very good for a man who has been traveling this long, Rashid. So tell me, what did you find out?'

'Well, Al-Hajj, where should I start?'

'Just from the very beginning,' Al-Hajj Abdul replied excitedly.

Rashid breathed in deeply. 'Okay. When I arrived at Imela, I found transportation to the slave market. I went there, hoping to learn something. The name Isa Faquil was mentioned as one of the men who bought slaves and I was told where he lives. I managed to get on a truck that was heading west towards Rokon, but I got off a few towns after we crossed the Nile because I needed to go north. I spent days in one small town looking for transportation northward. I finally found some traders who were going in the same direction and we started talking. I told them I had heard of a businessman named Isa Faquil who dealt in camel hides at a good value, and the hides were in demand in the south.' Rashid paused to drink some tea and quickly lit a cigarette.

'You know, smoking weakens your speed like an old mare. I thought you would have stopped by now,' Al-Hajj Abdul commented.

Rashid smiled and drank some more herbal tea before he continued, saying, 'Old habits die hard, my friend. Anyway, one thing led to another, and these traders decided to show me a marketplace where I could find Isa Faquil. It took us two days to get there. On the way, they complained that business was slow because of the impending guerilla war; and the only safe times to travel were the early months of the year, which were rough because of the rainy season.' He paused to sip his tea.

'We finally arrived at the marketplace. I thanked them and offered them money for letting me ride their horse, but they refused, saying, "Men meet one another but trees don't." I still haven't figured that one out. Anyway, they left me at the market—'

Al-Hajj Abdul cut him short. 'Rashid, I hope you didn't go through all these towns asking a lot of questions.'

Rashid puffed on his cigarette and smiled before answering, 'Al-Hajj, you know very well that the one thing one doesn't do is rush an Arab trader.'

Al-Hajj Abdul smiled and nodded in agreement. 'Please continue.'

'At this marketplace, I happened to meet a man who was selling a good stallion for forty thousand . He finally took thirty-eight and sold me the beautiful animal. I changed my story, of course. I told him I needed the horse to deliver a message to a Sheik Nadim, but first I would have to see a man named Isa Faquil, who would tell me where to buy some good ornaments, since I wasn't interested in the garbage they were selling in that market,' Rashid said.

The older man smiled. 'I knew I needed a smart person like you to accomplish a sensitive mission like this.'

'Well, this trader knew of another trader who came from the area, so after the market closed down late in the afternoon, he took me to this man, who was selling camel and donkey hides. His business was slow that day and he wanted money, so we came to an understanding. Again, I was fooled. I thought the journey would be short, but it turned out to be a day and half. I was glad he was with me because I wouldn't have managed to make it alone, not knowing the little makeshift bridges and paths in the area. We finally got to a small town about fifteen miles from Isa Faquil's residence. I thanked the man and made plans for my next move.'

Rashid lit another cigarette. Al-Hajj Abdul waited patiently for his friend to continue the story.

'Al-Hajj, do you remember the cheetah hide I tried to sell to you and you declined, saying you didn't deal in animal hides anymore?'

Al-Hajj Abdul thought about it for a moment before he nodded.

'Well, after a couple of days and after finding out where Isa Faquil's place was, I decided to go there with my stallion, which was already well rested. I found Isa Faquil in the process of cultivating some land near his residence. Apparently, the man had become prosperous since he got into the hashish business. Nevertheless, I pulled out my cheetah hide and tried to sell it to him.'

Rashid glanced at his tea and then took another sip. 'Al-Hajj, you gave me instructions, and I had already spent too much money with nothing to show for it.'

Al-Hajj Abdul interrupted impatiently. 'Don't play with me, Rashid, just tell me everything. You will get your money.'

Rashid nodded and resumed his story. 'There were a lot of slaves working in his fields. When Isa left to get the money, I took a good look at the slaves and saw your young man talking to another slave. I remembered him from the picture you showed me. After a while, Isa came back from his tent and saw me examining the slaves. He laughed and asked me if I wanted to buy any. I said I was interested in only two, and I showed them to him. He said that those didn't belong to him but he could sell me any of his. I shook my head firmly and threw him off-guard by accepting two camel hides in exchange for my cheetah hide. I rode back to this little town and made plans to visit Mullah Sadiq Bin Fahad, who owned the two slaves. A few days later, on my way to see Mullah Sadiq, I saw army trucks packed with slaves, so I turned back to find out what was going on.'

Rashid puffed on his cigarette. 'I went back to Isa's pretending to want another hide. Incidentally, I met your friend, the Arab trader from here, Saleh Salim, who was there trying to buy some ornaments. A few questions later, I found out that all the able-bodied slaves, including all of Mullah Sadiq and Isa Faquil's slaves, had been taken away to work in a town outside of Juba.'

Al-Hajj Abdul shook his head in despair. 'By Allah, that was a missed opportunity,' he said.

'I pretended I wanted to buy something. Saleh got up to show me some things, and I walked outside with him. Since I had seen him with you numerous times, I knew he was working for you, so I told him where I was staying and made an appointment to see him later. He said he would pay Mullah Sadiq a visit before we met.'

Rashid looked at Al-Hajj Abdul and asked, 'Shall I continue?'

Al-Hajj Abdul's eyes opened wide. He knew it was about money. Traders were predictable. 'Rashid, you know me very well. Have I ever gone back on my word?'

Rashid shook his head. 'No, of course not, Al-Hajj, I will tell you everything.' He paused. 'Anyway, Saleh paid a visit to Mullah Sadiq before we met. He then told me that hundreds of slaves had been taken to unload heavy equipment to be used in the oil fi elds and other places where they had discovered more oil. I convinced Saleh to follow the trucks and see for himself. I figured he wouldn't have the same problems I would, considering the fact that I am only half-Arab and dark. So Saleh left and followed the truck route.'

'Did you see Saleh again?' Al-Hajj Abdul asked.

Rashid nodded. 'Yes, I saw him about three weeks later. He had come to buy other merchandise to take with him. He told me that when he reached the trucks' destination, he crossed a bridge and saw a large ship being unloaded by the slaves. He stayed in the area doing some business and finding out more information. He had taken clothing items, which he sold to some soldiers. He heard the soldiers saying that the slaves would be moved soon to begin digging trenches for the summer campaign against the Sudan People's Liberation Army—the SPLA. Saleh told me that it would probably take about two weeks to unload a large ship like the one he saw.'

Rashid paused to drink some more tea from a fresh pot. 'I thanked him and gave him all the money I had left; all fifty thousand pounds,' Rashid said, shaking his head.

Al-Hajj Abdul had not become wealthy by accident. He knew that the price Rashid was quoting was of course exaggerated, but there was a life at stake. If he paid Rashid well, word would go around and people would rush to work for him.

'Tell me, Rashid, how much did you spend altogether?'

'Well, I bought the horse, which—'

Al-Hajj Abdul cut him short. 'Don't tell me the details of horses and meals, Rashid. Just tell me how much everything cost and give me the information you wrote down.'

Rashid reached for his bag and unzipped it, taking time to look inside carefully. He finally pulled out a lot of papers on which he had written all the information he had gathered.

'Here is the account of what I have been doing for you since I left,' Rashid said as he handed over the papers.

Al-Hajj Abdul took the papers and slowly perused the details on every page. It was an eleven-page, handwritten report, and it took him about thirty minutes to read it.

'Good work, Rashid. I appreciate this, and I won't hesitate to call on you when I have more work. Now, how much did you use in addition to our agreement?' he asked.

Rashid removed another piece of paper from his bag and made the calculations. 'The final figure I come up with, Al-Hajj, is two hundred and forty-five thousand pounds,' he said humbly.

The older man reached into his small, unique-looking, brown camel-skin bag, counted five hundred thousand Sudanese pounds (two hundred dollars), and handed the money to Rashid, whose eyes opened wide with surprise. He knew that traders like Rashid made less than half of that money in a month.

'You see, Rashid, not only do you get your bonus, but I've added more for your patience and good work. May Allah be with you, and don't hesitate to call on me anytime you hear anything,' he said, getting up and patting Rashid on the shoulder before walking out.

* * *

Al-Hajj Abdul reached his residence as the sun was starting to set. His daughter brought him a light meal.

'Aisha, where did the young men go?' he asked her.

'They went to play football.'

'Football!' Al-Hajj Abdul echoed, laughing himself hoarse. 'When did this start?'

'They started a few weeks ago. They bought some sneakers and a ball and took Ghani and a few other boys to play. I believe they have a team now,' she said.

Al-Hajj Abdul continued laughing as he stood up. 'I will go and lie down. When the boys come back, you wake me up, Aisha, you hear?'

'Yes, Papa,' she answered humbly as he walked to his room.

When the boys got back, Aisha told them that Al-Hajj Abdul was looking for them. They quickly took showers and changed their clothes before dinner. It was a custom at Al-Hajj Abdul's residence to eat their evening meal exactly at eight. They joined Al-Hajj Abdul at the dinner table and greeted him one by one before taking their seats.

'So, young men, I hear you were playing football. Did you win?' Al-Hajj Abdul asked with a smile.

Ghani nodded affirmatively. 'Yes, father.'

'It is good you boys have found something to pass your time while you are here,' he said as they started eating.

It was a local custom to eat first and talk later, so they ate silently until they finished. The ladies removed the utensils and bowls, but Al-Hajj Abdul stopped the boys from leaving.

'Young men, don't leave yet. Ghani, please make sure the camels and the donkeys are all in good shape,' he said. Ghani left and Aisha brought some tea, which she served and then left.

'How do you like the tea, boys?' he asked.

'It is the best black tea I have ever tasted,' Wilbur responded.

Al-Hajj Abdul sipped his tea slowly before he spoke. 'I have some good news for you. Our quest has not been for nothing, and I hope Allah will give us more success,' he said slowly.

All the boys put down their teacups and turned their eyes on the older man.

'You remember I sent a few people to investigate the slave camps,' he said as he poured himself more tea.

They all nodded.

'Today I met with one of the men I had sent north, and he had some news. Your friend Edgar is indeed alive,' he stated.

The boys couldn't control themselves. They jumped up and down hugging one another.

Al-Hajj Abdul interrupted their cheer, saying, 'Young men, cool down—we still have problems. Before my man Rashid could get Edgar released, all the slaves were taken away to unload equipment.' He then told them the whole story, including what his other man, Saleh, had witnessed. Nevertheless, the boys were smiling.

'Young men, I want you to understand that the struggle continues,' Al-Hajj Abdul stated. 'There is one problem that we have right now. Last week I got information about a rebel build-up, suggesting that this summer there is going to be a military offensive here in southern Sudan. This means traveling from one area to another will be very dangerous in the coming months,' he concluded.

'But, sir, isn't there a way we can smuggle him out or even buy him back?' John asked with enthusiasm.

'No, what you are suggesting would put your friend in a lot of danger. I have learnt that the slaves will be taken to the front line to dig trenches sometime after they finish unloading the ship. I want to send Ghani to see Al-Hajj Musa Lara to find out anything he can about this coming campaign ... Don't worry about this now. I know you boys need to celebrate the news, so why don't you go to town and enjoy yourselves. Remember, however, we still have a lot of work ahead. Don't lose hope. I will talk to you tomorrow,' Al-Hajj Abdul said, dismissing them.

* * *

All three of them bowed to pay their respect to Al-Hajj Abdul before going to their quarters to prepare themselves for the night out in Nimule town.

'I will go and talk to Ghani. He may be able to suggest a good place in this town,' John said as they neared their rooms. Shortly after, Ghani and John came back.

Surprise and confusion was written all over Ghani's face. 'Guys, are you sure that my father gave you the go-ahead to go out and celebrate, at night?' he asked, still not believing what John had just told him. The boys nodded.

Ghani shook his head. 'This is the first time I have seen my father do this. Okay then, I will show you the town, but first I have to change,' he said as he rushed out.

'Well, boys, let's be thankful that we know where Eddie is. Remind me to cross over the border tomorrow to call my uncle with the good news,' Wilbur said.

'Now let's paint the town red, gentlemen. Are you ready?' Sam asked as he led the group through the hallway.

Ghani soon caught up with them, and they walked cheerfully towards the town. 'Nimule is a small town with all kinds of people, but it is relatively safe,' Ghani said with a smile. They walked through the town very relaxed.

Chapter 34

We had been working at the docks for more than a week, but the ship wasn't even halfway unloaded. I began to appreciate the technology I had seen in movies where unloading was done by a machine. The days were long.

On this particular day, some of us were chosen to stay in the camp. Courtesy of my friend Jimmy, I stayed behind to take care of the sick men and arrange the burial details of the ones who had not made it.

There had been a little bit of confusion before the burial because apparently the soldiers who had brought us had only written the number of slaves from each Mullah, but not the names. Every day after work, they would ask the leaders from each camp to count how many slaves were present and how many were not and just record the numbers. We buried many bodies without names.

I was put in charge of taking care of patients for sometime. Most diseases that affected the men were malaria and dysentery. Others had different infections that arose from injuries that were not properly treated and resulted in sores and sometimes tetanus and eventually death.

I made up my mind to ask one of the chief soldiers, through Jimmy, to get us some medical supplies and isolate cases of dysentery so as not to infect others. After dinner, I approached Jimmy and explained the problem to him.

'Look, Jim, I am not a doctor, but we need medicine, not just boiled water.'

'Tell me what you need and I will ask for it,' he stated.

I knew the medication that we needed because these diseases were common at home, but I was trying to decide what should take precedence.

'First, we have to separate those with dysentery from other patients. It should be done tonight if possible, otherwise all of us will be infected. We need antibiotics like tetracycline or even penicillin injections, and we need chloroquine or any other medicine for malaria. That would be a good start,' I said as we headed to our tent.

'Eddie, why don't you come with me and talk to the Commandant. It might be a good idea.'

I shook my head. 'I thought about that, and I realized that being too popular might make me a permanent fixture here, which I don't want.'

Jim nodded his head. 'You are right, Eddie. I will handle everything and also choose another person to assist you,' he said, before heading to the chief soldier's office.

Jimmy chose one of the Sudanese slaves to help me. He was from the Dinka tribe. The people infected with dysentery were put in another tent, and we dug them their own latrine. The chief soldier was worried that a lot of the slaves had fallen sick and some were dying, so the next day deliveries were made and the Dinka and I started to treat people.

Although I had given an injection to Jimmy at the oasis, I really didn't have any training. All I knew was that the needle had to be injected in a vein, so the Dinka and I started giving injections and used boiled water to sterilize the needles. We used old cloths to cover our mouth and nose. Everything was guesswork and people continued to die, but the death rate slowed down.

'I am impressed by your work, Eddie. Ever thought of joining the medical profession?' Jimmy joked with me that night. We had devised a way of relieving our stress through jokes and teasing.

'Maybe I should be a slave doctor and relieve the Mullahs and their slaves of diseases,' I said sarcastically.

He ignored me and said, 'I heard that some slaves will be taken to help with the building of military trenches. Word has arrived that the SPLA intend to mount a guerilla campaign soon. This is the only week I will let you work with the patients. If they need workers to dig the trenches, they will choose among the ones at the dock.'

I kept silent for a while before answering. 'Yes, you are right, Jim. See if you can get someone else to work with the Dinka.'

'Yup, I will take care of that tomorrow, now go to sleep. Goodnight.'

The next day Jimmy found somebody else who spoke both English and Swahili and we continued working. The death rate had decreased although people were still developing some preventable diseases like tuberculosis.

A few days later, when I tried to stay with the patients a soldier walked up to me and pushed me into the line for the workers. I went with them to the dock and easily rejoined the hard labor. The time I had spent in the slave hospital had given me some rest, and luckily I hadn't yet contracted any disease.

The ship had been unloaded fairly quickly, and by the time I rejoined the crew, it was only a quarter full. Jim nudged me to follow him into the back of the ship. 'Isn't this very risky?' I asked as we walked.

'Shh ... just keep quiet. I want to tell you something,' he said.

He took me to a small room. 'Look, Eddie, I just heard that some of the slaves will be leaving very soon to go further inland to dig trenches. We have to be in this bunch. It's our only chance if we are to ever escape,' he said.

'But they won't let you leave, Jim. You're an overseer,' I said perplexed.

'I have already taken care of that. Shortly after you left to help the sick, I found out that some of the other slaves spoke Arabic but were very afraid of being close to Arab soldiers. I managed to convince some to work with me as my assistants, and the soldiers are happy with them. Just stay close to me from now on.' He paused. 'Now, pick up one side of that bag of nails before they begin to wonder where we are,' he said as he reached for the other side.

We carried the bag to the dock, where we passed it over to the crew and went back to the cabin for another bag. The pipes had all been unloaded, and what was left to unload were bags carrying all kinds of screws and nails. We finished with the work an hour before sundown and walked to a ditch where as a rule everybody bathed before we went to the counting area.

We counted the men and walked back to the camp. I hadn't realized that so many people had died. The only burial I had attended was the first one, but now I estimated that over thirty slaves had perished in this place.

There was a sense of urgency in the air. I could tell that something was going to happen. We all had dinner, and then everybody retired to their tents, after relieving themselves. Jimmy and I lay down quietly for a little while, before he broke the silence.

'So are you ready for the trip to the front lines tomorrow? I have devised a plan to con these soldiers into choosing only the slaves that are fit for the journey!' he said easily.

I didn't doubt what Jimmy said anymore because he was never wrong. He knew how our captors' minds worked and was much smarter than they were, so he could anticipate their next move or reactions. 'I am ready, Jim. It's better than staying here waiting for death to come. Did you know that over thirty people have perished and about sixty are now in the makeshift hospital?' I asked.

Jimmy was silent for a moment. 'I am surprised it was only that number considering the miserable conditions we are in. There is one thing to remember. Death in any place is a destiny that nobody can change. Now go to sleep. We have to preserve our strength.'

I closed my eyes thinking about what he meant by that statement, but I fell asleep before figuring it out.

Something was nudging me and kept at it.

'Get up, man. I don't want to shout,' Jimmy said with urgency in his voice. 'Eddie, I will be somewhere near. I will do the counting. The trucks have already arrived. Now go,' he said before he left to talk to the Commander.

I walked slowly out of the tent and found a little water to wash my face. Soon after, Jimmy started shouting instructions. We lined up and waited for him to count us. Instead, he walked to the front of the line and started picking one person here and a few there and told them to make another line near the gate.

He closely checked each person from the chosen group, picking out certain people and telling them to step aside. He told me to count the selected group, which I quickly did and gave him the number. I was told to write down the group that each chosen person came from. All they wanted was numbers, not names.

Jimmy sat near the soldiers as the commandant argued with the man who had come to take the slaves. The man had camouflage uniforms just like the ones worn by soldiers in my country of Uganda. The little gate was opened.

The chosen group, including Jimmy and I, were loaded onto trucks. Jimmy sat next to the soldiers as the trucks started moving. He was speaking Arabic with them as the journey continued, and I wasn't surprised that they soon warmed to him. They had to do that anyway since he was the translator.

The trucks headed south on a tarmac road for about two hours before they turned onto a sandy dirt road. I observed Jimmy and noticed that he was also looking closely at the area. I tried to read some road signs, but most of them were written in Arabic, which I didn't understand, so I gave up.

Several hours later, the trucks stopped to be filled up. We were allowed to stretch our legs. We re-entered the trucks and continued for many hours before we finally arrived at a small camp with a few houses and numerous tents and were told to get off the trucks. I was glad we had arrived. The journey had been long and tiring.

We all got out of the trucks and were re-counted by Jimmy and the soldiers. Jimmy made sure that I didn't come along to count the slaves; I knew that he had a good reason for that. He gave us our tents, and we erected them quickly. A small clearing had been prepared for our tents, but all around there was short grass. I could tell by the wind that we were in the semi-equatorial region of the country.

As the sun was going down, we were given food and were told to eat quickly and then go to sleep; a lot of work awaited us the next day. At last I had a moment alone with Jimmy before we slept.

'Listen carefully, Eddie. Starting tomorrow we will be digging the trenches for these soldiers. Wherever we are, we are not too far from Torit because I saw signs that said the city was sixty miles east. This means we are near the black section of Sudan. When I tell you it's time, you just start crawling away, okay?'

I didn't try to argue with him because I had tried too often and failed.

'Eddie, if I get the opportunity to bail out, I will not hesitate. However, right now it's a lot easier for you to go alone. That's why I did not select you to help me. It's good that you keep a low profile. These new soldiers don't know you yet. Now, get some sleep,' he added as he covered his head and went to sleep.

I thought about what he had said and realized that Jimmy was talking about escaping by crawling away from the place. I prayed for a successful escape and for my mother. I fell asleep late and had a restless sleep. I dreamt of people running and leaving me behind even though I tried to call to them.

The next morning we were told to carry our tents, and we walked for two hours before stopping. The place was full of grass, but we put up our tents anyway. The cooks started working, and the rest of us were taken to dig holes and trenches of different shapes. That day we were told that soon we would be taken to another place where we would dig other trenches.

For the next few weeks we worked on the trenches. Each of us was given a hoe and a shovel. The soldiers liked to space their trenches, but they were always built in a zigzag pattern. Jimmy was again the overseer, checking on the slaves. When he came to me I decided to ask him what had been on my mind.

'Tell me, Jim, where do you think these SPLA soldiers are based? It seems to me they are trying to defend a single direction,' I said, a little confused.

'I don't know, but it can't be far from here,' he said. He leaned closer to me. 'Eddie, did you notice that there were some soldiers living in the hills?' Jimmy asked me and I nodded. 'Well, that is their current front line, but this is built on low land so that they can surprise the SPLA in the hills by heavy bombardment.'

A few days later, after another hard day of work, I noticed that Jimmy was worried. When I asked him why, he ignored me, which made me more worried. Finally he told me what it was.

'Eddie, I heard the Commander tell the soldiers to reshuffle the laborers so that they don't get to know one another. I don't think we shall see each other much during the day. Just always remember what we discussed. Good luck, my friend,' he said, patting me on the shoulder.

'I hope we get to escape together, Jim. I have come to realize that I don't have anything to lose by running, so if I get a chance I will go for it!' I said as we looked at each other for a moment. There was nothing more to say.

As Jimmy had told me, they soon reshuffled us and new people were brought into the tent. This act hurt me very much and made me more determined than ever to try my luck at getting away from this place.

We woke up one morning to the sound of heavy guns shaking the ground. We were told to stay inside the tents because there was a military operation going on. We slept all morning and were very thankful for the break. I managed to peep through an opening in the tent. I couldn't see much, but I was sure it was the big guns they had planted in the ground that were being used. Having lived in Uganda during wars, I had a good idea of the sound of guns.

After a couple of days without any work, the chief directed the soldiers to take us to another place further west so we could continue working. This was good because I managed to talk to Jimmy at lunchtime.

'So how have you been, Eddie?' he asked quietly.

'Fine, Jim, and you?' I asked.

He merely shrugged and kept eating 'Eddie, did you hear that heavy bombardment of the hills?' he asked but did not wait for my answer. 'I believe they are trying to dislodge the SPLA from that area. I heard them talking yesterday.'

'Jimmy, I noticed you were made a worker like the rest of us. Isn't that bad?' I asked.

He merely smiled. 'Nope, on the contrary, I am the one who proposed another man who could speak Arabic. Now I can listen to the soldiers' conversations since they can't easily identify me.' He paused to eat more food. 'Plus, I don't want to be responsible for anything that might happen in this camp,' he added, picking up his cup of water.

I had started to become very independent since we had separated. I just prayed daily and waited for an opportunity to take off. Going now would mean suicide, and since I didn't want to die my timing depended on when a good opportunity arose. We could still hear the heavy guns, which sounded like thunder from a distance.

There was a sense of urgency, and the soldiers were getting nastier by the minute. They took us two hours inland for work. We worked until it got late, and since we had left the tents behind, we slept in the prairie grass until daylight.

The area we were working in had a lot of trees and dense vegetation. The slaves were often bitten by rattlesnakes. Most could be cured, but there was a little snake called the 'black lizard' that killed some workers. Anyone bitten by it died within a few minutes. Nobody, not even the soldiers, knew the antidote for this bite. We were allowed to get some sticks to defend ourselves.

Every time we finished digging a trench, the soldiers put gadgets inside but made sure we were not around when they installed them. My opinion was that these were some kind of marking so that they knew the location of the trenches.

A few days later, we were taken to another place that was closer to the mountains. Though the mountains looked near, they were actually miles away. The soldiers demanded total silence. All that could be heard were hoes and shovels digging dirt from holes. We slept outside near the trenches, and the soldiers slept in tents.

We always carried our blankets, which were infested with lice and God knows what else. Some workers developed sores on their hands, but when they complained they were punished, so the best way to avoid the wrath of the Arab soldiers was to keep quiet and do the work.

Every morning after the mist had cleared we were at work again. I was feeling very sad and tired, but at the same time I silently resolved to escape from this hell. One day were told to pick up our things and head back to camp earlier than usual. Something was happening, but I couldn't tell what.

The soldiers quickly marked our trenches and we walked back to the original camp. First we passed the area where our tents were. We folded them up, and then we walked to the camps. We arrived late at night, but we were able to eat and put up our tents before turning in. During the night, I was able to squeeze into Jimmy's tent. He made me promise that I would wake up very early before anybody noticed. Jimmy told me that somebody had snitched on us, most probably a slave in our original group, so we needed to avoid being seen talking.

'I think we are going to be working in the hills, so be alert. Eddie, I must tell you, I won't be able to warn you if I make my run. If we're separated, good luck,' he said quietly.

'Jimmy, I will never forget your friendship,' I added before turning over to sleep.

I woke up early and walked to the water ditch for some water. My tendons and feet were hurting. It would be like this for the rest of my life, probably, but that didn't mean I didn't want to live. On the contrary, I wanted to live more than ever before.

We were quickly counted and divided into three groups. Our breakfast was put together with lunch, and we were told we would eat later. I noticed that Jimmy had been put in the third group. Our eyes met as if he was trying to tell me something.

They told us not to bring any blankets along and to be silent. I tried to run back to the tent to get a piece of cloth to rap on my tendons, but I was slapped and told to get back in line, which I did. Once again, the soldiers enforced silence.

We walked until we climbed a little hill, and just before we got to the top we started working on trenches. There was an air of impending danger, though the soldiers had relaxed and were sitting in the shade of a tree. Suddenly there was a loud explosion and then another. I was so scared that I dropped my shovel and prayed.

For some reason, I felt a sense of hope as loud bullets flew all around me. I thought about my mother and slowly eased out of the trench and started crawling uphill. I crawled faster, though dust was hitting me left and right, and I kept on crawling upwards. I did not dare to look back.

Prayers were on my lips. I prayed to the Lord to save my life, and I asked him to give me strength to continue crawling. After crawling for a short while, I saw a figure running towards me. I lay still and prayed. Nothing happened. I could hear shouting as I continued to crawl. After crawling for about an hour, I turned left and continued southwards.

Chapter 35

I had managed to distance myself from the shooting, but I could still hear explosions. I looked ahead and saw another hill. I decided to crawl through the valley adjacent to the hill. I wanted to rest but didn't dared to, remembering what had happened to the slaves who had tried to escape. I kept praying, asking God to intercede for me and give me another chance in life.

I don't know where the strength to keep crawling came from, but I continued though the ground had thorns and sharp grass. I finally reached the point when I couldn't crawl anymore because I was so weak and tired. I saw a little bushy area on my right and crawled there. I managed to gather enough courage to look back.

There was nobody in sight and no noise except for occasional explosions. I passed out soon after that, only to wake up in moonlight. I slowly got up and prayed for strength before climbing again. I decide to walk on the lower end of the hills to avoid being exposed.

I was half running and half walking. I gathered that if I could make three miles in an hour I would cover over twenty miles before dawn, and then I could rest during the day. There was too much risk involved in walking during the day. I walked until I felt the wounds on my Achilles tendons almost open up, but I knew I had to keep going.

Rain started falling hard, and I removed my gown. I decided to move on higher ground so that I would be able to see farther come morning, but when lights from a little town appeared, I was terrified and quickly went down the hill and stealthily walked as far from the area as possible. The rain subsided a little, and I believed that soon people would be awake and moving.

I crossed a main road and continued southward. By the time the sun started rising, I had already traveled so far that the town was out of sight. I was glad I had the sandals they had given us at the slave camp. Though I felt weary, the rain had given me some strength.

I kept saying prayers as I continued moving ahead. Although my feet were numb and my Achilles tendons were giving me a lot of pain, I moved on with caution. Since the land was uneven and had a lot of snakes, I got hold of a stick.

The only thing that worried me was being caught and tortured by the Mullahs. I had been a slave a day ago and now I was an escapee, and only God knew what would happen to me if they caught up with me. Somehow I felt that I owed my strength to Jimmy, the other slaves, and most of all, my mother.

The vegetation wasn't exactly equatorial, though there were more trees than before. My elbows had taken a beating from the crawling and the thorns that had embedded themselves in my flesh. As I walked I realized that I was more thirsty than hungry, so I prayed that I would be able to find a flowing stream or anything I could get water from. I dug deep in my head for the little geography I had learnt in class.

Since crossing the Nile, I hadn't seen it again, which meant that it was still somewhere on my right. I started focusing my walking south-eastwards, hoping that somehow I would be able to find a tributary of the Nile. I felt exhausted but kept on. I had walked for about five hours, and I was happy that I hadn't seen anything resembling a human being.

The snakes in this area were rattles and would reveal themselves before I stepped on them. Avoiding them wasn't difficult. I realized that the sun was getting hotter, and I found a concealed place between trees and decided to rest.

I rested for a long time, and I woke up feeling cold. The sun was setting and I could tell it was about to rain. I sat up and slowly recollected the events that had led me to where I was. I had walked for a long time, and had possibly already covered fifty miles. I believed the river slanted to the east, so I just decided to keep going south.

I got up slowly and thankfully realized that my feet were feeling better, so I put on the sandals and started walking down the hill. My journey seemed impossible for a slave who had his Achilles tendons cut, but the alternative was chilling. The wind refreshed me as I walked and prayed even harder. I asked God to forgive me for the bitterness I had against Him and to give me the strength to continue.

I still wasn't sure if I had walked enough miles to be sure I was safe from the barbarian soldiers and the slave traders. I remembered the journey from the LRA's camp up to the slave market, and I didn't intend to fall into their hands, come what may.

Jimmy had told me that towns in these areas were infested with Muslim militants who practiced Sharia law, which included killing people for different sins, and I believed escaping from a slave camp was among the sins they killed people for. I looked to the sky and swore never to be a slave again. People had to be told the truth about institutionalized slavery in this country, and I had made a promise to Jimmy that I would tell the world about it.

As I walked I noticed something shiny in the distance, and there was a full moon but I couldn't tell what it was. I slowed down and walked towards it with caution. As I got nearer I noticed that it was some kind of river or canal.

I looked around the whole area but didn't see any dwellings, so I moved nearer and realized it was a little river that flowed eastwards. I gathered it was a small tributary of the Nile. I removed my gown and sandals before I bent over and drank my fill.

I was not afraid of catching cholera or dysentery; I had heard somewhere that flowing water didn't carry as many diseases as still water. Moreover, I had drunk the water from the oasis, which stayed still in one place and was filled with filth, and it hadn't killed me.

After drinking, I bathed and thoroughly washed my elbows and my feet. I thanked God I had found some water to soothe my feet. I climbed the bank on the other side and got dressed. I was feeling refreshed and strong. I had stopped feeling hungry, which only meant that my body was adjusting to hunger, and that was very dangerous.

I made up my mind to eat anything that was edible even if it was grass; I had to survive. Although I didn't have a watch, I could tell it was past midnight. I couldn't go far, but I wanted to distance myself from people, so I walked away from the river as quickly as possible.

I still couldn't afford being seen by anybody and didn't know exactly where I was. I had never been to the south of Sudan until I was brought by force. What I had read was that most of the south belonged to the SPLA, but then again I knew that the LRA was also camped in the south of Sudan. *I can't trust anybody in this area*, I thought as I walked a little faster.

I was now walking on flat land, and that gave me the creeps; I had to get to higher ground—a hill or even a mountain—to stay safe. Th e pain in my feet increased, and I decided to sit for a little while in order to help the blood in my feet circulate again.

When I sat down I had a vision of my mother kneeling down and praying to God. Her eyes were looking up in the sky, and her hands covered her cheeks. I got up instantly, prayed for strength, and then continued walking southwards. I had been sitting there for anywhere between thirty minutes to an hour. Resting had relieved some of the pain I felt in my feet, so I decided that after every two or three hours of walking I would rest. This would not only give me strength but also relax my veins.

I now understood why the Mullahs had cut our Achilles tendons. They wanted to maim us so that we wouldn't be able to walk far without resting. I felt a lot of hatred for the slavers and everything they represented.

Their so-called religion wasn't Islam, because I had known good Muslims all my life. They were kind and generous. In my country Muslims and Christians got along very well. These barbarians lived by mistreating others and doing whatever they felt like, and the government just turned a blind eye. *How else can you explain the work we were doing—unloading a ship full of oil equipment and digging military trenches?*

I kept asking myself these questions as I increased my pace. My estimate was that I had about two hours left before daylight. I jumped over a big log, and then from the corner of my eyes I saw that it had moved. I instantly knew what it was and managed to look back only to see a python moving westward through the grass. I didn't want to be its breakfast, so I walked faster until I was fairly sure I was away from it.

My feet hurt tremendously, so I took a chance and sat down again, but I kept looking backwards and westwards. I wasn't a match for a python, not even before I was maimed. It was huge, probably the size of a full-grown tree trunk, and that meant twelve inches or more thick.

I finally got up and started moving again. I moved slower now but with more determination. I had to find a hill where I could rest before morning. Though I felt a lot of pain in my Achilles tendons, somehow the sting made me more determined to achieve my goal of freedom.

I recalled Father Benedict, an Italian man who had left his country and come to northern Uganda, a war zone, where he had spent the past fifteen years. Every day he put himself in danger and helped people because of his belief in God. I used to help at the centre during the summer, and sometimes I would clean his bedroom. He only had a few pairs of trousers and shirts and maybe two pairs of shoes. During the northern insurgency, he had sheltered people amid the chaos and fear. Some rebels had threatened his life, but he had stood firm and all the people who had run to the Catholic mission had survived the killing and abduction by LRA rebels.

I kept walking, but my mind was moving in different directions. I realized that it was almost daylight and I could see some hills in the distance. I thanked God again for having helped me get this far, and I was determined to triumph. My mind went back to my friend Jimmy, and I wondered how he was. By now he must have noticed my absence. I was determined to help him and every other slave by telling my story; all I needed was a little strength to get to the next hill.

Step by step we will get there, I told my body as I struggled on. I thought about the poor girl slaves that I had left at the Mullah's farm. They had been made into tools to breed more slaves. They would see their children being taken away to work and later maybe re-sold. The thought of it was heart-wrenching.

It had suddenly become bright. On my left I noticed a little bushy area not more than half a mile away, so I hurried as fast as I could. As it got a little lighter, I looked all around and behind me. The area where I had come from was bare without any kind of life. I continued at a slow pace until I finally arrived at the green grove, surrounded by tall elephant grass.

It had been two days since I had eaten, and I knew that if I didn't get anything in my body I would starve to death. I started looking around me and finally spotted some wild berries. I hesitated to eat them not knowing what would happen to me, but the hunger took over and I took some and chewed. They were so bitter that I quickly spat them out and felt downright dejected.

Deep in my heart the realization had come to me that I would need some kind of help, and it would have to come soon. Sleep came instantly due to the pain and exhaustion in my body. I dreamt of slaves working in the hashish fields and being beaten up by their guards; the Mullahs kept laughing. Suddenly the slaves, including me, attacked the guards, overpowered them, and escaped. During the escape we came to a big river that was too large to cross and swift flowing, so we didn't have anywhere to go. Going back would mean instant death by the Arab swords, and jumping in would mean death by drowning. We chose the latter and drowned.

I woke up instantly, scared and horrified. I looked around and realized that I was surrounded by bushes and trees. It was still hot but bearable. I stood up hesitantly. The area was very quiet —too quiet. Only vultures hovered in the sky above me. I became frightened and decided to try to walk again even though it was daylight. Since there wasn't a soul nearby I decided to risk it.

I walked for a long time and didn't see anything edible like a crop or an animal. I knew that if I was to survive I would have to eat something, even grass. I was also thirsty. I had almost given up on finding anything when I spied a small settlement built on a hill. I crawled close to it and saw a woman go into the shed and come out with some kind of foodstuff.

Oh, God, I am hungry, I thought. I could see the woman had a dark complexion, but I had seen black Arabs abuse other black people so I didn't feel safe. I still had to take a chance and get some food. It was fast becoming dark, and my best bet was to wait until the people were asleep before I grabbed as much food as I could carry.

The noises in the house ceased. I then crawled towards the shed and carefully opened the door and went inside slowly. I felt strange stealing food, but for some reason I didn't have any fear. I had removed my gown, so all I had on were my shorts, which had holes in them. I reached inside the shed not knowing what I would touch. My hand felt around, but I couldn't feel a thing.

I went further inside and touched something, but being without light I couldn't tell what it was. I just laid my gown down and felt it. It was a sack. I opened it, removed what I guessed was millet, and poured some of it on the gown, which I carefully folded. I was about to leave when I heard a slight noise outside that sounded like someone's footsteps. I instantly closed my arms to my chest and said a few prayers.

The door opened and a flashlight scanned the area. I pressed myself against the wall and stopped breathing. After a few seconds the flashlight switched off and the door closed. I didn't understand a word of the language the person had spoken, but somehow I felt that the woman who had the flashlight had seen me. For some strange reason she had decided not to say anything. The two women continued to talk outside.

I stood in the same place for a long time, and then I knelt down and said a quiet prayer before I opened the door of the shed and silently closed it behind me. I retraced my steps and felt very lucky that somehow I had been spared. Sitting down on the ground, I chewed on the millet I had stolen. Slowly strength returned after digesting the millet. I failed to break open the cola nuts I had found on my way out of the shed.

My next step was to get far away from this settlement as soon as possible. It was late at night, and there was no telling what the next day had in store for me. I got up, slowly walked around the shelter, and then continued southwards. I felt stronger and more confident, and I increased my pace as much as I could. Something deep inside me kept urging me to hurry; the woman could change her mind and turn me in.

It was very dark and the cold was becoming unbearable, but I knew I had to persevere. All I had on now were shorts because my gown was now my food sack. The darkness caused me to bump into trees, and sometimes I would make bad judgments and fall. I knew that the more distance I put between me and the little settlement the better.

I remembered how my mother had worked hard so that she could send me to school, and look where I ended up. I also kept thinking about Father Benedict, who always told us that a human body was like a vessel which God used to reach out to non-believers. He used to give examples of the thirty-seven martyrs who defied the king by refusing to denounce Jesus. Their punishment had been death by fire; the martyrs were not afraid and voluntarily entered the blaze.

My situation wasn't exactly the same because I had a lot of unfinished promises and debts I had to pay in this world before sacrificing myself; I believed my God knew that. I thought about my friends Wilbur, John, and Sam and thought about the things we used to do. They must be worried about me. I knew they had tried to find me, but also thought they would have given up by now.

I thought about how I had walked for about three days and by the grace of God had come to a settlement located on a hill close to nowhere when all the strength in my body was almost all gone. Miraculously, I had seen a woman leaving a food shed, and I had gone in and taken a little food. All these things hadn't happened by accident. There was a reason why by some undefined power things happened.

The moon suddenly appeared, and the darkness had almost lifted. Though I was conscious of my near nakedness, I had come to terms with it by a simple choice; either get rid of the food and dress warmer, or keep my hard-earned food and stay cold. I was able to get my bearings in the moonlight, and I resumed my method of walking a few miles and then sitting for a little while.

I ate a little millet and swallowed using the little saliva I had in my mouth. The wind was refreshing though my body felt cold and numb. I somehow generated a little heat in my body by walking and thinking a lot.

The terrain wasn't as hilly where I was, and that worried me. One thing I didn't want to come across was a big tributary. *How would I be able to cross it?* I couldn't even swim; I barely stayed afloat. When I was a student I always stayed in the shallow part of the pond.

The wind meant that morning wasn't very far off, so I increased my speed. In an hour or so I would rest, but now there was an opportunity to cover some distance in this beautiful moonlight. By then I gathered that I had put twenty miles between the settlement and me. I saw a hill to my right with dense vegetation and decided that it would be an ideal place to rest until tomorrow night.

With any luck I should be in the vicinity of Uganda within a week. I walked on and finally, when it was almost morning, I eased up the hill, almost crawling. Halfway to the top, I found a place that appeared concealed. I tore my gown in half and carefully tied my food into the bottom part of the gown and wore the other part as a long shirt, which descended just below my knees.

I slept peacefully and only woke up when something strange disturbed me. I carefully looked around and listened, but there was total silence though I was positive I wasn't alone. I slowly crept uphill in order to examine around the area and discern my surroundings. I knew I had heard something.

Suddenly I heard some kind of crack in the valley on my left. I carefully got on my knees and peered through the tall grass. I saw a lot of soldiers in battle fatigues crossing the mountains. I kept looking carefully, but it was hard to tell if these were the Sudanese Army troops or the SPLA, so I decided to stay put.

They were moving in a single line, otherwise I doubt it would have taken them long to see me. I decided to get closer to have a better look. Whoever these soldiers were, they didn't belong to the Sudanese Army. Their uniforms were different and most of their guns were small, automatic weapons.

They were all black and I felt relieved, but I still decided to keep my distance. I had heard of black people who worked for the Sudanese Army, and I wasn't going to take any chances. I remembered Jimmy telling me that the SPLA was not as united as it appeared and had separated into different groups. Some of the soldiers worked with the Sudanese government and were paid to weaken the SPLA. Matters got worse when oil was discovered in southern Sudan and some people became greedy.

I carefully retraced my movements back to my original hiding place. My mind was fairly competent, so I tried to calculate the distance I had covered in the past three and half days. I hadn't done any walking since the soldiers had passed. After about thirty minutes had elapsed, I decided to walk on. The advantage being that I would be able to map my journey more easily in daylight.

I picked up my cane and my food sack and climbed the hill, after which I carefully went down and continued to head southward. The journey was a lot easier, though I had developed sores in my mouth, which I believed were caused by thirst. I walked due south, but once in a while I turned eastward.

I remembered the sign I had seen at the bridge where we had unloaded the ship. It had said, 'Juba to Kit' and then something else, and since I didn't understand Arabic I guessed the something else meant how many miles it was from the town of Juba to Kit. At the rate I was moving, I didn't think I had covered over two hundred miles, so I kept walking.

Every time my feet felt numb, I would sit for a while before walking again. I couldn't bear the thirst anymore, so I decided to break some cola nuts to get the juice inside. I found a rock and started breaking them up. I only had four small ones and broke all of them, but I ate only two of them. It was getting late, and I knew I couldn't stay here in the open. I walked during the day, but I knew I would have to travel a little at night to cover more distance. I stood up and continued southward.

Lots of questions were going on in my mind. *Should I reveal myself to people? What if they can't speak English and are Arab collaborators? How do I know who I can trust?* These questions bothered me for some time until I decided to hold on before making any decisions. I was probably in Mahdi territory, and the punishment for a runaway slave was something I didn't care to find out again.

I finally saw what looked like a plateau and made a mental strategy to walk there at night. I slowed down, looking carefully for some water. I didn't find any, so I left everything to God. I hadn't called on Him all day, the last time being when I stole the food from the village. I located a nice shade under a tree, sat down, and started praying.

During my prayers I fell asleep and had a peaceful dream with a vision of my mother and plenty of food to eat. I dreamt about working at the Christian Catholic Centre, being in charge of food distribution, and having a lot of help. Everybody was very happy there. I woke up and reached out my hand only to realize that I was in a bush. I spent a moment collecting my thoughts.

I felt sad and frustrated with my circumstances, but after a while I stood up and started walking with my cane and my little package of food. It became dark and impossible to see anything beyond a couple of yards. My feet felt numb as usual, but most of the pain was in my mouth, which had sores that I now believed were caused by infection.

I had calculated my bearings during the day, so I didn't have any problem moving ahead at a constant pace. I walked, thinking of my dream. I wondered if it was true that some people were able to interpret dreams. *Did my dream mean that the people at the Catholic mission were happily eating plenty and had no problems, or did it mean that somehow I would be part of the group that helped others at the Catholic centre?* I hoped it was the latter. The more I thought of my dream, the more determined I became. If I succeeded in getting to Uganda, I would start believing in miracles

I must have covered about four miles in darkness before I decided to rest my feet. I ate some millet and another piece of cola nut before I said a few prayers. I was having a mental rejuvenation, and walking was easier than before, though the pain in my mouth persisted and the sores got worse.

The night progressed with clearer moonlight, which only meant that it wouldn't rain soon, but I still kept up my pace. I felt that I would somehow survive if only I succeeded in getting some water. I stopped again in the middle of the night to rest. I only had a handful of millet left and one piece of cola nut. I made an attempt to piece together as much information as I could remember about Sudan. I had heard of mass starvation and disease being the norm in this part of the country, caused by the constant movement of people.

I tried to recall something positive about this place, but my mind drew a blank. The news usually ignored the good and only dwelt on the negative. I truly believed that the country, especially the area I was in now, was fertile and could be a good agricultural land if only the wars would stop.

I stepped in some marshy ground and quickly retreated a few steps backwards. I had to wait for a few hours for the moonlight to be pronounced before I was able to see properly. In the meantime I decided I could still make progress if I walked east for a few miles, and that's exactly what I did. Sitting down and waiting for light wouldn't only waste precious time—it would also possibly be a trap for me if there were people nearby.

After I had walked a few miles, I tried moving again. My mind kept going back to the marshland. The only conclusion that came to me was that some sort of river wasn't far from where I was and would soon reveal itself, most probably the next day. I sat down to rest. I estimated was that it was about three a.m. and that I had just two or three hours before daylight.

I slowly got up and began to travel south again. I had stopped counting the days that I had traveled, but I felt I had a few more days of walking before feeling safe. My throat was very sore, and I felt pain every time I opened my mouth. I knew I had to have some water soon if I was to survive.

I walked south-east and endeavored to remain positive. My resilience held on until I reached a little hill overlooking a small village that was located in a valley. The morning breeze kept blowing as I looked for an appropriate shelter in the grass. I became disoriented and I knew that if I didn't get any water soon I would die. I fell asleep the moment I eased into the elephant grass on the far left side of the hill.

Constant pounding woke me up, and I realized that it was raining. God had answered my prayers. I held out my hands and sipped a few drops of water. I finally stood up and looked around. There was a palm tree nearby, but I didn't have the strength to climb it, so I started walking, feeling a little rejuvenated and thankful for the rain.

As I skirted the village, careful not to be spotted, I heard a noise ahead. It wasn't loud, but became more audible the closer I got to it. It turned out to be a little waterfall that had been caused by the rain. That was exactly what I needed to quench my thirst. I put my little bundle down and stepped into a ridge where the water came down. I only drank a little at first, trying to get my tongue accustomed to water again.

The way I felt after drinking enough water was indescribable. The water and the rain had rejuvenated my mind, but I still felt weak. I reached for my bundle and ate my last handful of millet before washing it down with rainwater. I eased myself up slowly with the help of my cane and continued walking around the village. Though it was daylight nobody was visible, which I thought was strange.

At this juncture my body was just moving automatically. I endured and finally put some distance between the village and me. I was weak and cold. I knew deep in my heart that I was developing some kind of malarial infection or pneumonia. Whatever it was, sitting down would increase it a hundredfold, so I kept walking southward, while asking God to heal my body.

I had come too far to lose now. *How can I allow a little disease to take me down when I risked everything to get away from captivity? And how can I even think of abandoning my mother when I am so close to my goal?* I asked myself aloud. I knew I had no other choice but to persist until I couldn't do anything anymore.

The sun had started shining and the cold eased off a little, but I still felt like a log that just kept moving ahead. Finally the land became fairly flat and walking became easier. The heat from the sun quickly dried my gown, and shortly afterwards I started sweating. I continued moving south.

I realized that I needed help if I was going to survive. I had spent many days walking and had contracted a fever. If I didn't get help soon, I would not survive for long. I started becoming dizzy after a few miles, and decided to sit down and rest.

I recalled an incident in Gulu when Father Benedict prayed for a young boy and told him to have faith in Jesus Christ so as to be healed. The boy was suffering from chronic pneumonia. This disease usually killed young children in a few hours, but miraculously the child had become better without having received any drugs. I didn't have much to lose, so I got on my knees and prayed to God, not feeling too confident.

I fell asleep soon after and woke up at night feeling stronger. I thought about my previous state of mind. *Was it emotional or was I really sick?* I asked myself, not believing that one could get better immediately without any kind of treatment. Nevertheless, I thanked God for the miracle, got up, and started walking again.

It was dark and there wasn't any moonlight, but I knew I had to take advantage of my renewed strength, so I kept walking slowly but at a steady pace. I finally sat down to rest when the moonlight was visible. I didn't know if what I had felt the day before had been sickness. Maybe it was a reaction of my body after many days without water.

I recalled my friends and I talking about the hopes and dreams for the future, and I slowly shook my head. *Only God knew a man's destiny.* I didn't have any idea what time it was, but I knew a long time had passed since I had woken up feeling rejuvenated. I continued walking, but the sores in my mouth kept getting worse. Every time I moved my tongue around, I felt a lot of pain, so I decided to sit for a few more minutes, which became hours because my feet were numb.

I started walking again, but this time with a lot of difficulty. I had slowly lost the confidence that I had originally possessed. All I was thinking of now was having enough strength to reach some people; any kind of people as long as they were not slave traders. I prayed that someone would be able to help me. I walked ahead though I was feeling very dizzy.

Suddenly I saw something that glittered and hurried towards it. I missed a step, however, and I felt myself falling slowly but couldn't stop myself. Everything became peaceful.

Chapter 36

Mrs Rita Aribo decided to go fetch some water from the stream down the hill from her home. The day before she had used most of her water to wash the clothes she needed for church. The little water that was left was not enough for cooking.

It had become a habit for most women and girls in their little village of Langabu to just take some soap and wash their bodies in the stream before fetching another can of water to take home for other chores. Life had been even more difficult before they started receiving aid from international organizations.

The aid had helped the town acquire hoes and seeds for sowing food so as to be self-reliant. Now that the rains had come, Rita expected a good harvest in a few months. Her two children were in a boarding school in the nearby town of Gangala, where a church group sponsored them.

Even though it was hard to accept living without her children, common sense had prevailed and she had painfully let them go. She visited them whenever she got a chance. Her husband, Ben Aribo, came home once in a while from his duties with the SPLA, but she hadn't seen him for over a month.

Usually Mr Aribo disappeared for many months and came home at the end of the summer. Most women in this little village lived with their young ones until they were old enough to either go to school or join the SPLA. They had come to accept this as a way of life.

Ben had told Rita of a very important campaign that might give southern Sudan their independence. Rita kept agreeing with most of her husband's goals even though she believed that she wouldn't live long enough to see that dream realized.

She and her friends had started women development programs in the village to help them cope with the constant absence of their husbands. Rita was a member of the group that cared for the sick, and they received training and medication from the International Red Cross.

As she walked down to the stream, she saw somebody she knew and waved. The day before it had rained a lot, and walking was a little difficult. She finally got to the well and dipped in her container, filling it to the brim.

This was also her opportunity to take a bath and get refreshed. After looking around, she chose to wash behind a small bush a little way from the well. She picked up the container and headed for the bush. The soap was in her right hand as she carried the water basin in her left and chose a good place that was fairly concealed.

She undressed before starting to wash her hair and then her body. She had a habit of singing when taking a bath, so she sang away as she scrubbed herself down. After a few minutes, she thought she heard a noise to her right but ignored it, thinking it might have been caused by the numerous small creatures that lived in the area.

She kept singing happily as she rinsed herself. She heard the noise again, but this time it made her jump back and dive for her clothes. Her heart almost stopped and her eyes were wide open with fear as she quickly put on her clothes. For some reason the noise stopped, but she knew it had come from her right.

She wasn't sure if investigating it was the right move, but there weren't any large animals in this area, so her fear disappeared and curiosity took over. How can I run away without finding out what it is? What will I tell my friends? *Something groaned and I took off without finding out what I was running from?* They will laugh at me for being a coward.

Rita decided to look around for a good stick, which she found very quickly. Taking a deep breath, she headed in the direction of the sound. Her mind wasn't playing games with her. She had heard the noise coming from somewhere to her right, she thought, as she moved ahead stealthily, not wanting to make any unnecessary sound.

Suddenly, she heard another groan a few steps from where she was standing. It sounded like someone sleeping soundly. She kept walking, her stick raised in case there was trouble. The first things she saw were feet that were scratched and wounded. As she stepped closer she saw that it was a young man sleeping. He wore a long, dirty, white shirt, and torn shorts. Near his head was a small bundle of cloth tied around a stick.

She used her own stick to push away the bundle, and then began to prod him with her stick but there was no movement. She bent down and carefully touched the young man on the forehead. He was very hot and shivering.

Rita stood up quickly and decided to rush back to the village to get some help. This young man had serious fever and would die if nobody helped him soon. The wounds on his feet meant that he had walked through the bush for a long time. He certainly wasn't from here—his attire testified to that.

Rita ran uphill towards her village. She arrived there in a few minutes and quickly went to see Miss Dorothy Auso, who worked as a doctor for the village folk. Dorothy was not actually a qualified doctor, but she had been a nurse for a long time and everyone called her the village doctor. Rita entered the room where Dorothy Auso was examining a patient.

'Doctor, I have to talk to you. It's an emergency!' she exclaimed breathlessly.

Dorothy asked her assistant to take over and then invited Rita into her inner office. 'What is it, Rita?' Dorothy asked.

Rita took a deep breath before explaining everything to the doctor.

'Do you think he can walk?' Dorothy asked. Rita shrugged.

Dorothy told Rita to get two other women to help while she prepared some first-aid medicine and also filled a bottle with sterile water.

By the time she finished putting everything in her bag, Rita had arrived with two other women. The few men who lived in the village were either old or had been injured during the struggle with the Sudanese government and had taken to drinking alcohol, so they would be of little use.

The young man was still groaning when they arrived. Dorothy bent down and poured a little water around his mouth. She gave instructions to Rita to use a wet cloth to bring down his temperature.

One of the women fetched water, and every once in a while Rita would pour it on the cloth and put the cloth on his forehead.

They had just decided to get some more help to carry the young man to the village when suddenly he opened his eyes. He looked scared, and then he screamed.

'Oh no, please …' he said. Rita put her hand to her mouth.

'Shh. Please don't be afraid. You are very sick, and you need immediate medical attention. Can you walk?' Dorothy asked the young man.

Dorothy was among the few people in the village who could speak English. She attended primary school in Nimule before going to high school in Uganda. She had hoped to go back to Uganda for further education, but the international organization that worked in the area had offered her a job with good pay and six months training in the medical field, so she had decided to stay in her village and help her people. She could treat most tropical and other basic diseases.

To her delight this young man spoke English; he had screamed in English. He slowly sat up without speaking and looked around him. Dorothy handed him the bottle of water. At first he sipped it, and then he drank the water down, almost emptying the bottle.

'My name is Dorothy. Can you speak now?' she asked in English.

The young man nodded.

Dorothy smiled, relieved that the young man could understand her. The other women were standing quietly nearby.

'Look, you are very sick. I don't know how you got here, but you need close attention. Swallow this medicine and see if you can stand up,' she said, grabbing a handful of pills.

* * *

I still wasn't sure about the women in these parts. I looked at their faces first before I swallowed the pills using the little water that was left in the bottle. Having traveled all that distance without meeting any people, I found it difficult to trust anyone.

'I don't know if I can get up to go with you. Where are we going?' I asked.

The woman who spoke English looked at me from head to toe and said gravely: 'Young man, wherever you are going, you can't get far with that fever. Our village is just up the hill, so try to get up.'

She reached for my hand and got me on my feet with the help of the other women. Another woman handed me my stick while a large woman put my arm around her neck and literally carried me. We walked like that up the hill. I didn't know where the other two had disappeared.

The women took me around the village. They probably didn't want to attract a lot of attention, which was what I wanted. I wondered if this little village was owned by the Arab Sheiks. Slowly we moved behind a few houses before one of the women opened the door of one of them and we stepped inside.

The house wasn't large, but after a candle was lit, I realized that it had at least three rooms and maybe four. The strong woman helped me to sit on a chair while the English-speaking lady prepared some medicine. I gathered she was a doctor of some sort. The other two women soon joined them and started talking in their dialect.

The doctor noticed my concern and smiled. 'Young man, what we are doing is delegating duties to help you,' she said but then suddenly looked at me carefully. 'You don't trust anybody and that's understandable. Do you have pain anywhere else besides your feet and mouth?' she asked me. I shook my head.

She looked at me very carefully. 'You seem to have traveled a long distance. You have thorns on your legs and feet and sores in your mouth, most likely caused by dehydration, but we are going to make you feel better,' she said, looking at me.

As an afterthought, she added, 'By the way, my name is Dorothy and this is Rita.' She pointed to the large woman who had helped me to the house.

Another woman brought some hot water in a basin, and Dr Dorothy took it from her, poured some solution in it, and mixed it before she put it before me.

'Okay, young man, put your feet inside the basin,' she ordered.

I hesitantly put my feet in the water. The pain was so terrible that I nearly screamed.

'I know it hurts, but you have to be strong,' she said as she put on gloves and started washing my feet.

The dirty water was poured outside and fresh water was added into the basin. The same substances were mixed with it, and the process continued. It hurt again but not as much as before. Dr Dorothy finally told me to remove my feet and put them into an empty basin. She applied some more stuff to my wounds using white gauze.

'You have a few splinters and thorns in your legs and feet. I'm going to try to remove as many as possible before bandaging your feet.' She paused and looked at me. 'God only knows what you went through, young man,' she added.

'My name is Edgar, but you can call me Eddie,' I said at last. All the women looked at me and smiled; their smiles were genuine, and I silently gave thanks to God.

Dr Dorothy opened her bag and removed a pair of tweezers. She held my feet closer to the light and carefully removed the small pieces of thorns that had embedded themselves in my flesh. She finished the first foot and moved onto the next and did the same.

Sometime later, when she had almost finished removing the thorns, she stopped and looked at me. She has seen my scars, I realized.

I put one finger on my mouth as a sign to not say anything. She quickly finished, removed some bandages from her bag, and carefully bandaged both of my feet and ankles. I could see she was in shock and wanted to finish quickly.

She avoided my eyes and kept looking at her work as she mixed salt with something else and gave instructions to Rita, who was standing nearby. I hadn't heard Rita speak at all in English, so I assumed she couldn't speak any.

Dr Dorothy turned to me and handed me a few tablets and some water, which I swallowed. Then she gave me a solution to rinse out my mouth.

'Swallow these now. I'm going to put others into packets that you will take three times a day. Rita will bandage your injured feet daily and apply some medicine,' she said.

Rita left as I drenched my mouth with the solution.

'I have sent them to make your bed because you need a rest. Is there anything you want to talk about?' she asked without turning around.

'Dr Dorothy, I know you saw my Achilles tendons,' I said gravely.

She was silent for a moment before she finally turned around and faced me; there were tears in her eyes as she tried to speak. She removed a handkerchief from her pocket and dried her tears.

'Eddie, four years ago my brother and two of his friends got involved in selling exotic leather from Congo. One day while they were on one of their journeys, they were captured by Arabs who robbed them of their money, tied them up, and took them up north. We heard this from a trader. They have not been seen since. We did all we could and spent our last pennies trying to rescue them, but all was in vain,' she finished and looked away from me.

I was shocked and saddened by her pain. What could I say to her that would change anything? I finally gathered myself together and quickly spoke.

'Dr Dorothy, I am truly sorry to hear about your brother, but I beg you to keep faith.' She turned and looked at me and smiled a little. 'You don't know what those few words have done to my spirit. I thank you.' She picked up her bag and turned to leave but stopped suddenly.

'This village isn't very safe. It has spies who would jump at a chance to make some money by reporting you to the warlords, but we will do all we can to hide you. Meanwhile, you should rest,' she said as she opened the door, went out, and closed it behind her.

I didn't know what to do, and my mind kept jumping from one possibility to another until Mrs Rita came back. 'You all right, Eddie?' she asked.

Rita spoke English? I was shocked and lost for words, but I immediately recovered.

'I feel better, thank you,' I answered. I was in Rita's house. Rita's English wasn't very good, but I understood her. I spoke slowly. 'Do you have a husband?' I asked.

'Yes. We have to be careful. Most dangerous thing is to enter a man's house when he is not home. Now you go to sleep,' Rita said with a smile. 'I will bring food to you later,' she added. I nodded, but her statement had made me nervous.

Rita gave me a change of clothes—probably her husband's— and then helped me up to the bed. I still wanted to ask her a few questions, but she left soon after she tucked me in. I slept dreamlessly and soundly for many hours. However, when I finally woke up I was very afraid and tried to get up from the bed. Rita rushed to my bedside and lit a candle.

'Eddie, you're all right?' she asked.

I must have been dreaming loudly because she looked concerned. I sat up in the bed and collected my thoughts.

'I am fine—I just didn't remember where I was. I'm sorry if I woke you,' I said.

She smiled and handed me a plate of food, which she had put near my bed.

'Eat now. You become strong,' she said as she reached for a jug and poured some water into a cup. I ate slowly because of the wounds in my mouth. I finally finished eating and washed it down with some water.

I didn't want to sound suspicious or even ungrateful, but in order to rest my mind I had to ask the question that was bothering me. I also had to talk slowly so that Rita could understand.

'Rita, you know I'm in danger and some people may have seen me entering your house. Won't it bring you some trouble?' I asked as slowly as I possibly could without appearing to frighten her.

She nodded her head in understanding. 'Eddie, we know people saw you come here and warlords have many spies in this place, but you're sick. Not good for you to travel,' she said in a serious voice. I nodded even though I didn't feel safe in the village.

The drugs that Dr Dorothy had given me made me sleepy. I drifted off and woke up the next day feeling rested, though I still felt slightly disoriented.

Dr Dorothy came over and checked my temperature and also checked me for other signs of infection. 'I am glad to report some improvement in your condition, Eddie. The fever has subsided, and you are responding well to medication,' she said, checking my pulse.

There was a little commotion as one of the ladies who had helped me the day before came in and talked to Rita. Her tone of voice told me that there was trouble. She kept looking at me as she spoke. Rita and Dr Dorothy were trying to calm down the woman.

After a few minutes, Dr Dorothy came to where I was lying down and put her hand on my forehead. 'Don't worry, Eddie. Whoever they are, we shall counter them. Just take your medicine and try to sleep. We might have a long night ahead,' she said quietly.

She walked back to where the other women were and talked to them in a low voice.

I started to think of the many potential dangers that faced me. The warlords could take me to be a spy, or they could discover that I was an escaped slave. All the possibilities were very worrisome, I concluded.

Rita gave me some food, but I could tell she was worried. I controlled myself though I was dying to know what was going on. I wanted to be part of the decision making of my fate, but I could tell that they were not ready to tell me.

I finally fell asleep and woke up when someone whispered in my ear to get up.

'Shh,' they cautioned, and I got up and quietly put on my sandals. I wanted to ask what was happening, but I kept quiet as they slowly walked me outside and further away from the village—in silence. We finally stopped on a hill, a good distance from the village, where they put me on a horse that was waiting there with a rider.

A familiar voice spoke. 'Eddie, it's not safe for you to stay in this village, so you will be moved to another place where you can get help to move on. I have put some medicine in your shirt pocket,' Dr Dorothy said.

'Dr Dorothy, why are you going through all this trouble for me?' I asked.

She shook her head and didn't answer for a while.

'You see, Eddie, I feel like by helping you I'm doing something for my brother. Go now. It's going to be a long journey,' she said, so we took off.

I kept looking back until the silhouettes of the ladies disappeared.

The man who was riding the horse was very quiet; the only sound I could hear were the hoof steps of the horse. I tried to figure out what could possibly have gone wrong but finally gave up. I had almost become accustomed to the silence when suddenly the man decided to speak in Swahili.

'You know, somebody fingered you and you could have been caught, but Dr Dorothy took pity on you and made arrangements to get you out.'

I was very grateful to God for setting Dr Dorothy on my path.

We kept going south for hours as I thought about what the man had just said. 'How many groups do you have in southern Sudan?' I asked, trying to make conversation.

'Oh, we have many aside from the SPLA, and the others always change allegiance as they please,' he said.

We were making better time on the horse than I had ever made on foot, which was good in itself, but then these reports of numerous warlords in the area were not good. I wasn't sure how they would treat an ex-slave. In a few days I had experienced some kindness mixed with a lot of sadness. It was hard to imagine a united Sudan sometime in the near future.

We stopped a few times since we had begun our journey, but we didn't talk much. When we came to a hill, the man stopped the horse and pointed to lights in the distance. 'That's the town of Geranja, where we are going. It's only an hour away,' he said. We rode the rest of the way in silence.

When we got to the outskirts of the town, the man pointed to a little white building. 'That is our destination,' he said with relief. I could tell this fellow didn't much like being a babysitter and was glad we had finally arrived. He dismounted his horse, walked to the door, and knocked.

A man wearing a black cassock came out, and they talked for some time. The man who brought me handed a note to the man in the doorway, which he read before telling my escort to help me dismount. He opened the door wide and motioned me inside.

The fellow who had brought me jumped onto his horse and rode away without looking back. He just left without saying goodbye; I didn't even get his name. I was still thinking about that as I was led into the building.

'I'm Pastor Joseph Janda. Welcome to my home and church. I understand your name is Edgar, right?' he asked, shaking my hand.

I nodded and smiled, still confused by the quick turn of events but also grateful that I was in the presence of a clergyman. Pastor Janda showed me where I would sleep and also gave me some food.

'This town is constantly involved in sectarian wars, so it's better that you stay inside most of the time,' advised the Pastor after I had eaten. 'Do you know why you were brought to this place?' he asked.

I shook my head. 'No, Pastor. I was told that I was in danger but wasn't told from what. The fellow who brought me told me that I was fingered but I don't know for what,' I answered.

The Pastor looked at me closely before pulling his chair next to my bed. Then he walked away and made sure that the door was locked before coming back to where I was.

'I will tell you this,' he began. 'The village where you left Dorothy is controlled by different warlords. They are afraid of anybody from outside, thinking they are spying for the Arab government in Khartoum. Your presence was reported to some warlord. That's why you were moved here,' he said quietly.

I nodded my head in understanding. 'Would they execute me, just like that?' I asked.

Pastor Janda nodded. 'Most of these warlords are not honorable men, and I'm constantly surprised by some of their actions,' he answered.

I didn't have to ask many questions to know what he meant; my immediate problem lay in being able to work out my present location in terms of my country's border, so I decided to ask the question on my mind.

'Excuse me, Pastor, how far is this town from the border of Sudan and Uganda?' I asked.

He shrugged. 'Quite far,' he said, standing up. 'Maybe a day or two by car.'

He reached for a tea kettle, put it on the stove, and then came back to sit.

'How safe is this place, Pastor?' I asked.

'This place isn't safe at all for travelers unless you are from around here or you have the support of a warlord. That's why you have to stay inside,' he answered uneasily.

Chapter 37

Wilbur and Sam had been trying long-range football shots with John as the goalkeeper. John had been improving on his goalkeeping skills since they started the football team. The boys had settled into their new town, and the people liked them.

Across town Al-Hajj Abdul was having a meeting with Saleh Salim, an Arab trader who was one of the men he had sent up north to investigate Edgar's whereabouts.

Al-Hajj Abdul looked at the handsome trader in front of him. He was a light skinned Arab, of medium height and weight, and was probably a little over thirty. He was always in a good mood, but today Al-Hajj Abdul noticed that Saleh was not his usual self.

'Saleh, are you okay?' Al-Hajj Abdul inquired as he poured some tea into his cup.

'I am okay Al-Hajj. I stopped at your place yesterday evening and I was told that you had gone out. I met the young men from Uganda. Very nice young men. I didn't tell them why I came to see you… Sorry I couldn't wait, but I didn't have any urgent news until today,' Saleh said.

'No problem, Saleh. Do you have something for me?' Al-Hajj Abdul asked.

'Al-Hajj, I believe Rashid told you everything I told him, about my talk with Mullah Sadiq and my trip to Juba,' Saleh began.

Al-Hajj Abdul nodded. 'Yes, we met a month ago. Thank you.'

Saleh reached for his tea and drank a little. 'Al-Hajj, as I was coming I learnt of some things that made it imperative to see you as soon as possible. When I was in the town of Langabu trying to sell cloth and some ornaments, I heard the SPLA guerillas had attacked the government forces, and during this attack some slaves managed to escape. There is a possibility that your boy Edgar was among those that escaped,' Saleh added.

'You are not sure about any of this, Saleh?' Al-Hajj Abdul asked.

Saleh shook his head but reached in his pocket and pulled out an envelope. He handed it to Al-Hajj Abdul, who took it, opened it, and removed a small letter, which he read in silence. After a moment he folded it and put it back into the envelope.

'This letter says you should go and meet this man immediately. It states that he has found what you were looking for but doesn't explain anything,' Al-Hajj Abdul said as he passed the envelope back to Saleh.

Saleh took the envelope back and carefully put it into his trouser pocket.

'I received the letter today. You see, Al-Hajj, this fellow, Aisis Haddu, has done numerous deals with me, mainly in leather, but when I saw him a few months ago the only thing we talked about was the slave I was looking for, so there isn't anything else he could be contacting me for beside that,' Saleh said firmly as he motioned for the waiter to bring another pot of tea.

Al-Hajj Abdul pondered over this silently. The fellow in front of him had already proved his reliability, according to Rashid. Al-Hajj Abdul had no reason to doubt Saleh, and besides, the rumor about the guerillas ambushing the government soldiers in the process of digging trenches had been substantiated by reliable sources. There was a possibility that what Saleh reported was feasible, albeit remote. In any case, Al-Hajj Abdul decided to encourage Saleh.

'Okay, Saleh, I will give you the money for your services so far, and you will get the rest if you succeed in rescuing our boy.'

'Al-Hajj, I will need his current picture to carry along with me, and I'm ready to leave anytime.'

Al-Hajj Abdul got to his feet, smiling. 'Let me rush to the house and see if I can get a photograph of the boy. I will be back soon,' he said, walking away quickly.

Saleh shook his head as he watched the old man leaving. For a man who has great grandchildren, Al-Hajj Abdul has aged nicely, he thought. He sat back in his seat and waited.

Al-Hajj Abdul sat down in a rundown taxicab. 'Take me to the football field,' he ordered the driver.

The taxi made good speed, and in little time they arrived at the field. Al-Hajj Abdul got out of the car and called out to Wilbur. The young man sprinted towards him.

Wilbur's heart had already missed a beat thinking that, for Al-Hajj Abdul to come to the football ground himself, something important had definitely happened.

'Wilbur, can you tell me where to get Edgar's identity card?' Al-Hajj Abdul asked with his hand on Wilbur's shoulder.

'It's at the house. I will come along and give it to you,' he said, jumping into the taxi, but not before he signaled Sam indicating that he will be right back.

Al-Hajj Abdul waved to the other players to continue as the little vehicle moved away then he gave the driver directions to his home and sat back.

Wilbur was anxious to know what the old man was up to, but knew he had to wait until Al-Hajj Abdul was ready to talk. They arrived at the house a few minutes later. Wilbur jumped out and ran inside.

Al-Hajj Abdul and the driver waited for him as the driver engaged the old man in small talk about the weather and business. Wilbur rushed back with the card and handed it to Al-Hajj Abdul.

'Thanks, son, I will let you know everything later,' the older man said.

Wilbur ran back uphill towards the football field feeling hopeful. More than a month had gone by since they had learnt that Eddie was still alive though still in bondage. Wilbur had passed on the news to his uncle, who had encouraged him to continue with the mission and expressed confidence that they would eventually succeed in getting their friend back.

Al-Hajj Abdul arrived at the restaurant a few minutes later. He paid the cabby before joining Saleh at the table.

'That was quick, sir. Did you succeed in getting the photograph?' Saleh asked.

Al-Hajj Abdul nodded. 'Yes, I did. I wouldn't have come back without it,' he answered as he pulled back a chair. 'Now, Saleh, let's talk about this upcoming trip of yours. When are you leaving?' Al-Hajj Abdul asked.

'I just found out that there is a small truck going to Okaru in about an hour, so I am taking it,' Saleh answered.

Al-Hajj Abdul nodded again. 'So sometime tomorrow you'll have arrived in Okaru?' he asked.

'Yes. If everything goes as planned, tomorrow afternoon or evening I'll be in the small town of Ame, where Aisis Haddu is waiting,' said Saleh.

'That brings us to the finances you will need. But first I want you to brief me about the extra costs you incurred during your trips up north,' Al-Hajj Abdul said.

Saleh had compiled a list of things he had done on his journey. The deal they had made was for Al-Hajj Abdul to sponsor him to continue with his usual business since he had had a bad year. Al-Hajj Abdul had financed his initial costs with an understanding that he would find out as much as he could about what had happened to the young man. Saleh had listed the additional costs he had incurred on the journey.

Al-Hajj Abdul read the list in silence and looked up. 'You mean you only used one hundred and fifty thousand pounds?' he asked in astonishment.

Saleh nodded. 'I made some good profits in the beginning. The only time I started experiencing any kind of loss was when I ventured into territories I didn't know.'

Al-Hajj Abdul pulled a bundle of Sudanese pounds from his pocket and counted two hundred and fifty thousand and gave it to Saleh, who took the money instantly. He couldn't believe that the old man was giving him even more money.

Saleh thanked Al-Hajj Abdul and put the money in his pocket slowly, as if expecting Al-Hajj Abdul to take it back.

'I tell you, Saleh, you have an opportunity to make even more if you bring back the boy. By Allah, I will give you double that and I will forget about the loan I gave you to continue your business,' Al-Hajj Abdul said, passing the identity card across the table to Saleh.

Saleh took it and looked at it carefully, wondering what kind of boy this was that made people commit that much money to get him back. He put the picture in the pocket where he had put the money.

'Al-Hajj, I don't want to hurry you, but I believe I should check on my transportation. It's getting late,' Saleh said, getting up from his seat.

'Certainly, Saleh, I wish you a safe journey,' Al-Hajj Abdul said, checking his watch. It was coming up to six p.m. which meant the truck was leaving shortly. Saleh picked up his bag, and Al-Hajj Abdul walked him outside.

'You don't mind if I see you off?' Al-Hajj Abdul asked.

Saleh was surprised. 'Not at all. That is the truck over there,' he answered, pointing to a small pickup truck that was already pulling over. 'I think we have arrived just in time,' he added.

They were met by a small man who apparently owned the truck.

'Are you ready to go, Mr Saleh?' the man asked.

Saleh nodded. 'Al-Hajj, this is Habib. He is originally from Moli, but has business here also.'

Habib bent down, almost touching the ground as he greeted Al-Hajj Abdul. 'It's my pleasure, sir. I will make sure Mr Saleh has a pleasant trip,' he said.

'Thank you, Habib. Let me wish you a good journey, Inshallah,' Al-Hajj Abdul said as he shook his hand.

Habib's truck had two rows of seating in the front. The back of the truck was loaded with different goods, mainly manufactured items that Habib would be delivering to towns up north. Saleh waved to the older man as they took off. Al-Hajj Abdul sat watching as the truck headed north.

* * *

The first two towns they stopped in were Pageri and Moli. Habib loaded or unloaded some goods and picked up passengers each time before restarting their journey. The road was bad, and the truck stalled a few times.

Saleh remembered his conversation in the town of Okaru with Aisis Haddu where he had told Aisis the name of a boy he was looking for, not expecting the man to find any information. The fellow was a regular trader in small towns between Okaru and Ngangala. Saleh had not paid attention to Aisis when the other man had written the name down in his book.

The more he thought about their short talk the more he realized that by all counts they hadn't exchanged much in the way of conversation. Saleh had tried to sell Aisis some cloth, which he had bought in Arua, but the man's price was too low and somehow the talk had shifted to the boy Saleh was looking for. Saleh had mentioned that he was willing to pay a lot of money to get the boy back.

The truck passed through numerous roadblocks with soldiers insisting on seeing their identification. The truck finally made a stop in the town of Magwe close to midnight.

'All right, everybody, we shall be here for thirty minutes. It should give everybody enough time to stretch,' Habib stated.

People disembarked and went to do various things. Saleh headed for a nearby restaurant for a meal and some hot tea. They stayed in Magwe for a little over thirty minutes before the driver called everybody back who was continuing the journey with him. They got underway at almost one a.m. and continued north.

It was very cold and Saleh could hear complaints from the people on top of the truck. He thought about the letter from Aisis. It had been written the day before yesterday. Aisis Haddu had given him until tomorrow, or rather today, to get to the town of Ame or else he would leave. It was only by chance that the driver of the truck he was in had brought the letter and found Saleh in Nimule.

Saleh had been planning to go to Arua to buy some clothing to bring into Sudan after his meeting with Al-Hajj Abdul, but the truck driver Habib had given him the letter from Aisis and his plans had changed.

The journey north-east to Okaru got more difficult, but they got to the station in Okaru by early morning. Everybody disembarked. Some looked for restaurants to buy tea and use the toilets while others gathered around the fires that were scattered around. Saleh realized that it wasn't a good idea to rent a hotel room at this time of the morning, so he opted to drink tea and listen to gossip for a few hours.

At around eight, Saleh walked to the outskirts of the city to get transportation to Ame. The morning breeze was refreshing but there was anxiety everywhere. Rumor had it that the Sudanese Army was planning to attack this area, but Saleh was used to this type of gossip, so he ignored it, as did most people since they heard it every summer.

He found a horse carriage an hour later that was going to Ame. They soon picked up a few more passengers before getting underway. Riding in a carriage wasn't comfortable, especially when moving through valleys and hills. In the past, people were robbed of their money and other belongings when they traveled through uninhabited areas like this. Luckily, this time the journey was quiet, though very slow.

The old man who was driving the carriage couldn't stand the silence anymore, so he started speaking. 'The marauders attacked this area last week. They took off towards the north. They belonged to the warlord Taban Nasir. All they do is take advantage of the summer turmoil to rob people.'

'What about the black Arab slave trader Hamis and his boys? I have heard that they're very active in these parts,' Saleh asked, trying to dig up some information.

'No, sir, it couldn't have been Hamis and his men,' the driver said, shaking his head. 'Hamis doesn't get involved in local squabbles—he buys his way through the warlords' territories.'

'Did they attack the town of Ame, sir?' Saleh asked.

'Oh! You were not in the area, I guess. The town was attacked on Saturday. There were about sixty bandits on horseback. Two were shot off their horses, and that's how we found out that they belonged to Taban Nasir.'

The sun was too hot and it was humid. The women in the backseat and their children had already fallen sleep.

'You see that big rock over there?' the driver asked. Saleh nodded. 'Well, I have timed the distance from that rock to Okaru. It is exactly one hour and a half,' he said.

Saleh was thinking about Edgar and not paying much attention. The letter had cautioned him to hurry. *Has Edgar escaped? Is he safe?* An escaped slave cost more than any other slave. The thought of the young man being kidnapped again made his body sag. For some reason, Saleh had become attached to the boy.

'Could you please hurry up, sir? I am worried about my wife,' he lied.

The driver looked at him before he commanded his horses to gallop harder. They finally arrived in Ame at noon. The journey had been long and treacherous. Saleh paid the man and walked down the street. He was shown a rundown hotel where travelers spent the night before proceeding to their next destination.

He went inside and inquired if a Mr Haddu was registered there. The hostel man looked at him suspiciously before answering that he didn't know anybody by that the name. Saleh understood the man's apprehension.

'My name is Saleh. I am a businessman. I believe he is expecting me.'

The man didn't answer but motioned Saleh to take a seat. He told somebody else to take his place at the counter and walked away.

'Are you from around here, sir?' the man at the counter asked.

Saleh shook his head. 'I am from the southern town of Nimule. I heard that some hoodlums invaded this little town on Saturday.'

'Yes, that's true. They have been very active in this area. That's why everybody is suspicious of strangers,' he stated.

There was some commotion in the back, and Saleh turned his head to see Aisis Haddu coming towards him.

'Allah-Akbar (God is great),' Aisis said as they walked towards one another and embraced. He looked at Saleh again. 'By Allah, it's you. You got my letter?' Saleh nodded.

Aisis took Saleh by the shoulder, and together they walked towards the hotel verandah. He shouted to a boy to bring some tea. They sat down as Aisis told him the latest news of marauders in the nearby areas. Finally the boy brought the tea and left.

'Now, Aisis, I am sure you didn't send for me all the way from Nimule to tell me about these marauders that attack every summer,' Saleh stated.

Aisis gazed at him and smiled. 'Of course not, my friend. The reason I wrote to you was to inform you about the boy you told me about last time when I saw you,' he answered.

Saleh took a deep breath, relieved that he hadn't made the journey from Nimule for nothing.

'Saleh, I sent for you because I think the young man is in extreme danger.'

'Wait a minute, Aisis. Why don't you start from the beginning,' Saleh said, confused.

Aisis looked at him undecided about where to begin. 'Okay, I'll tell you most of what I know,' Aisis said and Saleh nodded. 'A young fellow had been walking for about a week and was near death when he was discovered by a lady named Rita from my village, who had gone to the stream to bathe and fetch water. She and her friends and a local doctor moved him to her house and started caring for him,' he said and then paused.

Saleh motioned for him to continue.

'Apparently the boy had acquired a fever and was dehydrated, so the doctor gave him medicine and Rita gave him some food and a place to sleep. To cut a long story short, one of the old fellows who saw them started rumors that there was a spy in the village. Mind you, the only men left in this town besides me are old or disabled because most of the others have joined the SPLA or their factions.'

Aisis sipped some more of his tea before continuing the story. 'Well, anyway, word came that the old fellow had told the hoodlums of the warlord Taban Nasir about the spy in our village. This doctor, Dorothy, asked me for help to get the boy out of town. At first I refused until I remembered our conversation and recalled that the doctor had called the boy Edgar. I was told to take him to a priest who lives in the town of Geranja, south of our village. I took him there, accompanied with a letter,' he said and drank some more tea.

Saleh reached into his pocket, pulled out an identity card, and passed it to Aisis, who looked at it and gave it back.

'It's him,' he announced.

'What do you mean? You haven't looked at it carefully!' Saleh stated, passing the card back angrily. Aisis shook his head as he took it back and looked again.

'You will know what I mean when you meet him. The look in his eyes is unforgettable. Moreover, the reason I called you is because I remembered the name you told me and that's what the Doctor called him.' He paused. 'This morning I learnt that a warlord has offered a horse to anybody who catches this boy, so getting him out of Geranja won't be easy. You will need some help.'

Saleh knew that his biggest problem was what the warlord would do to the boy if he was caught and found out to be an escaped slave. 'I have to write a letter to Nimule,' he said, walking to the counter for paper.

'I will get you an envelope,' Aisis said, heading to his room.

Saleh started to go back but stopped midway and turned around to face a boy who was hanging about. 'Young man, can you call the carriage driver for me? He is down the street.' The boy nodded excitedly. He had realized that this man looked important, so he was happy to go.

Saleh sat down and started writing a letter to Al-Hajj Abdul in Nimule. He explained the situation and the distressing possibility of the boy being recaptured by warlords. Saleh further told Al-Hajj Abdul that he was going to see the boy but the situation might prove tricky.

Aisis brought the envelope, and Saleh put in the letter and turned to see the carriage coming to the hotel.

'What is this? Did the man change horses?' Saleh asked.

Aisis nodded. 'They are three brothers, and they have a couple of horses,' he said.

Saleh walked to the carriage. 'Mister, are you going back to Okaru?'

The man nodded, 'Yes, I am, sir. I found a driver, so I will have some sleep in the back,' he said. Saleh looked at the driver, who had a woman next to him, and noticed that there was a blanket in the backseat.

He turned to the older man. 'I want to give you a letter to take to Habib, the driver with a pickup truck. Do you know him?' The man nodded. 'Tell him to get this letter to Nimule immediately,' Saleh stated.

He gave the man ten thousand pounds. 'Thank you, and give this to Habib,' he said, handing him another ten thousand Sudanese pounds and the letter. 'There will be more for you the next time I see you if the letter is delivered. You are leaving now, aren't you?' Saleh asked.

The man was lost for words as he looked at the money, but he managed to say, 'Yes, yes … now.' He shouted and the carriage took off down the street.

After tipping the boy, Saleh turned around, went back inside the hostel, and sat opposite Aisis. 'You said that the warlord will pay to get this young man?' he asked again. Aisis nodded.

Saleh had a bad feeling about the whole thing and realized that the sooner they started moving the better. 'Aisis, let's go and see this young man. Is he still in the town of Geranja?' Aisis had been expecting this and had prepared an answer.

'You see, Saleh, I went through a lot of problems to contact you, and as you can see I have been waiting in this place though it wasn't part of my plan …' Aisis started, leaning on the table. 'I would say I've spent close to twenty-five thousand pounds, and that's not considering the money I've spent on food and lodging.'

Saleh nodded. As a fellow trader, he knew how things worked. 'I will give you fifty thousand pounds on the condition that you take me there now, and if I see this young man I will give you a bonus,' Saleh said, counting fifty thousand pounds and passing them to Aisis.

Aisis didn't need any more convincing. He took the money; he couldn't believe his luck. He had expected Saleh to try to negotiate, being a trader and all.

'I will go get my bag and we'll be on our way,' Aisis said enthusiastically. 'Hey, young man, can you bring my two horses in front of the hotel?' he yelled as he walked towards the back. Aisis had brought two horses—one carried his goods, and he had hoped that Saleh would meet him. He knew that Saleh would not have ridden his horse all this way.

Saleh stood up, picked up his handbag in his right hand, and walked to the outside balcony. He sat down and lit his pipe; it was time to put everything into perspective. This was his chance to make real money. Failure to achieve it now, since he was approaching middle age, meant he would be poor for the rest of his life.

He puffed on his pipe; a friend had given him a large roll, which he had acquired in Arua, where the best tobacco came from as far as he was concerned. The boy brought two horses to the front of the hotel and tied them to a pole. Aisis came out shortly, carrying his large bags which he put on his horse.

'We should go now, before it gets dark,' Aisis said as Saleh joined him.

Aisis gave Saleh one of the horses after putting a satchel on its back, and they walked to the nearest shop to stock up on supplies.

It was after four o'clock in the afternoon when they rode out of town. They traveled for a few miles in silence. Saleh was smoking his pipe, thinking about the trip ahead of them. 'Tell me, Aisis, when and how did you hear about the young man being in danger?' Saleh asked.

Aisis was silent for a little while before answering. 'Actually, I believe it was all started by the old fellow in my village, but I personally didn't hear anything or even know of his existence until the lady doctor approached me,' he answered as he took a swig from his flask, which he had filled with tea.

'Now, the next time I heard anything was that the warlord had put a price on the boy's head. That was after I had dropped him off in Geranja and was riding towards here. I heard it at a station stop a few miles from here. I will show you when we get there,' he added. 'At the station stop north of here, two men were talking and one of them mentioned that he had heard about a young man being hunted down by a warlord,' Aisis added. He sipped some more tea before capping the flask.

Saleh digested all this information, and his heart felt heavy and uneasy. 'Were these fellows headed back north?' he asked.

Aisis nodded. 'Yes. As a matter of fact, they were headed to Geranja.'

'When was that, Aisis?' he asked.

'Most likely yesterday. The only reason I didn't go with them was because I wanted to go to Ame and send you a message to meet me,' he concluded.

Saleh had heard all he could about this issue, but this time his heart was even heavier. He didn't like depending on luck, and this is what it was turning out to be. He only hoped that the letter would get to Al-Hajj Abdul in time to send reinforcements.

Aisis changed the topic and asked Saleh about the prices of leather, because lately there had been demand from Torit. Saleh promised to look into the current trend of leather that came from Congo when he got back to Nimule.

They arrived at a stop station at about eight o'clock in the evening and tied their horses outside a little teashop before going inside.

The old man who owned the shop served them hot tea. Saleh went outside, removed some rolls from the satchel, and brought them into the shop.

The three of them talked a little about how business was in Okaru. Saleh smoked his pipe in silence, but he noticed that the fellow's eyes were constantly on him.

'Would you like some tobacco, old fellow?' he asked.

The old man jumped up, came to where Saleh was sitting, and bent his knees in respect. Saleh gave him a huge chunk from his own, and he asked him about the rumors he had been hearing concerning spies. The man mentioned that he had heard that a large group of men were looking for a spy, but he wasn't sure about all this because the information was secondhand from traders from the north.

Saleh decided to ask him a few questions. 'Did the traders say they had seen the spy, old man?'

The old man shook his head. 'No, but they saw armed men on horseback.'

'Did they say how many there were?'

'Oh, they said there were about twenty, riding fast stallions.'

'When did they say they saw these horsemen?'

'They said they saw them a few miles from here, so I imagine that it was a few hours ago.'

'Thank you,' Saleh said as he reached into his pocket to pay the bill. 'Come on, Aisis, we have a long journey ahead of us,' Saleh said, walking outside. Aisis Haddu ran after him, and together they jumped on their horses and rode off.

Saleh was very watchful and silent as they rode. Every once in a while he turned on his flashlight and examined the ground ahead and around him. Aisis saw how serious Saleh had become and kept his mouth shut. The pace was slow but consistent. The horses had had enough rest, and the journey wasn't difficult. It was night and they were not thirsty.

After they had traveled for a few hours, they noticed some horse tracks and stopped to examine them. Saleh got off his horse and followed the tracks using his flashlight until he found their origin. He examined them closely, guessed how many they were, and also estimated at what time they had gone by.

'Aisis, they are at least five hours ahead of us, so we will have to hurry,' he said, jumping on his horse. Deep inside, Saleh knew five hours was an eternity, especially if he was chasing thoroughbreds. The situation had become unpredictable. It was now a game of chance.

Chapter 38

I woke up feeling weak and a little chilly. The priest was kneeling next to me, and he had a cup of steaming tea in his right hand.

'Morning, Edgar, how are you feeling today?' he asked kindly.

'I am feeling better now, Pastor, thank you.' I tried to smile as I took the cup of tea from him and sat up. At first I used the spoon to drink the tea, afraid of upsetting the wounds in my mouth, and after a few sips I started to feel better.

My mouth was not as tender as I had thought, and I was able to drink from the cup. I remembered that someone had once told me that wounds in the mouth heal faster than other wounds. Maybe it was true. The kind priest had even given me a pair of pants and a shirt to supplement the clothes that Rita had given me. I still had a cold and a slight cough, but my feet had healed reasonably well and the fever had subsided.

Pastor Joseph was a very kind man, God bless him. I had been staying with him for the past three days.

'Pastor Joseph, will you tell me exactly what you meant when you said it wasn't safe to be here and that you would arrange for me to be moved?' I asked.

He sat down on the edge of my bed before he answered.

'You see, Eddie, I couldn't tell you everything since you had a fever and sore feet.' He paused before continuing. 'There is a warlord who has been offering money to anybody who knows anything about spies and escaped slaves in the area. Since you are a stranger in these parts, you fall into those categories. The longer you stay here, the more dangerous it becomes for you.' He paused again. 'I have decided to find somebody to take you south,' he concluded.

I did not want to be an inconvenience to the man. 'Pastor, I feel strong now. Just show me the direction and I will go.'

He smiled and poured some more tea into my cup. 'First, gain back your strength. Don't worry, we will get you a horse and you'll travel with the Lord,' he said, getting up. 'Now take your pills and get some rest. I want to see you healthy,' he said and walked away.

I slept soon after that and had beautiful dreams of green vegetation and abundant fruits on trees. I woke up in the morning and went into the kitchen to make a cup of tea.

There was a woman named Margaret who knew of my presence at the church. Every day she brought roasted wheat pancakes to Pastor Joseph, who in turn paid her at the end of the week. She worried me very much because of the way she looked at me and rolled her eyes. I had told the Pastor about her, but he had just laughed at my fears. She knocked at the door and I opened it.

'Hello, how are you?' she said. I responded that I was okay.

'Tell me your name,' she said as she moved closer to my bed.

'Did you bring any pancakes for Pastor Joseph?' I asked.

'No, I came to see you. I will bring the pancakes later on today.'

I shook my head in wonder. 'Look, Margaret, you haven't said much to me since I have been here, so this is a surprise. How do you expect me to react?'

Her features changed instantly, and she looked at me with anger. 'What do you think I am, a prostitute? Do you think I flirt with every man I see?'

I was shocked at her reaction. She acted as if she was hurt by my answer. I knew I had to try to be friendly, especially under the circumstances. It was the only smart thing to do.

'Oh, Margaret, forgive me—my name is Edgar,' I said.

She sat on the bed, but for some reason I didn't feel any affection for this woman. There was something cold about her, and when I looked into her eyes, I knew I was right.

I told her I needed to take a bath and she left. I took a bath and tried to go back to sleep, but my mind kept going back to the little incident with Margaret. *What did she want with me? Was I being paranoid?*

Pastor Joseph came back at around two p.m. 'Edgar, how come you are up? Do you feel better?' he asked, sounding very concerned.

'Yes, I do feel rested, but I couldn't go back to sleep after the incident that happened about an hour ago.'

'Why don't you share it with me, son?' he asked, pulling up a chair.

I sat next to him and told him about Margaret's visit and how she had asked my name, pretending to like me though I was very sure she didn't. Pastor Joseph reacted calmly, but I could tell what he was thinking.

'I saw Margaret's mother this morning when I passed by her shop, and she told me that her daughter wasn't there so she put the pancakes in a bag for me.' The Pastor was quiet for a while, thinking. 'I don't see why she came to see you. She has a husband who does some trading up north, but some say he is a marauder. What exactly did she say, son?' he asked.

I was quiet for some time, trying to fully recollect what she had said.

'Well, she said that she wanted to know my name and be my friend, but she was acting strangely and rolling her eyes at me. She then said that she hadn't brought the pancakes because the purpose of her visit was to see me, and she said she would come back later with the pancakes.' I then told Pastor Joseph about her reaction when I refused to give her my name. 'On seeing her reaction, I apologized to her and told her my name, but, Pastor, when I looked at her eyes, they were as cold as steel.' I shook my head.

Pastor Joseph stood up and walked towards the window. He was silent and deep in thought. He finally turned around and faced me.

'Son, I am going to do a little investigation of my own. If there is anything fishy going on, I will find out. Meanwhile, you should stay in the bedroom until I get back,' he stated firmly as he walked towards the front door.

I finished my tea and I went to the bedroom in the back of the church to lay down. The events of the past few days, coupled with Margaret's strange actions, smelled of impending trouble. I needed to get out of here, but there wasn't much I could do but wait for Pastor Joseph to return.

Pastor Joseph came back about an hour later, and I could tell by the look at his eyes that something bad had happened. He went straight to a chair and sat down, putting both of his palms to his face.

'Son, we have big problems,' he began. 'Margaret's husband was here a few days ago, and you can guess why she asked all those questions. The problem we have now is that we don't know when he intends to come back,' he said. 'I have arranged a horse to take you to Okaru tomorrow morning,' he added.

He got up and walked to a little opening on the far side of the room and motioned me over. 'You see this opening? It leads to the little shop at the end of the main road. It was used to escape from the soldiers of the Sudanese Army. Just take this flashlight and see if it's still usable,' he said, handing me the flashlight.

I bent over and crawled through the opening. It was about two feet high, and although it was narrow, one could crawl through the passage. It wasn't as dirty as I had expected. I crawled until I reached an opening to a room. Though it was daylight, the little room was dark. I used the flashlight to look around.

There were two doors, and I half opened each of them and quickly shut them. The door on the left-hand side faced away from the road. When I was satisfied that I was in the right place, I crawled back into the tunnel and retraced my steps back to the room where Pastor Joseph was waiting.

'How was it, son?' he asked.

I shrugged my shoulders. 'It's not bad, Pastor, but what I am wondering is how much time I will have to escape.'

Pastor Joseph nodded. 'I have already thought about that, and I have decided on a diversion to buy us some time. I want the whole town to think you went back to Langabu,' he suggested. Pastor Joseph checked his watch. 'It's almost six o'clock. I need to inform Dorothy about the imminent attack,' he said as he reached for a paper and a pen and began writing the note.

I thought about the selflessness of what the Pastor was doing and was deeply touched, but I was also concerned about him. I wondered if the Pastor had a plan in case the gang came.

'Pastor Joseph, what do you intend to do if the group comes here?'

The Pastor looked at me closely before he replied. 'Son, I can understand your concern, but this isn't the first time we have had problems with warlords. They know better than to touch any natives of this town. I will go and find a messenger for this note and also talk to Charles Anuko. Just sit tight,' he said as he left with the note.

I wondered who this Charles Anuko was.

Pastor Joseph came back at seven p.m. and had the look of a man in a hurry. 'Look, son, if these hoodlums don't come tonight, they will be here sometime tomorrow, so listen carefully,' he said as he pulled a chair next to my bed. 'There has been a change of plans. We begin right now, so start getting ready,' he said and got up from his chair and paced the room. Suddenly I felt very chilly as I contemplated my future. I grabbed a plastic bag and put in some pancakes and the few clothes I had acquired from Rita and the Pastor. I sat down and waited. The Pastor must have seen the worried look on my face, because he suddenly came to where I was, touched my shoulder.

'Don't worry, son, God will take care of you,' he said.

For some reason his words made me feel better.

At exactly eight, there was a knock on the window. Pastor Joseph motioned for me to hide in the other room. I heard him tell a man that I had left a little earlier, and then he closed the window.

'You will take the passageway. Charles Anuko will meet you at the corner store, but first he will announce himself.'

He opened the door to the passageway and prayed for me before I left.

With my flashlight in hand, I moved backward facing the room while at the same time cleaning my prints; the Pastor had insisted on me taking a little broom for that very purpose.

I finally made it to the little shop, sat down in a corner and waited. There was a gentle knock on the door and a low whisper.

'This is Charles Anuko. Are you there, Edgar?'

I hesitated for a second before I said, 'Yes, I am here. Should I open?'

'Yes,' he whispered. I crept to the door and slowly released the latch.

'Come, let's go. Just follow me as quietly as possible,' he said.

I moved out of the shop and pushed the door closed. It was extremely dark, which was good for us. I followed the man quietly for about a half a mile before he turned to me and told me to relax.

'You know, Edgar, I saw a woman peep into the keyhole of the Pastor's room in the back and watched her move to the front of the church. It was Margaret. I think she wanted to see for herself if the rumors were true that you had left.' He paused. 'Pastor Joseph and I spread the rumor that we had sent you back for your safety. Now, let's hurry. I left my horse a little further down on the left side road.'

For the past week and half I had almost forgotten the hardships I had endured during slavery, but as we walked it suddenly dawned on me that I was still a slave, though I was on the loose. All the physical and mental abuse I had suffered came back to me like sharp needles being inserted into my head.

Mr. Anuko looked at me and asked me if I was alright. I nodded, but I could tell he didn't believe me.

'I know it's tough, son. Just continue to trust in God and everything will be fine. If you didn't have faith, you would not have got this far,' he said.

Is he psychic? I asked myself. How else could he know of my hardships and my prayers? We finally arrived at the place where Charles had tied his horse behind a little bush.

'We'll ride for some time until we get to a hilly area,' he said as he helped me sit on the large beast. He sat behind me, and we slowly rode further away from the town.

'Tell me, sir, why did we have to leave tonight?' I asked.

'First, you can call me Charles,' he said and paused. 'Yesterday one of the boys went out looking for firewood and came upon tracks of a lot of horses, and then there was the incident of Margaret peeping into the Pastor's room. There is no question in my mind that there is an imminent attack. The place I am taking you isn't very comfortable, but it is very safe. We used to use it way back when the Sudanese forces attacked our towns unceasingly,' Charles added.

My thoughts were all mixed up, and my mind traveled through the length of the journey from the time I was captured and sold into slavery. I hoped that one day I would make it back home. Though it was deep in the night, the moon had started shining and the sky was clear.

We arrived in a hilly area, and Charles helped me to dismount from the horse. We walked up the hill for a while before Charles stopped and pointed to a dark-looking hole.

'What is it, Charles?' I asked.

'That is the place I told you about earlier. It's actually a cave. I used it a few months ago, so it should still be clean,' he said as we walked towards the opening in the hill.

'The only precaution you should take is to make sure that after you relieve yourself, you cover the ground properly with soil. Better yet, you should dig a little hole some distance away from the cave. It is easy to do with a stick because the earth is soft this time of year,' Charles added.

Normally I would have been embarrassed to have this conversation, but at this point any topic was okay. Charles tied the horse to a nearby tree and removed two bags.

'Come! Let's check out your new hideout. Do you still have your flashlight?' he asked.

'Yes, sir,' I answered as I turned it on to locate the exact entrance.

The first impression I got when we entered was that it was narrow, but as we went further inside, the passage swung to the left and the room became larger. There was a bed, a lamp, and some utensils.

'You are sure nobody lives here, Charles? I see a mattress and a lantern in the corner!' I commented.

'I had to make sure I was comfortable every time I came here. Let me show you something,' he said.

He reached behind the bed and pulled out a small box and a gun with two large barrels. I was shocked, and Charles saw my reaction and came towards me.

'Edgar, you have got to learn to protect yourself in case there is trouble.'

He patted my shoulder and headed back to the makeshift bed. He sat on the bed and motioned me to come near.

'Now, Edgar, this here is a shotgun, and these are the shells you load it with. Have you ever loaded a gun or shot one?' he asked quietly. I shook my head. 'Now, I want you to watch very carefully. Your life might depend on it!' he said as he struck a match and lit the lantern.

Charles showed me how to dismantle the gun, put it back together, and put the shell in the chamber. He made me practice this numerous times. I was afraid at first, but I finally got the hang of it. Then he took me to another part of the cave and taught me how to shoot the gun.

'But, Charles, isn't it dangerous to shoot this weapon in here?' I protested.

He shook his head. 'No. First of all, the noise can't travel far because we are underground. Secondly, we are many miles from any kind of settlement.'

After practicing, Charles led the way as we re-entered the room we were going to sleep in. He cleaned the other side of the room using the little broom I had, and then he removed a mattress from underneath the other ones.

'What! I didn't realize—' I started saying, but he interrupted me.

'I keep more mattresses here in case there are more people to shelter. You can take this bed,' he said, pointing to the higher bed.

It bothered me to take his bed and I started to protest but he stopped me again.

'No protesting. You are still not well, son,' Charles said.

There was another question bugging me. 'Charles, won't the light be a liability if someone comes looking for me?'

He shook his head. 'No, but why don't you go outside with a flashlight and prove it for yourself,' he said, handing me a flashlight.

I walked outside and then turned around to look at the mouth of the cave. Not a single sign of light was visible; the place looked uninhabited. I walked back inside, shaking my head in disbelief. As I turned to go to the inside room, I realized that I had made two left turns coming in, one after another.

'Tell me, Charles, was this cave built by your people? It could not have happened by accident.'

Charles shrugged his shoulders. 'I believe it was created by our ancestors. We discovered these caves much later, after the arrival of the colonialists,' he answered.

Charles stood up and paced the cave. 'You know, Edgar, I have to go back for a little while to avoid suspicion. When I come back, I will say my name three times before I enter the cave so that you know it's me,' he emphasized.

'Thank you very much, Charles, and please thank Pastor Joseph for me,' I said as I walked him out to his horse.

He turned around suddenly and his voice changed. 'Son, in these parts death comes instantly, and any movement towards you most likely means danger. Remember that I will call my name three times. Make sure you have the gun next to you at all times,' he stated as he galloped away.

I listened to the hooves until the whole area was silent, and then I made my way back inside the cave. Sitting on the bed, I visualized my past and also had a glimpse of what my future would be if the slave traders recaptured me. I felt fear mixed with anger, and I reached for the shotgun and pumped it before laying it next to my bed.

I wasn't going to be a slave ever again, I promised myself quietly. My thoughts went back to my friend Jimmy. I wondered if he had also managed to escape.

Chapter 39

Habib the truck driver got the message from the old man with the carriage. At first he ignored him, but the old fellow mentioned that he had a letter from Saleh that needed to be delivered to Al-Hajj Abdul in Nimule immediately. At the mention of Al-Hajj Abdul Asuman, Habib paid more attention. Al-Hajj Abdul was an important man with lots of financial ventures, and a favor to him would mean a lot of money.

An idea crossed his mind; what if he opened the letter in private and then put it in another envelope? Nobody would know. He excused himself and walked to the nearest shop and bought an envelope. He then walked to a nearby restaurant and asked if he could use the restroom. The waitress handed him the key, and Habib rushed into the bathroom and shut the door behind him before he tore open the envelope.

What he read made his heart skip a beat. *This is a gold mine.* This was his big opportunity to make some money. He would tell Al-Hajj Abdul that he had seen some fighters who were looking for an escaped slave. He put the letter back into another envelope and wrote Al-Hajj Abdul's name on it before sealing it.

Habib rushed out of the restaurant and headed for his pickup truck, explaining that an urgent family matter required him to go to Nimule immediately. In thirty minutes Habib had acquired most of the goods that he normally took to Nimule and filled his tank with gasoline.

Habib left Okaru quickly without warning and drove at full speed towards Magwe. He had a few customers with him, but the money he anticipated getting from Al-Hajj Abdul would be more than enough to cover any losses. Instead of begging soldiers on roadblocks to let him go, he used a little cash to bribe them until he finally arrived in the town of Magwe. Luckily a few passengers jumped on the truck whenever he stopped in small towns for gasoline, and this additional funding helped to finance his costs at the roadblocks. He bought some tea, which he poured into his travel flask before beginning the last part of the trip. If all went well he would be in Pageri by midnight and Nimule at about one-thirty.

He continued giving the soldiers lame excuses and a little money at roadblocks until he finally arrived in Nimule a little after one o'clock in the morning. Habib collected his fares from the passengers before he headed for his shop, where he banged on the door for his wife and children to open up. They took their time doing this, making him agitated; he would complain later.

He rushed towards Al-Hajj Abdul's house on foot, leaving his workers and children to unload the truck. When he got there, he banged on the door and was lucky that somebody opened it almost immediately.

'What do you want at this time of the night?' the voice demanded.

'I have an important message for Al-Hajj Abdul from Okaru that can't wait,' he stated.

Finally the door opened, and a young man scrutinized him with a flashlight.

'Aren't you Habib the driver?' the young man asked.

'You know I am. Now get me Al-Hajj Abdul quickly. I have an important message for him,' he said again.

'Follow me,' the young man said as he led Habib to a large room and turned on a bright light. 'I will go and get him,' the young man said as he slipped away.

A few minutes later, the old man came into the room.

'Eh! Habib, how are you and what brings you by in the dead of the night?' he asked as he offered his hand to Habib, who bent down in respect.

'Al-Hajj, I have an urgent letter for you from Mr Saleh Salim,' Habib said, handing Al-Hajj Abdul the letter from Saleh.

'Have a seat,' the older man said as he opened the letter and perused it.

'Al-Hajj, sir, when I was in Okaru I was told that some warlords were looking for escaped slaves. I came as quickly as I could,' he said.

Al-Hajj Abdul shook his head and sent Ghani to get some tea. 'Habib, you mean you drove all the way from Okaru to this town to give me this?' Al-Hajj Abdul asked as Ghani brought them some tea and served them.

'Yes, Al-Hajj, I even gave money to soldiers on the roadblocks to let me pass quickly. And I was not able to get customers because I was in a hurry,' he lied, knowing that Al-

Hajj Abdul had no way of finding out for sure.

Al-Hajj Abdul reread the letter and realized its urgency. The letter stated the fact that Saleh had met the trader Aisis and showed him the boy's photo, and Aisis had confirmed beyond a reasonable doubt that the young man was Edgar.

'Ghani, get me a piece of paper and pen, and you should wake up the boys. This is urgent,' he said.

The young fellows came to the room all perplexed and sleepy and took their seats.

Al-Hajj Abdul cleared his throat. 'Sorry for waking you up, boys. We have just received information that your friend escaped and is alive, but he is in danger of being recaptured. Some warlords are looking for escaped slaves, and our only chance is to get to him before they do.'

'Sir, do you know where he is, exactly?' Wilbur asked.

'No, but one of my men is on the trail and should find out soon,' he answered. 'Young men, one of you may have to go and get help from our friend Adam Wani. Ghani will escort you,' he said.

He turned to the driver. 'Thank you, Habib. I will pay you well for this. I want to caution you about the delicacy of the situation. It requires complete secrecy. Can you take the young men tonight?' he asked.

'Yes, sir, Al-Hajj, I am at your service,' Habib answered.

'Good,' Al-Hajj Abdul said.

The three young fellows talked to one another for a moment and finally came to a decision. The boys thought Wilbur was better equipped, having gone through the rebel encounter in Madi Opel.

'Al-Hajj, we have decided that I should be the one to go,' Wilbur said seriously.

Al-Hajj Abdul nodded his head in agreement.

'We will get a few warriors from Adam Wani to help. Ghani, you and Wilbur should pack up a few clothes now. Time is against us. Hurry!' Al-Hajj Abdul said as he picked up a pen and started writing a letter to Adam Wani explaining the extreme urgency of the situation. He also wrote another letter briefing Al-Hajj Musa Lara about everything. After he finished writing, he put the letters in envelopes.

'Are you ready to go now, young men?' he asked Ghani and Wilbur, who had just got back carrying small bags. They both nodded affirmatively.

Al-Hajj Abdul stood up. 'Ghani, get my coat. I want to walk you boys out,' he said, heading for the door.

Habib and the three young men, John, Wilbur, and Sam, followed the older man; Ghani would catch up with them later. Everybody was silent as they walked towards Habib's shop.

When they arrived, the pickup truck had already been unloaded, and Habib's brother and some other people were busy arranging a few things inside the shop. Habib immediately took charge of the vehicle, checking the oil and other small items.

Ghani arrived with his father's coat. Al-Hajj Abdul gave Wilbur some money from his wallet and went to the front of the truck to settle the payment with Habib.

'Young men, let's go,' Habib shouted.

Sam and John were silent for a while until finally John broke down and hugged Wilbur. 'Hey, Willy, bring him back,' he said emotionally and stepped back.

Sam hugged Wilbur next. 'Willy, please take good care of yourself,' he murmured.

The two young men entered the vehicle, which had started up.

'My sons, may Allah be with you,' Al-Hajj Abdul said, and then the vehicle headed down the street to the only petrol station in the town.

Luckily the attendant was awake, and one beep of the horn from Habib brought him out of the small house.

'Fill up the truck,' he ordered the man, who yanked the hose loose and put it in the tank nozzle. 'So, boys, are you ready for the trip?' Habib asked, making an effort at conversation.

'Yes, I suppose so, but you have had a long trip. If you get tired, I can drive,' Ghani offered.

'I am used to this, but I will let you know if I need help. I take it you have a driving license,' Habib said. Ghani nodded.

Habib paid the man for the gas and turned the truck around for the journey. They passed by Al-Hajj Abdul, Sam and John, who were still standing in front of the shop, and waved to them without slowing down. The time was approaching two-thirty in the morning when they left Nimule.

'You know, we have to move fast if we're to make it in time,' Ghani said, and Habib nodded.

'The road isn't too bad this time of night. The only problem we might have is the roadblocks on the way,' he said.

'Do they bother you every time?' Wilbur asked.

Habib laughed a little and shook his head with a smile. 'Not if you give them a little money,' he said.

'In that case we will give them some money,' Wilbur stated firmly. *Some things don't change no matter where you go*, he thought. Wilbur's thoughts went back to the matter at hand. He knew that he would have to go with the warriors to fetch Edgar if they let him. It was the only sensible thing to do since he was the only one that Eddie would trust—if they found him alive. He shivered at the latter thought, but there was also a sense of relief that their mission might finally be coming to an end.

They went through a few roadblocks which Habib paid off quietly so as to avoid any hassle. They finally got to Magwe towards the morning, and Ghani mentioned that he was happy they were making great progress. They filled the tank again before continuing on their journey.

'Boys, we still have quite a few miles before we arrive in Okaru, so I suggest that if you feel like sleeping should do so,' Habib said.

Wilbur decided to shut his eyes, but Ghani refused to sleep because he didn't trust the man they were with. Years back he had heard people say Habib was a smuggler, and he had also been in the SPLA jail numerous times for different crimes.

Habib continued talking nonstop, which was good for Ghani since he wanted to stay awake. The truck got to Okaru safely after a few more roadblocks. Ghani told Habib to stop when they saw a restaurant. They drove through the town until they saw a petrol station that had a restaurant next to it.

'What! We haven't arrived yet?' Wilbur asked, astonished as the car came to a standstill.

'We have at least two hours to go, Wilbur,' Ghani said. 'I will get some coffee from the restaurant,' he added, getting out of the truck.

The tank was filled up, and Habib eased the truck next to the restaurant where Ghani was. Wilbur got out and helped Ghani with the coffee, which they sipped while standing outside. Soon they were on their way again. The road was now very bad and at times sand covered the whole road for miles, but Habib managed to pick up a few passengers that were heading in the same direction.

It was surprising to Wilbur how sparsely populated the area was; they traveled for miles without seeing a soul. After almost three hours of traveling, Ghani told Habib to slow down and make a left turn. The area had suddenly become familiar to Ghani, who had been to Mr Adam Wani's place at least twice.

'Habib, he lives a few miles down the road on your left,' Ghani said.

The other passengers disembarked, thanking the driver. The three of them kept moving down the narrow bumpy road for some time before they came upon a large house surrounded by several small huts and enclosed by a big fence.

'Slow down, Habib, we have arrived,' Ghani shouted.

Habib decelerated and proceeded slowly, stopping just before the gate. Someone dressed like a nomad warrior came and asked them a few questions. After he was satisfied, he opened the gate for them. Habib drove through and parked the car in the middle of the large compound. A lot of people were seated or standing in front of the different huts and gazed at them until someone came from the house and walked towards them.

He was a tall and lean and was dressed like any businessman that one might meet in Kampala.

'Hello, Mr Wani,' Ghani said, bowing over to greet the older man.

'This is Habib who drove us here, and you remember Wilbur Ochom from Kampala. We just came from Nimule with a message for you from my father.'

Mr Wani shook hands with Habib and Wilbur and patted Ghani on the shoulder. 'So how is your father?'

'Not too good, I am afraid. Everything is in the letter,' he said as Mr Wani led them inside. Ghani gave him both letters, including the one for Al-Hajj Musa Lara, Wani's brother.

Mr Wani offered them some seats and told a young woman to make tea while he read his letter. He stopped from time to time and looked at them in alarm. He tensed a bit before he quickly put the letter back into his pocket. Then he turned around with his eyes on Wilbur.

'Is this definitely the young man?' he asked Wilbur.

'Yes, sir, we received the information from a reliable source.'

Mr Wani walked to the door and shouted verbal instructions to one of his men.

'Young men, please feel at home. I will be back soon,' he said before he walked out. There were sounds of shouting outside.

'I hope we are not too late,' Wilbur murmured to himself as the woman brought them some tea which they drank in silence. Habib started saying how this area could be good for business if they only had a little peace.

'The only way Sudan will have peace is if they divide it into two; one part for the blacks and the other for the Arabs,' Ghani argued.

Wilbur was about to interject when he suddenly heard the sounds of numerous horses hooves. Everybody fell silent. 'I believe we have company,' he said.

'Friendly company, I hope,' Habib said, but nobody was listening to him.

Seconds later Mr Wani entered.

'I hope I didn't keep you. Some of my men had gone to town,' he said, sitting down. 'The way I see it, we are pressed for time, so my warriors will leave immediately to look for the young man,' he said.

'Sir, I would like to go with the warriors,' Wilbur said.

Mr Wani was taken by surprise. 'What? No. It's too dangerous for you to go, son. Do you realize that there might be a gunfight? Do you even know how to shoot a gun?'

'Yes, sir, I know how to shoot, and I have been in a real gun battle before,' Wilbur stated as everybody looked at him with surprise. 'Moreover, sir, Edgar knows me and trusts me, and he may not trust your men,' he added.

Mr Wani nodded, seeing Wilbur's last point. 'Okay, if that's the way you want it, I won't stop you. Let's go, we don't have much time. Do you know how to ride a horse?' he asked.

Wilbur nodded. He was glad about those lessons he had taken in Kenya when his father took him on vacation. They all stood up and walked outside.

'Wilbur, you will take my stallion. He is strong and reliable and doesn't tire quickly. There is a gun in the holster, and the bullets are in the saddlebag, on the side,' Mr. Wani said, pointing to a big black horse.

'Thank you, sir,' Wilbur said as he reached inside the truck and removed his bag. He walked to where Habib and Ghani were standing and shook their hands.

'See you soon, guys,' Wilbur said before he walked purposefully towards the stallion and mounted it.

Ghani and Habib just stared at the determined young man with admiration.

Mr Wani went towards his men, who numbered close to thirty, and approached one of them. He talked to him for a few minutes and then handed him an envelope. He turned and went over to where Wilbur was and patted his stallion.

'Son, you can trust these men. You shall be moving most of the day and night, and I believe by midnight you should be within sixty miles of the town of Geranja. Ahmed, the man I was just talking to, speaks English in case you want to ask him something,' he said and walked away towards the car.

Ahmed shouted some orders, and suddenly everybody followed their leader. The journey had begun, and only fate could turn Wilbur back.

Chapter 40

Pastor Joseph had been waiting behind the town market for Mr Charles Anuko for about forty-five minutes. He had a Bible in one hand, and his eyes were raised to the sky as he prayed that all would be okay.

He heard the sound of horse hooves behind him and turned around to see a large number of men on horseback riding into town. It was already after midnight, and nobody entered the town on a peaceful mission at such a late hour. They headed straight to the church and surrounded it.

Pastor Joseph had a good view of the church and the road that led to it. Suddenly a figure appeared from the same side of the street that he was on and crossed the road. On further examination, he noticed that it was woman. She went to the church and talked with the riders before quickly turning back.

Pastor Joseph followed his intuition and walked towards Margaret's mother's house, but just before he could leave the dark and walk into the light, the woman hurriedly crossed the street ahead of him, not more than ten paces away. Pastor Joseph realized that it was Margaret.

He turned and walked back to where he had been, shaking his head in disbelief. He almost bumped into Charles. 'There you are. I was waiting for you. Where did you leave your horse, Charles?'

'It's down the road. I couldn't bring it on the main road with all those bandits moving around.'

'What about you, Pastor? You look perplexed.'

Pastor Joseph just shook his head as they walked to the place where he had been sitting earlier. 'I saw someone cross the street to where the bandits were, so I decided to walk in the shadows and have a closer look; I almost bumped into the person.'

'Let me guess, it was Mrs Margaret Chachi, right?' Charles said and the Pastor nodded.

'I see that the riders have gone off. I assume towards Langabu, and with any luck they won't be back for a day or two.' Charles commented.

'Thanks, Charles, I will see you in a few minutes at your house,' Pastor Joseph said as Charles walked down the street.

* * *

Unknown to them, someone else was watching them from across the street. The town cobbler, Simon Galu, had been on his way to the shop to get something from his toolbox when he noticed that the town was about to be attacked. He quickly hid behind a tree only to realize that the hoodlums were heading for the church.

Surprised, Simon saw another person standing in the shadows and watching the scene. He soon identified the person as Pastor Joseph. Simon almost called out to the Pastor but held himself back when he realized that the Pastor was hiding.

Simon got another surprise when he saw a lady hurrying back towards the little shop and realized that the woman was none other than Margaret Chachi. She must have been talking to her hoodlum husband, he reasoned. After the thugs left, another figure appeared, talked to Pastor Joseph, and left soon after.

The person passed a few yards from Simon, and in the moonlight he could tell it was Charles Anuko. Simon didn't want the Pastor to know that he had been spying so he stayed put. *Now what the hell were those two talking about?* Simon asked himself. They couldn't have met at this time of the night without an appointment. This was getting more interesting by the minute.

A moment later, the Pastor walked down the street and Simon followed closely behind. He didn't know exactly why he was doing it, but he had seen too many things and curiosity was killing him. Pastor Joseph knocked on Charles' door. It opened and the Pastor entered. Simon hurried towards Charles' residence and put his ear to a hole by the front window. He could hear them talking.

The Pastor asked Charles if he was sure nobody saw him.

'Don't worry, Pastor, everybody in this town believes the boy went back to Langabu. Nobody would suspect the caves,' Charles assured the Pastor.

'Just make sure that you cover your tracks,' Pastor Joseph said.

Simon had heard enough. He withdrew quietly and walked to his shop to remove the tools from his box, which after all had been his original intention. He was sure that the information he had heard was valuable, and would afford him passage to go to Juba and look for work. He went back to his home, thinking of the best way he would use the information. Simon had stopped caring for his fellow man when his mother had remarried and abandoned him with his grandmother, who died soon after and left him alone to fend for himself at a very young age. One thing Simon had learnt in life was that it was every man for himself unless one joined the SPLA, but Simon had never liked guns.

He slept peacefully, knowing that there was some hope for him. He woke up late the next day, having slept more than eight hours. He made some tea and ate some stale pancakes that he had bought a few days earlier, and then he left for work. He had gone home with a few customers' shoes and some tools the night before, which he had in a bag.

He closed the door of his room and headed out. Everything had to look normal for his plan to succeed. That day he had a few customers and kept working, though his mind was elsewhere. The more Simon thought about what to do, the more he realized that the safest choice was to approach Margaret and demand payment in return for some information.

He could not possibly bribe the priest. That would be blasphemy, and as much as he didn't believe in God, he thought he would be punished if he dared bribe a priest. Approaching Margaret was the only solution.

Although Simon had started work late, he decided to close shop early when he realized that the marketplace was almost empty and he had no more customers. He locked his toolbox and walked down the street towards Margaret's residence to buy some pancakes.

It was five o'clock in the evening, but the town was empty because most people had stayed indoors after hearing about last night's raid on the church.

The pancake shop was open, and luckily Margaret was behind the counter. Simon bought some pancakes before he started talking to her.

'Mrs Chachi, I believe I have information you may need, but it will cost you.'

'What kind of information are you talking about?' she asked scornfully. It was known all over town that she despised poor people.

'Well, I saw you last night, and I know the person you are looking for is not in Langabu,' he answered as he picked up his bag and started to walk away.

'Wait, Mr Galu,' she called, her tone changing as she followed him into the street. 'How do you know all this? Do you have proof?' she asked as she followed Simon, who hadn't even slowed down a bit.

'Sure I do. When the horsemen came last night I saw Pastor Joseph in the shadows. He also saw you going towards his church, and you almost bumped into him when you were heading back to your shop. A few minutes later, he met another man and they had a conversation, which I overheard, word by word. That's when I knew that you, like everyone else in this town, had been fooled by Pastor Joseph,' he said with finality.

There was no need to tell Margaret who the other man was.

Margaret's hand flew to her lips in astonishment. 'Okay, how much do you want in exchange for telling me where the boy is?' she asked.

'Twenty-five thousand,' Simon said.

'Come and see me at nine o'clock, after my mother has gone to sleep,' she pleaded.

'Make it thirty and I will be there at nine,' the cobbler said and walked away quickly.

He despised the woman and everything she stood for. All he wanted from her was money, and then they would part company. Simon went home and started cooking some vegetables to eat with the pancakes. 'Life is too hard here for an honest worker. I am going to begin afresh,' he said out loud as he lay down on his bed and waited for the vegetables to cook.

* * *

Meanwhile, two other men had also been following the events in Geranja. The two were Aisis and Saleh. They had arrived in Geranja the night before while the horsemen were still at the town church, and they had watched and waited.

On closer examination, they had concluded that the boy had already left the town of Geranja. Both had taken the decision to approach Pastor Joseph the next day, after the hoodlums had left town. They arrived at the church at about eight in the evening and knocked on Pastor Joseph's door.

There was a moment's hesitation before they heard a voice. 'Who is it?'

'Pastor, it's me, Aisis Haddu. We met the other day when I brought the boy,' Aisis answered.

The door swung open, and Pastor Joseph emerged, smiling. He motioned for them to come in. 'Welcome, come in.'

'Thanks, Pastor. This is my good friend, Mr Saleh Salim,' Aisis said.

'Hello, Mr Saleh, welcome to my home.'

The Pastor closed the door and motioned for them to sit down.

'Pastor, I will try to be as brief as I possibly can, though the story is long,' Aisis said and then paused a little to put his thoughts together.

'Wait. Let me put on the kettle for some tea,' the Pastor said as he walked towards the kitchen. He came back after a moment and sat down. 'Sorry about that, gentlemen. You can now tell me everything,' he said.

'After I left the young man here last time, I rode towards the town of Okaru to see if I could purchase some good leather. On my way there I remembered that my good friend here has spent the past few months trying to find the whereabouts of a boy who was captured and sold into slavery. Saleh had told me that the name of the boy, and it matched the name of the boy I left with you.

'When I reached Okaru, I learnt that Taban Nasir was looking for escaped slaves, and that's when I decided to write to Saleh. To cut a long story short, I sent a letter to Saleh in Nimule, and he arrived with a photograph of Edgar, which I confirmed was the young man,' Aisis said. The priest looked dumfounded as he listened to Aisis.

'Pastor, Edgar's friends have been in Nimule looking for him. After we talked, Saleh sent a letter confirming the young man's identity and the danger he was in,' he continued. 'We arrived a few minutes behind the group that attacked your church, but we were afraid to show ourselves because we were outnumbered, so we resorted to spying on them from the shadows. We even saw you, Pastor, and the man who was following you,' Aisis said.

'A man!' Pastor Joseph exclaimed in alarm.

'Yes, Pastor. That short man who works in the market as a cobbler. He followed you until you entered another house, and he leaned his head against the window. I think he was listening to your conversation, Pastor,' Aisis said.

Shaken, Pastor Joseph stood up and paced the room up and down. 'So the location of the young man has been compromised. I have to think of something else,' he said, holding his face in his hands.

'Pastor, you may also be in danger. We are camped three miles from here. Maybe you should come to our tents and lie low for a while,' Saleh chipped in. It was the first time he had said anything.

'That's a good idea,' Pastor Joseph said. 'You will need to go round as if you are going back out of town and double back on foot. Do you remember the house I went in last night?' The two traders nodded as the Pastor brought the tea kettle.

'I will be there at ten o'clock. Now drink your tea,' he said, pouring some into their cups.

'Pastor, can I use your toilet?' Saleh asked. The Pastor showed him the door to the back. 'I will be right back,' Saleh said as he stepped out to the outhouse.

While he was coming back, he heard footsteps further down on the other side of the street, and he knew that they must be what he had heard while he was in the Pastor's house. He had felt strange then and decided to follow his instinct. He hadn't needed to use the toilet, but that was the only excuse he could come up with without raising suspicion.

The footsteps stopped by a door and somebody—a lady—opened it. The light shone on the man who entered the shop. It was the cobbler. Saleh quickly removed his sandals, tiptoed to the shop, and put his ear to the door.

'Do you have the money?' the man asked.

'I only have twenty-five thousand pounds,' the woman begged.

'No. That's not enough,' the man said.

'Okay, twenty-eight is all I possess,' she quipped.

'Bring the money,' the man said harshly.

The lady must have brought the money and given it to the man, because Saleh could tell that money was being counted.

'He is at the caves,' the man stated.

That's all Saleh needed to hear before he tiptoed away and then walked towards the church. When he arrived at the church, he entered and sat down in silence as if nothing had happened.

'Pastor Joseph, that shoe cobbler has already sold our boy out to the girl across the street for twenty-eight thousand pounds,' he said, pouring himself some more tea.

'Dear Lord, please help us!' the Pastor exclaimed.

'Pastor, Aisis and I will ride out of town in case somebody saw us and then walk back to your friend's house,' Saleh said, standing up.

'Pastor, we will be back by ten o'clock,' Aisis added.

Pastor Joseph opened the door and waited for them to mount their horses and ride off before he closed it again. The two men rode their horses back the way they had come until they were sure that nobody was following them. They dismounted and tied the horses to a tree. They walked back towards the town and stayed out of sight until they were at the house the Pastor had indicated. Saleh looked around to check that they weren't followed before knocking on the door softly.

'Who is it?' someone whispered.

'Aisis and Saleh,' came the answer.

The latches were removed, and a man motioned them in.

'You are sure that nobody saw you come in?' Pastor Joseph asked.

They shook their heads simultaneously.

Pastor Joseph was already seated. 'Gentlemen, this is Mr Charles Anuko, and Charles, meet Mr Aisis Haddu and Mr Saleh Salim.'

The three men shook hands and then sat down.

'I have already briefed Charles on the situation,' Pastor Joseph said.

'Gentlemen, it's a pleasure to meet you, though I must admit I was shocked by the number of people who know about the boy,' Charles said.

They nodded their heads in understanding.

'So what do you suggest?' Charles asked.

'I will go with you to the caves. I have a rifle with me and I am a warrior, so I can hold off anybody for a while until we get support from Al-Hajj Abdul Asuman,' Saleh said.

'Well, I tend to agree with you, Saleh. I am not handy with guns and neither is Pastor Joseph, I presume. I believe that it's better if you and Charles go to the boy while the Pastor and I wait for help,' Aisis said.

Pastor Joseph nodded. 'I brought my overnight bag along in case we all agreed on that very action. So what do you think, Charles?' he asked.

Charles shrugged, 'Well, we don't have any other choice.'

'Good, let's get going, gentlemen,' Pastor Joseph said.

'I will pack a few edible items to last for a few days,' Charles said, going into the other room. He came back shortly with a bag and two rifles. He handed one to Saleh.

'I know you have a gun, but it won't hurt to have an extra one. Okay, let's go,' he said, going towards the door. He peered outside to make sure it was safe before opening it wide.

They walked in complete silence until they reached their horses.

'Do you think I should bring this stallion along?' Saleh asked nobody in particular.

'Yes, I think we should ride to the caves so that everybody becomes familiar with the area, and then I will show you a shortcut back to Geranja,' Charles said as they walked to where he had left his horse. They mounted and headed for the caves.

'The caves are well structured for fending off attackers. There is a main entrance and two small holes that I will show you when we get there,' Charles added.

Pastor Joseph was riding with Aisis Haddu, and they had fallen back a few paces. Saleh and Charles were riding together ahead.

'Have you been in a gunfight before, Saleh?' Charles asked.

'Numerous times, mostly in self-defense against robbers, but I'm pretty good with all kinds of weapons,' he answered.

'Good. The young man hasn't been in a gunfight before, and we shall need experienced hands,' he said.

They finally arrived at the caves, and Charles had to use the signals to make sure Edgar didn't panic and shoot, and then they entered the cave.

Charles made the introductions and also explained that there was an imminent attack on the cave and that's why he had brought an extra hand.

Pastor Joseph and Aisis were shown a shortcut they could take back to the horse path, and they left after the Pastor had said a small prayer wishing them all blessings from God. Saleh, who was a Muslim, was as happy to get blessings regardless.

'Say, Saleh, do you by any chance have a rope I can borrow?' Charles asked.

Saleh nodded. 'Yes, as a matter of fact. I carry a few ropes in case I have to build a tent.' He opened his bag and removed some ropes.

'Give me all you have. I have to make traps for any intruders,' Charles said, taking a bunch of them and heading outside.

'So, young man, I have at last seen you face to face after spending months looking everywhere for you,' Saleh said, turning to look at Edgar.

* * *

I was puzzled when the Arab-looking man said that. He had the same complexion as the Mullahs but his face had different features. *Why would this Arab man be looking for me?*

'Let's backtrack, sir. We don't know each other. How come you have been looking for me?' I asked suspiciously.

Saleh smiled, reached into his pocket and handed me a document. It had my picture, and it said I was a student in both English and Arabic.

'Call me Saleh. I was hired by Al-Hajj Abdul Asuman to look for you. Your friends have been staying at his residence in Nimule. I believe their names are Wilbur and Sam, but I can't recall the other guy's name,' he said as he scratched his head.

'John,' I said.

'Yes, that's the name,' Saleh said. He then told me he had met the boys when he went to Al-Hajj Abdul's residence just before he came north looking for me again. Saleh went on to explain how, on his first trip looking for me, he had arrived at the Mullah's farms but was too late to do anything. He had followed me and the other slaves to the docking place near Juba.

I was astonished by what he was saying, and I didn't know how to reply so I simply nodded with gratitude. *My friends had been looking for me all this time.* I remembered telling Jimmy that they would but that was a long time ago. *They never gave up.* I felt so blessed.

Saleh cleared his throat and brought me back from my thought. 'I received information that you were here from the man who just left with the Pastor, and that's why I came.'

The face of the man, Aisis, was familiar, but I couldn't place him until Saleh explained that Aisis was the man who had moved me from Dr Dorothy's town to Pastor Joseph's place.

'I've already sent a letter to Al-Hajj Abdul telling him about the circumstances, so I assume help will be here soon. I just hope they arrive in time,' Saleh said, lighting a pipe.

This man was on my side, and he had told me quite a bit about people I knew, but I still felt strange around light-skinned people in Sudan, especially Arabs, and I was glad when Charles came back inside the cave.

'I don't believe anybody can just sneak in our cave unless he followed us here, but it's always better to be prepared,' Charles said.

We all pitched in and prepared some food and ate. Soon after, everybody took turns taking a flashlight and relieving themselves.

'Now, gentlemen, we need to decide where each of us will be in case we are attacked,' Charles stated. He showed us the two side openings and also showed Saleh the extreme end of the cave, which he had showed me sometime earlier.

'I believe it's best if Edgar mans this smaller hole. You and I will be switching every now and then between the other hall and the main entrance,' Charles said to Saleh.

Saleh nodded in agreement. Again Charles asked me to practice shooting and re-loading. We spent the next hour setting up a strategy in case we were attacked.

Chapter 41

Wilbur, Ahmed, and the whole group had ridden for many miles before they decided to rest. After three hours, Ahmed had ordered the men to mount again and ride so as not to lose valuable time. They did not rest again until they came to the road going to Geranja. Ahmed told the men that this would be their last stop before entering the town. Wilbur silently observed how Ahmed commanded his men.

'Ahmed, how come we are resting when it's already dark?' Wilbur asked.

Ahmed laughed. He and Wilbur had bonded since they began the trip from Mr Wani's residence.

'You see, Wilbur, it's about nine-thirty and people are still awake, but by eleven-thirty they start retiring. At one o'clock, all of them are in bed and that is the time to take the city unawares. Even the gunmen become easy targets because they are unprepared. Now rest,' he said and pulled his bag closer below his head as a pillow.

Wilbur, who had not had much sleep in the past few days, stayed awake for some time, but finally sleep took him.

Ahmed woke him up later. 'Come on, Willy, it's time to go.'

Wilbur stood up and shook himself. To his surprise he was wide awake. Everybody else had already mounted their horses, so he reached for his bag and headed straight for his black horse.

'Hey, Ahmed, I didn't keep you guys waiting long, did I?' he asked.

'No, don't worry. Let's go,' he said and started giving orders to his men as they resumed their journey.

This time they rode through the valley, always moving parallel to the main road. Ahmed rode in front, talking to his men about what Wilbur believed were plans for going into the town of Geranja. After about an hour he fell back.

'How are you feeling, Willy?' he asked.

'Not bad at all, just anxious,' Wilbur answered.

'Everybody gets very anxious before an encounter with an enemy. Just try to think about something else,' Ahmed advised, 'I believe it is almost one o'clock. The town can't be more than a few miles from here.'

* * *

Meanwhile Pastor Joseph and Aisis had just reached the traders' camp. The tent was still in place. The only thing they had to do was clean out the sand and dust.

'I will prepare the tent, Pastor, you just rest,' Aisis Haddu volunteered.

'Thank you, my friend,' Pastor Joseph said as he bent down and opened his bag.

Suddenly he heard the ground shake and stood to listen properly.

'Did you hear that?' he shouted to Aisis.

'Yes, Pastor, those are horses; a lot of them, at that,' he replied.

'I don't think it's the first gang. They can't be back from Langabu that fast. I will go and meet them before they go into Geranja in case they are the help we are waiting for,' Pastor Joseph said, heading for the horses.

Aisis helped the Pastor mount his horse.

'Be careful, Pastor. They might be the enemy,' he said, but Pastor Joseph was already galloping towards the sound.

* * *

The men didn't hear the horse until it was less than a hundred yards from them, and then they all dispersed, turning their mounts around with their guns held up, ready to shoot.

'Don't shoot, please, I am not armed,' the Pastor shouted.

Ahmed said something, and everybody lowered their weapons. The moon was high in the sky and most things were visible. They could see that the man had no weapon as he came closer to them.

'By any chance are you men from Al-Hajj Abdul Asuman?' he asked.

'Who wants to know?' Ahmed questioned.

* * *

Pastor Joseph was a steady man, and that was how he had managed to stay in this wild place for so long.

'I am Pastor Joseph Janda from Geranja. Saleh sent me to wait for men that would come to help him.'

Wilbur couldn't control himself any longer.

'Pastor, do you know where Saleh is now?' he asked.

'Yes, I do, son, but they are expecting problems any minute.'

'Take us quickly, Pastor,' Ahmed said as he ordered his men to follow.

Pastor Joseph looked at the young man who had asked about Saleh and knew he wasn't from this area. He spoke perfect English. The Pastor's hunch told him that this was one of the young men Saleh had talked about who were looking for their friend Edgar.

'I left another fellow on top of that hill,' the Pastor said, pointing at the traders' camp.

Ahmed nodded in the direction the Pastor pointed, and one of his men went to get Aisis.

'Let's go, Pastor. You said they are in danger,' Ahmed said firmly as other fighters made way for them to go ahead.

'We will take a shortcut,' Pastor Joseph said, spurring his horse on.

* * *

There was a tiny noise outside, and Charles crawled towards the entrance. Then the noise came again, and this time he was sure what it was. He went back inside the cave and woke Eddie and Saleh and motioned to them to take up their positions. Then he crawled back to the entrance, positioning himself against the wall.

Next came the sound of someone cursing as he tripped on one of the ropes. Charles had brought the spare rifle and he also had the shotgun, but his instincts told him to hold on.

The moonlight was shining hard, and he counted twelve figures. He waited till the figures were near the mouth of the cave, to be visible. *The hoodlums couldn't be back from Langabu that fast. These had to be other local thugs.* He took a step to the left and started shooting. The people fell one after the other, but more were coming towards the entrance.

* * *

Saleh and I woke up suddenly. Saleh started shooting, but I hesitated. Then a thought came to me in the form of a question: Are you going to die without a fight?

The answered was obvious, so I peeped through the small hole and aimed my rifle. I squeezed off a few rounds until the people started retreating while aiming where I was. I was surprised when one of the slugs actually entered the cave, so I aimed and squeezed the trigger several times. Then I moved my body from the line of fire.

I peeked out, but I couldn't see anybody although there was occasional fire from one of them. I almost got hit again when someone sprayed bullets at my side of the cave. I squeezed off a few more rounds and pulled back, angry at myself. *Am I enjoying this crazy episode?* I rationalized that it was because it was the first time in months that I felt in control and could actually defend myself.

The place became silent, so I stole another peep before I walked to the front of the cave.

'How are you doing, Charles?' I asked.

He turned around and glanced at me. 'Get out of the line of fire, young man, I'm doing just fine. I believe they're regrouping for the second attack.' He paused. 'How are you doing back there?' he asked.

'Well, I emptied one magazine and I'm on the second one,' I answered.

'That's my boy, but go easy on the ammunition,' he said, looking back at the entrance. I hadn't even walked five steps before I heard him squeeze his trigger. I ran and took my position again. I peeped into the hole and saw people running towards my position.

I squeezed off more shots and then quickly pulled my head back. Then I realized that somebody was coming towards me.

'How are you doing, Edgar?' Saleh asked as he got closer.

'I'm doing fine. How about you?'

'I'm out of ammunition,' he said.

'I've got about fifteen rounds left.'

'That's not enough. Let's go tell Charles,' he said.

We went to the front and broke the news to Charles, who just shook his head. 'It will all depend on how many of them are left. I'll use the shotgun for a little while before I join you. Stay far from the holes. Take the clip, Saleh,' he said.

Saleh was thinking about letting in some thugs, so that they could get their ammunition, but he kept this thought to himself; there would be time later, if it came to that.

* * *

Meanwhile, Wilbur and the fighters were nearing the caves.

'It's up this hill,' Aisis said, pointing to the centre of the hill.

Suddenly they heard the sound of a shotgun firing.

'Pastor, does your friend or his companions have a shotgun?' Ahmed asked.

'Yes, Charles does. I believe Saleh also has a gun,' Pastor Joseph answered.

Ahmed told a few of his men to stay back and cover the road going to Geranja. He, Wilbur, the Pastor, and the other fighters kept on going up the hill.

'Where is the mouth of the cave?' Ahmed asked, and the Pastor showed them.

'All right, Pastor, you and Aisis stay here. Are you coming along, Wilbur?' he asked as he glanced at him and walked ahead.

Ahmed had briefed his men on what to do. He told Wilbur that some of them would go to the top of the hill to neutralize the thugs facing the cave, and others would pounce upon those that had stayed with the horses. He warned Wilbur that some of the coming fight was going to be a sword deal, but Wilbur still decided to go along.

They started moving up. Some gunfire was still coming from the cave. When they saw the thugs, Ahmed used his hand to signal his men to start firing.

Then all hell broke loose. The thugs started falling like dominoes while others ran toward their horses only to be met by a similar fate. None of the men that had attacked the cave got away. Nobody could believe how fast this combat ceased. There was total silence.

* * *

Charles was the first to notice that something was different when he stole a look. The new people were dressed differently from the bandits that had attacked them, and they had swords.

'Hallelujah!' he shouted, but nobody heard him amid all the gunfire.

Then I heard the voice and so did Saleh.

'Did you hear that?' I asked him and he nodded.

Charles came in the room shouting happily. 'Gentlemen, I think help has arrived,' he said with a big smile and left.

Saleh and I went to my little window to steal a glance. What we saw we shall never forget; I quickly looked away.

Saleh looked for a while and then sat next to me.

'Look at it like this, Eddie, they came here to massacre us and take you back into slavery, so they got what they deserved,' he said, getting up and starting to light his pipe.

I started to like this man. I realized that I had misjudged him. Saleh managed to change my mind about Arabs. Not all of them were bad. It was the same everywhere in the world. Some people were evil and others were good.

Charles retrieved a lantern, which he took outside, walking cautiously. He put the lantern where they could see it and shouted for them to come into the open and avoid the traps, which he pointed out to them.

'Is Edgar Lapyem there? I am Wilbur Ochom,' a voice said.

* * *

I didn't wait for him to finish. I stormed past the lantern, temporarily forgetting that I couldn't run. Willy also ran towards me, and we embraced each other.

I started crying loudly like a baby, and I couldn't stop. All the tears I had held back in the past months streamed out like a river.

'Oh, Willy, it's you …it's you…' I kept crying.

Willy was crying also as we held each other. We stayed like this until Ahmed announced that there would be a lot more time to socialize later. Right now we had to take care of the business at hand.

Charles and Saleh cleaned out the cave as they talked about some leather deals, but Charles told Saleh that he lacked the capital. Wilbur took a bundle of Sudanese pounds and gave it to him.

Charles' mouth flew open in surprise, but I went to him and hugged him.

'I don't know how to thank you,' I said to Charles. Next I hugged Saleh and thanked him.

Pastor Joseph and Aisis joined us while most of Ahmed's warriors gathered the bodies and searched the surroundings. Pastor Joseph said a little prayer for the dead while Ahmed told his fighters to catch up with us after completing the burial.

We mounted the horses and rode off. I rode with Wilbur, and we talked about the events that had led them to conclude that I had been taken into bondage. He told me about their search for me and their stay in Nimule. I was overcome with gratitude and amazed at the zeal with which they had searched for my whereabouts. Wilbur did not ask about my time in slavery, which I appreciated. Instead he talked about football and Sam's rules, which made me smile. Sam was always a bully when it came to football.

We finally arrived at Saleh's tent at around five o'clock in the morning, and Saleh gathered his things. Pastor Joseph didn't want to go any further but prayed for us and wished us the best of luck.

'Pastor, I would like us to make a contribution towards your church,' Wilbur said, handing Pastor Joseph some money and his contact information.

Saleh and Charles made an appointment to meet in Nimule in two weeks, and Aisis also told Saleh they would be in contact.

I thanked Charles and Aisis for all their help and promised to keep them in my prayers. I hugged Pastor Joseph and thanked him for everything. I promised to write. Pastor Joseph told me that when he came to Kampala he would contact me through Wilbur.

We waved to the three men until they had disappeared behind the hill. The men that had rescued me made jokes that they had made more than they ever would have dreamed. Only two of our men were injured and expected to recover fully. Ahmed interpreted all this to us. I didn't feel guilty anymore about what I had done, thanks to the pep talk that Saleh had given me.

The weather started becoming warmer as daylight approached. We rode at an average speed until one in the afternoon, then stopped in order to eat and rest the horses. We did not stop again until we reached a spot where we parted company with the fighters.

Wilbur went to talk to Ahmed in private while I went around thanking all the fighters one at a time, speaking in Swahili.

Ahmed gave us five men to escort us to Mr Wani's house. As we were leaving, Ahmed called out to me very loudly. 'Hey, Eddie, come visit us soon. Please don't let those primitive idiots discourage you,' he shouted.

'Thanks for everything, Ahmed,' I shouted back.

I could not tell him that I had no intention of ever coming back, even if I had met good people who had helped me.

Chapter 42

A young boy stopped us, told us that he had been told to meet us, and asked us to please follow him. Saleh put the boy on his horse, and we followed along until he pointed to a restaurant. Indeed, Habib's pickup was parked in front of the restaurant.

We rode slowly and dismounted, then Saleh paid the boy. There were three people standing in front of the pickup. I was introduced to Mr Wani, the driver Habib, and Ghani. They all hugged me as if they had known me before, and I was deeply moved. I thanked Mr Wani and promised never to forget the favor.

Finally we climbed into the pickup and waved to Mr Wani as we left the restaurant and got on the main road to Nimule. I sat at the front of the pickup with Habib, while Wilbur, Ghani and Saleh and Ghani sat on the second row.

There were a few roadblocks on the way, but the driver, Habib, bribed them and we drove on. Wilbur and I slept most of the way while Habib, Saleh and Ghani continued talking.

We arrived in Nimule at noon the next day and drove straight to Al-Hajj Abdul's residence. Ghani and Wilbur jumped off the truck, but I had to climb down carefully because I couldn't jump.

I eased myself down with the help of Saleh and Willy. Habib kept honking the horn, and finally the boys arrived and saw us.

There was a lot of hugging, shouting, and crying, and my tears flowed freely as I embraced my friends, Al-Hajj Abdul, and all the other people in the residence.

After some time my friends gave me new clothing to wear and I went to take a shower. It was the best shower I have ever taken and I didn't want to finish.

I finally joined everyone in the backyard. A whole goat had been slaughtered and was being roasted by two experts who had been brought from the neighborhood. Though Al-Hajj Abdul did not normally permit drinking, beer was plenty.

He said something I will never forget. 'Son, before the white men and other people brought us religion, we celebrated by sacrificing an animal and drinking plenty. This occasion calls for such a celebration, so you are welcome to drink liquor, though I will personally have a soda.'

Saleh was also drinking soda. I wasn't sure if I would ever see him again but I knew that I would make an effort to write. I thanked him and promised to be in touch. *How do you thank somebody for saving your life?* Saleh patted my shoulder and said that he would like that. Shortly after midnight he said goodbye and left.

We ate meat and drank beers until the wee hours of the morning. The whole celebration was so surreal that I felt like I was in a movie. I still couldn't believe that I was free. I was happily tipsy by the time I got to bed

In the morning Ghani woke us up, reporting that Hon Ochom had rented a small plane to pick us up in Arua town at one-thirty in the afternoon. We had to leave Nimule in the morning in order to reach Arua on time.

Tearfully I said goodbye to all the people I had just met.

Al-Hajj Abdul decided to escort us to Arua. The happiness I felt as I crossed the border and stepped back into Uganda cannot be described. As we neared the airstrip, Wilbur begged Al-Hajj Abdul to go to Kampala to see his father and meet Wilbur's uncle, which he accepted after some persuasion.

The plane was already on the runway when we arrived at the airport, so the car drove straight to the little six-seater plane. The airport, or rather airstrip, was very small and could only accommodate a few planes at a time. After we embarked, I approached the pilot, whispered into his ear, and he nodded.

I came back and took my seat. Nobody seemed to have noticed my little talk with the pilot, which was fine with me. The plane taxied on the runway, and soon we were airborne. I had dreamt about this moment for a long time, but I never thought it would happen.

I was looking forward to seeing my mother again. I was the only person who understood the extent of her pain after she realized what had happen to me. I also wanted to see Father Benedict and be able to fulfill the promise I had made to myself to work at the Catholic centre.

The time I spent as a slave had taught me to value my life and to respect other peoples' lives. I had also learnt that as bad as things got, there was always someone somewhere worse off than you, and in most cases their suffering was not by choice.

I looked at my friends and realized that as much as I loved and appreciated them, they would never again understand me completely. How could they? I was a different person. The only person who understood me as I was now was Jimmy Abiriga. I would never forget him. I had left as a boy and had come back as a man.

Someone nudged me, and I turned to see John's beaming face.

'So, Eddie my man, how do you like the small aircraft?' he asked teasingly, trying to cheer me up.

I smiled at him, and frankly I had missed him a lot. 'Well, my friend, I wouldn't exchange it for a Boeing 747 right now,' I answered.

Sam laughed hard and patted my back. 'Me neither, Eddie,' he said, still laughing. Wilbur laughed too, and soon everybody was laughing. I couldn't remember the last time I had laughed this hard. I really loved these guys.

The pilot told everybody to tighten their belts. The small plane slowed down, and soon its tires touched the ground.

'Gentlemen, welcome to Gulu,' the pilot's voice echoed through the speakers. Everybody fell silent, and I knew an explanation was due.

'I am the one who asked the pilot to land here. I believe you all know the reason why,' I said, facing them. They all nodded, including Al-Hajj Abdul.

Wilbur got out of the plane first. 'My brother, we are with you all the way. I should have suggested the same thing myself,' he said as everybody started getting out.

I stepped out of the plane and looked at the vegetation surrounding the airstrip. Gulu had never looked more beautiful. I took a deep breath and followed the others.

There was only a single small building that was used as a receiving terminal, and an old man was attending it. I believed he did everything from sweeping to writing reports about any plane that landed or took off. Wilbur talked to him, and in a few minutes an old car pulled up in front of the entrance.

'Our ride has arrived. The pilot will wait for us,' Wilbur announced, heading for the door. We followed him and squeezed into the taxi. I gave the driver directions to my mother's residence.

Everybody was quiet, as if there was an unspoken realization that this part of the journey was a delicate one. The taxi finally stopped in front of my mother's house. I was a little perplexed and hesitant. Wilbur, who spoke my language, volunteered to break the news to her slowly and walked towards the back of the small house I had lived in all my life.

What happened next was a vision that will be with me as long as I live. My mother came out of the house and ran towards me, and I responded likewise, forgetting again that I couldn't run. I almost fell, but she had already reached me, and she stopped my fall. She held me tight, crying loudly and thanking God at the same time. I also held her close with tears running down my cheeks. She kept looking into my face and cried harder each time she did so.

Finally, after what seemed like forever, we separated and talked to one another softly. I introduced everybody who was with me, and my mother embraced each one of them, thanking them for bringing me back.

The taxi, which had left while Mother and I were embracing, came back shortly with Father Benedict, who ran towards me before I could even stand up and embraced me strongly.

'My son, God has answered our prayers. You are here as he promised,' he said.

Nobody could have noticed the difference between the holy man from Italy and any of us. We were all one as we entered my mother's small house.

My mother insisted on preparing a little feast and started running around doing different things as we kept up the conversation.

'Excuse me, everybody,' Father Benedict said, cutting the conversation short. 'I have an announcement to make.'

Everyone was suddenly quiet, and all eyes were on the Father.

'Our boy Edgar passed his exams with honors; four principles, all As. He has the grades to attend Makerere University.'

My eyes popped and my mouth opened wide, but no sound came out. I merely stood up and hugged him. I looked at everyone with tears in my eyes, but this time the tears weren't of joy but of sadness; I wiped my eyes before I spoke.

'I have something to say. I made a promise to a fellow slave who helped me escape that if I succeeded in getting away I would make sure the world knows about what happened to us. It's a promise I intend to keep. If it wasn't for him, I would never have survived. His name is Jimmy Abiriga,' I stated.

Wilbur smiled. 'We are with you, brother, all the way.' He paused and looked around at the gathering. 'To Jimmy Abiriga!' he announced, raising his glass.

All of us toasted to my new best friend.

Author's Note

This book was inspired by actual events that happened to many young men and women who had the misfortune of being captured in Northern Uganda by the rebels of the Lord's Resistance Army (LRA) in the 1990s.

Although what the LRA rebels did to their people is well documented with regard to turning children into soldiers, the story of slavery is not widely talked about. Many former captives are still afraid of retribution and will not come forward. The ones who agreed to tell their stories insisted on remaining anonymous.

This particular story is about a young man we shall call Edgar, who is captured by the LRA and sold into slavery. His journey takes us deep into Sudan's hinterland and also follows Edgar's friends as they attempt to rescue him. The names of characters and the places have been changed.

Edgar is an unquestionably brilliant young man who has the misfortune of being in the wrong place at the wrong time, just like so many others. Looking at Edgar's story, one realizes how a young innocent person can be transformed into a scared untrusting adult. The young men and women who managed to escape these atrocities have been affected psychologically to the extent that they prefer to be left alone, or simply limit their communication with other people.

While in captivity most of the men were physically maimed or raped, as were the women. The young men were used in the fields for hard labor whereas the girls were used for domestic chores and breeding other slaves. Seeing first hand evidence of some of their wounds, coupled with the fear in their eyes, one is confronted by the horrible truth of what happened to these young people in captivity.

As horrifying as it is, slavery is still an accepted way of life in many primitive cultures. Edgar's story has a positive outcome but not all captives have the chance to escape or be rescued. It is difficult to accept that there are many more captives who are still in bondage. This barbaric practice is a menace to the new era of modernity.

Acknowledgements

I would like to thank Ivan Rugyema who brought this story to light. His work on this incredible narrative made this book possible. Without him, this story would not have been told.

Special thanks to Jennifer Freedman, Elizabeth Martinez, Jenny Rice and Christine Comeau for their editorial input.

Made in the USA
Lexington, KY
02 May 2014